P9-CAL-535

A MADMAN CALLS

"Can you see the parking lot from where you are?"

"Yes."

"Watch."

He was speaking with a horribly exaggerated calm, a calm he couldn't possibly be feeling, but she could barely make out the words because her mind was careening wildly. All the air seemed to leave her lungs in a rush, and she had to force herself to say, "What do you want?"

"Do you doubt I will do as I say?" His voice had gone slightly wondering, as if he really wanted an answer.

"No," she managed. "No." And she thought: That voice! My God, I've heard that voice before.

In the parking lot, the truck exploded.

The voice whispered, "Pretty, wasn't it?"

Ellen felt rooted to the floor. Her hand, still on the window, trembled as the glass shook from the blast. People were streaming from the Civic Center, running into the parking lot, waving their arms. Black smoke rose to the sky in a single, feather-like plume.

"Call home," the man said softly.

"What?" Her mind suddenly refocused. "What did—"

But there was only a dial tone.

"Brimming with rich characters, romance and suspense, the plot resolves in a breathtaking denouement. This sure-handed debut marks the advent of a strong new talent."

—*Publishers Weekly*

WILLIAM H. LOVEJOY
YOUR TICKET TO A WORLD OF POLITICAL
INTRIGUE AND NONSTOP THRILLS. . . .

CHINA DOME   (0-7860-0111-9, $5.99/$6.99)

DELTA BLUE   (0-8217-3540-3, $4.50/$5.50)

RED RAIN   (0-7860-0230-1, $5.99/$6.99)

ULTRA DEEP   (0-8217-3694-9, $4.50/$5.50)

WHITE NIGHT   (0-8217-4587-5, $4.50/$5.50)

*Available wherever paperbacks are sold, or order direct from the
Publisher. Send cover price plus 50¢ per copy for mailing and
handling to Penguin USA, P.O. Box 999, c/o Dept. 17109,
Bergenfield, NJ 07621. Residents of New York and Tennessee
must include sales tax. DO NOT SEND CASH.*

ALL FALL DOWN

ZACHARY ALAN FOX

Pinnacle Books
Kensington Publishing Corp.
http://www.pinnaclebooks.com

PINNACLE BOOKS are published by

Kensington Publishing Corp.
850 Third Avenue
New York, NY 10022

Copyright © 1997 by Zachary Alan Fox

All rights reserved. No part of this book may be reproduced in any form or by any means without the prior written consent of the Publisher, excepting brief quotes used in reviews.

If you purchased this book without a cover, you should be aware that this book is stolen property. It was reported as "unsold and destroyed" to the Publisher and neither the Author nor the Publisher has received any payment for this "stripped book."

Pinnacle and the P logo Reg. U.S. Pat. & TM Off.

First Printing: September, 1997
10 9 8 7 6 5 4 3 2 1

Printed in the United States of America

For David and Ginger

In essence, the second law [of thermodynamics] says that everything in the entire universe began with structure and value and is irrevocably moving in the direction of random chaos and waste.

Jeremy Rifkin, *Entropy*

JUNE 11

LAS CRUCES, CALIFORNIA

Chaos is the oldest of the gods.

—*Hesiod, 8th Century B.C.*

1. Do It!

There were twenty-seven children on the school bus when Lowell Alexander DeVries stepped on board in a clown suit, put a gun to Linda Sowell's head and said, "I'll kill you right now if you give me any trouble."

Linda laughed as she turned to look at him while automatically easing the door shut—a towering figure in a wild orange wig, red and white polka dot suit, and painted-on happy face, who had climbed on behind Monica Ochoa, the little Down syndrome girl. A parent, of course, coming along on the bus for a birthday party later at school. Parents were always doing crazy things like that. But then she saw his eyes and the downturned mouth hidden within the gaudy red clown-smile, and she started to scream.

DeVries shoved the revolver furiously against her forehead, upsetting her glasses. "Believe me, I'll do it."

Linda Sowell began to stammer. "What do you—"

"Drive up to Palm and turn left. I'll give you directions. If you try to signal anybody, I'll kill you and every damn kid on this bus."

Then he turned to the handicapped students in their special seats and smiled, Chaos smiling excitedly with him as he pointed the revolver at a child chosen at random. "Hey kids!" he said happily. "Have I got a surprise for you!" And pulled the trigger.

8:33 A.M.

Standing in her tiny kitchen Ellen Camacho jumped back and swore softly as the coffee she was pouring splashed over the edge of the cup and onto the tile countertop. She couldn't afford to get any on her clothes; they were the only ones ironed. Hurriedly mopping up the mess with a paper towel, she picked up the ceramic cup and took a quick sip, putting it down as the weather report came on the radio. Four-year-old Denise was seated at the table behind her, watching Woody Woodpecker over her Lucky Charms, and Ellen had to turn up the sound to hear. "Hot," the morning DJ was saying needlessly, "a hundred and eight here in Las Cruces, a hundred and twelve up at Palm Springs, a hundred and twenty in Needles . . ."

Hot! Ellen agreed and flicked it off. Desert heat. But she could stand it. Better than L.A. heat, or anything else about Los Angeles. Four years in La La Land working downtown street patrol—gangs, crack heads, homeless, and crazies—and she had jumped at the chance to return to Las Cruces, heat or not. The fact that the police chief was a childhood friend and her marriage had just spun apart had made the decision easier. Three years ago. Almost to the day. It had been 108 then, also—or 106 or 110—with humidity down near 15 percent. Dry. Like the inside of an oven. And *hot*.

Denise giggled excitedly, dropping her spoon into the bowl as Woody chased Wally Walrus across a parking lot.

"Turn it down, hon, you'll wake Grandfather."

The girl jumped off the chair and sprinted to the television. She never walks anywhere, Ellen thought with a touch of envy for the manic energy of the young. Even the heat didn't slow her down. Of course, Denise thinks this is normal; she's not used to anything else.

"Bye-bye!" Denise said suddenly from in front of the TV, opening and closing both hands in an exaggerated wave, then dropping to the floor and disappearing behind the couch. Ellen hurriedly put down her coffee and raced around the couch, arms outstretched. *"I'm going to get you,"* she whispered with mock seriousness, and Denise giggled breathlessly, scrambling away on her hands and knees. Ellen marveled at the joy her daughter took in repeating the rituals of daily life. Every morning at breakfast she would wave bye-bye and Ellen would have to chase after her. Pleasure in the familiar, she thought, something we all experience. And maybe why Ellen had moved back to Las Cruces.

Denise had scurried around to the back of the couch. Ellen caught up with her, reached out, and loosely grabbed the girl's ankle, but Denise squealed and pulled free, continuing on to the other side. This time I won't follow the script, Ellen thought, and turned around and came at her daughter from the other direction. Surprised, Denise scrambled to her feet and started to run. But her shoe became tangled with the couch and she tumbled suddenly to the floor next to the glass-topped coffee table. Ellen gasped, reaching out frantically, but the girl was already sitting up, laughing.

"Don't scare me like that," Ellen said, her heart pounding. "You know what the doctor told you about banging your head." She looked at the girl with concern.

"Didn't bang my head," Denise said happily. "My *seat!*" And she began scrambling away again. "Bye-bye."

"Not this time, hon. I've got to get ready for work. And you've got to finish your green eggs and ham." That was Denise's term for breakfast, after the Dr. Seuss book she always insisted Paul read to her when he came over in the evening.

The girl pranced to the table, sing-songing, "I do not like them, Sam-I-am. I do not like green eggs and ham."

Ellen glanced at the clock. Only ten minutes until the sitter arrived. She started tidying up, arranging the pink and green floral cushions on the couch and neatly stacking Denise's toys on the bottom shelf of the coffee table. This place is too cheerful for an adult and too neat for a child, a girlfriend of hers had once said, peering critically around the living room, and Ellen had laughed. Okay, so she was a little compulsive about cleaning. Maybe it was her way of drawing a curtain against the past; the years with Pete had been messy in more ways than one, and she didn't want to be reminded of them. Anyway, she didn't want Mrs. Garcia—Julie—to have to do any straightening up. Julie was a godsend, with good sitters, or any sitters, for that matter, almost impossible to find nowadays. Ellen guarded Mrs. Garcia's identity as if it were a state secret, mumbling off-handedly about neighborhood teenagers when acquaintances asked about her child-care arrangements. Actually, Julie was probably fifty. Like Ellen, she had been born in Las Cruces, but they'd never met until Ellen had arrested the father of one of the kids Mrs. Garcia had been watching. He'd only been cited for public drunkenness, but both parents had returned to Mexico two days later with their three-year-old and suddenly Julie had had an opening. Paul had given her a look and said something about abusing her authority to find a sitter, but Ellen had laughed and told him that all's fair in love and war. And baby-sitting.

The telephone next to the toaster rang and Ellen grabbed it quickly before it woke her grandfather. She knew it had to be dispatch. But what could be important enough to call about when they knew she was on her way in?

"It's Jeannie, Ellen. Better saddle up. You won't believe this one. No one else does."

2. Lock Up

Still in his clown suit Lowell DeVries stood by the open door of the bus in the oppressive heat of the aged building and screamed, *"Off! Now! Go, go, go, faster, faster!* You—" He grabbed Linda Sowell by the wrist and yanked her off the steps, sending her sprawling to the ground. "Get these kids down that ramp now. *Now!*"

Trembling with fear, Linda struggled to her feet. "Please," she gasped, but the man was out of control, screaming at the top of his voice. Two boys about seven and nine stepped uncertainly off the bus, crying loudly, their faces contorted with terror as they looked at the clown, waving his gun and screaming at the driver. DeVries instantly seized them by the arms and hurled them viciously toward the ramp leading to an underground room. *"Move, move, move!"*

Other children were coming off the bus now, convulsed with sobs, howling, moaning, staring in horror around the huge, frighteningly dark building. With a fierce backhand swing DeVries struck Linda Sowell across the face with the barrel of his revolver. "Faster, damn it! Get those bastards down there."

"Some of them can't walk," she managed through tears, but he screamed, *"Do it!"* then hopped onto the bus and began pulling children from their seats and pushing them furiously from the door to the ground below. They were all crying now; some seemed unable to speak, moaning and blubbering and howling, and DeVries grimaced with distaste as he yanked them by the arm and forced them off. Linda was trying to comfort the most disabled, leading them toward the ramp, when DeVries jumped down, grabbing her and yanking her back on board. "Use the lift, get them off of here," he shouted, indicating the five children in wheelchairs.

Hurriedly, Linda dropped into the driver's seat, her heart pounding too wildly to think, and operated the power lift to accommodate the wheelchairs. DeVries stood outside watching, then, as he had thousands of times before, put the first two fingers of his right hand on the underside of his left wrist and felt his pulse. Seventy-eight. Too high, he thought, too high. But to be expected. It was finally happening. It was natural to be excited. Suppressing an urge to smile, he shouted, "Hurry up, goddamn it, or I'll kill every one of these little bastards."

He reached in his shirt pocket, drew out a list, and used a pencil to tick off the first two items.

1. DO IT.
2. LOCK UP.

This time he did smile. Just wait, he thought, his excitement growing as he stared at the bus. *Just wait!*

8:49 A.M.

Speeding along Van Buren, Ellen could sense the excitement a mile away—too many cars out, too many people, too much noise. Still, it didn't seem real; someone must have gotten their information wrong, thought they'd seen something they hadn't, panicked, and called the police. When she turned on Date, though, and saw four of the town's six police cars jammed in the intersection, doors thrown open, lights flashing, radios blaring, she knew it had to be true. With a sinking feeling in the pit of her stomach, she thought, Just like L.A. She wondered how long it had been since Las Cruces had experienced a major crime of any sort. Probably last year when Rona Two Crows had shot her husband in the leg when he'd come home drunk and tried to beat her up. She couldn't think of anything at all previous to that.

Yellow crime scene tape had already been haphazardly run across the intersection and along the sidewalk of the determinedly middle-class neighborhood, and twenty or thirty people hovered uneasily behind it with the half-wondering, half-excited look observers always had. Two uniformed patrolmen were hastily setting up saw horses at the far intersection while another waved traffic onto a side street. Ellen pulled her Toyota in behind Chief Paul Whitehorse's red Jeep Cherokee and stepped out just as a squadron of F-14s thundered low across the sky, heading to the navy bombing range in the hills twenty miles east. It was such a common sight this time of year that only tourists and newcomers glanced up, the natives merely pausing automatically for fifteen seconds before continuing their conversations.

Whitehorse detached himself from two patrolmen who were moving along the middle of the street with evidence envelopes and trash bags, heads bent to the ground as they looked for debris, and walked over to her. He was a tall, thick-set man of forty-three, with a rugged, dark face and black hair pulled back into a short ponytail. His gaze lingered on her for a moment.

"Hard to believe, isn't it?"

Ellen's eyes narrowed as she stared around at the officers and bystanders and squad cars. Everything seemed to be in a heightened state of confusion. "You don't really think it's a kidnapping, do you, Paul? A school bus? The driver probably just got lost or had engine trouble."

Whitehorse shook his head, spoke calmly, as he always did. "The driver's been doing this route for two years. Her son was on the bus. He's retarded. The whole bus was learning-disabled and mentally and physically handicapped kids. They all go to a special class over at Kessler."

There were only two grammar schools in Las Cruces, Kessler and Fremont, and one high school. Both the grammar schools had gone to year-round scheduling because of overcrowding. Ellen looked at her watch. "What time was the bus supposed to arrive?"

"Twenty-five to eight. School starts at a quarter to."

"More than an hour ago."

"At eight the vice principal got in her car and started looking. She figured like you—breakdown, flat tire, something like that. She backtracked the whole route. All the kids had been picked up. The last one would have gotten on at that house on the corner at about twenty after. So something happened between here and Kessler."

Ellen looked around. The crowd behind the yellow tape had quickly doubled in size, and some of them were shouting to the two patrolmen nearby. Parents, she thought; they must be frantic, their children disappearing like this, and her heart went out to them. She said, "Did anyone see anything?"

"Woman in the house up there, the yellow and white one, thinks she might have seen someone get on the bus. Fergy's going door to door taking statements." He paused, looking at her without emotion, waiting for the inevitable.

Ellen said, "You get a description?"

"Yeah. Pretty good one, too. Six feet tall, wearing red and white polka dots, orange hair, painted face."

"You're kidding me."

"A clown."

"Jesus."

A man in civilian clothes was snapping pictures with a 35 mm camera. Howard Stines, Las Cruces' one-man crime lab. Chief Whitehorse said, "Kind of a toss-up who I give this to—you or Zach."

There were only two detectives in the department, Ellen and Zachary Harris. Zach handled robbery and homicide, Ellen everything else.

"So far as we know there's no homicide, so I guess it's you."

Ellen glanced at him with the sort of secret look that passes only between lovers, which they had been for two years. "You try giving this to Zach and I'll shoot you in the kneecaps. Has the department ever had a kidnapping before?" There certainly hadn't been one in her memory, and she had lived here most of her thirty-four years.

"Custody dispute, five, six years ago, when you were playing big city cop. Ricky Cruz—remember him from school? Little guy from the reservation, used to race around on an old Harley? He took his two-year-old girl for a weekend visit—he and Lela split up the year before—and never came back. San Diego police picked him up in Balboa Park a few days later. That's it. I know what you're thinking—we've got no protocol, no established procedures. So we'll make it up as we go along. Can't be too much different from any other crime scene: look for witnesses, talk to folks at the school, see if anyone had a grudge against the teachers or administrators, collect physical evidence. We both know time is the important thing here if we want those kids found alive, so we'll put everyone we can on it. I already called the F.B.I., asked 'em to hurry in some suits from L.A. to help us in-juns. Cross your fingers and hope they show up soon. Till then, you're in charge."

"The media know?"

"Not as far as I can tell. You better have someone call the radio station right away and have them ask over the air if anyone saw the bus after seven-twenty or so. Big yellow school bus, someone must have seen it."

"People see it every day, Paul. They're used to seeing it. I don't think it'd attract anyone's attention. Have the parents been notified?"

"The principal's doing it. I suppose most of them know. Some of them are over there." He nodded toward the knot of men and women behind the crime scene tape.

"Someone's going to have to talk to them. They've got to be pretty upset."

Whitehorse shook his head. "My job. But I don't like it." He smiled thinly at her. "How you feeling this morning? Seems like I kept you up a bit late last night."

"I was a little slow getting going until I got the call. It kind of got my attention. You put out a statewide A.P.B.?"

"Soon as I heard. But you gotta figure the first thing he'd do is dump the bus someplace, put the kids in a couple of vans, maybe, or a truck."

"Maybe," Ellen said. "But he'd figure no one would start looking right away. He had forty minutes or so, even longer until the police would be notified. Forty minutes could put him in Palm Springs or Riverside. Or Mexico."

"Chief." One of the patrolmen had come up and was holding a see-through plastic bag at eye level. Inside there was a silver dinner knife. "Found it in the gutter up by the date palm yonder."

"Looks like sterling," Ellen said, staring at it. "Too expensive for me. Pretty dull, isn't it? Not the sort of thing to commandeer a bus with. And why would it be in the gutter?"

"Send it along with Howard," Whitehorse said. "Probably doesn't mean anything. Don't want the F.B.I. saying we left things behind though."

As the patrolman wandered over to Howard Stines, a few of the parents began yelling at Whitehorse. He turned at once to Ellen. "You organize it. Have someone talk to the folks at the school, get the media involved, get people looking. You set things up the way you want. You can use the whole department if you need to. But we gotta move fast. A bus load of disabled children—it's going to be tough on them."

"Something like this happened in central California years ago. Two or three guys hijacked a bus full of kids and hid them in another bus they'd buried in a rock quarry after putting in an air shaft so they wouldn't suffocate. Must've been in the mid-seventies."

Whitehorse nodded. "I remember that. Don't recall what happened though."

"It was a ransom snatch. I think they wanted a few million dollars. They weren't very bright. They didn't leave a guard at the quarry, and the kids and the driver dug themselves out the same day."

"Maybe we got ourselves a copycat."

"Maybe," Ellen agreed. "Let's hope not. If I remember my criminology classes at Arizona State, the one common trait of ransom kidnappers is brutality. Brutality and stupidity."

"That's why we gotta come down quick on this." He considered a moment. "If you snatched a bus load of mostly poor kids, who the hell would you ask for the ransom?"

Another squadron of F-14s zoomed by, out of sight but loud, vibrating the ground with shock waves. Ellen stuck her hands in her pockets, waited until she could be heard again, then said, "There's a lot of options, I guess. The school, the police, the radio station. I suppose you'd expect the state to come up with the money."

"You better set up some recording equipment on the school's phone system then. Do it as soon as you can this morning. I'll have Charley Deets over at the radio station record all in-coming calls. Everything coming into the police station is already taped. I reckon I ought to call the D.A.'s office over in El Centro and see about getting authorization for tracing calls, too."

"Better call the sheriff and get their helicopter checking county territory for the bus."

"They're already up. Lots of places to hide it though."

The parents on the sidewalk were becoming louder. "Where's our children?" a woman shouted angrily, and a man screamed, "Damn it, talk to us!"

"Guess I better go over there," Paul muttered. "What the hell am I going to say? Don't worry? It's going to be all right?"

Ellen looked into his face. There was an ugly two-inch vertical scar along his right eye where he had fallen off a rock, hunting rattlesnakes when he was eleven. The incident had become legendary in Las Cruces. Paul's leg had broken in two places and he lay in the midsummer sun less than ten feet from a huge granddaddy rattler for five hours before his uncle found him. Just the boy and the snake, staring at each other, neither of them moving. Then the rattler turned its head and slowly slithered away. Ever since, a couple of his buddies from the old days called him Snake or Snake Eyes. He was giving her that look now.

"You want me to help talk to them?" she asked. "Maybe a woman—"

"No sense both of us doing it. It's me they want to see."

Repressing an urge to give him a kiss, Ellen patted his arm. Paul nodded curtly and walked over to the yellow tape, where the crowd had grown to about sixty people. Ellen could hear the buzz and hum of anxious voices as he neared and felt a tug of empathy for him. How do you tell a group of parents not to worry about their kidnapped children, especially handicapped children like these?

"Hey, Sarge."

Ellen turned to see Manny Rios standing behind her. She was never sure what to think about Manny. He did his job adequately, but there was something of the smart-ass about him, a constant smirk on his face as if he were laughing at some private joke at everyone else's expense. He was shifting from foot to foot with his typical nervous tension. "You running things?"

"Yeah, Manny. What've you got?"

"Just the knife." He shrugged and put his hands on his hips. "We covered two blocks in every direction. That's it, along with two bags full of trash. Fast-food wrappers and the like. It's all going to the lab. But don't bet on nothin'."

Ellen moved out into the center of the intersection and stared around. They were in one of the newer housing developments—three and four bedroom homes, grass in the front struggling to stay alive in the dry, rocky soil, scraggly palm and yucca trees lining the street like exhausted sentries. She remembered when all this was scrub. As a kid she used to come out here with boys from the reservation to ride her bike and chase jackrabbits and lizards. Sometimes her grandfather would have her collect jimsonweed for visions or for medicine. Who would have thought then that people would pay $100,000 to live in a cheaply built house on a tiny piece of hard-scrabble desert? Manny Rios followed along behind her, taking off his cap and wiping sweat from his head. "No tire tracks, no witnesses except for the old biddy up there claims she saw a clown. Probably had a little peyote for breakfast."

"Is anyone from the school here?"

Rios glanced around. "Vice principal was. Must have gone back. Didn't want to face the parents, I guess. Don't blame her."

Ellen turned and yelled to a patrolman standing by his car. "Lou, I got a job for you."

Louis Sharperson, forty-four and the oldest uniformed officer in Las Cruces, ambled over. Every time she looked at him Ellen couldn't help but think he'd have long ago been bounced off any big city force; at two hundred and seventy pounds he was at least eighty pounds overweight and always looked as if he were one hamburger from a heart attack.

"Ellen." Sharperson mopped his face with a handkerchief as he approached.

"Stop by the station and pick up some recording equipment, then hustle out to Kessler and tap into their phone system. You know how to do that?"

He grinned sheepishly and shoved the handkerchief back in his pocket. "Yeah, I think maybe I done something like that once or twice. Always legally, of course."

"Show the principal and office staff how to operate it, then just leave everything. I'll be out there pretty quick, might even get there before you do."

"Gotcha."

As Sharperson left for his car, she turned again to Rios, who was staring blankly down the broad street. "What are you thinking, Manny?"

"I'm thinking, don't jump to conclusions. We don't know if this is a kidnap. Could be something else. Could be nothin'."

"But if it is?"

He turned to look at her. "We don't find the bad guy real soon, these kids are going to be real dead."

"So get moving, Manny. You're looking for a big yellow bus. Or anyone who saw one after about seven-twenty. First thing you do is go to KDJX and have them make an appeal for witnesses. When you've done that call the Palm Springs TV station—get people involved, get them looking. Then you're going to have to get in your car and dog it. Start from here and go west on Date. Forget the houses for now, but stop at gas stations and convenience stores and so on. Talk to people. Make something happen. Maybe someone out there saw something."

He looked at her and frowned. "But you don't believe it."

"Got to do it, Manny. There're twenty-eight lives at stake."

The house where the bus had last stopped was about fifty

feet from where Whitehorse was conferring with the distraught parents. Ellen walked over by herself and stood a moment on the sidewalk, trying to imagine what it had been like. She closed her eyes. Is he a psycho? Why the hell a clown outfit? Did he burst on board the bus and yell and scream and wave a shotgun? What did the driver do? How did the kids react?

Madness, she thought with a chill. It must have been complete madness.

Going back into the middle of the street, she began to walk toward the far intersection, where Howard Stines and a patrolman were sprawled on their hands and knees peering intently at something in the gutter. As Ellen approached, Stines took a pair of tweezers from a molded plastic kit on the ground. He glanced up at her briefly, then hunched down again in the gutter and probed in a quarter-inch of murky water. "Glass," he muttered. "Four shards so far. None over six centimeters in length. More on the sidewalk, probably some on the grass, too. I haven't checked yet."

"From the bus?"

"Looks like. Safety glass, you know. From the way it's distributed I'd say he must have shot the window out. It's the only way it would have ended up way over here." He picked up a piece with the tweezers and held it to the light. It appeared to be smeared with something opaque. "Blood," Stines said. "Almost certainly. I can tell you as soon as I get back to the lab."

Ellen's stomach turned over. "You think he shot one of the kids?" It seemed incomprehensible. What possible reason would there be?

Stines dropped the fragments in an evidence envelope. "Blood's fresh, Ellen. Could be the kidnapper's or the driver's. But never bet on good luck."

"My God." But why? she again wondered. What value would the children have for him dead?

Stines completed picking up the shards. "Safety glass

shatters rather than breaks. That's why there isn't much of it." He turned and stared at Ellen through his thick spectacles. "Doesn't look good for the children, does it? Guy must be a psycho. Better hope he didn't shoot more than one."

"Better hope we get to him before he does." Ellen paused a moment. "Keep this to yourself, guys. We don't want the parents going crazy with worry." Turning away, she glanced at her watch. Time to get to the school. "Bobby!" she yelled, and Bobby Muledeer, the patrolman who had discovered the dinner knife, hustled over.

"Wrap it up," Ellen said. "Howard can finish here. You go help Paul deal with the parents, then get back to the station house."

Muledeer squinted at the knot of parents. "Come on, Ellen. I'm not any good at that sort of thing."

"Just do it," she said. "And now, Bobby. Not in ten minutes. We've got to get moving here."

8:52 A.M.

Linda Sowell could see nothing in the darkness.

Where am I? Oh God, where . . .

Panic gripped her so that she couldn't think, couldn't make her mind work. Her heart pounded wildly and a strange sound like a half-cry came from her lips. What has he done to us? Where are we?

All around her the children were crying, screaming, all of them, afraid of the dark, terrified of the clown who hadn't played with them at all but had shot his gun in the bus and grabbed and shoved and hurt them. Some must have had their arms and legs broken, so fiercely had they been thrown down the ramp.

Why'd he shoot at a window? When Linda had heard the shots she whirled around to see what had happened, but the man had screamed and struck her in the face and wouldn't let her look. It was just the window, wasn't it? He hadn't shot a child!

Oh my God! Where's Eric? she wondered suddenly as her mind began to function again.

Dear God, he hadn't shot Eric, had he? No, no—she'd seen him running toward the ramp as the clown had shouted and waved his gun at them.

"Eric!" She screamed his name above the wailing. "Eric!"

There has to be a light someplace. There has to be! She couldn't even tell how large the room was. Tiny, probably, the way the children's howling was everywhere, pounding at her, drilling into her ears.

She shouted her son's name again and a girl close by began sobbing louder. Linda's pulse began to throb. "Eric!"

Panicking, she took a quick step, hit something with her foot, kept moving.

He's here, he's here somewhere. I know he is. I saw him go in.

"Eric!" Her voice had become shrill.

God, it was so dark!

"Momma."

Fingers touched her frantically. Linda reached down, seized them eagerly; wet with slobber. The cerebral palsy boy, she thought and instantly yanked her hand away, feeling both revulsion and hysteria and knowing it was unworthy of her but unable to resist. Her voice cracked as she yelled her son's name again, then heard him nearby this time.

"Momma!"

He grabbed at her leg, clutching with both hands, letting go as another child fell against him. Linda bent down, scooped him up. "Eric, it's Mommy, it's okay Eric, it's Mommy." She held him close, pressing tightly so his face was next to hers, kissing, soothing, cradling the back of his head with her hand.

The screaming and howling around them was deafening. She had to find a light and console the children. Still holding her son she began to walk slowly sideways, carefully putting her left foot out half a stride to make sure the floor was clear, then dragging her right foot behind it. On her fourth step she hit a wheelchair with her shoe and moved cautiously around it. Two more steps and she was at a wall. Bare cement or plaster. What kind of room is this? she wondered.

Light switches were about five feet off the ground, she thought, placing her hand at shoulder level and advancing slowly, running her fingers up and down the uneven surface of the wall. Nothing. Cautiously, she began to move forward. Then her fingers discovered what she was looking for. She quickly flipped the switch, and at once the whole horrible scene jumped alive in front of her: twenty-seven children, some sitting on the floor, some sprawled on the ground, others standing uncertainly, all blinking in the sudden light, rubbing their eyes, and crying. The five wheelchairs were grouped together near the ramp where they had landed after being pushed inside. Six-year-old Emily Scranton, a favorite of Linda's, was sprawled on the floor, sobbing uncontrollably.

Quickly Linda put Eric down and rushed over to Emily, lifting the tiny girl and trying to comfort her. "It's all right, Emily, all right." Then with a sense of horror she again recalled the gunshots—how many had there been?—and the shattering glass and terrible screaming that had rocked the bus.

He shot at the windows, not the children, she thought. He was trying to scare us.

She had heard the window break. It was the glass exploding as much as the gunshots that had made the boys and girls scream so. Quickly she counted the children, just to be sure. Twenty-six! Please, no, don't let it be. Please.

"Who's not here?" she said loudly, hearing the hysteria tearing at her voice.

A little girl—Linda's mind was so confused she couldn't remember her name—half-sobbed with fear and excitement, "Emilio. The clown shot him. I saw the blood on his shirt."

Linda put her hand out to steady herself against the wall. Emilio was a six-year-old dyslexic from the reservation who was scheduled to enter a regular classroom in September. Why would the clown shoot him?

"Teacher, teacher, why are we here?" Arturo, the little Salvadoran boy, asked frantically, grabbing onto her hand and pulling. Many of the Hispanic children called her "teacher," and Linda never attempted to correct them, thinking it improved their behavior if they thought of her as a teacher rather than a bus driver.

"I don't know, Arturo, I don't know why we're here." Then she recognized her mistake and immediately tried to rectify it. Bending down, she smiled broadly and looked into his face. "It's a game, Arturo. The clown put us here for a game. It's funny!" She tried to laugh but was so deathly frightened that it came out as a gurgling sound, and she quickly added, "We'll get out pretty soon. Then Mrs. Harvey and Mrs. Agostino will have snacks for us all. Would you like a snack?"

Arturo began to cry. Linda looked in despair at the madness and confusion around her and raised her voice. "Boys and girls, quiet! Be quiet, please."

Two little girls, about five or six but still in diapers, were lying on the ground, kicking and screaming hysterically. Oh God, they're having a fit, Linda thought with panic. I don't know what to do. I don't know how to care for them. I can't do anything.

Her eyes raced around as if something might be nearby to help her deal with these children. The room was larger than she had first thought, maybe thirty by thirty feet, but oppressive like a dungeon, with bare cement walls and ceiling and floor. A badly decayed red and blue braided rug covered part of the floor and provided the only color. Against a wall she spotted a television and she hurried over and turned it on. Static. No antenna or cable, evidently. A VCR rested on top. She pushed the Play button, and suddenly the television sprang to life with Disney's *101 Dalmatians*. Eagerly she turned up the sound. "Look, kids. A movie!"

But no one was paying attention. Even Eric was crying at

her feet. Dear God, she thought as a terrible sense of hopelessness began to clamp itself on her heart. How am I going to deal with this?

"Mommy, Mommy," Eric was saying between sobs. "What's that? What's that?" He was pointing toward a filthy curtain that hung from the ceiling at the far wall. One of the children, Tiffany, the eleven-year-old mute child, was clutching at Linda's waist. Linda took her by the hand and crossed to the curtain. It was perhaps six feet long and hung from a corner of the room to create a small three-sided alcove. Behind it there was a chemical toilet, the sort that people take on camping trips.

"It's a toilet, Eric. A bathroom."

Just then her eyes lighted on a door adjacent to the curtain. She crossed to it quickly. Locked. The handle wouldn't budge, felt as though it hadn't been turned in years. But maybe it was a way out.

At that moment the door up the ramp banged loudly open and Linda spun around. DeVries, in tailored slacks and a striped short-sleeved dress shirt, pointed at her and said, "You! Come here!"

9:30 A.M.

Hurrying to the school in her car, Ellen's mind turned to the cliché she'd heard so often from L.A. homicide investigators: if you don't solve a murder within twenty-four hours, you won't solve it. Not strictly true, perhaps, though close enough. But the time-line in kidnapping was different: if you don't get the hostages back within six to twelve hours, you aren't going to get them back alive. Except for the occasional politician destined for public humiliation, hostages are liabilities, nothing but trouble to a kidnapper. Easier to kill them and be done with it.

And the offender? She tried to recall again what she had learned about kidnappers in her criminology courses. But that had been ten or twelve years ago, and whatever she had read then had been transformed over time into a set of amorphous, vague memories that ran together in her mind. Kidnappers—ransom kidnappers, at any rate, not the political brand—tended to be stupid and brutish, she seemed to recall, losers desperately seeking that one quick score that would make up for a lifetime of futility. But inevitably they were caught because there was a single inescapable flaw in every kidnap scheme—the pay-off. There is simply no way to exchange a large sum of money in such a manner that the kidnapper can be assured of escape. It can't be done.

Of course, as she remembered one of her professors saying, statistics on kidnappings come only from those that are reported to the police. Who knows how many industrialists or film stars or politicians followed kidnappers' instructions to tell no one when their child or spouse disappeared? It had to happen sometimes. Money quickly changed hands, the victim returned, and no one was the wiser because everyone kept quiet. That was the key to success, of course: keep it quiet.

But not this time.

Whoever took those kids knew there'd be an instant hue and cry, knew they'd all be the center of attention until the children were released, that time would stand still.

Wait until the press finds out, she thought, and remembered the central California kidnapping; even though the children were free within hours, it had been a media circus for weeks.

So whoever's behind this, she thought, knows for a certainty there's no way to keep it quiet. Maybe doesn't want to. But there's no way he can get away, either. He has to be psychotic. Or political. A terrorist group, making a statement and not caring if they got out alive. Must be.

Just then a helicopter from the Palm Springs TV station appeared out of the haze to the north and cut obliquely across the sky, heading in the direction of City Hall.

Less than an hour since the crime was reported and already it's starting, she thought. God help us.

3. Warning

Lowell Alexander DeVries stood calmly by the open door, the revolver in one hand, a child's lunch box in the other, and stared down at Linda Sowell in the underground chamber. Perfect, he thought. There hadn't been a sound until he'd opened the door. Although he'd experimented with a radio, he couldn't be certain until all twenty-seven of them were actually down there. But the room had worked fine, just fine, exactly as he had planned.

How lucky he had been to find this place! There couldn't be more than a half-dozen people in the world who were even aware of its existence. DeVries, though, knew it as well as he knew his own house, had spent hours carefully—obsessively, yes!—studying its plans before first coming out here thirteen months ago and removing the aged chain on the door with a pair of bolt cutters, then grinding through the lock with a portable power drill. A mangy half-wild cat, attracted by the noise, had limped up nearby and watched with curiosity and fear, occasionally jumping back and snarling at this intruder into its previously inviolable territory. Ignoring the animal's angry complaints, DeVries had yanked open the door, then grabbed the five-cell flashlight and camp lantern he'd brought with him, and stepped inside.

For a long moment he'd stood completely motionless, eyes squeezed shut, breathing air no one had breathed for forty years, forcing himself to savor and experience the moment, committing not just the impressions but the emotions to memory as the hairs on his neck and arms stiffened and his senses intensified. Then he allowed his eyes to blink open and he peered into the incredible, still darkness, his heart pounding. "Now it begins," he'd said aloud, and the cat, overcome with curiosity, padded up close and also stared around. Time to go to work. Switching on the lantern, DeVries had advanced cautiously into the room, holding the flickering light aloft, shadows leaping ahead on the walls and ceiling as he moved. The room was thirty by twenty-eight, he remembered: eight hundred and forty square feet. No windows, of course, but the twelve-foot ceiling gave it a sense of space.

For three weeks DeVries had come out on Fridays and stayed over until Sunday afternoon. The cat set up housekeeping somewhere nearby, and Lowell, who normally loathed them, found himself anticipating its visits. Soon he surprised himself by bringing it milk and scraps of food. He named it Ellen as a sign of . . . what? Respect? Or to heighten the anticipation?

It had been necessary to tap into the powerlines to bring in lighting, and he'd installed a chemical toilet, as much for himself as the hostages, in the curtained off area. A table and TV and VCR were brought from his own house. The night before the kidnapping he'd dropped off two cartons with several boxes of breakfast cereal and a five-gallon bottle of water. He didn't ask himself if he had forgotten anything. It simply wasn't within the realm of the possible.

And now it was all coming together.

Linda stared fearfully at the man as he stepped halfway down the ramp.

"What do you want with us?" she asked, trying to make her voice angry and demanding but mostly, she knew, sounding scared. She shoved her hands in her shorts pockets to keep them from trembling.

DeVries looked at her without emotion, then glanced at the turmoil in the room below and winced. He must have been in his early forties, Linda thought fleetingly—well dressed, nice looking, dark hair receding a bit. Summoning up what remained of her courage, she said, "Where's Emilio? What have you done with him?"

DeVries glanced idly around the room again, his gaze unexpectedly coming to rest on one of the older children. His body seemed to stiffen. "Who's she, the pretty one in the sun dress?"

Linda instantly recognized the look in his eyes and started to panic. "Stay away from her. Don't you ever—" Her voice shook and she began to move toward the child but DeVries took two quick steps down the ramp. Dropping the lunch box, he seized her by the wrist and twisted painfully. "What's her name?"

"Tiffany," Linda managed between sobs. "She's mute. Leave her alone. Please! Please!"

"Mute?" DeVries looked at the child with fascination. "Interesting." He walked over to the girl, who stared at him without emotion. "How old is she?"

"Eleven."

"Can she hear?"

"Yes."

"Why can't she talk, then?"

Linda shook her head helplessly.

DeVries dropped to one knee and peered into the girl's face. "Can you hear me, Tiffany?"

The child stared at him but gave no indication of understanding.

"Do you like me, Tiffany? I'm your friend." His hand went to the beautiful French braid that fell halfway to her waist, then to her bare leg, and began to move slowly up and down, caressing. "You're very pretty. Did you know that? I like you. I like you a lot."

Linda rushed over to him in a panic. "Get away from her. Do you hear me? Get away!"

With his other hand DeVries drew the girl closer. Gently, he kissed her on the forehead, his lips lingering on her flesh. "So pretty."

"Get away from her," Linda screamed again, and two of the other children began howling.

DeVries came slowly to his feet. "I'm afraid I need to leave for a while. I have to give the police something to do. But I'll be back shortly. You'll wait for me, won't you, Linda? And you, too, Tiffany?" He hugged the girl to his body with one hand. "We have much to accomplish, all of us. In the meantime, there's a video for the VCR, and two boxes of food. Make the best of it. You're going to be here for thirty-eight hours."

"Thirty-eight hours?" Linda shouted. "You can't do that! The children need special care, most of them need medication."

DeVries smiled at her as he retrieved the lunch box. "Every kid who's gone missing in the last twenty years has 'needed medication.' Forget it."

"But you don't understand." Her voice began to race out of control. "They do need medication. They're handicapped, most of them have medical problems, diabetes and—"

"You're not helping things," he interrupted. "Most of you are going to remain here thirty-eight hours. You have food, you have entertainment. I expected you to complain, it's only normal under the circumstances. But it does not alter the situation in any way. I suggest that you try to organize things, calm the children down. It will make the time remaining to you easier."

"You can't do this!" Linda pleaded. "You can't—"

"I can and I have. Please understand that this is not a caprice, Ms. Sowell. I have given it a great deal of attention. Every possible contingency has been considered and dealt with. Every move has been gone over a hundred times. There is simply no way for this plan to go wrong. Nothing remains but the inevitable." Turning abruptly, he disappeared up the ramp, and the door slammed shut.

Linda's resolve, which had been slipping since he'd rushed them off the bus, finally gave way, and she began to sob uncontrollably.

9:40 A.M.

Kessler was the newer of Las Cruces' two grammar schools, a low-slung, bunker-like building without windows, looking, Ellen thought as she sped past the tiny parking lot, probably very forbidding and institutional from a child's point of view. There was a tiny, perfectly trimmed triangle of grass in front by the flagpole and another larger patch in the rear, but most of the play yard was blacktop and probably 130 degrees in the summer. Fremont School, where she had gone as a child, was over on the opposite end of town, near the reservation, and probably fifty years old, but there were windows in every room, a huge playground in the back with shade trees, and a rutted circular area near the bike racks, where a half-century's worth of kids had played marbles.

Kessler was where Denise would be going in September if they took advantage of the Early Admissions Program, Ellen realized with a start. She wasn't sure if she liked that. But was it important enough to sell her house and move across town just to get Denise into Fremont? Motherhood, she thought with a smile, comes with more decisions than we anticipated, doesn't it? Maybe that's the price we pay for the joy of children. God, if some of my L.A. friends could hear me now! Pregnant? How did that happen? Like it was a terminal disease and her life was suddenly over. She'd have to spend every minute of the next few years changing diapers, cleaning up vomit, and taking temperatures, to hear them tell it. Pete had sulked for days when he'd found out, accused her of planning it even though her doctor wouldn't let her take birth control pills and Pete wouldn't use a condom. But the marriage was pretty much over by then anyway. All except the shouting, she thought wryly.

Pete, you jerk, the only thing you taught me in life is something I didn't want to learn: when it comes to love don't trust your feelings!

Instead, do a background check.

Why didn't he vanish from her memory the way he'd vanished from her life? "Disappear, you bastard. Disappear!" she said aloud, pounding her fist on the steering wheel. Sometimes she'd find herself staring into Denise's face, seeking traces of Pete and finding none, as though nature had taken its final revenge and erased all evidence of paternity.

Ellen had already ensured that her daughter wouldn't suffer by the absence of a father. Besides Paul and her grandfather there were any number of people, men and women, on the reservation to take her places and teach her things that a single mom didn't always have time for. Occasionally, Ellen would find herself fantasizing about all the things the two of them would get to do together in the future: going to movies and picnics, sewing a dress for the junior prom (only twelve more years to choose the color and material), struggling over algebra. Then Ellen would warn herself: Don't try to make up for your own mother's neglect. You can kill with love, too.

The small parking lot was full, so Ellen left her car in the loading zone and checked her watch as she hurried up to the door marked "Office." Already more than two hours since the children were taken. Inside, two frantic women in shorts were talking to an older woman behind a counter. The older woman—a secretary, Ellen assumed—was trying to calm them without success. "We don't know anything. I'm terribly, terribly sorry, but I think you'd be better off going down to the police station."

"But where can they be?" one of the women, a young Hispanic with an infant in a backpack, was saying in heavily accented English. "Why would someone do this?" She was in tears and put her hand on the counter as if she were about to collapse. The other woman, a stark, heavy-set blonde, said accusingly, "You must know something."

The secretary spread her arms in a futile gesture. "Really. All we know is the bus didn't get here."

"But someone—"

Ellen said, "Maybe I can help," and introduced herself. Smiling gently, sounding concerned, she said, "The F.B.I. should be here within the hour. With the announcement of the kidnapping on radio and TV, everyone in the desert will be searching for the children." She took a breath and looked at the two mothers. The best thing they could do

now, she went on, is go down to the police station. Someone there would be talking to the parents; maybe one of
them had some idea why the kids had been taken or who
might be behind it.

The blonde woman wasn't mollified, and the fear she felt
expressed itself in anger at Ellen. "Why can't the police
find them? How could you allow this to happen?"

"They're bound to turn up soon," Ellen said, hoping her
tone sounded convincing but at the same time feeling angry
with herself; the patronizing dead-calm voice people always
used at times like this never seemed to make things better.
But she didn't know what else to do.

The younger mother broke down into sobs. Ellen turned
to the other woman and said, "She needs your help. Perhaps
you could drive her to the police station."

The older woman's eyes flared as she started to object,
and Ellen immediately thought, She's probably never had
a Hispanic in her car. Then she reproached herself for
being unfair. This was no time for hostile stereotyping. The
woman hesitated just an instant, then took the other by the
elbow. With Ellen's help they got her into the blonde
woman's van. Hurrying back to the office, Ellen said, "Let
me use your phone for a moment."

The secretary handed the phone over the counter and
watched as Ellen punched out the number for Paul Whitehorse's secretary. "Better call Dr. Sanderson, Maggie. We've
got a lot of very worried parents. I'm going to be sending
them down to the station so we can group them in one
place." Fear, she thought, was more easily handled when you
had others to share it with; alone it can be overwhelming.

"But Dr. Sanderson has private patients today," Maggie
protested.

Ellen felt a spark of irritation but damped it down. Las
Cruces wasn't big enough to keep a psychologist on staff
and had to contract with Sanderson for his occasional assistance. Ellen didn't have much faith in the efficacy of
mental health "experts," but anyone was better than no one
in a situation like this. "Call him, Maggie. It's what he does.

Better call Father Raul and the minister down at First Baptist—Griffith or Griffin, I think. Tell them what's going on. They'll want to help. You can put everyone in the multi-purpose room. Have the janitors put out about a hundred chairs if we have that many. We'll have whole families there."

"I don't know if Paul is going to like having all these civilians here," Maggie said doubtfully.

Ellen sighed, annoyed at having to deal once again with the secretary's customary recalcitrance. Anything out of the ordinary was sure to be resisted by Maggie, who had been the previous chief's secretary and couldn't be fired. "It's okay, Maggie. And don't wait. These people have had their children stolen. We'll do whatever we can for them."

She hung up and said immediately, "The principal—"

"She's waiting for you," the secretary said and lifted up a panel in the counter so Ellen could come inside. The principal's office was down a short hallway. They stepped through the open door and into the neat, if somewhat cheerless, room. The principal was standing with her back to them, staring out the tiny vertical slice of tinted glass that served as a window to the playground. "Mrs. Gantt, this is—"

"Detective Sergeant Camacho," Ellen said and stepped across to shake hands with the woman, who turned to greet her. Mrs. Gantt was about sixty, petite, with gray hair and thick glasses that dangled from her neck on a chain. She was wearing a dress and heels, unusual for Las Cruces in the summer. Behind her on a wall were several plaques with official-looking seals and pictures of Mrs. Gantt standing small and insignificant next to local politicians and businessmen. As though the years had fallen away, Ellen's mind immediately slipped back to when she had been summoned to a similar principal's office to wait, even smaller and more insignificant, for a ride home when her mother had been too sick or angry or distracted to pick her up. Usually her grandfather would come, or her mother's sister, and Ellen would feel the sting of embarrassment for a week, though her friends never mentioned it.

"Sergeant." The principal stepped forward and shook hands nervously, then motioned Ellen to a chair before seating herself behind the desk. Her manner was stiff and unnatural, Ellen thought, like someone trying desperately to appear calm but not able to pull it off. "Do you have any news?" the woman asked at once. "Do you know where the children are?"

"I'm afraid not. I was hoping you'd be able to help us. Can you think of any reason at all why someone would want to do this? Did you have any intimation that something like this might happen?"

"Me?" Her voice rose abruptly as if she had been accused of something. "Why would I know anything?"

"I don't know," Ellen replied gently, trying to calm her. Evidently a lifetime of dealing with irate parents and school district bureaucrats had left her nerves frayed. Ellen said, "I thought someone might have been upset at the school. A neighbor angry at playground noise or—"

"No, of course not."

"No threatening phone calls? No strangers hanging around?"

"No." She was becoming more agitated.

"Schools can be flash points for community problems," Ellen said reasonably and added, "often quite unfairly." She was in a hurry to get back to the station but hoped for some help from the school, which meant getting this woman on her side. "You must have a thousand students—"

"Nine hundred and five," Mrs. Gantt said distractedly.

"That's quite a few families. Parents get angry at teachers about their children's progress or because their children were disciplined. Kids get in fights, break windows, get expelled for cheating. There's a lot of potential trouble with that many students."

"But nothing like that has happened. Nothing serious anyway. No one has gotten angry enough to steal our children."

The telephone on the desk buzzed, and Mrs. Gantt picked it up at once, listening to her secretary a moment, then turning to Ellen with a flustered look on her face. "It's the Palm Springs newspaper. They want to ask me about the kidnapping."

"Tell them no. We don't want a dozen different sources dealing with the media. Have them call the police station."

Mrs. Gantt spoke into the phone. "Tell them we have nothing to say, Luz. If anyone wants to talk about the kidnapping, have them call the police."

As she hung up, Ellen said, "I'm having someone come over with recording equipment for your phone system. There's a possibility the kidnapper might call here with a ransom demand."

The principal seemed to shrink within her clothes. "I can't believe this is happening."

"Have you had a chance to talk to their teacher yet? Does she have any idea at all why this has happened?"

"There are two teachers. Mrs. Agostino has kindergarten through third and Mrs. Harvey fourth through eighth. They can't imagine why—"

"Are they here now?"

"Of course. They're in their classrooms, waiting."

"I want you to send them to the police station. Perhaps they could help calm the parents. We'll want to interview them anyway. The handicapped kids are the only students bused in Las Cruces, aren't they?"

"They're the only ones the district transports. We can't afford more than one bus, with the people here always voting down bond requests."

"And your bus follows the same route each day?"

"More or less. Students move in or out of the district all the time. And we get a lot of migrants from Mexico who might only be here two or three months at a time. The driver gets a new map each time a child is added or deleted."

Ellen took her notebook from her pocket. "What do you know about her, the driver?"

"Linda Sowell? She's wonderful. It's a very difficult job. It involves much more than just driving a bus, you know. Sometimes she has to actually go up to the door and pick

the child up bodily if he or she can't walk or use a wheelchair. There are three or four who are so tiny they have to
be placed in car seats. And the wheelchairs have to be secured. Linda's marvelous at it, very helpful and loving.
She's never complained about anything, even when the
children get sick or lose control of their bladders."

"And her son was on the bus?"

Mrs. Gantt nodded. "He's retarded, I'm afraid. Brain
damaged, I believe. His mother took this job so she could
spend more time with him."

Mrs. Gantt hesitated for a moment, as if debating with
herself, then said in a more subdued tone, "Linda Sowell
graduated from Fremont and Kennedy, you know. I consider her one of our real success stories. She's had a very
difficult life. Her mother was a drug user, and Linda started
smoking crack cocaine when she was twelve or thirteen.
She spent six months in jail when she was about twenty. But
when her child was born, she began to turn her life around.
She doesn't even smoke cigarettes or drink alcohol now. It's
taken her seven years, but she's finished three years of college. She wants to be an L.H. teacher—learning handicapped."

"Do you have her home address?"

"Of course." She spun her Rolodex and read the address.

Ellen jotted it in her notebook. She didn't expect anything to come from it, but the house would have to be
searched. As she finished, Mrs. Gantt said, "Sergeant, I don't
mean to be telling you your business, but you need to find
those children and not waste your time here at school. I'm
familiar with their medical problems. If you don't get them
back by tonight—"

"We are looking, Mrs. Gantt. But without more information we're stymied. At this point, the only clue we have is a
witness who thinks she saw a clown get on the bus."

The principal nodded vaguely. "I heard someone mention that."

"Does it mean anything to you? Does a clown indicate

something? Do you sometimes have a clown come to school?"

"Of course. Parents, especially in the lower grades, like to put on parties and celebrations—birthdays and Fourth of July and Cinco de Mayo. They're supposed to clear it with us first, but sometimes they just go to the classroom. Usually, of course, they don't dress up. They just bring treats."

"Then the children might be used to a clown. They wouldn't be unduly frightened."

"Oh, no. They wouldn't be frightened at all. I don't think there's ever been a circus in Las Cruces, but the children have seen them on television, I'm sure."

Ellen flipped her notebook shut and put it back in her pocket. A feeling of disappointment moved within her; she hadn't expected to learn anything dramatic from the children's school, but she still felt let down. As she made ready to leave, Mrs. Gantt leaned forward in her chair. "Sergeant, I want you to know that we at Kessler did nothing improper. We followed the procedures set down by the board concerning busing and classroom visitation. I'm sure none of this can be blamed on the school."

Ellen debated a sarcastic rejoinder—Don't worry, we're not going to get you fired—but bit it back and said instead, "I'm sure you did exactly what you were supposed to do, Mrs. Gantt. No one blames you."

The older woman smiled uneasily. "Well, you know how people like to sue nowadays. Part of our new culture of victimology." Her gaze shifted away, and her voice took on a surprisingly accusatory tone. "This never would have happened a few years ago. If only the police today were better able to protect us—"

"How could the police have prevented this, Mrs. Gantt? I'm sure the chief would like to know what he's doing wrong."

The principal's jaw tightened, and her face turned red as she looked back at Ellen. "I didn't mean that the police were derelict."

"I'm sorry," Ellen said, looking at her steadily. "What did you mean? I'm not following you."

"Only that—" She became flustered. "I'm sure I didn't intend to imply that—"

"Don't imply anything, Mrs. Gantt. Don't talk to anyone about the kidnapping. Do you understand?"

The woman was taken aback at Ellen's aggressive tone. "Yes . . . . Of course."

"And be sure to send the teachers downtown." Ellen came to her feet. She wasn't in the mood for any more of the principal's cover-your-rear maneuverings. She took a business card from her pocket and handed it across the desk. "Have them ask for me. I want them there within the hour."

On the way out, she decided that maybe she would try to get Denise into Fremont School after all. Even if it meant selling her home.

10:21 A.M.

Hurrying across town to the police department, the air conditioner already on high, Ellen glanced at the dashboard clock. Almost three hours. How are the children holding up? she wondered, reaching forward and switching on the car radio. The lone station in town had dropped its country music format, and the DJ and newscaster were talking about the kidnapping with the mother of a little girl who had been on the bus. But she was so frantic she could scarcely be understood. Ellen didn't want to hear it, didn't want to have to share the woman's grief. What if Denise had been on that bus? The thought had been with her since she'd arrived on the scene. What if my child had been taken by a madman? How would I react? How would any mother? She thought of the fairy tales she and Denise read together—children murdered or stolen or locked up in secret rooms. Hansel and Gretel. Little Red Riding Hood. Rumplestiltskin. Or the Pied Piper, kidnapping the children of Hamlin because he was angry at the city. The real point of these stories was not to frighten kids but adults. The greatest fear of parents is the death of their child. She punched the button of a San Diego news station and heard about the kidnapping. It was the same in Palm Springs and Escondido.

It's going to be madness, Ellen thought. And once more she wondered why a kidnapper would want to do something so public, something that would turn Las Cruces into the center of the world. Why not keep it quiet? The child of some millionaire Palm Springs businessman, for example. What did he hope to accomplish by initiating a media carnival? More important, what could he possibly gain by shooting one of the children, if that in fact is what happened?

Maybe he's trying to frighten us; he didn't harm a child at all, merely put a little blood on some glass to make us think he means business. He wouldn't turn this into a capital crime for no reason, would he?

Again, she felt a rush of sympathy for the parents. It wasn't fair—first coming to grips with the special problems of their children, now this.

A moment later she turned on Main and hit the brakes in surprise. For the first time in her life traffic was backed up around the Civic Center. Cars were lined up to enter the public lot in front, and a half-dozen panel trucks bearing the logos of TV and radio stations had been illegally left along the traffic circle leading to the main entrance. Only ninety minutes since the news got out, Ellen thought. God, wait until tonight.

Leaving her Toyota in the gated employee lot in back, she entered the Civic Center through the rear door. It was a new, boxy, three-story concrete building put up as part of a government jobs project for reservation teenagers, most of whom were unemployed or underemployed. The west side was given over to city offices—personnel, building inspector, local permits, city council chambers. The east side was the police station and twelve-cell jail.

Hurrying along the deserted hallway toward the sound of anxious voices, Ellen came into the two-story marble-floored entry foyer in the front of the building. Several dozen men and women with cameras and microphones were grouped around Paul. She stood back against the wall and watched as Paul, facing away from her, finished reading a prepared statement. Ellen could catch only a few words and phrases above the murmuring of the crowd and the hum of cameras: twenty-seven children . . . possible kidnapping . . . no ransom demands . . .

When he finished, the reporters became more animated, surging forward, shouting questions and shoving microphones and tape recorders in his direction. Paul said something she couldn't catch and again the reporters' voices boomed out as flashbulbs repeatedly lit up the side of his face.

"No questions," she heard loudly as he jerked stiffly away from the press of the crowd and began to walk rapidly in her direction. His face was flushed but otherwise without expression. Not stopping, he turned abruptly toward the reporters, his tone frustrated, angry, and final. "I'll come down at noon if we have anything."

But it was as though he hadn't spoken and again questions shot out. Their voices were hostile and insistent, like neighbors arguing over a fence and about to come to blows. Ellen felt a pang of sympathy for Paul. He was the most intensely quiet man she knew, and this had to be hell for him. He hated public functions, hated even having to appear in the city council chambers to report on police matters, despite having known most of the members for years.

His expression didn't change, but again she could feel the emotion in his voice. "I'll let you folks wait in here because it's too hot to be out in the sun. But you stay in the lobby. If anyone tries to go upstairs or in one of the department offices, I'll have him arrested. You got that?"

The front doors swished open and another group of reporters bustled in with minicams and sound equipment. When Paul turned once more toward the rear hallway, they started yelling and rushing forward. He ignored them, striding purposefully toward the hallway where Ellen was standing. As he passed by, he muttered, "Let's go," and she followed him through the double glass doors and into the first-floor reception area of the police department. Jeannie Wheatley, still in her probationary year, was behind the counter, talking excitedly on the phone and running her hand through her stringy, blonde hair. When she saw Paul, she shouted, "Channel 7 in L.A. wants to talk to you, Chief. And I've got CNN on hold."

Whitehorse quickened his pace, and Ellen had to hurry to stay with him. "No media," he yelled over his shoulder. "Tell them they can come and camp out like everyone else, but I haven't got time for phone calls. And you get someone from the jail to come down here and keep order out front."

They hurried through the empty squad room, where Ellen's desk was, to the small elevator in the rear and rose swiftly past the second-floor jail to the third floor, where Whitehorse's office and the conference rooms were located. Like Jeannie Wheatley, the chief's secretary was on the phone. Before she could say anything, Whitehorse said, "No reporters, Maggie. No calls at all. And phone Washington and find out where the hell the F.B.I. is."

Still hurrying to keep up with him, Ellen followed Paul past Maggie's desk to his own office beyond. When they were inside, he slammed the door with a crash, and they were engulfed by silence.

Whitehorse crossed to his desk, sank into the leather swivel chair, and said, "Jesus Christ! Where the hell are the goddamn feds? They expect us to handle this ourselves?"

Ellen sat in one of the two upholstered armchairs and tried to relax him with a smile. "City Council's not going to be too happy if the press gets nasty, Paul. We're supposed to be 'Friendly Las Cruces' like the sign on the highway says."

Whitehorse began to rummage through the papers on his desk. "Don't worry about the council. I can handle them."

Which he could, Ellen knew. For the most part the council members liked Paul, or liked him as well as they could like any police chief. Crime was something they tried desperately not to think about. It was, in fact, why they had fled L.A. or San Diego or San Francisco for the desert. More to the point, she reflected, they trusted him. Whitehorse wouldn't get drunk on the job like the old chief or allow his people to use force unless absolutely necessary. Any officer who even removed his gun from his holster had to appear before a civilian review board to explain his actions. In an early stroke of genius that showed he understood his superiors completely, one of Paul's first actions had been to hire, out of his own pocket, the sixteen-year-old daughter of his sister on the reservation to paint over the occasional graffiti that appeared on fences and buildings. Graffiti, to the nervous people of Las Cruces, was a sure sign of the beginning of the end. So all the patrol officers knew unofficially who to call when they spotted any. And the town leaders patted themselves on the back for finding a chief who was doing one hell of a job keeping the gangs out of Las Cruces.

Outside the council, most people thought Paul competent, if a bit difficult to get to know. "Complex," someone had once said to her. He had few friends among the newcomers in town, and even some of the old-timers considered him aloof and a little cold. But he also played poker once a week with some good ol' boys down at the Elks and took off every year to hunt deer in the Rockies and ducks in northern California.

If anything, "complex" may have been an understatement, Ellen felt. Paul's mind was like a house with an infinite number of rooms, each with a different but interesting assortment of furniture. He enjoyed chess and war games and target shooting and studying Native American history. He could talk for hours about the battles of the southwest—Horseshoe Canyon, Big Dry Wash, Dove Creek—and how the Anasazi came to leave their pueblos or what the Apaches were thinking when they drifted into Mexico.

His real love, though, was his horses. Paul went riding for

at least an hour every day, sometimes with Ellen, sometimes alone. He had eight horses now, six Appaloosas and two mangy-looking wild stallions rescued from Nevada, though he had had as many as a dozen in the past. Last month he'd finished building new stables and a corral behind his house and was planning to refence his pasture area once it cooled down in the fall.

Ellen liked that Paul could be passionate about his interests without being obsessive, something he had lately become about his job, putting in sixty-hour weeks and seldom taking time off. Except for hunting, he had little interest in getting away from the city. He'd been outside, he'd say if asked, eight years in the army as an M.P. before getting out as a sergeant and unit supervisor. He'd spent two years in Germany, two in Korea, and four in the vastly more alien New Jersey. By the time he'd left the army, he'd seen enough of the world to appreciate Las Cruces. A year after returning, he'd married an Agua Caliente girl from Palm Springs said to be worth ten million dollars. She'd died five years ago. Whitehorse didn't need to work, and Ellen figured that was another reason the City Council liked him. A rich police chief is likely to be an honest police chief.

Still angered by the reporters, Paul stared across the desk and asked, "What'd you learn at Kessler?"

"Nothing. The principal's mostly concerned about protecting her reputation. But I don't think this has anything to do with school."

Paul was glaring around the office, only half listening, his eyes darting from the bronze Remington copy the mayor had given him to the wall where a half-dozen plaques and awards hung next to a hundred and thirty-year-old Navajo rug he'd inherited from his father. Suddenly he tossed a ballpoint pen on the desktop and bolted to his feet. "Goddamn it, Ellen, we can't just sit here! We need to do something! Where the hell's that bus? Why hasn't it turned up by now? You're the one with the damn criminology degree. What the hell are we supposed to be doing?"

Ellen spread her arms. "What we are doing—interviewing witnesses, searching the area, waiting for a ransom demand. Usually it's pretty low-key at this point so as not to panic the offender. Without any physical evidence, there's not much more we can do until we hear from him—or them."

Paul's expression went suddenly soft. "Christ, I hope he didn't hurt one of those kids. They weren't any threat to him."

The phone rang, and Paul leaned down and snatched at it. "The mayor on line one," Maggie said.

Determinedly keeping his voice calm, Paul asked, "What exactly does 'no phone calls' mean, Maggie?"

"But the mayor—"

He slammed the receiver down. "F.B.I. will be here soon. They're the kidnap experts. Or so they keep telling us in those bulletins they're always sending out. Sheriff's department's got its helicopter up. They've pulled all their cars from regular duty and got them checking out the county. I've got everyone I can spare out looking. Hell, everybody in southern California is looking for that damn bus." He sighed and sank into his chair. "Well, we better get organized. Be ready for the feds, show them what pros we are." Yanking a binder from his top drawer, he began to take notes. "Physical evidence?"

"The glass fragments and the knife. That's it. Don't expect anything else. This is a very clean crime."

Without looking up, he said, "Howard told me he lifted a print from the knife. He's already sent it to Sacramento. And it was definitely blood on the glass, but he hasn't typed it yet. Any witnesses?"

"The woman who said she saw a clown. And anything Ferguson and Rios have come up with."

Whitehorse shook his head impatiently. "Nothing so far."

"Lou's putting in the recording equipment at the school. You get permission for a phone tap?"

"City attorney's working on it. Probably by noon." Paul looked at his watch. "Only three hours since the kids were snatched. You believe it? And all hell's breaking loose. You ever have your life turned upside down so quickly before?"

"Yes," Ellen said slowly. "When Denise was born and Pete couldn't make it to the hospital because he was doing poppers with his fourteen-year-old girlfriend in West Hollywood."

"Heard from him lately?"

"Every six months he sends one month's child support payment. Just to show he cares."

Whitehorse looked at her, wondering whether to pursue that line of thought, then asked, "How's Grandfather doing? I didn't see him last night."

"He hasn't come out of his room all week. Just sits and stares. He won't even talk to us. The doctor thinks it's the stroke, but I think he's given up. He wants to die."

"Old people remember how it used to be, how the family used to treat the elderly with respect, ask their opinion, do things for them. They remember what it was like when they were young. Now children got their own agenda." Paul's own daughter was at Berkeley studying political science. She called home maybe once every two months. She didn't dislike her dad, just had little to say to him.

Ellen said, "Grandfather would be worse off in a home. At least here he can see a few friends from the reservation."

"He walking yet?"

"I bought him a walker. He won't use it if I'm around though. He won't use the wheelchair either. When I'm not home, I think he goes out to the living room and watches TV sometimes. I don't know if he understands though. It's sad."

Paul nodded. "Tough to get old." He went back to the notebook. "What else?"

"I'll run background checks on the bus driver and teachers and principal. I can't believe they're involved, but we might as well check. I'm going to divide the city up in sections, assign one car to each, have them searching for the bus without being too obvious about it so we don't spook the guy. What'd you do with the parents?"

"They're downstairs, I guess. Probably in the cafeteria."

Ellen jerked to her feet. "Damn it, I told Maggie to set up the multipurpose room." She went over and banged open the door to the outer office. "Maggie, I told you—" but the older woman interrupted. "They're working on it, Ellen. They can't put up a hundred chairs in ten minutes, you know. They're government workers. Everything's *mañana* to them. What do you want me to do when it's set up?"

"Herd the parents in there. Get a TV in there, too, so they have something to do. But no reporters. When the teachers from Kessler show up, I want you to put them down there. You got all that or do you want me to write it down?"

"No need to get nasty," the woman snapped. "I'm as worried about those kids as you are."

Ellen yanked the door shut and sat down again.

Whitehorse said, "Where the hell's he hiding the damn bus? Town this size, there can't be that many places."

"Doesn't have to be in town, Paul."

"Yeah . . ." He winced and began to rub his neck with his left hand. Watching him, Ellen felt an instant of alarm, but it quickly passed. Paul had suffered a mild stroke eight months ago, and his left side was still sensitive. He had insisted that no one be told, and other than his doctor Ellen was the only person who knew. He looked up at her. "We haven't got the manpower for a case like this. A town of thirty-two thousand, twenty-four sworn officers, a few hundred thousand acres of desert, Mexico practically next door—"

"Maybe that's why he chose Las Cruces. He figures wherever he goes the F.B.I.'s going to be involved. That part's a given. So the only thing he can do to alter the odds a bit is pick on a small town, a place without the manpower to do a significant search."

"Christ." The chief stood up abruptly and crossed to the huge tinted window that looked down on the parking lot and the aging commercial district of the old downtown. In the distance lay the mountains and arroyos the military had been using for bombing and gunnery practice for more than half a century.

"Helicopter coming in over at Landers' parking lot. KNBC it says. L.A., isn't it?"

Ellen wasn't paying attention. "We need someone who saw something. Without a witness we've got nothing."

The phone rang, and Paul turned back to his desk and picked it up. Zach Harris in the squad room said at once, "Bad news, boss. We've got a body, a boy about five."

Paul felt as though he had been kicked. He put a hand on his desk to steady himself. After a second he asked, "Where?"

"House on Tortuga. Woman's a waitress at Zuni's, came home a few minutes ago and found him on her couch. I got her on the line now. She's about to lose it."

"Jesus."

Ellen instinctively had come to her feet. "What?"

"Kid's nude except for a clown hat and clown makeup on his face. Sitting in front of the TV like he's watching it. Probably been shot but she didn't get too close. She's calling from her neighbor's house next door. What do you want I should do?"

"Tell her to stay where she is. I'm going down to Dispatch. I'll take over." He slammed the phone down and was through the door to Maggie's office before Ellen caught up to him.

"My God," she whispered as he hurriedly told her what had happened. But why? she wondered. Why kill an innocent child?

They were already in the hallway when Maggie's agitated voice came rushing after them. "Jeannie Wheatley on the line, Chief. F.B.I.'s on the way up."

Paul halted and went back to the door. "Christ, about time. Tell them to hang on. We'll be down there in a minute."

But as they neared the stairwell, three men in suits emerged from the elevator alcove at the other end of the corridor. Paul stopped, waiting impatiently, then began racing down the stairs as the federal agents quickly introduced themselves: Matthew LaSalle, a good-looking man in his thirties, evidently the team leader; Charles Middleton, fifty-ish, heavy-set, with a ruddy, scarred face; Vince Garibaldi, studious-looking and probably in his late twenties.

At the ground floor, Paul hit the stairwell door with his fist, and a couple of civilian employees quickly moved to the side as the small group hurried down the hall toward Dispatch, Paul briefly telling the agents about the child's body.

Jeannie Wheatley was bent over her console, talking into her headset as everyone crowded behind her in the tiny combination Reception/Dispatch area.

"Give me a car in the north area," Paul demanded, then turned toward the open rear door and yelled, "Zach, get in here."

Jeannie shoved a headset toward Paul while speaking into her own microphone. "Seven echo, stand by."

Paul recognized Freddy Durand's "Seven echo" response.

"How far are you from Tortuga?" Paul asked, then spun around as Zach hurried into the room. "What was the address of that house?"

Harris said, "Thirty-seven-oh-one."

Paul repeated the number and Durand said, "Two minutes."

Paul quickly explained about the boy. "I want you to go Code One and stash your car in the garage. Don't let that woman talk to anyone, and I mean anyone! Tell the neighbors to keep quiet, too. I don't want the press to find out about this. I'll have Howard come out and take the body to the medical center in his own car. We'll have to get the medical examiner up from El Centro to do the autopsy." He turned toward Matthew LaSalle. "I can't take my people off the street to process the house. You got any more bodies?"

"Crime scene people are coming in any minute. A man named Adam Richards is in charge—"

Paul barked into the microphone, cutting him off. "Someone called Richards will take over the investigation,

Freddy. You stick around long enough to make sure he knows what he's doing, then get back on the street. I want that goddamn bus found." He threw the headset down and turned to Zach standing just inside the doorway. "Find Howard. He's probably in his lab. I want him to get that boy's body to the med center. As soon as there's an I.D. or cause of death, I want to know. When an F.B.I. guy called Richards gets here, show him how to get to the house. He's going to do the crime scene." He wheeled around to the F.B.I. agents as Zach left and exploded with anger. "Christ, why'd he kill a five-year-old boy? What kind of threat was a child to him?"

Feeling sick, Ellen rested against a desk and shook her head, her eyes on the floor.

Matthew LaSalle said, "You better fill us in. We still don't know exactly what's happened." He looked over at Garibaldi. "Vinnie," and the young agent took out a tablet and made ready to take notes.

Still wound with emotion, Paul's eyes swept around the semipublic area they were in. "Next door," he said, and everyone tramped into the squad room, where Zach sat hunched at his desk talking into the phone. The other three desks were vacant. Only Garibaldi sat down. Paul turned to Ellen. "You might as well explain. You're in charge."

Ellen summed it up quickly: twenty-seven severely handicapped children snatched about 7:20, probably by someone dressed in a clown suit. They'd searched the area and turned up nothing but the knife and several small pieces of safety glass stained with blood, probably the dead boy's. There had been no contact with the kidnapper and, until a moment ago, no victim. And so far no one has reported seeing the bus.

"Just disappeared?" LaSalle said. He glanced at the other agents.

Ellen nodded.

"And no ransom demand?"

"Nothing."

LaSalle shook his head. "Should have heard from them

by now." He rested his seat against the corner of a desk, eyes fixed on the floor as he thought it out; then he straightened abruptly and began speaking rapidly. "Well, we're not going to have much time, given the medical state of the hostages, so we better prepare as much as we can right now. I could get a lab team sent in to process the abduction location, but I don't suppose there's any point. Your crime scene people took pictures, didn't they?"

Ellen glanced at Paul, then back to LaSalle. "We *are* the crime scene people. And yes, we took pictures."

"How large an area did you search?"

Ellen tried to recall where the glass had been found. "Two blocks in each direction."

Charles Middleton, looking very un-FBI-like in a western style suit and cowboy boots, started to say something, but LaSalle asked, "And there weren't any surfaces for prints?"

"Not unless we find the bus."

"Until," LaSalle said and gave her a half-smile. "How are you searching for it?"

She gave an uncomfortable laugh. "Everyone in the state's searching for it. Sheriff's working county areas with cars and a helicopter. Our patrol cars are looking in the city. Announcements on radio and TV—"

"How many cars have you got out?" Charles Middleton asked. There was an edginess to his manner that Ellen found vaguely off-putting, and when she said "Six," he raised his heavy gray eyebrows and glanced at LaSalle.

"Parents have any ideas?" LaSalle asked.

"Not the ones we've talked to so far. We're not done though. Some are still at work, probably haven't heard yet."

LaSalle seemed interested. "How many parents are unaccounted for?"

Paul said, "We're rounding them up. One of my men's in charge. You'll have to talk to him about it." He took a half-dozen steps away from the desk he was leaning against, as though to work off excess emotion, then came back and stood next to it again.

"Any reason to suspect the driver?"

Ellen shook her head. "Not really. She had some minor drug problems as a teenager, but she's been clean for six years."

"Got her picture?"

"The driver? I don't know. I suppose we could get it."

"And pictures of the kids. The school probably has class pictures. Get them on TV. Do it as soon as possible so the TV stations can cut into their regular programming. Maybe it'll jog some memories. At least it'll get people thinking. Do you have the interview notes on the woman who saw the clown?"

"The officer's still in the field," Ellen said. She was beginning to feel like a student who hadn't completed her homework.

"Have the notes typed up when he gets in. D.C.'s sending in a psychologist from the Behavioral Science Unit. He'll want to go over them. He's flying into March Air Force Base up in Riverside. Luckily he was in San Francisco putting on a training seminar. He should be here by noon. I asked for an army hostage removal team, too. They're coming in from New Mexico."

Whitehorse looked surprised. "Hostage removal?"

"Twenty-six children hidden away somewhere—our first priority has to be getting them home safe. When we locate them, we're going in if we have to."

"You don't think between us—F.B.I., Sheriff's Department, Las Cruces police—we've got enough people to do it on our own? We need the army, too?"

"They're experts," LaSalle said reasonably. "They know how to go in and get out fast, without casualties."

"Casualties." Ellen shook her head. The word seemed out of place, a television news term that had only an abstract reality—casualties in the middle east, casualties in Cambodia, Bosnia, Armenia. It seemed to change the nature of the crime, intensifying it, if anything could make it worse than it was, while at the same time depersonalizing the victims. She asked, "Why do you think he shot that child? What's he thinking?"

LaSalle shook his head. "I don't know. Doesn't make sense. Dead hostages don't have any value."

"What about the other children? Do you think he could be planning to kill them, too?"

"Always prepare for the worst and hope for the best," Charles Middleton said. His gaze settled on Ellen's face. "The point is to be ready."

"We don't even know what to be ready for," she said as Paul sank down in a chair. "It's frustrating. There's nothing to go on, nowhere to focus our energy. We don't even have a ransom demand."

LaSalle agreed. "It's tough. But he wants something. Until we know what it is, we don't know how to plan."

"It doesn't have to be money," Charles Middleton said, beginning to roam around the small room. "Could be one of the kids. Or even the driver."

LaSalle shot a look at Vince Garibaldi. "Check with the parents. Find out if any of these kids is involved in a custody dispute." He turned back to Ellen. "Probably ninety percent of kidnapped kids are snatched by their mom or dad. It's unlikely in this case, though, I suppose."

Ellen said, "Most of these children are on medication of some sort or another. They're going to be in pretty bad shape unless we get to them soon—hours, not days. Even then it might be too late for some of them."

LaSalle turned again to Garibaldi, obviously the errand-runner of the group. "See what kind of medicine is needed and have it ready. Maybe we can get it to the kidnapper somehow. At least we can prepare for their release." As Garibaldi made a note, LaSalle said, "Exactly what disabilities are involved here? Are they all medical problems?"

"Medical, emotional, physical. Cerebral palsy, AIDS and drug babies, retardation, paranoid schizophrenics—"

"Jesus." LaSalle looked at the other agents.

Garibaldi said, "I've got a three-year-old. Just one and it's still a madhouse with all the noise. Wherever he's keeping these kids, it'd have to be soundproofed."

"Or out in the desert," Middleton replied, still pacing

around the room in a display of nervous energy. "There's a hell of a lot of territory out there. No way we can search—" The building shook briefly, and he halted in mid-sentence. "What's with the goddamn fighter planes? Someone declare war and forget to tell us?"

"The marines and navy use the mountains for bombing and gunnery practice," LaSalle said, turning toward him. "My brother used to fly an A-10 out there. I think the Blue Angels still train here, too. It's one place I can guarantee they aren't."

Whitehorse said, "There was a school bus taken once before in California. Up north somewhere."

LaSalle reached down and popped open his briefcase. "Chowchilla, 1976. I had the file faxed to me before leaving. Three guys, still in prison. They did it for money."

Ellen's mind locked onto something, and she said, "Haven't I seen you before? On TV maybe?" The way the words blurted out without thought surprised even her, and she could feel her face color with embarrassment.

Garibaldi looked up from his notes and smiled, but Middleton laughed out loud. "We call Matt 'Pretty Boy' because the press officers like to trot him out for TV interviews. Guys like me and Vinnie aren't photogenic enough for D.C. New-look F.B.I. and all that."

LaSalle seemed annoyed. "I've been involved in a few kidnapping cases. It's the sort of thing TV likes to cover. So people tend to remember me, I guess." He took a quick glance at his watch, anxious to move on. "Quarter to eleven. I wish to hell B.S.U. was here. We've got to get moving. But it gives us an opportunity to prepare." He stared at Ellen and Paul. "The Bureau has a kidnap plan ready at all times, and I've been through this enough to know the options. Our most common approach is to saturate the pay-off location with agents in unmarked vehicles so we can tail the bag man. We've also got a variety of microphones and surveillance and tracking devices. We can use the psychologist from B.S.U. for telephone contacts and that'll give us a feel for their emotional makeup. Until then we've got some things to do. Like I said, we haven't got much time, especially with this bunch of hostages. So we'll split the duties. Everything's got to be at double time." He looked at Paul. "Maybe someone should write this down."

Ellen sat at a desk and took a pen and paper out of a drawer.

LaSalle snatched up a ruler from the table and began to tap it nervously against his leg as he thought things out. "Number one: Finish interviewing the parents." He glanced at Ellen. "This has to be your priority. You need to put more than one person on it. Tape record everything. Ask about neighborhood feuds, personal vendettas, arguments, anything like that. Also, more tricky under the circumstances, where were they at seven-thirty this morning? Then run the names of every parent, boyfriend, and girlfriend through the National Crime Information Center computer for priors of any sort. I'm not ready to rule anyone out yet. I'll have some technical people here, and they can do the actual data processing for you.

"Two: Unaccounted-for parents. Where are they? At work? Vacation? Don't take anyone's word for it. Have your people verify it in person.

"Three: Strangers." He began to pace around the small room, his eyes on the floor. "Ask around the school as well as the kidnap location. Has anyone noticed strangers hanging around any time in the last month? People taking pictures? Asking questions? Get descriptions, vehicles, and so on. I'll give you people to help out on this also.

"Four: Have someone take a list of the parents' names to local banks. Every parent. Go directly to the manager. Speak to no one else. Have them check their records—unofficially—to see if anyone has applied for a large loan recently or appears to be in financial trouble. Then have the bank request a T.R.W. credit report for any parents they have a business relationship with. Don't ask T.R.W. to do this for you; they won't without a court order, and we haven't got the time.

"Five." He stopped his pacing but didn't sit down. "I'm

bringing in more bodies—technical experts: surveillance, electronics, crime scene people, and so on. I'll try to keep them out of your way, but it's going to start looking like F.B.I. headquarters here. We're going to need them though. Expertise is the only advantage we have in a situation like this. Also, a dozen field agents to help in questioning. They'll be in their own cars, so when we get to the pay-off we can use them to swarm the area. I'll get into details later." He looked at Ellen. "What are we up to?"

"Six."

"Okay. We need at least two dozen detailed maps of the area so everyone can follow the drop routine once he calls. It might also give us some idea of where he's hidden the bus. The important thing now is to be ready. Once he calls, it's going to be madness around here. We won't have time to plan."

He looked at the others, still tapping the ruler on his leg. "Can anyone think of anything I missed?"

Ellen stood up. "I'll get some more people questioning the parents."

Paul stared at the wall. His voice was disbelieving.

"A clown! How the hell does he expect to get away with it?"

11:52 A.M.

Linda Sowell didn't think she could stand it another minute. The children hadn't stopped crying since being thrown in here and she didn't know what to do. She wasn't trained for this, she didn't know how to comfort them. She sank down on the floor, her back against the wall, while Eric and Arturo clung to her. Tears of rage and frustration rose in her eyes and she wanted to scream, but she didn't dare.

Tony, a twelve-year-old autistic boy, was shrieking and pounding his fists on the cement floor because his routine had been disrupted. The first thing he did each day at school, Linda knew, was take all twenty-two Sesame Street books from the shelves, spread them out on the floor, and name them in order. The moment he stepped on the bus after school, he counted the windows, then the seats. But whenever his routine was interrupted, he became uncontrollable.

"Teacher, I have to go to the bathroom."

Arturo was pulling her foot and crying. Linda pushed herself to her feet and took his hand. "Come on, Arturo, I'll show you."

With Eric trailing after her, she led the boy to the curtained-off bathroom and showed him the chemical toilet. "Here, Arturo."

But when he saw the unfamiliar-looking device he began to cry. "No, no, no—"

"Please, Arturo," she begged. "It's a toilet." She began to unzip his pants, but he became panicky and started to run away.

In a cheerful voice, Linda said, "Let Eric show you! Eric, do you want to go to the bath—" But Arturo was already wetting his pants, the urine streaming down his leg onto his shoes and the floor.

Linda sank to the floor again, a wave of despair coming over her. Her mouth felt dry and her head swam with nausea. I'm going to be sick, she thought. I'm going to vomit in front of these kids, and it's going to scare the hell out of them.

A boy in a wheelchair began to rock his body back and forth, back and forth, faster and faster, until he tumbled face first onto the floor. Linda leapt up and ran over to him, pulling the boy close and comforting him. She didn't even remember his name. He wasn't crying, but his body continued to heave and lurch in a rocking motion. Linda soothed him and was finally able to put him back into the chair. As soon as she did, he began to rock again.

We can't take it much longer, she thought. These children are going to die if we don't get out of here. Eric suddenly began pulling heavily on her hand, his voice excited and fearful. "Look, look." He was pointing at a five-year-old girl sprawled on her back, her body twitching as though from electric shocks.

Oh dear God, thought Linda, and began to panic. The girl was having a seizure and Linda didn't know what to do. The school district had never given her any training for this sort of situation. You're supposed to keep them from swallowing their tongue, aren't you? she thought. And keep them calm? *Calm?* She couldn't even keep herself calm.

Linda dropped to her knees next to the child. Veronica, wasn't it? Her parents called her Roni. Linda rolled the girl onto her stomach, worried that she might be making things worse. "It's okay, Roni. Okay." Could she hear? Probably not. The child's whole body jumped with convulsions. Linda put her hand on Veronica's back, and the girl's torso arched off the floor and fell again with a thud. I don't know what to do, she thought, I don't know—

But just as quickly as it had started, the seizure was over. Still, Veronica didn't wake up, lying quietly as though asleep. Linda felt the pulse. It was so faint.

Oh God, oh God, oh God, don't die on me, Roni. *Please!* And she could feel her mind start to slip, like a spring beginning to unwind. All around her the children were screaming and crying and pounding the walls as they worked each other into a frenzy. Linda came to her feet, her eyes darting around the small room, coming to rest suddenly on the interior door she had tried earlier.

I'm not going to let us die in here, I'm not going to let my life end, she thought, and hurried over to the door, trying the handle again. Frozen.

She needed a wrench or a screwdriver or a hammer, something to get the handle off. She stared wildly around the room. It had been stripped bare. There was nothing, nothing she could use as a tool. A curtain, the rug, two cartons with boxes of breakfast cereal. Maybe there were some utensils, then. She crossed rapidly over and looked in the cardboard boxes. Nothing! Not even any plastic spoons.

There has to be something, she thought, there has to be!

Then she remembered her purse. She had grabbed it automatically and slung it around her shoulder when hurrying off the bus. It was on the floor near the bottom of the ramp. She raced over, dropped to her knees, and began to rummage inside. There had to be something in there. She turned it upside down and shook everything onto the floor as the children around her continued crying. Dark glasses, makeup, lipstick, wallet, change purse—Dear God, let there be something, she prayed—Kleenex, nail clippers—

Nail clippers! With a small pointed nail file. She seized it eagerly and hurried over to the door. Using the file as a screwdriver, her fingers trembling violently, she began to work on the handle to the door.

I'm not going to end my life here, she swore. I'm not!

12:06 P.M.

Ellen was vaguely aware of everyone talking at the same time: Charles Middleton on a cellular phone to Quantico as he paced back and forth at the other end of the conference room; Vinnie Garibaldi, sounding angry, to someone at the National Crime Information Center; Paul, Matthew LaSalle, and herself bent over the coffee table, setting up sector lines on maps of the city and surrounding desert. When the door flew open, all the noise stopped at once as they spun around to see Maggie standing with hands on hips and feet spread. "You're going to have to talk to them sooner or later, you know," she said aggressively.

Paul came to his feet and looked at her with irritation. "Talk to who? What are you talking about?"

"The reporters! You told them noon. I've already had three calls."

"Jesus, Maggie, what can I tell them? We haven't gotten a ransom demand. We haven't found anything. Nothing's happened!" Except for the dead child, and he wasn't about to go public with that yet; they didn't even have an I.D. on him.

The secretary shook her head and looked exasperated.

"They need something, Paul. They need you. Doesn't matter what you say."

"Christ!" Paul looked as though he was going to kick something.

Middleton put his hand over the cell phone's mouthpiece and smiled at LaSalle without interrupting his pacing. "Come on, help the man out, Matt. You're the expert on reporters."

"Maybe it would be a good idea," LaSalle agreed, coming to his feet. "We can demonstrate an F.B.I. presence, show people what we're doing, and let the press as well as the offender know we're on top of things. If he sees he's dealing with us and the army and every law enforcement agency in southern California, it might convince him to give it up."

Whitehorse jammed his hands in his pockets and looked at Maggie with resignation. "All right." He paused and sighed. "Tell them ten minutes."

Maggie nodded and shut the door as Middleton shoved the phone in his shirt pocket and crossed over to the couch. Remembering her four years in the ultimate media city, Ellen said, "They're going to wonder why we haven't caught the guy yet. Four and a half hours, why isn't he in jail? Especially the L.A. stations. Another chance to make the police look incompetent."

Whitehorse swore to himself and strode over to the third-floor window. He didn't want to talk to the reporters again—not in ten minutes, not ever. But if not him, who? He wasn't going to make Ellen do it. With growing irritation, he stared down at the bizarre scene unfolding in the streets. "Civic Center parking lot's full. Landers' and Lucky's lots are full. Gridlock in the streets. Must be two or three hundred people standing outside in hundred and ten degree heat because they can't get inside. Any more reporters show up and I'm going to have to pull a couple of guys just to keep order. Christ, if it goes on much longer, the city offices will have to shut down; workers won't be able to get inside." He turned toward LaSalle, who had come up beside him. "Why haven't we heard from the kidnapper? That's what they're going to want to know. What the hell can we say? It doesn't make sense."

LaSalle looked uncomfortable. "He should have contacted us by now. If it's political, you'd think he, or they, would be on the phone to the media. Or if it's money he's after . . ."

That's what made everything so horrible, Ellen thought: we don't know why he did this. If he wants to trade something for the hostages' release, why doesn't he tell us what it is? It must be torture for the poor parents, wondering why this madman wanted their children. What was he doing with them, to them, right now, this very instant? She thought of Denise and her heart turned over. What if it had been my child? she thought again. Every parent in Las Cruces must be asking that right now and probably rushing to lock their doors. But how much worse it was for these children with their special needs.

Paul said to Middleton, "You folks can take your gear and set up in the conference room across the way. It ain't fancy, but it's what we got. I'll try to find someplace for your computer people. Let Maggie know if you need anything else." He turned to LaSalle. "We'll get together again after talking to the reporters." The phone buzzed and Paul picked it up. "Jesus, Maggie, I'm coming."

When he put the receiver down, he said to Ellen, "Want to come along, watch the media stars?"

"I don't think so, Paul." She smiled at him, hoping to relieve some of the tension he felt. "There's some things a man's just got to do alone."

But she rode down with them in the elevator so she could watch on the television in the lunch area. She was surprised to find the small room crowded already, two dozen or so noisy civilian employees taking up the molded plastic seats that had been repositioned in front of the TV. Maggie must have dialed into the rumor mill the moment Paul had agreed to talk to the press. A minute later the room went quiet as the station cut into its regular programming. Paul evidently started before they were ready because there was no time for an introduction from a reporter, only a hurried voice-over from the studio, then a quick cut to the chief, standing stiff and uncomfortable, his back against a wall, and, next to him, Matthew LaSalle, expressionless, handsome, relaxed, as though he had done this sort of thing a hundred times before. Paul was caught in mid-sentence, introducing LaSalle as the F.B.I.'s liaison officer. The Las Cruces police would continue to be in charge of the investigation, he went on, but the F.B.I. was offering its support and assistance, as were the army and sheriff's department. They were all looking for the children, but unfortunately there was no new information to report. They had yet to find the bus and had heard nothing from the kidnapper. The authorities weren't even sure how many people were involved or what they wanted, but something would probably turn up soon because so many law-enforcement agencies were involved now. He hoped to hear from whoever was responsible soon so they'd know what was expected for the children's return; the important thing, of course, was to get them back safely.

He paused, took a deep breath, and said he could spare five minutes for questions before they had to get back to work.

"How could someone hide a huge yellow bus in a town this size?" a man yelled. The aggressiveness in his tone made Ellen wince. He smells blood, she thought, like a shark who spots an injured fish. He wants to finish it off before it regains its strength.

"We're making a search for the bus," Paul repeated without emotion.

"Who's in charge of the investigation?"

"Detective Sergeant Camacho."

"Is it true they were kidnapped by a clown?" a middle-aged man shouted. There seemed to be amusement or derision in his voice, as if he didn't believe this fantastic-sounding story, or didn't want to be accused by his colleagues of being taken in; cynicism was acceptable, gullibility was not.

"We're not sure," Paul said. "We think so."

"Why haven't the kidnappers contacted you?"

"I don't know. I wish they would. We're getting medicine—"

"Why . . . ?" Fifty voices yelled at once, drowning each other in a sea of confusion.

Ellen didn't want to hear any more. Making her way out of the crowded room, she strode rapidly into the hallway. Paul has to be loathing this, she thought as she took the stairs up two at a time. Reporters thrived on the aggressive rough-and-tumble of a press conference; it's how they made their living. But that was the urban world, the world of clutter and noise and push and shove. People live in Las Cruces because they value quiet, civility, manners. Paul hated crowds, felt uncomfortable with strangers; his life was lived internally, within his consciousness. Who you are is what you are inside, and the superficialities of life, the surface externalities that meant so much to the media crowd from L.A.—the proper clothes and haircuts and restaurants and autos—were of no consequence.

They're two completely alien cultures, Ellen thought. And they'll never understand each other.

4. Patience

Lowell Alexander DeVries was completely at ease as he relaxed back in his lawn chair, the cat coiled loosely at his feet, and watched Chief Paul Whitehorse stare nervously into the camera as he said, "We're making a search for the bus."

DeVries laughed out loud. "You didn't answer the question, Chief. They said, Why can't you find it?"

"Who's in charge of the investigation?"

"Detective Sergeant Camacho."

"Yes, indeed," DeVries whispered as his heart quickened

pleasurably; his hand dropped to his side, and the tips of his fingers gently stroked the coarse black hair on the cat's belly.

The lovely Ellen, he thought. She, too, has her role in the scheme of things, a part long since worked out in the most precise and loving detail. Are you ready, Ellen? Are you prepared for your two flashingly glorious days in the limelight? By tomorrow her name would be known in Vladivostok and Cairo and London . . .

Ellen.

Ellen.

Ellll-en . . .

Perhaps he should call her, see how she's handling stress. How are you? How do you like it so far?

"Is it true they were kidnapped by a clown?"

"We're not sure. We think so."

DeVries's body rocked forward as he laughed again. "Maybe I should have had one of the kids tape it, you idiot. Then you'd be sure."

He lifted the video camera from the floor next to his chair and aimed it at the television, staring through the viewfinder. There was no tape in it yet; that would come later. The camera was a crucial part of the managed chaos and misdirection that was so important for the next few days, as well as proof that the children, or most of them, had indeed been alive until the incompetence of the police . . .

"Why haven't the kidnappers contacted you?"

That had been a woman from Channel 9 in Los Angeles. Nice looking, long black hair, huge indigo eyes, baby soft skin the color of wet teak. Oh Lord, he'd love to spend a few nights with that! Maybe he should have kidnapped her, he thought with a smile, then quickly corrected himself. No, no, this was better. This was foolproof.

12:40 P.M.

As Ellen crossed rapidly through Paul's outer office, Maggie bustled out from behind her desk, waving a dozen pink telephone slips. Ellen snatched them from her hand and quickly saw they were all from relatives of the missing kids. Why hadn't the children been found? What were the police doing? Ellen tossed them on the secretary's desk. "I haven't got time for this, Maggie."

"But I told them—"

"Then you call them." She started again for Paul's office.

"But that's not my job." The familiar refrain.

Ellen halted and turned toward the older woman. "Then I'm making it part of your job. As of this minute. Do you understand, Maggie? You call every one of these people in the next half-hour and tell them why we haven't found the children." Maggie started to protest, but Ellen pressed on. "If you don't, we'll have a personnel hearing next week, and you can explain why you shouldn't be fired."

Half ashamed of herself, Ellen stormed into Paul's office and slammed the door behind her. As a civil service employee Maggie couldn't be fired if she were stark-raving mad, and they both knew it. She sank down on the couch and let out a loud breath. Goddamn reporters! she thought. They were putting her on edge. No, it wasn't that at all. It was the kidnapper. Why hasn't he called? Kidnappers want something. Why doesn't he tell us what the hell it is?

She jerked to her feet and looked at her watch. Almost a quarter to one. Five hours since the children had disappeared. Where was Paul? The press conference was supposed to last only ten minutes. Were the reporters that hard to get away from? Maybe LaSalle was making a statement; he'd seemed to enjoy meeting the press, or perhaps had just learned the secret of doing it without showing his distaste. The phone on Paul's desk buzzed, and Ellen reached over and snatched it up. Maggie said, "Three FBI agents just came in from San Diego. Computer experts, I guess. Where am I supposed to send them?"

Ellen felt like screaming but determinedly maintained her composure. "Maggie, where did we put the F.B.I.?"

"I don't know. No one tells me anything."

"I'm going to let you work on this one by yourself, Maggie. Where did Chief Whitehorse put the F.B.I.? When you figure that out, it will tell you where to send the new guys." She jabbed her finger down to disconnect, then immediately punched the number for Zach Harris in the squad room downstairs. Maybe one of the patrol cars had something. Or the F.B.I. crime scene techs at the house where the boy's body was found could have preliminary lab results by now. But before he could answer, she slammed the phone on its cradle. Zach's not an idiot; he'd tell her if anything had come up.

Relax, she warned herself. Taking a deep breath, she leaned back against the desk. It wasn't like her to get so antsy. Normally, she had no problem disengaging herself from cases she was working on, automatically standing aside and looking at them dispassionately, as though watching a movie. It was a skill every cop developed sooner or later. Otherwise, you'd get so caught up in the never-ending tragedy of daily life, you couldn't function. So what was different this time? Children. Twenty-seven already helpless children. And the inexplicable cruelty of it all.

Damn it, she thought, where was the F.B.I.'s behavioral science expert? He had been due in almost an hour ago. Doesn't he realize how important time is in a case like this? Those poor kids: They must be terrified.

Five hours.

And all we have is a clown and a knife.

I'm as bad as those reporters, she thought with a sting of self-recrimination. How could someone hide a huge yellow bus in a town this size?

How indeed? But they had.

Anxious to do something, to make something happen, she left Paul's office and crossed through the reception area—now where was Maggie?—to the conference room across the hall, where the F.B.I. was set up. Middleton was prowling back and forth by the far wall, head down, talking into the phone, while Garibaldi sat hunched at the table, typing on a portable computer. While she was standing by the doorway, two men in suits came in and introduced themselves as agents from the L.A. office; there were three more outside looking for places to park, they added. Garibaldi glanced quickly over his shoulder while typing. "Matt wants them out questioning people around the school." Ellen took the two men down to the squad room so Zach Harris could brief them, then hurried back to the conference room just as a face appeared on Garibaldi's computer screen with as much detail as a 35 mm photograph. "Oscar Woodhill," he told her without looking up. "Convicted of kidnapping a Boston plastic surgeon in 1987. Captured the same day. Still in jail." He hit a key and another face appeared. "Roger Alan Gleason, a sex kidnapper. Took eight children between 1983 and last year. Killed them all. On death row now in Florida."

"Do you have every kidnapper in the country in there?" Ellen was not overly fond of technology but couldn't help but be impressed.

"Every felony kidnapper in the last twenty-three years. And all the data are correlated so I can ask for details of any case involving boys under ten, say, or kidnap locations in towns under 35,000 population and ransom over two million dollars, or whatever I want. The program does all the work."

At the other end of the room, Middleton began bellowing angrily into the phone. Ignoring him as well as she could, Ellen asked, "What happened to your computer guys?"

"I told the chief's secretary to find an office for them on the civilian side of the building. They need a place that's quiet. She said there's a conference room over there, too."

"Yeah, but it's the mayor's—"

At that moment Matt LaSalle walked in. "Paul'll be here in a minute. He wanted to wash up after meeting the press." He smiled grimly. "I know the feeling."

A bang came from the other end of the table as Middleton slammed down the phone. "Holy Christ!" He spun around and faced LaSalle. "Those cretins in D.C. want us to encrypt all communications from here on in."

"Why?" Ellen asked, looking at him and feeling suddenly peeved. Did they not trust someone at the police station?

"The walls have ears," Middleton replied, waving his arms histrionically and beginning to pace again. "The forces of darkness are everywhere, evil is rampant, trust no one, no one! Anyway," he added with a sharp glance at LaSalle, "that's what Washington thinks. They're afraid of the god-damn reporters."

Ellen was feeling increasingly uncomfortable with Middleton's edgy tough-guy mannerisms and constant ranging from place to place. She had immediately taken to Matthew LaSalle, though, and his quiet, in-charge manner. Of course, being that nice looking helped, too, she decided with a private smile, allowing her eyes to appraise him as though filling out an arrest form: six-two, two hundred pounds, early thirties. Narrow-waisted without being skinny; full in the chest, like a weight lifter or boxer, with thick ax-handle wrists and large powerful hands that gave him a rugged, outdoorsy look. Wearing an expensive gray suit and a long-sleeved white shirt with French cuffs, something you didn't see much in Las Cruces. And no wedding ring, she noticed, feeling a prickling of embarrassment for doing so. Ellen had worked with agents from the Los Angeles field office a couple of times when she was with the L.A.P.D. but had never run into him. She asked how long he'd been there.

"Eighteen months. Cleveland and Boston before that. You used to be with the L.A. police, didn't you?"

She looked at him with surprise. "How'd you know?"

He smiled. "I checked. I like to know who I'm working with. Guess you weren't happy with Los Angeles."

Ellen laughed uneasily. She didn't enjoy talking about her personal life and tried to terminate the topic by putting a note of finality in her voice. "I'm here, aren't I?"

But LaSalle wasn't put off. "What didn't you like, the city or the department?"

"Both, I guess." She paused, not wanting to go into it with a stranger. "Anyway, I was having problems with my husband," she said at last, the words tumbling out quickly. "It seemed better to leave."

"Problems work out?"

Middleton had taken a chair at the table and was sitting with his suit coat off, flaunting the long-sleeved brown shirt with western-style embroidery that he wore with a string tie and turquoise clasp. Ellen darted a glance at him before returning her attention to LaSalle and smiling uneasily. "We got divorced. So I guess they did work out."

Just then Paul came in, shutting the door behind him. He was as composed and unemotional as always, not even a flushed face or anxious eyes, but Ellen, who had known him most of her life, knew not only that he had been upset by the encounter with the press but that he'd never let them see it. His stoicism was both a shield and a sword, keeping people at bay and uncertain at the same time. Occasionally, it bothered her even now, leaving a part of him forever hidden and untouched. That was his right, she felt, anyone's right to retain some small vestige of privacy and uniqueness. But it had been difficult to get used to after living with Pete, who wore his emotions on the outside like his badge, where no one dared miss them. But that was because there was nothing inside Pete, no core to protect.

Paul waved Ellen and LaSalle to the table. "Must be a dozen F.B.I. guys wandering around in the squad room. Every one of them wearing a suit. You think they might be a little obvious in Las Cruces?"

As everyone was sitting down, the door opened and Marcus Cox, a sergeant in the sheriff's office, came in and was introduced around.

Ellen knew Marcus vaguely. About forty, black, large and muscular, like the sheriff's department used to like their deputies before the era of law enforcement "sensitivity." A good cop, she'd heard. Ambitious, hard working, anxious to move up.

That made six at the table. They had chosen their places almost ritually, Ellen noted, as though establishing territories: she and Paul at the ends, the three F.B.I. agents along one side, and Marcus on the other, an empty chair on either side of him. Everyone but Ellen seemed to be toying with a pen or pencil or coffee cup, and she began to sense something in the air, something she couldn't put her finger on. Its elusiveness discomfited her, but before she could wonder about it LaSalle turned to Paul. "Your jurisdiction, Chief. Your agenda." The mood seemed to ease a bit, and Ellen thought, He's going out of his way to do things right; he's trying not to step on toes. She liked that, his concern for protocol and protecting Las Cruces' role in the investigation. Most outsiders wouldn't have given a damn.

His face still without expression, Paul nodded toward Ellen at the other end of the table. "Sergeant Camacho's in charge."

Everyone's gaze shifted at once in her direction, LaSalle seeming to catch her staring at him as she was caught in mid-thought. She felt herself color and started to look away but, sensing that the F.B.I. was going to be the key to the investigation, began by addressing her remarks to him. "I guess I'm feeling a little uncomfortable about getting too many people involved here. Our department's too small to do everything by ourselves, of course, but with more F.B.I. people coming in all the time and the sheriff and maybe even the army, I think we're going to end up falling over each other."

Charles Middleton's pale eyes, until then on the notes in front of him, came up suddenly and fixed on her with impatience. "So let's get organized. That's what we're here for."

Ellen felt everyone's gaze as she paused and stared at Middleton, contemplating a sarcastic rejoinder, then changed her mind. It's a test, she sensed at once, the others seeing if she'd back away or lose her temper. But multijurisdictional investigations were like an intricate tribal dance that required agreed-upon movements by everybody. If people started bickering, the whole would dissolve in favor of separate parts that would never again fit together. She looked at LaSalle, then Marcus Cox, and wondered if they resented her being in charge; she was not only a small-town cop but a woman. It was probably something neither had experienced before and another possible source of friction. If so, she wasn't going to let it bother her. Turning her attention to Middleton before looking at the others, she said, "Las Cruces P.D. will coordinate. I want all information, all evidence, all leads, all hunches, everything, filtered through here. That okay with everyone?"

It was.

"Then we'll do it by the book and follow normal jurisdictional lines—sheriff in the county, police in the city, F.B.I. for advice and assistance and, of course, if another state or country is involved." Focusing again on LaSalle, she asked, "Where's your psychologist? He was supposed to be here by now."

"He got sidetracked in Riverside, getting some information from D.C. He should arrive in an hour or so."

Ellen didn't try to hide her annoyance. "It's getting late. An hour's going to be crucial to these kids."

"He knows that. Couldn't be helped."

"It probably could be helped," Middleton replied evenly. "B.S.U. has its own concept of time." He smiled and tapped his head with his pen. "All that right-brain thinking, creativity run amok. It's not the first time. We just have to work around it."

"All right, we'll focus on strategy for now," Ellen said. "Then get into the details later." She got out of her seat and went to the blackboard. Snatching up a piece of chalk, she looked at the five men staring at her from the table. "We'll do it in order." And looking straight at Middleton, added, "Organized, the way you like it. First problem." She jotted a "1" on the board and then "THE BUS" and said, "This has to be our priority. All the computer stuff and witness questioning is fine, but I want the bus. It can't have just disappeared. So where is it?"

LaSalle flipped open his notebook. "What do we know so far?"

Ellen looked at the sheriff's deputy. "Marcus?"

Cox glanced at his notes. "Our helicopter hasn't turned up anything so far. This is a hell of a lot harder than it seems, you know." His eyes came up, and his voice took on a defensive quality, as though someone had accused him of dereliction. "There's a lot of territory out there. Guy could have hidden it under some date trees, in a barn, large garage. Could be in an arroyo up in the hills."

"Or in Palm Springs or Mexico or anywhere within sixty miles or so," Paul added.

"In the Chowchilla kidnapping back in the seventies, they drove immediately to a river and hid the bus in some reeds, then put the kids in two vans," LaSalle said, looking at his notes. "They were in a hurry and didn't try very hard to conceal it."

"We'll keep looking," Marcus Cox went on, "but you'd need a fleet of choppers to do a good job."

Middleton pushed his chair back from the table and crossed his legs. "We could get a fleet," he said to Cox, then turned to LaSalle for confirmation. "Call them in from various local agencies, have them here in two hours, sweep the region from the air."

While Middleton was talking, Ellen put a "2" on the board and wrote, "THE KIDS." "Do we assume the children are where the bus is? If he was smart, he dropped them nearby, or got them out of here, like Matt said, and then dumped the bus. So, do we make an effort to find the kids, irrespective of the bus, or do we wait to hear from him?"

"What'd you have in mind?" Marcus Cox asked.

"Going door-to-door. I'm not suggesting it, just putting it out as a possibility. This isn't like kidnapping some middle-aged businessman, you know. These children all have special needs, and most of them require medication. It's getting on to six hours now. I don't think we can wait any longer. Again, concentrating on witnesses might be standard procedure, but we don't have the time for that. We've got to get hustling."

LaSalle thought about it. "You must have eight or ten thousand housing units in a town this size. Maybe two thousand business establishments. Where would you get the manpower?"

"I'm not advocating this yet, but if we had to, we could turn to the air force or the National Guard."

"They'd never agree," Middleton said. "This is a civilian matter. There's no way the military is going to get involved with providing manpower."

"They get involved in floods, riots, tornadoes—"

"That's different," he replied, not looking at her. "You don't understand how they think."

"Why is it different?" Ellen felt provoked, not so much by what he was saying as how he was saying it, the "don't question me" tone of superiority she associated with all federal agencies.

Middleton's blue eyes darted angrily toward her, then moved away. He shifted in his seat and his voice sharpened. "Believe me. I was in the army. They just don't do these sorts of things."

"You made policy for them?" Ellen's eyebrows arched in mock surprise as she stared at him from three feet away; in the back of her mind she was thinking, Don't do this, don't turn the F.B.I. against you. But she couldn't stop herself. "When you were in the army, they let you tell them what to do?"

Marcus Cox gave a short laugh but Middleton's face reddened, and he snatched his pen off the table as if he were going to break it in half. "I've been a federal employee all my adult life, *Sergeant*. I know what I'm talking about."

"The two don't necessarily follow."

"More important," LaSalle said quickly, trying to defuse the tension, "do we want to do it? Do we want a thousand people, especially a thousand uniformed people, out there banging on doors? Maybe we'd better talk to our psychologist first. Someone who tries to pull off a snatch like this can't be completely sane. He's already killed one child, seemingly for no reason. If he sees the military combing through the city, he could go off the deep end."

Looking down the table, Paul nodded his head. "We

don't know anything about him yet except that he's dangerous. We better step lightly. At least for now."

"Okay," Ellen said, not agreeing but willing to concede the point until the behavioral expert arrived. "But I'm going to call the governor and have Sacramento set things up with the National Guard. If we decide to go ahead with a full-scale search, I want the troops here and looking within an hour. If we don't find these kids by nightfall, some of them aren't going to make it."

To no one in particular, Middleton said, "We usually bring in a tracker with dogs when someone's missing. Had pretty good luck in the past."

"The kids didn't walk away," Ellen said, trying, though not succeeding, to keep the sarcasm from her voice. "They drove. You got a dog that tracks buses?"

"Greyhounds," Cox said and smiled.

LaSalle asked, "Did you run background checks on the teachers and so on?"

Ellen nodded. She had picked up the faxed information on the way to Paul's office. "The only one with a record is the bus driver, and we already knew that. Twice for possession, once for dealing when she was a teenager. No big deal." Quickly, she added, "We'll search her place when I can spare a body. It's going to be a dead end though. She's got a disabled child herself. He was on the bus. She wouldn't endanger other children."

"Still—" LaSalle said, looking uneasy.

"I know, I know. We'll get to it."

Cox leaned forward and started to say something, but Middleton beat him to it. "What exactly does 'get to it' mean? It's potential evidence. We have to move on it. There's sure as hell nothing else tangible to work on."

"I'll find someone!" Paul interrupted sharply. "Even if it means going myself."

The conference room door opened suddenly, and Maggie stepped in. "Chief."

Whitehorse pushed to his feet and went to the open doorway. A tenseness grew in the room as everyone waited, silently watching the whispered conversation, until Paul returned to the table. "Maybe we've finally got something," he said, sitting heavily. "A man walking his dog found a lunch box along the highway and figured it might belong to one of the kids, so he called us. It did. The kid's name was inside."

Ellen's pulse quickened. "Where'd he find it?"

"On Ridge Road, north of town. It was on the shoulder, like one of the kids threw it from the window."

"Where's the road lead to?" LaSalle asked.

"Doesn't lead to much of anything. It skirts the reservation, then heads out along the hills toward an abandoned Marine airfield before dead ending in some old silver and manganese mines."

"Mines?" LaSalle's voice rose with interest.

"I know what you're thinking," Whitehorse said. "I suppose it's possible. You could drive a bus right into some of those pits. But, like Marcus said, there's a lot of land out there—mountain and desert. No way to search it all." He looked down the table at Charles Middleton. "Even if you brought in a whole battalion of helicopters."

Middleton grunted indistinctly, pushed out of his chair, and began to wander around the room. LaSalle said, "But someone must know where these mines are located. They must be registered."

"Most of 'em haven't been worked since before World War II. That's going on sixty years now. No one around here would remember anything. Once in a while kids or rock hounds get lost in one and the sheriff has to send in a rescue team. But most of those places have been closed up so long you'd never find them."

LaSalle turned at once to Vince Garibaldi, an edge to his voice. "Get on the phone to the Department of the Interior. They must have a map of all the mines in the area. Tell them it's crucial. We need the information faxed within the hour." Garibaldi went to the telephone and LaSalle turned back to Whitehorse with a sense of urgency. "You're going to have to go out there where the lunch box was found. You'll need some people to search the area and more to search the road, as far north as you have to. I can have some staff brought in if you—"

"That's county territory," Cox interrupted, coming suddenly back to the conversation. "Our jurisdiction. We'll take care of it."

From the other end of the room, Middleton exhaled a derisive "Jesus!" and stared up at the ceiling.

Paul peered down the table at Cox. "I'd like a couple of my officers to go along."

"Have to ask Branson," Cox said, speaking of the sheriff. "Man's usually not too thrilled about city police tagging along. You know how that is." He smiled but his voice had hardened. "If we turn up anything, I'm sure you'll be the first to know."

"Not tagging along," Paul said. "Searching! Christ, Marcus, there's thousands of miles of desert out there."

As everyone stared at him sitting alone on the side of the table, Cox shrugged. "Like I say, talk to the man."

Exasperated, Ellen said, "Marcus—" It's starting, she thought with despair, everyone moving instinctively away from each other, as if there were some kind of reverse magnetism at work.

Keeping his tone level, LaSalle said, "I think it would be best if we funneled everything through the Las Cruces police, as we agreed earlier. We need to have some centralized control for an operation this size."

Middleton came across the room and leaned over the table, his fingers pressed against its top, and stared into Cox's face. "Maybe someone in the Justice Department should give your boss a call, tell him how things in the real world work. How's the United States Attorney General sound to you?"

Cox stared at the man a moment, then spread his large hands, but his eyes glistened with emotion. "I can't tell the sheriff what to do. You clear things with him. Protocol, you know—"

"All right, all right," LaSalle said and sighed. "But let's try to pull together on this. We're all on the same side." He gave Ellen a quick look and shook his head as though he wasn't certain of that at all.

Beginning to prowl once more around the room, Middleton said, "Let me try to make this point again, boys and girls." He stopped, jammed his hands in his pockets, and stared at everyone. "Trackers might be able to help now that we've got a starting place. Take the dogs out on that road, let them sniff the lunch box, maybe some clothing from the kids' homes, and turn 'em loose. It's something to do, for Christ's sake. What else have we got besides sitting around, waiting for the fucking shrink?"

Paul shifted in his chair and looked at Ellen. "It might be worth—"

Middleton interrupted as though Paul hadn't been talking. "There's an old guy in Kentucky with some magic hounds who does work for us sometimes. We found a mass murderer in a six hundred acre Ohio cornfield in ten minutes." He tried a smile on Marcus Cox. "Your territory, of course, Deputy. But we could fly them in and—"

"We got dogs," Cox told him sharply. "Don't have to go to Kentucky. We use 'em on search and rescue. I'll check into it."

"Search and rescue dogs are not the same," Middleton said. His tone became overly deliberate, as though he were talking to an idiot. "You need dogs that—"

Cox's whole body stirred belligerently. "Don't tell me what kind—"

As Middleton's voice shot up in return, Ellen shouted, "I don't believe this!" and the room suddenly quieted as she stared at the men in a fury of emotion. "Twenty-six handicapped children are being held captive by a madman and we're sitting here arguing about whose *dogs* to use?" Her body sagged as though all the energy had drained out, but her voice remained demanding. "Come on, guys! This is crazy! We've got important things to talk about."

The air was brittle as everyone's eyes fixed on her, not in embarrassment but resentment. After a moment, Middleton said aggressively, "Like it or not, the details have to be attended to. We have experience tracking. We know how to—"

"Not now!" Whitehorse snapped. He, too, was clearly upset at the way things were going. "We can take care of that later. We have too many other things to do."

"Like deal with the press," Ellen said at once, looking at Matthew LaSalle and taking a breath to calm herself. In the back of her mind she was thinking: We have three jurisdictions here, law-enforcement experts, and we're not getting a damn thing done because everyone's worried about defending their own territory. And suddenly she recognized what it was that had made her uncomfortable earlier: she had encountered this sort of unprovoked aggressiveness with coyotes out in the desert. For no apparent reason, a handful of males would begin to circle one another, sniffing and growling, getting ready to fight. It was how the social system was formed and a biological imperative. But weren't humans supposed to be above that sort of thing? Frustrated almost to the point of screaming, she tried to change the group's direction while she could; maybe if they could agree on a small problem, the large ones would follow. Forcing herself to sound calm, she said, "We've never dealt with the press on this scale before. I'd appreciate any suggestions."

LaSalle eased his chair away from the table. "Well, it's obvious you have to do something. We almost couldn't get inside this morning. Reporters are fighting each other for space down there. And it's going to get a hell of a lot worse. The first thing you'll need to do is clear the building, move everyone across the street."

Whitehorse said, "What if we open the high school for them? It's five miles east. At least it'll keep them out of the sun."

LaSalle went to the window, but it was on the wrong side of the building and all he could see was the crowded parking lot. "You can set up an information base there, but you'll never keep them all away from the Civic Center. This is where it's happening. Photographers and TV camera operators especially will need to hang around here."

Sounding suddenly accommodating, Marcus Cox said, "I'll try and get some baby cops from headquarters to loan you. You can set them up across the street to keep the reporters where they belong."

Ellen agreed and said she'd also see to opening up the high school. Maybe they could convince at least some reporters to stay there.

"You said that road where the lunch box was found heads out by the reservation," Middleton said to Paul, taking the conversation off into another direction. He stood with his back against the wall, arms folded on his chest. "Any chance Indians could be involved?"

"Attacking and burning wagon trains, stealing little white kids to raise them in the Indian Way? I don't know, Charles. We pretty much gave that up last year when we got civilized."

Middleton wasn't fazed. "It wouldn't be the first time militant Indians have created problems. Law-enforcement officers, including F.B.I. agents, have died. You know that as well as I do, so don't play dumb."

With a stab of resignation, Ellen jammed her chalk down on the narrow ledge of the blackboard. She had deliberately kept from thinking about it, but they were going to have to face it sooner or later. "There's always agitation of some sort on the reservation," she said to no one in particular. "It's just like a city council, you know. People disagree." She made a limp gesture with her hand.

"What are they disagreeing about?" LaSalle asked with interest.

Ellen looked at Paul, hesitating for a minute, then said, "There's a group of young people primarily who want to put in bingo and a card casino. Most are against it, don't want outsiders coming in, changing things. Paul's on the Tribal Council—"

Middleton pushed suddenly away from the wall. "You are?"

Whitehorse looked at him but said nothing.

Middleton's voice rose angrily. "Holy Christ! You think maybe you could have told us before?" He turned to LaSalle. "I'll call Washington. We need to look into this."

Whitehorse straightened his back and glared at the F.B.I. agent. "What exactly is there to look into? Something unusual about bingo?"

"Number one," Middleton explained, staring at Paul as if it were obvious, "militant Indians! Like I said, we've had these problems before. It's too much of a coincidence not to investigate, especially with that lunch box turning up out there. Number two, reservations are within our jurisdiction. We don't need your approval. Number three, how wise is it to have a police chief investigating a crime that he may have some connection to through the Council?"

Ellen saw Paul flush angrily, but before he could say anything LaSalle quickly jumped in. "Until we hear from the kidnapper, we don't have any reason to think there's tribal involvement. There's certainly no reason to be concerned about Chief Whitehorse's handling of the investigation. I'm much more worried about the circumstances of the crime. I've personally been involved in six kidnappings, and there's a few things about this one that bother the hell out of me. First, it was in broad daylight on a major street. Kidnappers just don't operate that way. They usually go after a single victim and snatch him where no one can see. Second, the dead hostage. What was the point? Especially with a five-year-old kid. And maybe most important, we haven't heard from him yet. That's contrary to the purpose of a kidnapping. We don't have any idea why he, or they, did it. Until we do, we're running blind, making plans we may not be able to implement."

"Your six kidnappings," Ellen said, feeling an unexpected new concern force its way in among the others. "How many turned out okay?"

"Depends on what you mean by okay," the agent said, staring at her. "All six, we caught the offender. It's a stupid crime. We always get them."

"And the victims?"

"Dead. Not always on purpose. Sometimes it was negligence or something unforeseen. But all dead. Like I said, a stupid crime."

5. Wait

Lowell Alexander DeVries strolled into the house, took a can of Diet Coke from a portable ice chest, and seated himself comfortably on a lawn chair. He would have preferred a more interesting, more celebratory, drink—a nice brandy would be fitting even at this early hour—but alcohol was unwise and DeVries prided himself on never doing anything unwise.

Taking the printed list from his pocket, he looked at it as Ellen curled languidly at his feet and meowed with excessive affection. From item 1, *DO IT,* to item 5, *WAIT,* everything had gone as planned, a fact that caused—not elation, not run-away excitement—but contentment, like the warming glow of satisfaction that followed a particularly delightful meal. He had known with a rigid and absolute certainty that there could be no foul-ups. There never were when one planned wisely. That was one of the great lessons borne in upon him from his adolescence. The race goes not to the swift but to the sure. Haste makes waste. Look before you leap.

Aphorisms.

Neatly written on three-by-five cards.

At the age of sixteen DeVries had begun to collect quotations the way others collected sports cards. The sayings of the wise and the sayings of the foolish. Words to live by, keys to success. At first he had merely jotted down those easily retrieved from memory, the well-known slogans and ready currency of everyday speech—*A penny saved . . . Early to bed . . .*

Waste not . . . . As he grew older, though, his tastes matured, and, his interest whetted, he began to actively and eagerly seek out the more obscure aphorists: Chamfort, Renard, Montaigne ("Men are most apt to believe what they least understand.").

Yes! he would tell himself with a shiver of cold excitement that moved like ice along his spine when uncovering a particularly cogent and telling statement, a dozen or so words that alone contained a library's worth of wisdom.

"*A learned fool is more foolish than an ignorant one.*" Molière. *Yes!* Feeling the thrill only a true collector can.

Each statement had been carefully and artfully inscribed on heavy-stock index cards with a calligraphy pen bought especially for that purpose, then placed in a box he later had constructed of Philippine mahogany, with polished brass fittings on the edges. "The Wisdom of the Ages" he printed on the outside, not without a dose of irony certainly because he knew that too much faith could be put in the written word.

On the other hand, each statement did carry the heavy weight of truth. How else could we explain its survival for hundreds or even thousands of years? The fact that oftentimes the advice could be inconsistent ("Look before you leap," but also, "He who hesitates is lost") was of little consequence. Intelligent people pick and choose wisely; they do not turn over their lives to astrologers or new-age channelers or card files, though they may use such information if it speaks directly to them. And Lowell was, he knew with certainty, an intelligent person.

So each morning, at precisely 6:00 A.M., he reached into the mahogany box, drew out the next card in sequence, and carried it the remainder of the day in his shirt pocket. The Wisdom of the Ages, helping to direct the life and times of Lowell Alexander DeVries. Today's card read:

"*Evil is easy, And has infinite forms.*"

—*Pascal, 1670*

"Yes!" he said aloud. *Of course, of course . . .*

There are infinite ways of doing evil.

But there was evil in not doing, also. Ineptitude, sloth, and inaction are the truly inexcusable sins, he had long ago learned, not from reading but where those few seminal lessons of life must be, in the harsh and closely ground crucible of experience. Lowell's parents, over-educated and ineffectual, had lived lives of astonishingly random carelessness, stumbling inexorably from mistake to mistake, yet never profiting, never learning from what should have been character-strengthening experiences. Instead, failure inevitably begat even greater failure, always an emergency or unforeseen problem suddenly springing up, then quickly becoming a calamity through a simple lack of planning and forethought. What was more evil than that? Vacations ruined, jobs lost, important people unintentionally alienated, evictions from a dozen homes for non- or late payment of rent. The list went on.

None of this had been obvious to young Lowell at the time, however. It had come to him later, at night, stealing up like a dream as he lay on his bed, staring darkly into the past. His entire existence had been spent surrounded by people of the grossest incompetence, not just his parents but friends, too, who, through their messy, ill-planned, and careless lives, had brought evil to him in ever-increasing amounts, laying it at his feet as though it were some sort of grotesque tribute paid by an inferior people to their master. Teachers, social workers, classmates. All inept. All. Especially (his heart began to pound as the memory rose), young Rudy Ayala—excitable, stupid, Rudy, who had lost his wallet in some bushes when the two of them had taken that thirteen-year-old girl from the projects out to the desert. Then letting it slip to the police when they showed up at his house (an accident, Rudy had insisted feverishly years later, staring into Lowell's stony face, pleading with him. Just a mistake! Jesus, Lowell, I didn't mean to!) that Lowell DeVries was the other guy involved. Rudy had been sentenced to "counseling," but the judge had put Lowell in juvie because it was his second, or second proven, forcible rape.

Not that the thought of jail had unnerved young Lowell in the least. Even at fifteen he felt he was able to accept just about any hand life dealt him. But that was before he found himself suddenly living cheek-by-jowl with members of the Desert Loco Killer Boys and SB Gangsta Crips. Bad things happened during his three years in Juvenile Hall, things which through the immense force of his will Lowell was able to push below the level of conscious thought. But the memories lingered, he knew, because sometimes in the middle of the night he'd awaken drenched in sweat, heart pounding like mad, and a horrible sick feeling expanding like a balloon in his stomach. Only a trace of the dream ever remained: Lowell, naked, running, running, running, falling on his face, then a horrible weight landing on him. When that happened, he wouldn't be able to have an erection for days.

And they say jail doesn't reform anyone! Lowell knew better. People can change, as he did when at age sixteen, lying on his bunk and staring up at the rutted swirls on the concrete jail ceiling, he decided once and for all that he would never again allow something like this to happen to him. Thus, the card file. And the library and the continuation school. And the plans.

Twenty-four hours after his eighteenth birthday, Lowell had walked out of Juvenile Hall with a high school diploma and had kept on walking until he got to San Bernadino City College, where, after talking to a counselor, he signed up for a two-year course in architectural drafting. He found he liked it and surprised himself by discovering he had some real talent in that area. Pretty soon he was working for a large engineering firm and life began to improve.

But also in the back of his mind—kept alive with periodic dream visits that made him hard and excited and frighteningly short of breath—was the memory of that thirteen-year-old girl squirming naked on the hard, gritty floor of the desert and the thrill he had felt slamming into her body, making her scream and scream and scream, begging to be let free. It never left him, this need to dominate, to force himself on others. (Power, he knew then, watching her trying to escape from under him, was the basis of all human relationships.) But the weight of those years in jail was too great and too current to risk anything that might lead again to incarceration. So now he satisfied himself with monthly visits to Miss Violet's, a large rambling pink and blue ranch-style house on the ragged, southern edge of Mexicali, where for two hundred dollars he could act out his fantasies with eight- to twelve-year-old Salvadoran or Mexican girls for one hour and come home sated.

Thus, it was largely in the name of self-defense, his determination not to lead the sort of meaningless life his parents had, to always be in control, that DeVries had, through the power of his mind, eliminated the painful uncertainty of randomness and chance from his existence and wrenched his life instead into the increasingly narrow and tightly controlled track that he was to follow to this day. The extraneous, unimportant, and frivolous were ruthlessly stripped away until only those facets of being that had some real value remained. He disciplined himself to a regimen that, even for the sexual urgings of his body, was as predictable as a bus schedule. Everything was spelled out, each action carefully detailed. There would be no surprises, no confusion, no messiness, in the life of Lowell Alexander DeVries.

Not that existence was without its pleasures, of course. As well as the obvious enjoyment of sex (more than just a pleasure—*the* pleasure, surely), two slight indulgences, two deviations from the unbending, monkish asceticism and self-abrogation of life, were allowed: clothing and food. His dress was without fault, always moderately priced, perfectly tailored English suits and sport coats that fit him like a model in a department store ad. A traditionalist to the end, DeVries loathed polyester and insisted on wool until summer turned too hot and then (reluctantly) permitted himself a wool blend, as well as an occasional seersucker, which

gave him a slightly rakish appearance, a bit like a young Jack
Nicholson, he thought with a stab of secret pride. His hair,
which was thinning slightly on top, was always neat and
short and combed straight back, and his fingernails mani-
cured. A scent, changed quarterly and not yet well known
but which he would see mentioned in the back pages of *Es-
quire* or *GQ*, trailed gently after him like a wink. Women
turned their heads and stared in open admiration at the obviously muscular body, the self-assured bearing, the bur-
nished movie star looks, then sighed to themselves when
they noticed the thick gold wedding band which he wore
like body armor to keep them at a proper distance.

If any of them had gotten to know him better, and there
had been two or three, they would have discovered beneath
the finely cut clothes and tight, leopard-print bikini underwear (purposely a size too small so he could always feel
its silky texture gently rubbing against the most sensitive
area of his flesh), a hard, well-muscled body indeed, as well
as an obsession with personal cleanliness that Lowell himself admitted was occasionally excessive. He showered without fail in the morning and evening, brushed his teeth after
eating or drinking anything, including water from the fountain at work, and washed his hands frequently but not, he
hoped, compulsively. The world could be a filthy place if
one permitted it to be. One could join it, mingle with its
abundant trash and disease and meanness, or rise above.

Food was naturally a more daunting indulgence when living in a back-water like Las Cruces, but the challenge of the
hunt merely heightened the joy of discovery. French restaurants were nonexistent in the area, and Italian seemed to
mean nothing more than pizza or spaghetti. The great mass
of Mexican restaurants were predictably second rate, but he
managed to find two that at least were clean, insisted on
fresh vegetables, and understood cilantro. The inevitable
Chinese storefronts that dotted the town were pedestrian
in their menus, often filthy, and always unworthy of a repeat
visit, but a surprise was an Indian restaurant named, of
course, Taj Mahal, where Lowell DeVries was a frequent

and honored guest, dining alone in Eastern splendor as swarthy young male servers in open-necked shirts danced attendance. Monthly visits to Palm Springs or San Diego served to meet the need for haute cuisine.

Life, in short, was steady, predictable in the extreme, and always enjoyable. And about to get infinitely better. He had been thinking about this day for seven and a half years. He'd taken the time to check his diary for the exact date the idea had first occurred to him. It was spawned by the need—"desire" was a better word, he decided, since he actually needed nothing—for more money to better indulge his few crucial interests.

But it was just over three years ago that he had begun to plan in earnest. Someone, a woman in an elevator at work, he remembered, had mentioned a new school bus for handicapped children only, and suddenly there it was, the whole idea, presented to him ready-made. How much is a bus full of missing children, not just children but disabled children—worth to the community? One million? Two million? Far more, surely, to a society where children are, in theory at least, elevated to the status of innocent and saintly icons. It was like a gift from heaven, God smiling on him and saying, "Here it is. Do it!"

And so he did.

No, he didn't do it. That again was the point, that was where Lowell DeVries differed from his parents and from the common run of humankind, from those fools, for example, in northern California who, after minimal planning, had attempted a similar snatch years ago. Don't rush into anything, he had needlessly reminded himself; don't be impulsive. Think. Prepare. Rationally, carefully.

Three and a half years.

Planning, reading, studying.

Preparing, preparing, preparing.

Perhaps the single thing one can never do too much of.

He began at the local library, quickly devouring the few books they had on kidnapping, mostly case histories. Then on to the small satellite campus of the junior college and their criminology collection. By now he had a library card under the name of Robert Louis Stevenson, author of *Kidnapped*, of course, but none of the minimum-wage slaves who stood automaton-like at library checkouts had heard of either Stevenson or the book, so the joke was, he had to admit, a private conceit. Amusing, nonetheless. Quickly he moved on to the far larger university libraries in Riverside and San Diego. Within six months he had a pretty good idea how to do it, but there were some F.B.I. documents on strategy he still wanted to see so he had to wait for copies from Washington on an interlibrary loan.

Finally, he understood F.B.I. policy and processes—how they think and plan, how they seduce and deceive their adversaries—as well as anyone in the Bureau. Along with awareness of their strengths came recognition of their weaknesses—the inevitable reliance on institutional memory and the procedures and routines that had worked in the past—that gave him a prescience, an ability to predict and misdirect, that, he knew, made his plan invincible.

There were four primary elements that had to be worked out: the snatch, the lock-up, the ransom exchange, and the get-away. The first and third were clearly the most crucial, but all four necessitated separate detailed procedures.

Almost two years were devoted to the specifics. He had, there was no doubt of this, thought of everything, anticipated every contingency. And because she played so vital a part in his plans, he had early attached himself to lovely, young Ellen Camacho (marvelous, marvelous figure, heavy black hair, eyes that glistened like flint), following her home from work or to Paul Whitehorse's house or out to dinner or shopping. Several times he broke into her house, and soon he knew Ellen perhaps even better than she knew herself—knew her secrets, yes, everything.

When he was through planning, completely satisfied that he had done all that was possible, that his strategy was without error, he began anew, this time approaching it from the F.B.I.'s standpoint. Again, the same four points: the snatch, the lock-up, the exchange, and the get-away. The F.B.I., not aware of Ellen's starring role, would look at number four as most important, followed in order by three, two, and one. And while they worked out their countermoves, while they strategized and planned, the melancholy history of Charles Singleton II, lurked like a ghost in their collective memories, recognized but unspoken, and doing its mischief as it reminded them all that the list of F.B.I. fiascoes must never be added to.

Armed with this foreknowledge, DeVries war-gamed it, much as the Bureau itself does with crimes of this sort: catch the bastard who took the kids—surveillance, SWAT teams, marked money, tapped phones. And, of course, their vaunted psychological profiling. (Dr. Walter Exley, *the* expert, would be assigned to a case of this importance.) Their charge would be clear: Find the lunatic who did this, save the children, and above all, maintain the image of the Bureau.

DeVries had attacked his plan relentlessly, looking for every foul-up, every loop-hole, every unforeseen contingency.

And then planned in—what would you call it if you had a sense of humor? Diversions, he decided. He planned in diversions.

1:15 P.M.

Six hours since the kidnapping, Ellen thought with a flaring of emotion, and the Civic Center overrun with dozens of F.B.I. people of one sort or another—surveillance, electronic, lab and computer techs—but still no one from Behavioral Sciences. Frustrated at the delay, she and Paul went back to his office and asked Maggie to bring up two sandwiches from the cafeteria since it was packed with reporters and they couldn't go down there. When the secretary appeared ten minutes later with a plastic plate, she was apologetic. "All they had left was egg salad."

Ellen took it from her. "Have the teachers shown up yet?"

"They're in the multipurpose room talking to the parents. Pretty hectic down there, I guess."

"How about Dr. Sanderson?"

"I think he's still in his office."

"Goddamn it!" Ellen tossed the plate on Whitehorse's desk, knocking a pile of papers onto the floor. Grabbing the phone, she spun the Rolodex around to where she could read it. A minute later she was saying, "Damn it, Herb, I don't care how many patients you have. You get over here or I'll have you arrested. You understand? I don't care, I'll make up a charge!"

She slammed the phone down as Matthew LaSalle, holding a walkie-talkie, ducked his head in the doorway. "Behavioral Sciences just showed up. We better get together again."

Paul pushed at once to his feet. "Christ, about time."

The psychologist was standing at the long conference table, pulling papers from a thick leather briefcase as everyone came in. "Dr. Walter Exley," LaSalle said, introducing each of them in turn and adding, "Walt's been in B.S.U. longer than most agents have been in the bureau."

Exley smiled and stepped forward to shake hands. Ellen recognized him at once and for the first time felt a tiny surge of hope edge its way in amid the despair that had taken hold of her. Sixtyish, completely bald, wide face, round glasses, he had become something of a celebrity as the F.B.I.'s expert on terrorist behavior. Officially a consultant now, he spent most of his time lecturing to local police departments and seldom worked in the field. As everyone sat she asked if his presence meant that the F.B.I. was assuming that this was a political crime.

"Not necessarily," he replied, looking at her and Paul as he continued to unload his briefcase. His voice had an odd edge to it, nervousness or impatience, Ellen thought; but all at once his tone softened and he gave them a half-smile. "I should apologize for being late. Time is always crucial in a kidnapping, and I believe especially so in this one, but I got hung up waiting for some data from Quantico. Terrorism? Politics? Maybe. Most kidnappings now are. If not, it actually makes things more difficult because ransom kidnappers tend to be less predictable. But in any case, negotiations have to be undertaken and that is where we can be of most use. Tell me what you have so far."

Just then Charles Middleton walked in, a Styrofoam cup of coffee in his hand, and quietly drew a chair back from the table. Exley stiffened and looked at him with mild surprise. "Charles." The name eased out, almost like a sigh; then he smiled uneasily and added, "I didn't know you had been assigned."

Ellen stared at the two of them, the room suddenly quiet, and wondered what Exley was saying; he was smiling now but not, she thought, convincingly.

"I wasn't assigned," Middleton replied as he sat heavily and gazed tranquilly across the table at the older man. "I volunteered. Just like in the army." He focused his wide blank face on the psychologist as he sipped his coffee. "You know how it is in the army, Doc. Always volunteering for something." Pushing his chair back, he crossed his long legs and smiled. He wants us to see his boots, Ellen thought. He probably has a story about the shoemaker in San Antonio who took measurements of his feet and had a steer slaughtered in Madrid, then aged the leather for three years.

"Well," Exley said, and shot a fleeting glance at Matthew LaSalle, "happy to have you on board."

Middleton looked at him. "Yeah?"

There was a pause for several seconds until Exley said, "We were asking Sergeant Camacho what was known about the crime so far."

Trying to regain control of the meeting, Ellen quickly recounted what they had. When she mentioned the child's body, Exley looked disturbed.

Middleton shook his head and grunted. "Clown makeup! A world-class crazy."

"Not necessarily, at least not in the sense you mean it,"

Exley replied, but he was clearly concerned. "By its overt-
ness and the unnecessary risks the kidnapper took to place
the body in the woman's house, I'd say it implies someone
with absolute confidence in his ability to pull this off. Interesting, isn't it? I wonder why he feels so sure of himself.
But the child's nudity, the makeup . . ." He turned abruptly
to Ellen. "What physical evidence do you have?"

"The home where the body was found is being gone over
now. From the abduction scene there wasn't much." She explained about the dinner knife and lunch box. The road
where the lunch box was found led into the mountains,
where there were dozens of abandoned mines large enough
to conceal a bus. But the area encompassed thousands of
square miles, most of it completely desolate and used for
bombing practice. It would be impossible to search it all.

Exley nodded grimly. "Our chopper pilot said the navy's
getting nervous about all the news helicopters in the area.
They're afraid one of them might stray into the bombing
range. I think the F.A.A.'s going to shut down this entire
area."

"That road also leads past the reservation," Middleton
said. While there was no emotion in his voice, it was clear
he was making a point, and Ellen felt her cheeks burn. She
glanced at Paul and their eyes met. "There's been some in-
ternal squabbles about gambling," Middleton went on, his
face without expression as he stared at the psychologist. "At
least from what we've been able to learn so far. Details have
been remarkably difficult to come by. But it needs to be
looked into. And someone needs to be searching the reservation. So far nothing's been done."

Exley seemed interested. "Indians, huh? Not exactly my
area of expertise, of course." He bent over the table and
looked around. "What's the area of contention?"

Trying not to show his annoyance, Whitehorse said, "It's
no big deal. The younger folk want to put in bingo, poker
machines, a card room. That sort of thing. But it's a local
problem, a reservation problem. It doesn't have anything
to do with the kidnapping."

"It's mostly a question of money versus tradition," Ellen added, trying to simplify a complex issue she didn't expect outsiders to understand. "There's a certain amount of resentment toward the Agua Calientes up in Palm Springs because they're millionaires, while most California Indians are dirt poor. Some people see this as a way to catch up."

"Is there any money in reservation gambling?" Exley asked.

Paul frowned and shrugged his shoulders. "Someone's making money, sure. But it's usually the game operators, guys from Chicago with a bunch of vowels in their names, not the reservation."

"Mafia," Middleton explained with elaborate blandness to the psychologist in case he was unfamiliar with the notion. "La Cosa Nostra. Marlon Brando. Very nasty people. They cut heads off horses."

Exley looked uneasily at LaSalle. "I suppose there could be something to this," he said with some reluctance and began to silently tap a forefinger on the tabletop. "Perhaps we better check with the Bureau of Indian Affairs. Time is definitely going to be a factor here and—"

No longer trying to hide his irritation, Whitehorse pushed his chair back and came to his feet. "You contact B.I.A. if you want but they're not real popular around here. I'll call Art Peña on the reservation and have him poke around. He takes care of things for the sheriff out there. But if there was a bus or two dozen retarded kids running around, we'd sure as hell hear about it. It's not like you can hide 'em all in one of those little houses or mobile homes without folks knowing." He stalked from the room without waiting for a response.

"The point," Middleton said brightly, "is not to leave loose ends. It is very bad, career-wise."

Turning to Ellen, Exley said, "What do you know about the teachers, bus driver, and so forth?"

"Everyone's clean except the driver. She had drug problems some years ago. Nothing big time. Her son was on the bus, so I don't think she would be involved."

"Gone through her house yet?"

"Still haven't had a chance," Ellen told him and felt a stab of irritation with herself at not having accomplished it yet. "We're pretty short on manpower."

Exley said to LaSalle, "How many people have you got?"

"Total? Fifteen field agents, half-dozen techs, three computer analysts."

Exley stared at him without comment.

Something's happening, Ellen thought, watching them as the silence lengthened uncomfortably. Her interest was piqued, but she was also beginning to feel like an outsider as the F.B.I. agents seemed to speak to each other with a sort of deliberate obliqueness, like the members of a secret club. LaSalle was beginning to look annoyed. After a moment, he added, "D.C. assigned me. It's my manning level. My decision."

Exley paused as though contemplating this, then asked, "Is that the new management philosophy I keep hearing about? Decentralizing control, decision-centers, something like that? Or is it still Total Quality Management? It's hard to keep up with the fad of the moment."

LaSalle seemed to be holding his body rigid as he looked steadily at the other man. "They want problems dealt with at the scene. People in the field are to handle things as quickly as possible, cut the red tape. We focus on results, not processes."

"Well," the psychologist said, looking benignly through his glasses, "they certainly can't fault you for bringing in too few people, can they? There might be arguments the other way though. The bureau's second guessers—"

"My decision," LaSalle repeated with finality. "We start with strategy; manning follows naturally. Let them second guess all they want. I'm going to get those kids back—"

Before he could finish Whitehorse came back and dropped noisily into his chair. "Peña's already checked out the reservation. Nothing. Forget it. It's a dead end."

"All right," Exley said. "We'll leave it unless we have some reason to think the reservation might be involved. Let's spend a few minutes going through what we've learned about kidnappers. That'll help you decide on the details of your strategy." He darted a glance at LaSalle, then turned his attention to Whitehorse. "The bureau's been extremely successful the past twenty years or so in dealing with these people. Kidnappers are invariably caught, so it's become a rare crime in the U.S. compared to Latin America or Italy. Although we'd never admit it publicly the bureau classifies some kidnappings as 'major'—those that involve significant victims, for example, or that otherwise attract public attention, as this case does, of course. In the past eighteen years there have been thirty-seven such incidents, and in each the kidnapper was either killed by law-enforcement personnel or arrested and convicted. I have been able to interview virtually all of those in prison and have come up with a pretty consistent picture of their behavior and how they think."

He came to his feet and slipped his hands into his trouser pockets, looking around at the others like a professor leading a graduate course, and Ellen realized: he is! This is Exley's seminar; he'd probably given this same talk to a hundred police departments. He turned from the table and began to walk away, then suddenly spun around, focusing the full force of his attention on her. "If you were going to kidnap someone, the wife of a local executive, say, how would you do it?"

Ellen was taken aback a moment but quickly recovered. "I guess I'd study her habits for a while, see how she spends the day. Then wait outside her house in the morning. When she left for work or to go shopping, I'd . . ." She paused a moment, still working it out. "I'd wait until she got in her car, probably in the garage, then come up beside her with a gun and make her drive off with me in the passenger seat. Then switch to another car as soon as possible."

Exley smiled. "Exactly. That's the invariable pattern. The abduction is carried out where it won't be seen, almost always at the victim's home. But this time it was not only observed but the offender dressed up so as to attract attention. Why?"

Ellen opened her mouth to respond, but there was nothing to say. It made no sense.

"And," Exley went on, "we haven't found the original vehicle. Why not?"

Ellen thought out loud: "Twenty-seven kids, some in wheelchairs. They would have needed another bus, or two or three vans, or a truck. Maybe it was easier this way."

"I don't know," LaSalle said at once. He began to fiddle with his ballpoint pen, nervously clicking it open and closed. "It's been bothering me, too. If you snatched a busload of emotionally disturbed kids, would you want to ride around with them? If it were me, I wouldn't want the hassle. They're probably scared to death, yelling and screaming and pounding on the windows. I guess I'd dump them nearby. But if I had to take them somewhere, I'd transfer them to another vehicle as soon as I could, then get rid of the bus before it's noticed."

"The kids might not have been a problem," Ellen guessed, trying to put herself into the situation as it happened. "They might not even know they were being kidnapped. They could think they're going on a field trip with a clown. They'd just sit there." A picture formed in her mind: the bus, twenty-seven kids cheering and clapping as they were driven off by a madman with a gun.

"Are these kids ever calm?" LaSalle asked. "Did you check with the teachers, see what they're like?"

"We haven't had time," Ellen said. It was one more thing that she should have taken care of by now.

"They saw him murder one of their classmates," Paul reminded everyone with an edge of annoyance. "I don't think they'd be very quiet—"

"Jesus Christ!" Middleton interrupted. "Drive it or dump it, someone should have seen the damn thing. Think about it, folks. We're not talking about a Ford Escort. It's thirty feet long, it's goddamn yellow! It can't just disappear."

"Nobody would pay attention to one more bus on the

highway," Whitehorse said. "I think they were counting on that. It gave them forty minutes to an hour to get out of town, hide the kids, and either hide or dump the bus. They could be fifty miles from here."

Exley turned again to Ellen. "Once you got the victim hidden away what would you do?"

"Call the husband. Tell him what I want."

"You wouldn't wait, hope he gets antsy first, make him sweat a little?"

Ellen shook her head. "I'd want to get to him before he even knows she's disappeared. That way he won't tell anyone—police, friends, co-workers. I wouldn't want any attention, anything out of the ordinary."

"Right. And this time?"

"Nothing's ordinary. It's the only topic of conversation."

"Again, why?"

No one had an answer. Exley sat at the table. "Let me play out some possible scenarios for you. Whatever's going on here, the kidnappers didn't snatch these kids on a whim. They want something. Until we hear from them, we don't have much to go on. But sooner or later we're going to get a call asking for money or release of someone in prison or aid to a revolutionary group somewhere. It's conceivable that it's a highly organized and trained group of terrorists we're facing. But with that child's body turning up like it did—costumed, as it were—I'd guess it's more likely a lone psychopath. In which case, he's probably after money and not some sort of political *quid pro quo*. If it is money, it at least gives us something to work with since political demands are almost always untenable. Even with a monetary ransom, they'll start by asking for something outrageous—a hundred million dollars, say. That's been the invariable pattern. But as soon as they make contact, we're a step closer to them. We'll begin to negotiate. I'll act as the primary negotiator. The objective is to drag things out as much as possible. The longer we keep them hanging, the more likely it is we'll be able to learn where they're holding the hostages.

"The difficulty we always have with this type of crime is

building up a body of evidence in a limited period of time. In the case of a serial killer, say, with each occurrence you learn a little bit more. You deduce, as it were, by accretion, by adding on pieces of information—a blood type, a piece of fabric, a pattern of attacks. Here, our deduction will probably have to come from hurried snippets of phone conversation. And our time will be severely limited, everything rush, rush, rush."

"*Deduce by accretion,*" Middleton repeated slowly, savoring the words as though they were chocolate morsels and smiling across the table at LaSalle.

"What if you do learn where they're being held?" Whitehorse asked. "There's twenty-seven—" He shook his head. "Twenty-six kids there. You're not going to attack the place."

"Indeed we might," Exley replied. "That's the decision-point I was talking about. It's Matt's call as team leader, of course. But I've already talked to the director twice about this. He is very concerned about these children. The president has even called him, wanting to know what can be done. We'll do whatever we have to. Going after victims is not actually as risky as it sounds. F.B.I. policy now is to rely on our strength and decisiveness. We'll go in if we're fairly certain of success or, if not, set up a siege, surround the locale, and make sure the perpetrators understand that there are only two ways for them to leave: alive with their hands in the air or dead. We're not going away. And we're not going to provide them a plane to escape in like some silly television show. There simply is no option other than surrender. It always works."

"Always?" Ellen asked dubiously.

The psychologist turned and frowned at her as though unused to being doubted. "There are never guarantees when dealing with human behavior, of course, but yes, always, or virtually always. If we don't get a line on the hostage location, though, we'll follow scenario B and try to set up the pay-off in such a way that we take out the kidnappers when they pick up the ransom. Whoever delivers the money can be outfitted with a microphone or tracking device. And since pay-offs are almost always at night, we can put 'fire-flies' on the ransom package: tiny lights that can only be seen if you're wearing special glasses. As soon as those lights move, we've got him. It's really not all that difficult."

"There's probably more than one bad guy," Whitehorse said. "You pick up the one with the money, what's to keep the other from killing the kids and taking off?"

"That's not been our experience in the past. We lay it on the line for the one we capture: 'You're going to jail, maybe for the rest of your life, maybe not. But why add to that the risk of a death sentence? Tell us where the hostages are and it'll go easy on you.' When they look at it like that, they usually see that the only reasonable option is to cooperate."

Ellen wasn't so sure. The F.B.I. was used to dealing with political terrorists who knew exactly what they wanted or people whose primary motivation was money. But someone who stole a bus load of retarded and medically fragile children and then killed one in cold blood did not seem the sort to react in a rational or predictable manner. This was probably the work of a desperate or wildly out of control person who would happily see the remainder of the children die if he was in danger of capture. The last thing you'd want to do in such a case was to confront him.

"The final option," Exley continued, "is to attempt to follow the pick-up man back to the hostage location. In any case, we'll try to get them to agree to a pay-off location that allows the field agents to visually monitor what's going on. We normally swarm the area with unmarked cars and take down the license number of every vehicle we see, then process it through the computer and see what turns up. Even if the ransom's not picked up, he's almost certain to be nearby watching, and, if so, we'll eventually be able to I.D. him. If we can't actually see the ransom package, we'll monitor it electronically. We've had enough experience to be able to get concessions from them—where to meet and so on. It's tricky though. They're almost always very tense and have to be handled gently. They don't like calling the police. They know the phone will be tapped. The most you get is thirty or forty seconds."

"There's another option," Ellen said, bringing up what she thought should be obvious to everybody. "Forget the heroics. Don't even attempt an arrest. Do what he wants, make the pay-off, get the kids back." That was the logical choice, she thought. Worry about the victims, rather than putting another notch in your belt.

Middleton's eyes widened in surprise. "Christ, why didn't we think of that?"

After a moment, Exley said, "Option one is find the children—quickly, before they suffer any medical emergencies—and bring them back with or without the kidnappers. Option two is try to apprehend the kidnappers when they pick up the ransom or follow them to the hostage location. Option three is do nothing, follow orders, give them what they want. And then deal with this situation again six months or a year from now when someone else decides it's a no-risk crime."

The door opened and a uniformed patrolman stuck his head in and said, "Chief."

As Whitehorse disappeared into the outer office, Middleton came to his feet and began to stalk around the room in a display of nervous energy. Exley removed a bottle of Evian water from his briefcase and took a sip before continuing to Ellen: "There is, of course, another anomalous element to this case, and that is the very public murder of one of the victims. Even when victims are murdered—which happens surprisingly often, by the way—kidnappers invariably keep up the fiction that they're alive since a dead victim has no value. But to kill one and then draw attention to it in the bizarre manner in which he did—"

Paul returned suddenly to the room, cutting off Exley and leaving Middleton standing by the window. "We took a print off that knife we found at the scene and sent it to Sacramento. They got a match already. I guess they ran it twice just to be sure." He paused a moment. "Turns out it's the governor's."

Everyone looked at him.

Finally, LaSalle said, "The governor of California?"

Paul nodded and glanced at Ellen.

"Guess our guy's got a sense of humor," Exley said, frowning at the tabletop.

"How the hell would he get the fuckin' governor's print on a knife?" Middleton demanded, as though one of them were responsible. The room was uneasy as they shifted in their chairs and fiddled with papers.

Ignoring Middleton, Ellen looked at LaSalle. "A couple of years ago we had a big dinner to dedicate the new high school. There were probably fifteen hundred people, maybe more. The governor was there. I suppose the kidnapper swiped the knife then."

"Two years he's held onto it!" Whitehorse shook his head. "The man must be a planner."

LaSalle asked, "Could you get a list of people who were at the dinner? It's likely to be someone local then."

Ellen shrugged and began to feel defeated, as though the knife were a symbol of greater losses to come. "The whole town was invited. Along with anyone else who wanted to show up. It was just hot dogs and chili and a five-dollar donation. Probably the governor's table was the only one with silverware."

"Jesus Christ," Middleton muttered and turned his back, staring fiercely out the window.

"This is not good, I'm afraid," Exley said thoughtfully. "Especially if he's really had it for two years. It means we're not dealing with a typical ransom kidnapper with an I.Q. of 90. But it does make for an interesting case. We've definitely got a thinker, all right, a planner." He smiled without humor. "Someone who knows exactly what he's doing." He looked over at Paul. "I think we need to at least entertain the possibility that the culprit is not only someone local but someone you know, perhaps someone who has taken the time to become familiar with how you do things and now is having his little joke with you. Or perhaps someone with whom you have a grudge—"

"You mean someone here in the department?" Paul interrupted angrily.

"Not necessarily a police officer but someone who could become familiar with your operations." Exley hurried on as Paul's face flushed red. "Let's think about it. We're dealing with a person who's obviously bright and probably local. In a small town people know people and know people who know people. He's been planning this for a long time. So perhaps by chatting with his policeman friends he could put together how the department would react to a kidnapping. It's possible he could even be getting updates as your investigation continues—"

"My officers are not involved in this!" Paul shouted.

Exley held up his hands. "I'm not saying your officers, Chief. Could be a friend of one of your officers or a relative or neighbor."

Paul was seething, but before he could say anything Exley asked, "Have you hired anybody in the last three years? Perhaps he joined the force anticipating this crime."

"Of course we've hired people. This is a growing city." Paul turned to Ellen. "Three, four, something like that. And half a dozen civilian employees. But I'd vouch for any of—"

"How about disciplinary problems? Is there someone you've discharged recently?"

"No!"

"You're sure? No one on suspension? No firings?"

"Goddamn it, no!"

"All right. We'll need to do background checks on everybody in the building though." Paul was getting hotter by the second, and Exley quickly added, "Not just police. Everyone. Including the civilian offices next door."

Paul looked as though he wanted to hit somebody. "Christ!"

"We'll work backwards, too," Exley added. "Anytime children are involved as victims it could be a crime of a sexual nature. Let us pray that it's not. But we'll ask Sacramento for all sex offenders registered in the county. As soon as we get the names, we'll check them out in person, find out where they were this morning." He turned to LaSalle. "Some of your agents can help with the leg work, can't they?"

LaSalle nodded. "Of course," he said, then asked, "Can you give us a profile? What kind of person are we looking for here?"

Exley shook his head. "Too early. If it's a political rather than sexual crime, we'd need to know who they represent. If a single individual, I'd need to hear his voice, perhaps talk to him awhile on the phone. We don't even know his age. Or if it is a he. What we do know is that this person is a killer. That should warn us to be careful, no matter what we do."

LaSalle sighed. "All right. Then maybe we better focus on the bus for now." He was beginning to sound frustrated, Ellen thought, as though he expected more assistance from the Bureau's behavioral expert. He straightened in his chair. "I need some ideas, Doctor. We've got to get moving. These children are troubled, many are sick. We can't afford to sit around and wait for a ransom call. If we started a search, how do you think he'd react? You must have some idea. What if we put up a dozen choppers and fixed-wing aircraft? Or sent people out in town? Ellen suggested using the National Guard."

"I didn't suggest it," Ellen said at once and immediately felt flustered. Why was she becoming so defensive? Quickly, she added, "I said it was a possibility. Something to think about. Those kids have to be found."

Exley frowned. "I wouldn't do it. Just because this fellow's methodical doesn't mean he's sane. You put a lot of people out there looking and he could snap. Even with the medical considerations, I think we should wait until he contacts us. Give us a chance to talk to him before we do anything rash."

Just then a dull thumping sound drew their attention to the window. Whitehorse tilted back in his chair and stared outside. "One of those big green choppers, looking for a place to land. It's too big to put down in the street. Probably have to go up to Fremont and use the play yard."

"The army hostage removal team," LaSalle said, standing and looking. "You better send a couple of vans to bring them in. They've got a lot of gear."

Whitehorse hurried into his outer office again to give the orders. When he came back, he said, "I got them on the radio. They're going to set up in the desert so they can get their helicopter in and out quickly." He turned to LaSalle, an edge to his voice. "You were talking about doing something—" and Ellen thought, Paul, too: he'd expected more help, to have made some progress by now, and was becoming frustrated at their stagnation. What made it worse was the certain knowledge that impatience could lead to measures they would later regret; without being able to specify the trade-off involved in sacrificing speed for caution, how could they decide what was best?

LaSalle began to pace around the room, staring at the floor, trying to work it out in his mind. "Normally, I'd agree with Dr. Exley and wait to hear from the kidnapper. But we all know that this is a special case with special hostages. Some of them are going to die without their medication. Damn it, we just can't leave them for days or weeks. Even hours could be crucial. What do you think those parents downstairs would want if we asked them?"

Dr. Exley started to object, but Ellen quickly said, "As far as I can see, no federal law's been broken. The F.B.I. has to wait twenty-four hours to get involved, right?"

"Not exactly," LaSalle said, stopping to look at her. His voice had gone cautious, and he seemed surprised at her question. "The law's been changed. It depends on the circumstances. What did you want to say?"

Ellen could feel everyone's gaze moving toward her and a sudden escalation of tension in the room. Sounding more confident than she felt, she said, "We're in charge. The Las Cruces police. We decide what to do."

"Okay," LaSalle said without emotion. The room was suddenly quiet. Ellen was feeling increasingly self-conscious as everyone stared into her face, but she didn't like the way the investigation was slipping into the hands of the feds, as though she and Paul were of no consequence. Although not at all confident about what she was going to suggest, it seemed the lesser of several evils. She looked over at LaSalle, who was standing near the door, watching her. She was aware of Middleton at the other end of the room, his hands jammed in his pockets and his eyes angry as he glared in her direction. "I think with the needs of these children we have to start looking for them immediately," she began evenly. "We've waited too long already. But I'm beginning to agree with Dr. Exley, too. We need to step gently. We don't know how this person will react to seeing a thousand people moving toward him as they search the town. He might panic, kill the kids, and run for it. You have to figure he's not too stable to begin with to attempt a crime like this."

Exley relaxed back in his chair, but Middleton muttered something she couldn't decipher and turned angrily toward the window again.

LaSalle said, "You want to hold off until we hear from him?" He was watching her, his unlined face without expression, waiting to hear her thoughts.

"Not exactly. I want to focus on the bus since we're more likely to find it than the kids. We'll put our departmental units out like they would be on normal patrol but looking for anyplace the bus might be hidden. We're a small town. There can't be that many structures big enough to completely conceal it. We don't have abandoned factories or warehouses to speak of. So we're looking for large garages or outbuildings, that sort of thing. We already have six patrol vehicles out. We can spare another eight officers from other duties and have them in civilian clothes and in their own cars doing the same thing. But that's the only overt action I want at this point. I don't want to spook this person. I want those kids untouched."

LaSalle showed no emotion but turned after a pause to Whitehorse, who was sitting at the end of the table with his legs extended, listening silently. "Chief?"

Paul's head nodded agreement, but his voice was uncertain. "We'll try it Ellen's way. I want to find those kids, but I don't want a massacre here."

Exley said, "The National Security Agency has satellites that can read a license plate from orbit. Maybe they could take a look at this area, especially out in the desert. See if they notice anything peculiar. That's what they do, as I understand it: analyze satellite data."

"We'll check it out," LaSalle said with a shake of his head. "Don't get your hopes up, though. The National Security Agency doesn't usually admit they have satellites. They usually won't even admit that they exist themselves. But we might be able to put up some planes of our own with photo equipment and get some people from Quantico or Langley to interpret the pictures. We can probably get the planes locally."

From where he was standing next to the window, Middleton said, "So for now we essentially do nothing?" He sounded incredulous as he stared from face to face. "Twenty-six kids who might die by tonight without medical assistance are missing and our plan is to *wait?*"

Whitehorse turned to look at him without expression, but Ellen didn't try to hide her irritation. "It's the children I'm worried about. We just hold off a bit and see what the bad guy wants before we get too overt."

Middleton grunted his disgust and stared away from her.

Whitehorse said to Exley, "It bothers me he hasn't called yet. It's been six hours. Whatever it is he wants, he should have called by now. What the hell's he waiting for?"

The psychologist shook his head. "We have to wonder. I wish I knew what he was up to. Something interesting, presumably. Something to get our attention. Else why the clown suit?"

Whitehorse came to his feet. "Ellen and I need to get going on the ground search."

Exley said at once, "Don't forget to get me a list of everyone in this building. We need to run a records check as soon as possible."

Ellen nodded. "I'll have Personnel send it over."

There was a shuffling of feet and chairs as Ellen and Whitehorse left. After the door closed, a silence descended on the room for several seconds, the vestiges of some unresolved emotion still alive in the air. Then Exley sat back and smiled at LaSalle. "So Matthew, again we work together. Career going along swimmingly, I presume? I hear good things about you."

"No complaints," LaSalle said, feeling a curious unease in the presence of his colleague, something he couldn't identify but that bothered him.

"Good, good. And you, Charles? Still in San Diego? I'm surprised DeCarlo let you come up here, with the personnel shortage they always seem to have. He still is the S.A.C., isn't he?"

"Hell, yeah," Middleton said, beginning to wander around the room, peering at the framed black-and-white photographs on the wall: desert scenes, the reservation, Las Cruces from the air. "It's part of my work-release program. I have to be back by five every night for my medication though. Wild mood swings, you know . . . . unpredictable behavior."

The psychologist looked at him.

"Joke," Middleton explained without expression, adding, "Hell, DeCarlo positively jumped at the chance to unload me for a while. Almost made me feel unloved."

"Yes?"

"Almost." He took a picture down, flipped it over, and studied the back. "You know who took these? Mr. Paul Whitehorse! An artsy cop! My, my, my. You don't see that in the Bureau, do you?" He turned around and laughed out loud as he saw Exley take a drink from his Evian bottle. "Unbelievable. Paying for what's free at any drinking fountain. I guess you know what Evian spelled backwards is, don't you, Doc?"

Ignoring him, Exley said, "Tell me what you think, Matthew. What's going on here? What are our chances?"

LaSalle sighed and leaned back in his chair. "I think I'm

not as comfortable with hostage situations as you are. Don't forget what happened in Texas with the Branch Davidians. Something like eighty people died. I don't want it to get to that point. I want to get the kidnapper when we make the money drop, if not before. And I want to do it before any more kids are killed."

"If there is a money drop," Exley replied. "We don't yet know what he's after. There's no sense in being alarmist, especially to the local police, but I think perhaps we've got something here beyond the typical kidnapping. As I said earlier, why the clown suit? Why kill a harmless child? Why such a need for attention? Something so unusual is cause for concern."

"Endangers our perfect arrest record?" Middleton asked as he began to wander around the room again.

Exley was annoyed but tried to remain civil. "I never said it was perfect, Charles. But it is something we should all be pleased about. Including you."

"Yeah, yeah, yeah. But I guess our marvelous record depends on whether you classify a case as 'major,' doesn't it? I can think of half a dozen snatches where we didn't turn up squat."

Exley flashed an annoyed look at Middleton's back, then turned again to LaSalle, his voice uncharacteristically tentative. "We had a kidnapping similar to this several years ago in West Virginia. Singleton, I think the name was. Charles Singleton II. Remember that?"

Middleton gave a short, derisive laugh. "God! Our finest moment!"

LaSalle shrugged as he looked at the psychologist. "The name's familiar. I don't remember the details though."

Exley reached down to his briefcase and pulled out a laptop computer of the sort Vince Garibaldi had been using. "Singleton . . ." he said, and began typing with two fingers. The screen filled suddenly with a color photo of a youngish, long-haired man. Exley hit a key and the picture gave way to text. He leaned forward and began to paraphrase aloud as he read through the material. "A 'survivalist,' lived in the woods, hated the government, public schools, taxes, police, authority of any kind. He dressed up in camouflage fatigues and combat boots like a soldier." He glanced briefly at LaSalle. "Probably imitating some movie hero of his. Then he broke into a little two-room school back in the hills and sprayed bullets all over the place with an assault rifle. There were seven students and one teacher inside. A nine-year-old boy died from a wound to his chest. It was never determined if it was intentional or not, quite possibly not. But Singleton left the child sitting at the teacher's desk, wearing a green beret."

LaSalle looked at him sharply and Exley nodded. "It's a curious similarity. Of course your kidnapper dressed the child in a clown hat and makeup, a playful rather than angry aspect. There was nothing at all playful about Singleton."

"What happened to him?" LaSalle asked.

Exley again hit a key and stared at the screen as he scrolled down with the cursor. "He took off with the other kids and the teacher, 'prisoners of war,' he called them. A week later he sent a video to a Wheeling TV station. They turned it over to the Bureau without broadcasting it. It showed the children and the teacher chained together with leg braces. He referred to them as agents of a terrorist state and promised to kill them and everyone else he found in public schools unless West Virginia put an end to property taxation, or property 'confiscation,' as he called it. It seems he lost his business, a little roadside bar and restaurant, when he couldn't, or wouldn't, pay his taxes.

"The state police found him more or less by accident a week later when a man out hunting thought he saw someone who looked like Singleton. He must have been hard to miss—this huge, gangly, fellow with filthy red hair to his shoulders and a long, bushy beard." He hit a different key and Singleton's face again filled the screen. Exley briefly spun the computer around so LaSalle could see it. "He'd been hiding out in an abandoned coal mine. Unfortunately, by the time the local police got there, he had booby-trapped the entrance. They tried to get inside instead of waiting for Bureau personnel. The whole thing blew up, killing everyone, including three sheriff's deputies. Singleton and the kids were so far back in the mine their bodies were never recovered."

"Another victory for psychology," Middleton intoned as though narrating an educational film. "The science of the mind."

"Once we learn where the children are being kept we need to bear this in mind," Exley said. "The last thing we want is another mass death like that."

"Well . . ." Matt said dubiously. "There are similarities in the cases, I guess. The kids, a dead victim, taking the teacher—"

"And the mines you mentioned outside of town," Exley added.

"Christ!" Middleton said, his back to them as he halted to stare out the window. "You're stretching, Exley. You're looking for parallels that don't exist. All kidnappings have some things in common. And they're all different. Forget it, we haven't got another survivalist." He paused a moment. "It's a rush, though, isn't it? This one? Jesus!"

The psychologist turned around in his chair to look at him. "Pardon?"

"Twenty-six kids disappearing into thin air, the crazy with the governor's fingerprints, a zillion reporters outside. Sure as hell beats doing tax audits or chasing wetbacks." He continued to look out the window. "I truly do hate the desert though. Goddamn Ethiopia was more appealing than this place." He turned back and let his gaze wander around the room. "They don't even have a coffee machine in here. How do they stay awake? Jimsonweed tea? Communal war chants?"

Exley began to stack the papers on the tabletop in front of him. "If we do get to a pay-off, Matthew, don't you think you should have Bureau people physically in the area? Especially if I'm involved in delivering the ransom. The police here are a little . . . unsophisticated, I suppose is the word."

"Primitive is the word," Middleton replied as he resumed wandering around the room.

"If the police can't handle things," LaSalle said, "we'll take over. I don't think you have to worry though. They know what they're doing."

Middleton's expression didn't change. "It's the squaw," he said at once. "I saw you staring at her. You're thinking with your crotch, *compadre*. Not surprising in the circumstances, but turn your back and she'll bury a tomahawk in it. Don't get your meat where you get your bread: old Apache saying."

"Such a way you have with words," Exley muttered with an unaccustomed edge to his voice. He scooped up his papers and shoved them in the briefcase. "You should try to see how you look to others sometime, Charles."

"Yeah? Would that help?"

"You do have enemies, you know. Not everyone in the Bureau is thrilled with this aggressive attitude you choose to affect."

Middleton chuckled. "Jesus, we're one big happy family, aren't we? Maybe tonight we could make up some popcorn and play Monopoly in front of the fireplace." He turned and gazed again out the window at thirty miles of desolate, white-hot desert. "A world-class crime in a world-class city. Friendly Las Cruces! You think there's kangaroos out there?"

No longer able to mask his annoyance, Exley leaned back and looked at the large man. "You harbor a good deal of rather undifferentiated hostility, don't you, Charles? I remember that about you."

"Yeah, well, it's because of my low self-esteem. When I was a kid the other boys would put me in a burlap sack and throw me in the river. I'm trying to learn to live with my pain."

Exley wasn't put off. "Perhaps when this is over we could talk, the two of us."

Middleton spun around and looked at him with contempt. "Don't try your psychological mumbo jumbo on me, ol' kind-hearted Doc. And don't try playing law-enforcement expert either. The locals buy into this shit because they don't know any better. But I do." Exley's pale face turned red as he started to say something, but Middleton didn't give him a chance. "Tell me something. How many mutts have you arrested in your life?"

"That's completely unfair, Charles. Apprehension is not B.S.U.'s charge. We're staff, not line. We advise."

Middleton crossed over to the table and yanked out a chair, spinning it around and sitting with his arms resting on its back. "Okay, fair enough, old pal. How many patients have you seen in the past ten years, then? None, right? Zero. Zilch. Nada. You're a book doc. A goddamn researcher! No patients, no arrests, no police experience. Probably never been in the military, never used a gun. You'd get hives if you had to go out on the range and qualify with an M-16 or Mac 10. You B.S.U. guys are running a scam and everyone in the field knows it. If we ever get a director with his balls intact after Congress approves him, your whole fucking department will get run out of here and you'll have to go to work for a living. Work! That'll be a shock, won't it?" He pushed to his feet and shoved the chair out of his way.

LaSalle said, "Charley," and shook his head but privately believed Middleton was at least half-right. Behavioral Sciences had had some early successes but for the most part was no more useful than a psychic palm reader. It was one of those organizational truths best left unsaid, though, since they were so beloved by the press and Congress.

The telephone rang and Matt picked it up. At once it was clear he was talking to D.C., and the others waited and listened, Middleton continuing to pace. When he put the receiver down a few minutes later, he smiled at his audience. "Just checking in to see how we're doing."

"They want to stay on top of things but not get too close in case it blows up," Middleton said with contempt. His voice rose. "They're saving you for the sacrificial lamb, my son. They're probably already preparing the fire. Hickory-smoked LaSalle, comin' right up."

"There won't be any need for a sacrifice, Charley. Things aren't going to blow up."

"Yeah, yeah, sure. Keep telling yourself that. If we don't find the kids by midnight, we'll put it on your tombstone." He strode again to the window and stared out at the vast expanse of desert stretching to the horizon and baking under the relentless heat of the mid-day sun. "Last year I made a list of places where I might want to retire. Las Cruces ain't on it."

In Paul's office, Ellen picked up the phone and dialed Dispatch downstairs. While punching out the number, she said, "What do you think?"

Paul lowered himself into his oversized leather chair. "I think we've got too damn many jurisdictions here: police, sheriff, F.B.I., army, air force. Every time you add a department, you create a chance for a screw-up."

Ellen said, "When I was in college I read about an experiment this guy did. When people came randomly into the room, each one was given a lapel pin to put on. Some pins were red, some green. It was completely random, but the people with the green pins drifted to one side of the room and the people with red to the other. When he tested them later, he discovered the people with the green pins thought they were smarter than those with the red pins and vice versa. That's what happens when you have departments, too. Everyone looks to their own group and loses track of the overall good."

Paul didn't appear to be listening. He spun around in his chair and stared out the window. "Fuck 'em. We'll do things our way. Fuck 'em all."

1:30 P.M.

I'm going to scream, I'm going to scream, I'm going to scream, Linda Sowell thought as the horrible cacophony of crying and wailing reverberated madly all around her. It was as if someone were taking a hammer to her ears and pounding and pounding. She dropped the fingernail clipper she had been using as a screwdriver and sank down on the floor, her back against the wall, and began to sob.

Alarmed, Eric threw his arms around his mother and clutched tightly. "Please, Mommy, don't cry. Please, please—"

But Linda couldn't help herself and Eric also started sobbing. "I want to go home. I don't like it here. Please, Mommy! I want to go home!"

Summoning up her willpower, Linda forced away the tears and hugged her son closely. "We can't go home yet, Eric. But pretty soon." And she thought, I can't break down. I'm all these children have. I can't break down!

Tony, one of the autistic boys, was racing around the small room, screaming at the top of his lungs, pounding his fists on the walls and floor. Trying to sound cheerful, Linda said, "Eric, why don't you play with Tony? Tony needs to play with someone. See Tony?"

Eric burrowed his face desperately into her shoulder. "Don't want to play with Tony."

"Please, Eric!" Hysteria began to rush again into her brain, making her dizzy and weak.

Lisa, a beautiful four-year-old schizophrenic, began pulling fiercely on Linda's shoe. "I have to go to the bathroom"

The front of the girl's dress was covered with urine.

Mechanically, Linda pushed herself to her feet. "Eric, please go play with someone. Or watch the television. *Please*, Eric."

Disengaging herself from her son, she took Lisa by the hand. The tiny child, with her Shirley Temple curls and frilly dresses, had always been one of Linda's favorites, never misbehaving on the bus, though the teachers said she could be a terror at school. "Come on, hon. I'll show you the bathroom."

Leading the girl to the curtained-off area, Linda helped

her remove her panties, then set her on the seat. On the other side of the curtain, the five wheelchair children were bawling loudly. They're scaring each other, Linda thought and then realized, We all are. The noise is worse than the confinement. The children are frightened to death. Anybody would be.

She raised her voice above the din. "Please boys and girls. Quiet. Quiet. Stop crying."

Except for Tiffany, the mute girl who sat staring at the wall as though in a daze, no one did. They were screaming so loudly they couldn't hear her. She picked up a little girl whose name she didn't know and hugged her close, her right hand comfortingly behind the girl's neck. "It's okay, it's okay," she said soothingly and immediately thought, It's not okay. I sound like an idiot.

The little girl did not calm down. Her face was wet with tears and saliva and she was screaming and sobbing at the same time. Linda began to walk with her, hoping the motion would have a soothing effect. Slowly, the crying began to subside and after five minutes it was only a whimper. Linda thought, I've got to do something about those wheelchair kids. I've got to get them quiet. Maybe the television would help. If I push them over to the TV they can watch the video. But the minute she moved the little girl from her shoulder and placed her on the floor she began screaming again. I can't hold her all day, Linda thought desperately and hurriedly shoved the five wheelchairs close to the television set. The video had played out and the screen was white with static. She pushed the rewind button on the front of the VCR and waited while it reversed. We're never going to get out of here, she thought as her eyes tried to focus on the flickering images. We're going to die in here.

Eric had come up and was clinging to her leg. The film stopped rewinding. Linda hit Play, turned toward the children, and said, "Cartoons, boys and girls."

She hurried to a little girl in a wheelchair. "Cartoon. See? Cartoon. Disney!"

She felt like grabbing the girl and forcing her to look but

restrained herself. After a moment the girl stopped crying, and Linda turned to the next child. "Cartoons. See?"

After twenty minutes she'd gotten half the kids to quiet down and stare at *101 Dalmatians*. She hurried back to the locked interior door and picked up the fingernail clipper from the floor. I'm not giving up, she thought. I beat drugs. I'm almost out of college. I'm raising a handicapped child by myself. I've done something with my life, goddamn it! I'm not going to die in here. I'm not going to let this bastard take it all from me.

Five-year-old Roni, the girl who had suffered the seizure, came over and sat down to watch as Linda dropped to her knees and began working on the screws that attached the handle to the door. "I want to go home," the girl said and grabbed hold of Linda's bare shin. "I don't like it here." The nail file was just a fraction too thick to fit the slots on top of the screws. It doesn't matter, Linda told herself. It doesn't matter, it doesn't matter, it doesn't matter!

"I don't feel good," Roni went on softly, continuing to grasp Linda's leg. "I sick."

I'll make it fit, Linda told herself. I'll widen the slot. I'll do it. I'm getting us out of here.

2:10 P.M.

Standing stiffly with his back to Ellen, Paul stared out the tinted double glass of his office window at the television and newspaper people gathered on the street below. How many were there now? Hundreds? Thousands? He had no idea. Dozens of panel trucks with satellite dishes, looking from his window like inverted mushrooms, sprouted from the edge of the crowd. Vendors had appeared from nowhere to sell soft drinks and ice cream. He sighed silently. How long before the T-shirt sellers showed up? A nerve in his neck began to twitch. "It's getting away from us. We're losing it. We look like yokels, like we don't know what the hell we're doing."

He was afraid more kids were going to die no matter what

they did, and the reporters just intensified his despair. It would be bad enough without them, but from the tone of their questions it was obvious they were looking for an angle, a slant to the story, and they hoped to find it in the incompetence of the local cops. Paul was more distressed than angered. Like a father with a favorite child, he felt an immense pride in the Las Cruces police. It was a professional and highly competent group and a far cry from the inept department he'd taken over eight years before. Only twenty-four officers but more effective for its size than any big city police force. Last year when Jeremy Watts, new to the city council, had suggested—"Just a thought," he'd insisted, smiling through his perfect insurance salesman's teeth and slapping Paul on the back—that the city hire an outside expert to do a "management audit" of the department, Paul's face had turned stony and he'd said, "I don't think so," and that was that. He wasn't going to have some criminology professor from Palo Alto buzz down in his B.M.W. to tell him how to run his department.

But this was something unique, something he had no experience of, and he knew it was making the department look bad.

"Interpol called from Paris," he went on, still staring outside. "They think there might be a terrorist link. Some German group I couldn't even pronounce. International terrorists in Las Cruces! I told them to talk to the F.B.I. A police chief in Italy faxed me twenty pages of information on Mafia kidnappings. What the hell's the Yakuza?"

"Japanese organized crime."

"Figured. A newspaper in Osaka faxed me a long list of questions. I'm supposed to answer by return fax. I told Maggie to unplug the damn thing." He paused, lost in thought, then his tone altered. "Goddamn it, why'd he kill that kid? He didn't even ask for anything. He planned it, had the hat and makeup ready and killed him in cold blood." He turned around and looked at her. "Something else bad's going to happen today. Real soon. Unless we get on top of things something very, very bad's going to happen."

Ellen turned toward the door. "I've got to get downstairs and talk to Zach about the ground search. You don't mind if I put him in charge of it, do you?"

"No, no, fine. He can put everything else on hold. It sure as hell can't be too pressing." Paul lowered himself slowly into his large leather chair. "We can't spook this guy though. He's already killed one. No telling what he'd do."

Ellen hurried down to the squad room, where Zachary Harris and two uniformed patrolmen, one of them at Ellen's desk, were answering phones and taking notes while other lines continued to ring without interruption. "People who think they saw the kids or the bus," Zach said as he slammed the phone down. Immediately it rang again and he made a face. "Or people with theories. Theories! People who live in Las Cruces shouldn't fuckin' have theories." He picked up the phone and almost at once said, "For you," shoving it at her across the desk.

Ellen raised her voice above the commotion. "Sergeant Camacho."

Nothing.

"Hello?" she said, and the hairs on the back of her neck bristled up as she thought she heard someone breathing.

"Who is this?"

In the background the sounds of the squad room faded and suddenly seemed a hundred miles away as she heard someone whisper, "How do you like it so far?"

"What?"

For a long moment there was no sound, then the line went dead.

Ellen stood frozen, unable to move.

"So?" Zach said, looking up at her oddly.

Ellen handed him the receiver. "How do you like it so far?"

"Huh?"

"That's all he said: How do you like it so far?"

"Idiots. Idiots and creeps. Christ!" He was exasperated, almost angry, Ellen thought, as though all the calls were somehow her fault. But his fury snapped her out of her thoughts and reminded her of what she wanted from him: fourteen officers to be assigned to different sectors of the city, with no overlapping; some in civilian clothes and driving their own vehicles, others in patrol cars. They were to concentrate on finding the bus but be low-key about it. They should take standard city maps and mark off each street as they cleared it. Everyone would be on double shifts until this was over. Zach could set up things any way he wanted as long as he got it moving within thirty minutes and kept her apprised of where each officer was at all times.

"I'm supposed to do all that and answer the phone, too? All right, Christ!" His phone started ringing and he snatched at it. "Sergeant Harris."

Hurrying back to Paul's office, Ellen was thinking of the phone call—"How do you like it so far?"—when she ran into LaSalle in the hallway. "I was just going for coffee," he said. "You got time for a quick break?" Ellen glanced at her watch and started to decline, then changed her mind. "Yeah, sure, for ten minutes or so. I've got something to tell you anyway."

The cafeteria was at the end of the next hallway. Even before getting there Ellen could tell it was still crowded with reporters and TV technicians and on-lookers. She stopped at the door and shook her head. "Uh-uh. They'll crucify us."

"Anyplace else we could go?"

"There's a lunch room next to the reception area. No coffee machine though."

"No one knows me. I'll get two coffees and meet you there. Cream and sugar?"

"Black. Get one for Paul, too. Black."

As LaSalle disappeared into the crowded cafeteria, Ellen retreated to the lunch room, where she had earlier watched the televised press conference. It was deserted, almost eerily so after this morning, the bright plastic chairs still scattered in front of the TV and the tables littered with newspapers. Five minutes later, LaSalle arrived, balancing three Styrofoam cups. He put them gingerly on the table in front of her and shook his head. "I'm not sure why people drink coffee when it's a hundred and ten degrees outside. Guess I'm about to find out."

Ellen smiled and pried the top off her cup, watching steam hiss out and curl around the tips of her fingers. "We do it to equalize our body temperature with the environment. Then it doesn't seem so hot."

LaSalle sat and took a tentative sip. "It was eighty-eight in Los Angeles when I left, and I thought that was bad." He put the cup down, looking at her from his clear blue eyes, and she thought at once of Middleton's derisive "pretty boy" comment. It didn't fit though: LaSalle's features were too sharp-angled and rugged to be pretty, and he was too big for a boy. She understood why the Bureau trotted him out for press conferences: he was the epitome of the calm, in control professional they wanted the public to think all agents were like. She smiled to herself: If the world could only see the Charley Middletons. LaSalle blew on his coffee and stared at her. "I guess you'd rather be here than in L.A. though. Despite the heat."

"Well, I'm from Las Cruces. This is home, where I belong."

"But you had to leave in order to come back." He was watching her with relaxed curiosity as he held the cup in front of his mouth. More than watching, she thought with a start. Staring, with an intensity she found discomfiting. He added, "So what took you away?"

Ellen's gaze shifted to the empty room as an uncomfortable sensation began to rise from somewhere deep inside. Odd, but she'd never thought about it like that before. As much as she loved Las Cruces, as much as it was home, she had left more than once. Longed to leave. First, at age thirteen to live for a year with a family in Utah, part of a church group, middle-class Anglos taking reservation kids to the city and giving them religion and clothes out of the L.L. Bean catalog. That was too cynical though. They were nice people trying to do good, and she still kept in touch with them. She'd left again at eighteen to go to college in Arizona, coming home only for a couple of weeks every year in the summer. And then she'd moved to L.A. after commuting daily from Las Cruces to the El Centro police department for eighteen months.

There was no doubt what she had been fleeing from all those years, though it pained and embarrassed her to think her first instinct had always been to run from trouble rather than face it. But with her father long gone and her mother slumped in front of the television all day, either sick or complaining or both, she loathed her home, a forty-year-old house trailer a quarter-mile from the nearest neighbor on the reservation. By the time she was ten or eleven, the other kids wouldn't come by because her mother would yell at them and throw rocks and call them names. Even her grandfather, the person who really brought her up, wouldn't visit, making Ellen go to his house trailer, where he would explain that it was not her mother's fault she acted that way; someone was doing magic on her. While Ellen was in L.A., her mother had died. A brain tumor, the autopsy had said; it had been destroying her mind for years. And somehow it had made Ellen feel a terrible weight of guilt, as though it were her fault.

All those years away from Las Cruces—escaping, running, fleeing ghosts that she could see only in retrospect—now seemed random and pointless. There had been no pattern, no meaning to her existence. Things happened. Or didn't. People came into her life, disappeared, came again. Work, home, shopping. There was no continuity, no sense of belonging, and she had felt every minute as though a part of her being were missing and had to be discovered again.

What did she think of now when she recalled those years in Los Angeles? A brown sky hanging over a cement landscape, though it wasn't clarity the air lacked so much as gentleness. A rotten marriage. Endless street crime. A politicized police force where merit seemed to play no role in promotion. And television. Television everywhere, as if it had become some strange new religion: shopping malls, restaurants, auto repair shops, offices, people's homes, hospitals. Endless newscasts, MTV, ESPN, soaps. Lives lived vicariously behind barred windows, hovering in front of twenty-seven-inch altars in search of a salvation that never came. Perhaps the final straw, though, was when a juvenile court judge had started sentencing gang members to ballet class. To learn "discipline and focus," he'd said. Forty hours of *pas de deux* for gang banging. When she'd told friends in Las Cruces, they'd thought she was making it up, but it was true. That was the ethos and the madness of Los Angeles.

Las Cruces was friends, people she had known all her life and could count on. Home. Paul. Peace. But even that was changing. A crime like this would have been unthinkable here when she was growing up. Maybe L.A. had been a little peek at the future; the madness that overlay the city like a blanket of smog had followed her home, trailing behind her on the Pamona Freeway as she fled east, and Las Cruces would never be the same.

All this passed through her mind like a flicker of light. But it made her start, and she felt her back stiffen and a little trickle of perspiration race along her ribs. Don't talk about it, she warned herself. Don't bring up memories better left buried unless you want to spend the rest of the day brooding and reliving the mistakes of the past. Glancing at LaSalle watching her, anticipating a response, her hands fluttered with a sort of schoolgirl nervousness from the tabletop, then flopped back down again as she said hurriedly, "Los Angeles was just a bad decision, a mistake. There aren't very many good memories. And a few real bad ones."

"Your ex?"

"Yes, mostly." My God, I am talking about it, she thought with a stab of panic but went on, as though once started she had no choice but to continue. "He was a cop, in Hollywood Division. And proof that the department's psychological screening doesn't work."

"He liked to push people around?" LaSalle guessed. It was a common enough problem on any police force, though seldom discussed openly. The people who most want to become cops shouldn't. And no amount of screening could catch them all.

Ellen made an off-hand gesture, a half-hearted attempt at appearing more relaxed than she felt. She definitely didn't want to get started on Pete. Putting the top back on the coffee as though needing to keep her hands occupied, she shrugged. "Mostly he liked to push me around." She tried a smile, but it faded quickly and she thought, Why am I so nervous? She put her hands in her lap and made them stay still. "I guess he never bought into the era of the sensitive male. When we were living apart, separated—it was just a couple of months before the divorce became final—he came over to my place one night and said he wanted to talk. I should have known better. Pete never wanted to 'talk' about anything. I opened the door with the chain lock on, but he kicked it and the screws came flying right out of the wood. He grabbed me and started whacking me around. I picked up my daughter and tried to run out of the apartment, but he knocked me off balance and Denise's head hit the wall and she blacked out. When she wouldn't come to, I called the paramedics and they took her to County Hospital. Pete had taken off by then, and I was too frantic to think or I would have insisted on somewhere else. Have you ever been to County?"

He shook his head.

"It's a level of hell Dante didn't know about." A chill that she could feel all the way to her toes went through her as she remembered. "Full of gunshot victims, stabbing victims, drug overdoses. Half the people in the emergency room were in handcuffs and shackles. Families screaming in the hallways, people yelling in fifty different languages, threatening each other, fighting. Gang bangers waiting outside with M-16s to see if they'd finished the job on their drive-by or would have to go back the next night. Armed guards following doctors on their rounds. It's like something out of some horrid science fiction movie. Foreign governments send their military doctors to train at County because it's the closest thing to working in a combat zone. Every evening the staff does a body count, just like on battlefields. The night we were there a guard killed a P.C.P. freak dressed up in a ninja costume who was attacking cars in the parking structure with a sword and a baseball bat.

"We had to wait two hours to see a doctor, then they put Denise in a ward with a dozen other children. She had a brain aneurysm, they said. She still hadn't come to. But the nurses were so busy with other patients they didn't check her monitoring equipment. A blood vessel in her brain broke and she almost died. She was in the hospital for a month. Even now she has to be careful not to get too excited or bang her head." Her gaze went to her hands and her voice tightened with emotion. "When you almost lose a child, it changes you. All the dumb little things you ignored before or never even saw suddenly become beautiful: the way she pushes up in her crib or smiles or grabs your finger." Her eyes came back to him and she gestured impatiently. "Does this sound corny?"

"Not at all. But I can see why you're glad to be out of there."

Ellen laughed uneasily. "Let me tell you how glad! When I left Los Angeles I got in my old Civic and drove as fast as it would go until I got to Palm Springs, where it died on me right in front of the Hilton. I figured that was a sign. Here I was with thirty-five dollars cash and a dead car in front of one of the world's most beautiful hotels. I had about five hundred dollars left on my VISA. So I picked up Denise and went inside and got a four-hundred-dollar room for the night. I had room service send up a lobster dinner and a fifty-dollar bottle of wine, and I had the best meal of my life, maybe the best night of my life, and buried the past right there. Zap and it was gone. The next day my grandfather came up in his twenty-year-old pickup and brought us to Las Cruces. I'm staying!"

"How long have you been back?"

"About three years. A lot less money but more fun, or at least more sanity." As she smiled—a fleeting professional interrogator's smile offered like an obligatory social pleasantry—she thought again, God, why am I telling him all this? A vague confusion moved like ground fog in her consciousness, obscuring all other thoughts. Almost at once, LaSalle asked, "Boyfriend?"

Ellen laughed, wondering what her face was expressing as another tiny ripple of panic shot through her, and tried to sound indignant. "Wait a minute! What is this? A cross-examination?"

LaSalle relaxed back in his chair, staring at her calmly from his pale eyes. "I told you, I like to know who I'm working with." He smiled suddenly and beautifully, a flash of brilliance in a perfect face, and leaned across the table in her direction. "Anyway, it paves the way for me to ask you to dinner when this is all over. How does Saturday sound? We can go up to Palm Springs and see if the lobster at the Hilton is as good as you remember. Or go to Sonny Bono's. Does he still have a restaurant there or has he given it up for politics?"

"Well . . ." Inexplicably her heart began to race as though it had suddenly become too light and little red flags sprang up all over her mind. She wasn't sure what was happening here or whether she liked it. Wasn't sure what to feel. Mostly, it was making her wish she hadn't accepted his invitation for coffee.

"Assuming we're done by Saturday," he was saying, and through a rising haze of confusion Ellen thought she heard herself say "I don't know" as her heart pounded, and it was hard to think rationally all of a sudden, and she wasn't looking for anyone anyway because there was Paul, whom she loved, she was sure, and who loved her.

"Or is there a boyfriend?" LaSalle asked abruptly, still smiling easily, interrupting her thoughts, and she was aware suddenly, almost against her will, of how attractive he was in his form-fitting suit and tailored shirt and the unsettling effect it was all having on her. Like a schoolgirl, she told herself with a stab of embarrassment. Like a fifteen-year-old when the best-looking guy in class unexpectedly smiles at her. Damn it, Ellen. Act your age.

"Paul and I . . ." she began and faltered.

LaSalle's eyes widened. "Chief Whitehorse?" He hunched

forward again, looking at her over the table, holding her gaze and not letting her look away. "Old friends. Of course. I should have known. Serious?"

"I—yes."

"Getting married?"

Ellen waved a limp hand, her mind racing, and thought, God, this is what murder suspects must feel under questioning. She needed time to formulate her thoughts before she could frame an answer but had to say something. "We haven't actually talked about it."

"Great!" He sat back in the chair and grinned, and she thought, How pretty his smile is, the way it rises into his eyes, making them glow with a soft illumination. But he was still talking, not giving her a chance to think things through. "Then dinner's still possible. You're not telling me no. You're saying maybe. I needn't vainly and painfully admire you from afar. There is hope." He was laughing easily now, gently poking fun at the both of them, and Ellen laughed, too, trying to tamp down her own emotions and give herself time to arrange her thoughts. "I like the chief," LaSalle went on. He picked up his coffee and sipped. "He seems like a good cop."

"He is," Ellen said, anxious to go to Paul's defense, though she wasn't sure he needed it. "He's proud of what he's done here. That's why this is so hard on him. He's afraid it'll make the Las Cruces P.D. look bad."

LaSalle shook his head. "He shouldn't worry about it. He's got a good department. You can tell just by walking around, watching people. They care about their jobs. Anyway, kidnapping's a no-brainer of a crime. We'll get the guy."

"I don't think that's our main concern. We need to find these kids before they have medical problems." Which provided a much needed excuse to leave. Fleeing again, she thought, but not caring, and started to come to her feet. "I'd better get back. I feel guilty sitting around while the children are missing. Even if there's nothing more we can do right now."

LaSalle put his hand on hers before she could get out of her chair. "You said you had something to tell me."

"Oh!" Ellen sank back in her seat. She had almost forgotten about the phone call. Suddenly it all seemed silly, but she told him anyway.

When she finished he said, "And?"

She looked at him uneasily. "I think it was the kidnapper. At least I did then."

Matthew's eyes narrowed. "What made you think so?"

Ellen fluttered her hand and began to feel stupid. "I can't explain it. It was like I sensed something. I could just tell it was him. He was asking me how I liked the kidnapping so far. And promising me that it was going to get better."

"But why? What would the point be?"

She shook her head. "Maybe he wanted to rattle me. I don't know. But he wanted to hear my voice. And talk to me. I feel it. Or did. I don't know. Maybe I'm just imagining things."

Matthew smiled. "Let me know if it happens again. We'll trace the call. But it was probably just someone who wanted to ask you to dinner and chickened out." They rose, LaSalle suddenly seeming to dwarf her as he stood at her side. "I'll go upstairs with you. I've got a call into the National Security Agency to see if they can maneuver a satellite into our area. And don't forget Saturday night. Either lobster at the Hilton or Italian food at a geriatric pop star's restaurant. Who could ask for more out of life?"

Ellen picked up the two coffees and smiled at him. "Well, we'll see." She felt an odd rush of pleasure like she hadn't experienced for years, as warming and pleasurable as a bath, then a piercing of embarrassment at her own coquettishness that remained with her like an unwelcome guest as they rode together in the elevator. On the third floor, LaSalle smiled and veered off for the conference room as Ellen headed back to Paul's office, arriving just as Howard Stines hurried up the stairs from his lab.

"Except for the glass and the knife, we've got diddly,"

Stines said with a shake of his head. He was a short, thin man with an aggressive manner, as though daring anyone to contradict him. He shrugged and looked at Ellen. "Nothing in the trash we collected but trash. No secret messages or smoking guns, but what'd you expect, Polaroid shots of the crime in progress? This guy knew what he was doing."

"What about the lunch box?"

"Interesting," he said. "No prints. Not even the kid's."

"Yeah, interesting," Ellen said. "So what does it mean, Howard?"

"The kid was neat, didn't get his hands all over it. Held it by the handle just like his mommy told him."

"You obviously don't have kids."

"Course I don't have kids. They're little barbarians, screaming all the time and peeing in their pants."

"Even if the child's prints weren't on it, the mom's should have been."

"Or maybe the governor's," Stines said. "He always looked like the kind of guy who hangs around parks with a Hershey bar."

"What about the house where the boy was found?"

"That F.B.I. guy, Richards, whatever the hell his name is, called in county lab techs from El Centro along with his own guys from L.A. There must be twenty people there, tripping over each other and playing expert."

"Any preliminary evidence?" Paul asked.

"Christ, it's only been two hours. Be realistic."

"I don't want to be realistic, Howard. I want help." He threw his pen down on the desk. "You're going to have to go out and take a look at the bus driver's house." He saw Stines start to protest and raised his voice. "I know you usually don't go by yourself, but we're short, Howard. Who the hell else can I send? Ellen can give you the address. Shouldn't take but an hour."

As Ellen ripped a slip of paper from her notebook and handed it to Stines, he squinted at Whitehorse through his thick glasses. "We don't need a warrant?"

"She's a victim, not a suspect, Howard."

Stines shoved the paper in his shirt pocket. "If you say so. I'll see you when I get back."

After he left, Ellen said, "I better dig up some more people to interview the teachers. I should have done it earlier."

Paul frowned. "There's got to be someone else who can take care of it, Ellen. We need you here. You can't do everything."

"Who am I going to get?" she asked with annoyance. "Maggie? Jeannie Wheatley? Everyone's on something already."

Just then Maggie came in dragging a large blackboard on wheels. Paul said, "What the hell is this for?"

"Mr. LaSalle said he wanted it."

"Well, take it over to the conference room and give it to *Mr.* LaSalle. And where the hell is Ferguson? I haven't seen him since this morning."

"I'll call downstairs and find out."

Maggie grabbed the blackboard and rolled it out of the office. A moment later she yelled from her desk. "He's still out interviewing people along the bus route. You want him?"

"No," Paul said, feeling a rising of frustration again at having too few people to get the work done. "But tell him to call me as soon as he's done." As he was talking, LaSalle and Middleton walked in.

"I forgot to ask," LaSalle said. "What did your officers turn up from the parent interviews? Our computer people are tied into D.C., but they need some data."

Paul glanced at Ellen, then at the F.B.I. agents. After a moment, Ellen said, "We haven't finished with that yet."

Middleton shot an I-told-you-so look at LaSalle and jammed his hands in his back pockets as though trying to control his temper. Still seated at his desk, Paul glanced from Middleton to LaSalle, trying not to show his annoyance. "We've got a personnel problem," he said finally. "There aren't enough people here to do everything. We're not used to dealing with problems like this."

Middleton stared at Whitehorse with exasperation. "Then

maybe someone else should have overall control of the investigation. We don't want to steal your thunder, Chief, but it's time you let us quarterback things. We've handled this sort of crime before. You haven't."

Ellen noticed Paul's neck stiffen, but his expression didn't waver as the tension in the room immediately ratcheted up. "Quarterback?" He sounded confused as he considered the word a moment, then gave up. "I don't get it."

"Let us run things," Middleton said testily. He clearly wasn't sure if Whitehorse was being sarcastic or stupid, but it didn't matter. He pressed on like a man determined to see for himself how thin the ice ahead was.

"Like football?" Paul turned a questioning look on LaSalle. "Is that it? This is a game to you guys?"

Middleton's face flushed, and he took a sudden step toward Paul as if he were going to hit him. Quickly, Ellen said, "There still aren't enough bodies. Your being in charge wouldn't change that."

"It would get things done!" Middleton snapped, gesturing angrily with his arm. "We're running out of time if we want these children back alive. Goddamn it, you know that! Don't be so damn proud. Twenty-seven lives are at stake. Give it up. Let us take over. We've done this before."

"And screwed up before," Paul replied calmly.

LaSalle, still standing by the door, put his hands in his pockets and sounded as though he was oblivious to the emotion around him. "Our primary objective at this point is to find out what the parents know. Or what they suspect. There could be something vital there. At any rate, it's the only hope we have now. Perhaps Charles could take over that aspect of—"

"Of course," Ellen said instantly, jumping at the chance to get Middleton out of the way.

"Wait a minute," the F.B.I. agent said at once. He looked around the room as though discovering he had mistakenly crossed into enemy territory and didn't know how to get back. "That's not what I meant. Goddamn it, I'm not going to waste my time with that."

"It's got to be done," LaSalle said patiently. "Like you said, the department hasn't got the resources. Looks like it's up to us to help. That's why we're here."

Middleton's gravelly voice was angry and baffled. "Come on, Matt—"

"The parents are in this building, aren't they? Downstairs?"

"Don't do this, Matt. I mean it. I didn't come up here to do Whitehorse's fucking clerical work."

Ellen tried to keep her voice steady as she said, "They're in the multipurpose room on the other side of the building. First floor." When Middleton turned to her with a look of rage, she felt absurdly like cheering, as though she were a seven-year-old who had just bested the schoolyard bully. She stared into his eyes and added pointedly, "Whole families. About a hundred people, maybe more."

LaSalle turned calmly to his colleague. "Make sure everything's recorded. And I want to know if any parents are unaccounted for."

Middleton stood for a moment staring angrily at LaSalle, then without comment stomped off, his boots pounding silent dents in the thick carpet. After a moment, Ellen crossed over and gently shut the door, finally allowing herself to smile as she looked at LaSalle. "Thanks."

Paul tilted back in his chair and began to toy with a pencil. "I like your style, Matt. I was thinking of shooting him myself, but your way's better." He paused a moment and added, "Maybe not though. Seems like you might've made yourself an enemy. My old army boss used to say the first rule of bureaucracy is never leave any wounded because they'll crawl through hell to pay you back."

Ellen couldn't read his emotion as LaSalle seemed to brush the comment aside. "Don't get the wrong idea about Charley. He and I go back a long way. He's a smart guy and probably the best investigator I know, even if he doesn't always show it. He's a good man to have on your side. But he's also his own worst enemy."

"Not anymore," Paul said deliberately.

LaSalle smiled despite himself. "Yeah, I know. This macho cowboy routine can be annoying. But it's no act. He was a Green Beret in Ethiopia and Honduras, did a lot of clandestine stuff, I guess. He won't even tell me about it. I know he was in an Eritrian P.O.W. camp for thirteen weeks. That's where those scars on his face came from. But sure, he can be a definite pain in the ass. It's why he never went anywhere in the Bureau, and he knows it. But Charley doesn't give a shit. It's how he is."

Anyway, LaSalle did not tell them, Middleton was the only one he asked who'd jumped at the chance to join him. This was the sort of case the careerists in the Bureau instinctively shied away from as a no-win situation: if it turned out okay, LaSalle would get the credit; if it blew up in their faces, there would be enough blame to taint everyone. Before asking for his help, LaSalle had called to see if Middleton was working on anything vital and the other man had laughed derisively. "Border crap. Running down illegals. The fate of the nation hangs in the balance."

"Pissed off the agent-in-charge again, huh?"

"Fuckin' DeCarlo hates my guts. Could've been worse though. He was going to file an insubordination charge against me last year, but I told him if he did I'd send the photos I have to D.C. So instead he's got me chasing busboys and hotel maids back to Mexico."

Unable to restrain himself, LaSalle had asked, "You really have photos?" It was possible. Middleton belonged to a tiny brotherhood of loose cannons scattered across the Bureau and other law-enforcement agencies whose confidential data rivaled Hoover's legendary dossiers on politicians. The "Government in Exile" they called themselves and sent their *samizdat* publications zipping around the world via fax.

But Middleton had run off on his own tangent. "Last week I found three hundred Chinese on a tuna boat out of Ensanada. They paid thirty thousand each to get smuggled into the U.S. Figure it out, my friend: thirty thousand dollars times three hundred. That's nine million. I'm thinking of buying a boat. Wanna go halvsies with me?"

Bringing LaSalle back to the present, Ellen asked, "Why does he dislike us? What'd we do to him?"

LaSalle shook his head and smiled. "Charley's just intense. He wants to catch the kidnapper and find the kids."

Ellen frowned. "He doesn't seem like the compassionate type to me."

"Oh, hell, he's not compassionate at all. But he figures anyone trying something like this is personally insulting his intelligence."

"Well, I don't like him," Ellen said flatly. "I don't trust him." And she thought, but did not say because it sounded melodramatic, He's evil. He'll do you harm.

LaSalle shook his head. "Don't worry about Charley. He owes me. He'll be okay."

"Owes you for what?" Paul asked.

"Once in a while he pushes too hard and someone pushes back. I've stuck my neck out for him. He knows it."

Paul said, "It's the people who owe you that you've got to watch out for. They don't like thinking they've needed someone else's help."

They paused while another group of F-14s passed by, probably twenty miles distant but shaking the windows with the force of an earthquake. Then LaSalle said, "All those planes out there got me thinking about how you said the children could be sixty miles away by now. So I dug through my memory for my seventh-grade math. A circle with a sixty-mile radius. Pi r squared. Remember? I haven't thought of that in years. But I worked it out. A sixty-mile radius gives us eleven thousand square miles. That's a hell of a lot of territory."

"Almost all of it uninhabited," Paul said.

"Some of that's in the bombing range. I suppose they could be out there, as long as they're not actually in an impact area. If they are, those F-14s aren't going to notice them, the speed they're going. It's more probable, though, they're somewhere else, assuming the kidnapper's not suicidal. That still leaves a lot of territory, and there's no way to do a good job with the single chopper the sheriff has. I don't think we can rely on the National Security Agency, either. So I called Washington to get authorization to hire a half-dozen fixed-wing planes and two helicopters, along with their pilots. We're going to send them out this afternoon to different parts of the county. They'll have orders to report anything in the slightest way suspicious. But we're also going to equip them with cameras we're getting from the Air Force. D.C.'s sending in some experts to read the photos. The planes will stay high enough that it shouldn't alert the kidnappers."

"Good idea," Ellen said. "But don't expect them to come up with anything. He's hidden that bus somewhere. Hidden it good."

"You're probably right. But we've got to try if we want the kids back before there are any more problems. I told them not to look for the bus so much as a place to hide it—outbuildings and so forth. They should be off the ground in the next two or three hours. I'll let you know what they turn up. I'm also having some more agents sent in from L.A. and Phoenix. Exley wanted some back-up if he's involved in a ransom delivery."

Ellen saw Paul's face go suddenly rigid as he asked, "How did the shrink get mixed up in the pay-off? I don't recall that discussion."

"It's just a precaution. We don't know what kind of demands the kidnappers will make. But we can never have too many bodies in this kind of situation."

"That's a typical D.C. philosophy, isn't it?" Paul said, staring hard at him.

LaSalle held up his hands. "Look, you people are in charge. If you don't want them, I'll get on the phone and have them recalled."

"A little late for that. Did you clear this with Ellen like we agreed?"

LaSalle hesitated. "We're getting off on the wrong foot,

aren't we? No, I'm sorry. I just didn't think of it." He looked over at her.

"Ellen's investigation," Paul reminded him. "Everything goes through her. We agreed."

"Consider me chastised," LaSalle said with an embarrassed look at Ellen. "Have you had any more mysterious phone messages?"

Paul looked at her inquiringly.

"Sorry," she said. "I've had too much on my mind." She told him about the call.

"Recognize the voice?"

Ellen hesitated just a second. "No."

Paul shook his head. "It's probably nothing. Unless it happens again."

LaSalle said, "That's what I told her. We'll keep it in mind though." As he was talking, the phone buzzed and Paul snatched at it. "Reporters have been calling asking about a dead child," Maggie said. She spoke rapidly, as though afraid of being hung up on before she finished. "I told them there isn't a dead child, but they insist. I guess someone called a TV station and claimed he was the kidnapper and told them he killed one of the children. Some nut, I suppose. What do you want me to say to them?"

"Goddamn it!" Paul felt miserable. "Do the parents know?"

"You mean it's true?"

"Maggie, damn it, I asked if the parents knew!"

"Well, I should think so! There's a TV down there and—"

"Get Zach on the line."

While Maggie connected him with the squad room, Paul hurriedly told Ellen and LaSalle what had happened.

Ellen swore softly to herself.

"Confusion," LaSalle said. "Shaking everyone up—" Before he could finish Paul spoke into the phone.

"Problems, Zach. The parents know about the dead boy. Have we got an I.D. yet?"

"Not confirmed. It's a five- or six-year-old Caucasian. There's only four possibles. You want the names?"

"Go next door and get the parents of those four. Bring them to the squad room. I want them separated from the other parents. See if you can make a preliminary I.D. on the child based on the description, then have someone drive the kid's folks to the med center for a positive. But get it done now. I don't want all those other parents worrying."

He put the phone down and said to Ellen, "Call the TV station and see if they have a tape of that call. Christ! What the hell else can go wrong?"

LaSalle said, "I'm going to see if anyone's back from the house where the body was found. They may have come up with something out there."

As he started to leave, Ellen interrupted him. "Thanks again for taking care of the parent interviews. It's a load off our minds."

"No sweat." He smiled at her, his gaze lingering just a second, then left.

Paul's eyes stayed with LaSalle as he crossed into Maggie's office. After a moment, he turned abruptly to Ellen. "What have you got Manny doing?"

"Talking to people along the route—stores and gas stations and such." She glanced at her watch. "He should have checked in by now. I'll have Jeannie ask him to give us a call."

As she reached for the phone, Exley came in. "It turns out there are forty-one thousand registered sex offenders in California. Mind boggling, isn't it? We're asking the computer for those within an eighty-mile radius. It'll probably still be several thousand. I'm afraid our check of employees was not very helpful, either. No hits at all in your department and only two minor problems on the civilian side." He looked at a piece of paper he was holding. "Bobby Ray Hoskins, felony spouse beating."

"He's a clerk over in payroll," Ellen said. "He's about sixty years old and five-foot-six. Doesn't sound like our guy."

"And Arthur Byer. Theft, armed robbery, and resisting arrest. All more than ten years ago."

"Don't know him."

"Custodian. I already checked. He was just getting off work at seven-thirty this morning."

"So nothing," Ellen said.

"Well, of course, we can't get into juvenile records, not most of them, anyway. They're normally sealed by the courts." His stare became intense. "Are you sure there's no one in the department with a grudge? No disciplinary actions?" Paul's face turned hot and Exley said, "Well, I have to wonder—"

Just then LaSalle ducked his head through the open doorway. "The National Security Agency called. They can't help. They don't have satellites over the U.S., they said. And weather satellites don't function that way. Sorry."

LaSalle disappeared again and Paul turned to Ellen, who was still standing with the phone in her hand. "Why haven't we got a ransom demand? Goddamn it, what the hell's he up to?"

> **"Passions unguided are for the most part mere madness."**
>
> —*Hobbes, 1651*

DeVries could barely restrain his excitement. Everything was falling into place. Everything!

Isn't it, Chief Whitehorse?

He laughed out loud.

Are your dogs out on the road yet? Finding that lunch box was a remarkable bit of luck, was it not? What about the shoe? I haven't heard anything about that yet. Am I going to have to draw you a map? And you, Dr. Walter Expert Exley! What do you think of my little boy-clown, so cute in his colorful hat and makeup? Doesn't that resonate with you?

So much information for them, so much to think about and contend with. It must be difficult, all this chaos.

He began to stride around the vacant house, taking quick, long steps to work off the emotion roiling within his soul. He would have to stay focused. He shouldn't have called Ellen—that had been foolish—but the anticipation had been too much; he wanted to hear her voice, wanted to live a moment with her fears.

How do you like it so far? Well, you ain't seen nothing. Just fucking wait.

But this was no time to relax. Once, just once, he had let his guard down during the planning process and the whole scheme had almost come crashing down around him. Even thinking about it sent a shiver racing along his spine.

"passions unguided"

My God, yes. *Yes*.

He had been following Ellen for months, had been inside her home several times, more than he should have, as it turned out. But Ellen was the key, it was she that made all else possible, made him invincible, and it was essential to know everything about her. Each time he had been extremely cautious, making absolutely certain that he was not seen, that he disturbed nothing, that he put things back the way he found them. And he took nothing, not even a beer from the refrigerator.

But he needed to know about her, needed to understand how she reacted and thought and felt, needed to experience the hopes and fears that swirled about her consciousness. The first time, he'd come in through an open window in the rear, stayed for two hours, carefully going through her drawers and cabinets and closets, taking his time to be methodical and think about what he was doing. In the kitchen he'd discovered two extra house keys and had taken one, getting it duplicated and later replacing it. After his second visit, there'd been no real need to return but he had, several times, because he enjoyed it. It gave him a thrill to know he could walk in any time he wanted and, taking his time, pick through the clothes and books and countless things that made up the life of the woman who was to play such a pivotal, if unknowing, role in his future. And fascinating it was.

On his second visit, under some sweaters in her closet (beautiful multicolored wool/acrylic blends and a single cloud-soft beige cashmere from Scotland that must have cost a week's salary), he'd come across a folder of papers dealing with her divorce and the subsequent custody hearing. Nasty, that, he thought and chuckled aloud, but ex-spouses could certainly be difficult; reason enough not to get married. Her ex's name was Peter. Three years with the L.A.P.D. had old Peter Peter Pumpkin Eater, until being booted out. Did a little jail time, too. DeVries had felt a sudden rush of emotion, and his heart had begun to race angrily.

How did you like being locked up, Officer Pumpkin Eater? Did they love you in jail, the other inmates? Did they throw you on the floor or against the wall, rip your pants off, and love you?

From the evidence in the papers, young Peter appeared to be a macho buffoon who drank to excess, raced around in a Jeep, and misused his power as a policeman. One of those odd people who always seemed to be in some sort of trouble, a circumstance they would inevitably blame others for. How could a bright, elegant woman such as Ellen be attracted to an idiot like that? Liked the way he spread her legs, no doubt. People could be so stupid about such things.

There was also a rather thick file on the little girl. Had her head banged up pretty good, didn't she? Good old Petah had been responsible for that also, it appeared. Not quite the loving father, was he? Three months prior to Denise's hospitalization, there had been a custody dispute. Petah Petah had tried to wrest young Denise from mommy, claiming abuse and neglect. My, my, my. There had been a formal hearing, testimony from Child Protective Services, neighbors, friends. Fascinating reading. According to daddy's attorney, Ellen was a terrible mom, a vindictive and cruel woman who was unfit to raise a child. And apt to flee to the reservation, a horrible and loathsome place to bring up a child, in addition to being a venue of murky case law regarding parental rights. Although the judge seemed to sympathize with Peter, custody had been divided equally between mommy and daddy. Several months later, in a hearing that appeared to be uncontested, Peter had lost even that right. DeVries had unexpectedly felt some fraternal interest in the case, sympathy even, for the aggrieved husband. Perhaps, he thought, we will exact our revenge together. Pay attention, Peter. The future will be fascinating.

Little Denise, it appeared from other papers he ran across, had been getting a lot of immunizations recently. School must be looming in the near future. Or so Ellen assumed. DeVries knew different.

The rest of the closet had been of little interest, as had the house in general. No thrilling little secrets, like homemade sex videos or love letters or illicit drugs. There had been a rather too luxurious magenta-colored, two-person spa tub in the expanded bathroom, though, the sort designed more to spur sexual fantasies than perform the more mundane duty of facilitating cleanliness. Somehow it hadn't surprised him; there were, he was sure, unexplored depths to pretty Ellen's psyche, depths he would love to plumb, if only time permitted. Birth-control pills in the medicine chest. And, when he carefully went through her dresser drawers, some awfully skimpy panties and see-through nightgowns. Blacks and whites, mostly, one nightgown with playful little red hearts scattered all over it. Ellen liked to vamp a bit, then, play sex kitten. Maybe she'd play for him someday, meow and curl against his leg and flick her kittenish tongue against his tensed flesh. He'd run his large hands through the neat piles of underwear, letting the sensuous texture of nylon brush against his skin, slip around and through his fingers like sand as he touched and touched and touched. Suddenly, a dizzy feeling moving rapidly through his head, the underwear was out of the drawer, and he lifted an armful to his face, rubbing his cheeks and lips and forehead through it before allowing everything to splash noiselessly to the floor around him.

His heart had raced.

Put it back! Put it all back!

Quickly DeVries had scooped up everything, neatly folding each pair, fingers moving rapidly as he restacked them in the drawer. What color had been on top? Pink? Was it pink, Lowell? My God, try to remember because she'd know. It's the sort of thing people remember. She probably had a pattern: white on Mondays, blue on Tuesdays, the way he himself did, everyone did. His eyes had closed as he'd concentrated. Think! White! White had been on top, yes, then pink, then white again. Working rapidly, he'd completed the pile, making sure everything was perfect, then hurried out to the living room, his heartbeat beginning to return to normal. Taking a breath, he'd stared around, taking everything in as if for the first time. It was as neat as his own house but feminine, overly feminine to be truly comfortable. Flower prints on the fabrics, too many soft pastel colors everywhere. Little knickknacks and ceramic figurines on the tables. Fussy. He'd picked up a primitive wood carving, mesquite probably; it was supposed to be a coyote, he'd supposed, a fetish or magic charm. In the Age of the Microchip! Next to it were two very old Indian baskets about eighteen inches across, rather attractive in a primitive sort of way. Something she inherited, perhaps.

The kitchen had not been to his liking, either: Denise's drawings and scrawls taped to the refrigerator, too much yellow and white everywhere, as though a child had chosen the colors. All very banal, middle class, and depressing.

It had been on what proved to be DeVries's final visit six months before the kidnapping that he had been almost discovered. He had been in Ellen's bedroom, drawn again to her underwear, looking and feeling and smelling, when without thinking he'd quickly shed his clothes and pulled on a pair of her panties. Standing in front of the mirrored closet door, he'd stared in fascination at his body, the muscled torso descending wedge-like to a narrow tanned waist and Ellen's marvelous pink bikini panties that weren't able to contain his penis as it stretched and fought against the silky smooth fabric. His stomach had tensed with pleasure as he'd watched. Then abruptly he'd spun around and hurried into Denise's bedroom and yanked open her top dresser drawer. Child's clothes—panties, shorts, socks. He'd run his hands through them, lifted everything in a bundle and let it fall to the floor, then whirled around and watched himself in the mirror. He pulled down Ellen's panties, staring excitedly at his body, tensing, posing, sticking out a leg like a fashion model, then heard a door open.

Stopped breathing.

His erection sagged.

Someone was in the house!

Balancing on one foot, heart pounding madly, he'd yanked the panties all the way off, then stepped quietly to the open bedroom door and flattened against the wall.

Listening.

Someone was walking around. *Idiot!* Recriminations had flooded into his mind. He never should have come back. There was no point in doing so; he had given in to a whim— passions unguided—and he knew by now that that was always a mistake. *Always!*

Footsteps moving softly in the kitchen. A cupboard door opening with a squeak.

It had been only half past two. Ellen must have come back early from work, he'd thought. He'd have to kill her; there was no choice. It was either that or abort the whole plan. That meant he'd have to find someone to take her place. Goddamn it, why hadn't the front door made more noise?

Footsteps out of the kitchen. They hadn't sounded right—too slow, too soft, too . . . what? Weird? *Yes!*

DeVries had kept his back pressed against the wall but slowly, carefully bent his head to stare around the doorjamb. Someone in a bathrobe had been standing alone in the living room, gazing in the opposite direction. A man! Thick white hair to his shoulders, like an Old Testament prophet, head bent forward, moving his right arm slowly up and down as he ate a cracker. He must have come from the vacant bedroom, meaning he had to have walked right by Denise's open door, yet had seen nothing. He'd come this way again though. DeVries would have to slip the door shut before he was noticed. But before he could do anything, the man had turned and started toward the bedrooms.

DeVries had yanked back his head. If the man had given any indication at all of being aware of his presence, DeVries would've killed him. He could've done it in a second; the old man's neck would've snapped like a pencil. DeVries had waited, sweat trickling along his bare sides as he'd heard the footsteps slowly come toward him down the hallway, tiny step after tiny step. At the open door, they hadn't even slowed, and Lowell had risked a look as the aged body edged past. Christ, he'd thought, he must be eighty or ninety years old, muttering something under his breath as he inched forward. Goddamn Alzheimer's case, probably wouldn't see me if I jumped out and spit in his face.

DeVries had let the man disappear into his own bedroom, but he had learned his lesson: don't improvise, don't do anything that might screw up the plan.

Still naked, the sweat suddenly as cold as crystals of ice on his bare skin, he'd begun to quickly straighten Denise's room.

Business before pleasure, he'd told himself over and over. He was too far along now to risk everything coming apart. Use your brain; there'll be plenty of time for fun when this is over.

But that night he'd driven to Miss Violet's and paid for two girls.

3:25 P.M.

The Sheriff's Department pulled two rookie cops from jail duty and sent them up to Las Cruces for crowd control. Ellen had the Civic Center cleared and told the reporters they could hang out across the street in the heat or go up to the high school. Despite the 109 degree temperature, most chose the crowded sidewalk. A half-hour later she was on the phone to the governor's secretary in Sacramento trying to determine if the governor recalled anything unusual about the dinner he'd attended in Las Cruces when Jeannie Wheatley at the reception desk downstairs called on the intercom line.

"You better send someone down here pronto before we have a riot with these parents. They're pretty upset—"

"But Bobby Muledeer's there. And an F.B.I.—"

"Bobby's outgunned, Ellen. And the F.B.I. guy's no help at all. He says he's got no information, you guys are running the investigation. I feel sorry for the poor bastard. He's trying to interview the parents, and they keep yelling at him. I can hear it from here."

Ellen suppressed a sigh. It was her fault; she should have handled this hours ago. "All right, Jeannie. We're on our way."

As she put the phone down, Paul, staring out the window, said, "Guess what favorite little froggy of ours just pulled up in his green machine?"

"Goddamn it!" Ellen snapped and crossed over to the window. Dr. Herbert Sanderson was just emerging from the air-conditioned comfort of his lime-colored Jaguar two floors below in the employee parking lot.

Ellen said, "Damn him! Next month he's out of here. I don't care if we have to go to Palm Springs to get a shrink."

They watched as Sanderson, a pear-shaped man in his forties with thick glasses and pale jowls, removed a powder blue sport coat from a hanger in his car and pulled it on. After buttoning it, he ran a hand over his bald head, then started for the door.

"We've got to get downstairs, Paul. The parents are having a fit."

Paul moved away from the window. "My job, Ellen. No sense you coming, too."

"I'll go with you. I want to talk to Sanderson."

Rather than wait for the elevator, they hurried down the back stairway, Paul putting his arm around her shoulder and giving her an affectionate hug before they emerged into the hallway. Crossing rapidly to the civilian side of the building, they headed directly to the large room where the parents had been assembled. A harried Middleton was standing with his back pressed against the wall, Bobby Muledeer next to him, as several dozen people shouted questions at them. Just inside the door, Dr. Sanderson was carefully draping his sport coat over the back of a folding chair, evidently oblivious to the tumult. He turned his wide head and, blank-faced, gravely whispered, "Paul, Ellen," as though giving a benediction.

Ellen, trying not to lose her temper in public, said, "Damn it, Herb, these people needed you. Where the hell—"

"Not now, Ellen," he said firmly. "I was with a suicidal patient. I couldn't very well leave her. I appreciate your problem, but you must try to understand."

At that moment, Middleton noticed them and said loudly to the parents, "I'm sure Chief Whitehorse would be happy to answer your questions."

Everyone spun around, and there was a silence that lasted for several seconds. Then they surged in Paul's direction. "What the hell's going on here?" a man about thirty asked. He was dressed like a construction worker and came up to Paul as if he were going to strike him. A woman grabbed Paul's arm, shrieking, "Where are our children?" as another woman broke down in sobs.

Paul held up a hand. "I'll tell you everything we know—" But before he could go on another man shouted, "No one's told us nothing but shit! Who took our children? Where are they? Why can't—"

"Quiet, quiet," Paul said, raising his voice, and a few parents joined in: "Give him a chance. Let him talk." But others kept yelling angrily at him.

Loudly, Ellen said, "If you don't let us talk, we can't help you."

"I'll tell you what we have," Paul shouted. "But you've got to promise to keep it amongst yourselves. We can't let the press get involved in this. We don't know how the kidnapper will react."

The crowd started to quiet. In a minute they were silent. Calmly, Paul said, "I'll tell you everything we know so far. Then I'll answer your questions. But when we're done, I want you to cooperate with us. We need to talk to you, too. There may be something you folks know that could help us find your children. Mr. Middleton over there is an F.B.I. agent. He's an expert. He's trained to deal with kidnappings. I want you to take turns talking to him or to Officer Muledeer. We also need to make sure that all the parents have been informed. It's possible that some are at work somewhere where they wouldn't have heard what's happened."

Ellen stepped up next to Paul. "Before Chief Whitehorse gets started, I'd like to see the children's teachers, if they're here."

Two middle-aged women held up their hands.

"If I could talk to you in the back," Ellen said, indicating the farthest corner of the room.

Paul looked at her a moment, his expression not changing but communicating something—let's get it over with—with his eyes, then turned to the parents. "Okay, this is what we know . . ."

As he began to go through it, Ellen detached herself from the crowd and motioned for the teachers to follow. In the rear of the room, they introduced themselves, Mrs. Harvey and Mrs. Agostino. Clearly distressed, Mrs. Harvey said, "We tried to keep the parents calm, but there's nothing we could do. What can we say to them?"

"Most of these children need medical attention," Mrs. Agostino, an attractive blonde in her forties, said emphatically. "Some of them are going to have a seizure if they don't get their medication by tonight. They won't last until tomorrow."

"I know," Ellen told her. "The news reports are making that clear. Maybe the kidnapper will release those children that need medicine. All we can do is hope. He's not contacted us yet." She thought of the phone call, the soft breathing in her ear—How do you like it so far?—then added, "We don't even know why he took them."

"Is it true he killed one of the children?" Mrs. Harvey asked. "I just can't believe anyone would do that."

"I'm afraid so." Zachary Harris had called her as soon as they had a preliminary identification. The parents were already on their way to the medical center with a civilian department employee. "We think it's a boy named Emilio."

"Oh my God," Mrs. Harvey said.

"But why?" Mrs. Agostino demanded, then began to cry softly. "He was so harmless!"

"He must be crazy," the other woman whispered, and Ellen thought, These women are with the children six or seven hours a day, probably as much as the parents, and it's affecting them almost as much. Rather than the teachers calming the parents, Ellen found herself trying to ease their minds. "Maybe he is crazy. If so, he may actually be easier to deal with than if not. Let me ask you about the children and their families. Maybe there's something that can help us."

Ellen talked to them for twenty minutes, stopping from time to time to glance at Paul and the parents. They were becoming raucous and angry again as he was unable to give them the reassurances they so desperately sought.

"What they must be going through," Mrs. Harvey said as a man began to yell angrily at Paul. Ellen looked over at them. What can they be feeling? she wondered. It was beyond her ability to comprehend. Their children, already weighed down with burdens most people would never experience let alone understand, ripped away from them by a madman. What words are there for a situation like this? She felt helpless and inadequate as she never had before. There was nothing anyone could do to help. Except get their children back.

Paul was trying desperately to explain: "We have helicopters and airplanes out, we have cars searching, people retracing the bus route. The sheriff and F.B.I. and army are here. But until we hear from the kidnapper—"

But how could this happen? they wanted to know. How could you allow it to happen, right in broad daylight?

At that point, Dr. Sanderson stepped forward. "Your grief is understandable," he said soothingly. "Express your anger, talk to me."

Ellen felt like screaming. You goddamn fraud, trying to calm these people with your textbook clichés when they need understanding, support, sympathy. Sanderson's voice droned on until Ellen couldn't stand it another second. Thanking the teachers, she left the room, taking the stairs hurriedly up to Paul's office. The moment she came in, Maggie said, "Your sitter called. Twice. She wants to know if you're getting home on time."

A flaring of anger went through Ellen at having to deal with such a trivial problem when the parents she'd just left were facing a tragedy of incomprehensible gravity. Then she warned herself, Don't take it out on others; it's not their fault. "Okay, thanks, Maggie." She went into the office and dialed her home number. Mrs. Garcia picked it up on the first ring. "I've been watching on television. I guess you might not be home, huh? You want me to stay a while?"

"Would you please, Julie? I don't know when I'll get there. Or, if you want, you can take Denise to your house."

"No, no. No one waiting for me. I may as well stay here. Anyway you got cable and I don't."

"Maybe you can find something to microwave for dinner. I didn't plan anything."

"I'll make enchiladas and beans. You got the stuff. I already checked."

"Has Grandfather come out of his room?"

"He comes out, goes to the bathroom, goes back to his room. Two or three times."

"Take him some food when you have dinner. Bring him a bowl of ice cream, too. He usually eats that. Let me talk to Denise for a moment."

Mrs. Garcia put Denise on the phone, and Ellen told her

to be a good girl tonight. Denise said she was always a good girl, then asked, "Can I stay up to watch *The Neverending Story*? It starts at eight o'clock."

"If Mrs. Garcia says it's okay, you can." When the baby-sitter came back on the line, Ellen said, "I'll try not to be too late, Julie. But I just can't tell."

"Don't worry, honey. We'll do just fine. You help those missing children. They're not doing fine at all."

Ellen hung up and immediately headed down to the squad room to see how the search was going. Time was running out. They had to make something happen.

6. Call

DeVries gently closed his eyes to the world, took a deep breath, and slowly expelled it. Reaching into his slacks pocket, he removed one of the four quarters he had ready and dropped it into the phone slot. It was exactly 7:00 P.M. Only twenty-nine hours to go, he thought. Everything in his life, he knew with a sudden rush of insight, had been leading up to this moment.

Everything.

How many truly seminal events can anyone look back to when summing up his time on earth? DeVries, when reflecting on the forty-one years thus far essayed, could identify several: the day when, aged eleven, he'd realized he was wiser in the ways of the world than his father; the day four years later when two needlessly abusive, blue-uniformed policemen had appeared at his parents' house and arrested him for rape; and the day he'd met Stephen Weir.

Dr. Stephen Weir, psychologist.

Part of the regimen, the half-believed-in "rehabilitation" for juvenile hall inmates in those days, was an evaluation by a clinical psychologist, to be followed by a number of one-on-one counseling sessions in the weeks to come. After three months, the boys—or young men, some were kept until their early twenties—could choose to continue meeting voluntarily with the psychologist if they wished.

Most did because it got them out of continuation school or a work detail for an hour or so and impressed those who decided when an inmate of the grossly overcrowded facility would be eligible for probation or early release. After two or three meetings, however, virtually all stopped coming since the psychologists insisted on asking them to talk about themselves, their experiences, their hopes, and why they did the things they did. Introspection was not only difficult but threatening to a generation that had no experience of it.

Except for Lowell, who, after a rocky beginning ("Fuck you, Doc! I'm here because I have to be here!"), found he actually liked talking to Dr. Weir. Learned some things, some important things.

Learned, for example, that psychology was a much less exact science than most people realized. DeVries had always thought of shrinks as mystics who were somehow able to peer into the secrets of the soul, who knew what people were thinking at all times and understood and perhaps even sympathized with the private urgings they harbored in the dark corners of their consciousnesses. But it wasn't like that at all, he realized on one of his early visits to Weir, who had asked him why he'd raped that girl. "Why?" DeVries had said to him, honestly surprised. "Because I wanted to!"

"But why did you want to? Most people don't force themselves on others. Why do you think you did?"

"Jesus, you tell me. You're the shrink."

Weir had settled back in his chair and shaken his head. "A psychologist can never know these things, Lowell. Trying to determine why another person did something is no better than a guess and oftentimes dangerously wrong. You're the only person who can ever know."

But Lowell hadn't wanted to know. Like most of his fellow inmates, most people he knew on the outside for that matter, he'd sensed intuitively that the examined life was not worth living. Better to do than think. So his chats with Weir had been enjoyable only so long as he wasn't required to delve too deeply into the mysteries of being. But he'd liked the way the psychologist, middle-aged and bald and somewhat overweight, had accepted him without judgment, had liked the way nothing seemed to upset him. For a long time, Lowell had been convinced that this was an act, the imperturbable shrink of countless bad TV shows, and it had incited him to try to break through the facade, get the guy mad and show what he was really like. Lowell would come to their meetings armed with a litany of insults thought up the day before: "You couldn't make it in your own practice, could you, Doc? That's why you're here, working for the state." "How come shrinks are always bald and ugly? That some kinda rule?" "How do you like spending all your time where everyone hates your guts? Guards, administrators, guys in the wards—they all think you're a pussy."

Nothing.

Man was cool.

It was Weir who'd gotten him interested in school. Lowell had been an indifferent student at best and had usually skipped as many days as he'd attended. Why not? His dad had a Ph.D. in chemistry and his mother a master's in music, and what did it get them? But Weir had complimented him on his intelligence, told him he wasn't like the other inmates, the majority of whom had I.Q,s or behaviors that precluded them from going into most types of work, allowing, if not encouraging, them to slip instead into a life of crime. ("Of course they're stupid or they wouldn't have been caught. I'm here because my partner was an idiot.") But Lowell had gone to the on-site high school every day and had soon begun to enjoy it. Part of this had been escape, of course—he could sit in the small library and not have to worry about being jumped by the gangs who loathed the aura of the upper middle class that hovered about him like a poisonous cloud despite his half-hearted attempts at working-class chic (tough-guy haircut, tattoo of a rattlesnake on one bicep)—and part the thrill of a superior intellect beginning to blossom.

He'd finished his work toward a diploma by the time he was seventeen, then had begun to study on his own. In the beginning a little history but that was boring, so he'd tried philosophy and had found it too arcane. Psychology, though, had been both fun and interesting. Freud, Jung, and Adler were a bit daunting for a teenager, but he became interested in the humanist school—Maslow, Rogers, and so on—and later the developmental psychologists, and was soon able to dismiss Skinner's behaviorism as reductive and self-evident ("People do things that are rewarding and don't do things that aren't. This is some sort of revelation?").

He learned enough to realize that there was nothing "wrong" with him. He fit none of the classic modes for criminal behavior—no abusive parents, no history of crime in the family, no mental illness, no poverty, or mistreatment at school.

"So why do you think someone with such an exemplary history ended up incarcerated?" Weir—was he smiling behind that beard as he asked it?—had wondered one day.

"Because I did the stupidest thing I could have done," Lowell had answered without hesitation. "I trusted somebody." Meaning Rudy Ayala of the lost wallet.

But it had been a relief to learn that he wasn't "ill," that there was nothing even problematic about him, except perhaps for a lack of focus in life, and *that,* Weir had insisted, could be remedied by a greater effort at self-control. He just needed a goal, something to aim for.

"Look at all the people who have triumphed over tragedy," Weir had said to him. "You're not the only person who's had a little difficulty in his life, you know. Grow up. Take responsibility for yourself instead of blaming others."

That was when the idea of collecting aphorisms had first occurred to him.

"There is no substitute for hard work."

—*Thomas Edison*

"To succeed in the world, we do everything we can to appear successful."

—*LaRochefoucauld*

"Failing to prepare is preparing to fail."

—*Anon.*

The world had seen a lot of successful people, Lowell had realized. And many of them had overcome early misfortune. So why not learn from them? He'd begun by noting down sayings as he heard them, then searching through the library, collecting. Still, there'd been a sense about it that struck him as slightly foolish. It was the sort of thing he'd have made fun of anyone else doing. So he'd told no one, not even Weir.

But he'd known he was on to something. The Wisdom of the Ages. Just knowing these phrases had made him feel more confident, as if he could do anything he wanted to do. Weir hadn't been just giving him a line. Education was the key to everything. Education and self-control.

"You're a human being, not a slug," the psychologist had told him more than once. "Tell your mind that it is in control. Your mind and not your body."

Weir had also suggested continuing with school once he was released, and Lowell had agreed, though it was at best a half-step in the right direction. Mind and body indeed function together, and while it was clear that he outdistanced his fellow inmates intellectually, physically he'd been no match. So he'd begun to work out in the gym, the most popular room in juvenile hall. For seventeen months he went every day—five hundred and sixteen days—an hour at a time, enduring from first day to last the taunts and threats of the other inmates, most of whom had made him look like an inferior copy of their own sleek, well-muscled selves. *Hey, pretty boy, you goin' to get some muscles? You goin' to be buff, white bread? Want to be strong enough to rape mo' girls, Lowell? Maybe we get you first. Maybe we'll love you tonight, Low-ellll.*

For five hundred and sixteen days he'd ignored the other inmates, refused to recognize their existence. If there hadn't been a guard in the gym, they would have killed him for sure. More than once he had been surrounded in the day room or showers, where the gangs had made good on their threats, pushing him to the floor, ripping off his pants, and having their way with him. But in the gym he'd wait silently in line for one of the Nautiluses, then position himself on the moist, ripped, vinyl seat, and begin his reps as grunting, sweat-smelly young men on either side turned their hard, expressionless faces and whispered threats while they worked on perfecting their own bodies.

Weir had suggested he try meditation. "Ignore them, tune them out. They're not worthy of your concern. Find a fantasy where you can lose yourself. Then, when you start your workout, concentrate on it, eliminate everything outside your own consciousness. You won't hear a thing, I guarantee it. But it takes concentration and self-control."

He'd experimented with sexual fantasies at first: reclining on a vast cushion of silk pillows, sucking the hard erect nipples of a huge-breasted blonde while another took him in her mouth and a third lovingly rubbed perfumed oils over his body with tiny, red-tipped fingers . . . being on a desert isle with six lustful high-school cheerleaders after a plane crash . . . but these visions had made him more aware of himself, not less, and he'd felt a secret embarrassment at their childishness. So he'd sought the more calming scenarios that Weir had suggested: a mountain pond, wild flowers, a gentle spring breeze. And soon he would be there, and the gym and the punks and the threats and the smells would disappear as surely as if their very atoms had ceased to exist. That alone had been enough to make him grateful to the psychologist; he had brought peace to Lowell De-Vries. The first he'd known.

The June before Lowell's eighteenth birthday, the continuation high school had held a graduation ceremony for its twelve successful students. Weir was the only guest in attendance whom Lowell knew. Sitting on a folding chair in the small audience, Weir had smiled proudly as the young man had received his diploma. DeVries was one of his successes: he had gotten an education, learned self-control, and had a focus in life. Too bad more young men didn't progress this well. Young men like Rudy Ayala, for example, who, Weir had heard through the jail grapevine some weeks later, had been shot to death by an unknown assailant in front of his house. Weir had recognized the name of Lowell's partner in the rape, but since Ayala had not been sentenced to juvenile hall they had never met. He wasn't surprised though; there had been a particularly star-crossed group of young men in the facility that year. Three others Weir knew to be incarcerated at the same time as Lowell—among his tormentors, in fact—had also met violent ends shortly after release. It wasn't the sort of future he would have hoped for them.

But now, almost twenty-five years later, DeVries was a successful man. He still kept in touch with his old mentor by mail, sending a letter every few months to Oregon, where Weir had retired. It was a nice gesture, and the psychologist appreciated it.

Sitting at the reception desk on the first floor of the Civic Center, Jeannie Wheatley yawned and slumped back in the chair, her long blonde hair falling behind her halfway to the floor. She was tired and annoyed. She should have gotten off at 3:30 but the chief was making everyone work double shifts until the kidnapping was solved. That meant not getting out until almost midnight. Her boyfriend was going to be one very unhappy dude. She was supposed to go over to his place at eight and whip up lasagna and an Italian salad. Of course, that was just an excuse for drinking a couple of bottles of vino and then trying out his new waterbed. He'd gotten a round one this time, with those silvery satin sheets that made you slip and slide and say *Ummm!* at all the right times. The phone gave an irritating electronic ring, interrupting her fantasy. Damn, an outside line. She tried to sound alert. "Las Cruces Police."

"Monica Ochoa's wearing red and white tennis shoes and she has a four-inch scar on her neck."

Jeannie bolted forward and her heart gave a thump. "I'm sorry, please repeat that." Just like she had been trained: when in doubt, tell them to repeat. Don't ask, tell.

"It's seven o'clock," the voice said, a man's voice. Obviously disguised, maybe even electronically distorted, raspy, assertive. "The clock starts now. You've got exactly twenty-four hours to get twenty million dollars. I'll tell you then what to do with it."

"Who are you?" she blurted out, her heart racing even faster. Stupid question! she immediately thought. Jesus, he's not going to tell me his name. She stared transfixed at the computer screen in front of her. The number of the calling party was automatically displayed along with its location on Palm Street and a "P" for pay phone. She whirled around quickly, looking for someone to alert, but there was no one else in the combination office–reception area. She grabbed the other phone and hit the intercom button connecting reception to the squad room. The light instantly lit up on her console as someone responded, but she couldn't risk going off the line with the caller. She began to panic. She had to let someone know. Covering the mouthpiece with her hand she yelled, "Somebody get in here now! Hurry!"

"You'll have to call the Federal Reserve," the voice on the phone said. He sounded so calm; it was as if he were reading a script. "I want three million in circulated one hundred dollar bills, no two numbers in sequence, of course. I want seventeen million in cut diamonds of one-half to three carats, D or E flawless, or V.V.S.I. Call the diamond center in Los Angeles. You'll need to bring everything in by helicopter. If it's not here in twenty-four hours, the children die. All of them."

Keep him on the line, Jeannie thought desperately as

her heart tried to beat its way through the rib cage. Keep him talking until I can get a patrol car to the phone booth. She covered the mouthpiece again and yelled, "Someone get in here," just as a female patrol officer rushed in. Jeannie jabbed a finger at the screen and whispered, "It's him!"

The woman lunged for the radio dispatch microphone. Don't let him hang up, Jeannie screamed at herself and asked, "What are we supposed to do with the money?"

"It works out to less than eight hundred thousand per kid," the distorted voice said as if he hadn't heard her. "Not a bad deal, everything considered." The line went dead.

"A pay phone at 1482 Palm," the officer next to Jeannie was saying excitedly into the microphone.

Jeannie grabbed her arm. "He hung up."

"He hung up!" the woman shouted. "Get everyone out there now!" She slammed the phone down and said to Jeannie, "Call the chief. I think we've got him."

DeVries replaced the receiver and looked at his watch. Twenty-eight seconds. Three over quota but not bad, not bad at all. Now to wait. He stepped quickly from the booth at one end of a mini-mall, where all the stores were closed for the night, and into the idling Ford Taurus he'd rented under the name R.L. Stevenson. Forty-five seconds up Stapleton Drive took him to the Wal-Mart parking lot, where he left the Taurus in a sea of other cars. A rapid walk up the block brought him to the El Matador, where his own car sat in the side lot. He came in through the bar entrance, crossing swiftly through the noisy, crowded room, and slid back into the restaurant booth, his half-eaten meal still warm. A trip to the restroom during dinner could happen to anyone, but it didn't appear to have drawn any attention. He stopped a passing waiter and ordered a margarita, adding, "Do you know what time it is? My watch has stopped."

"Sure," the waiter said. "A couple of minutes past seven."

"Good," DeVries said and smiled, making sure the waiter would remember him. "Got an important meeting later, and I'd hate to rush through a great meal like this."

While he waited for the drink, he placed his left hand in his lap so his watch would be hidden and took his pulse.

Seventy.

Perfect.

7:03 P.M.

As Ellen stood stiffly to the rear, Paul bent over Jeannie sitting at the communications console, listening to the screech of radio calls as cars converged on the phone booth. Bobby Muledeer was the first, just two minutes after the caller hung up. Within another minute, two more cars rushed up in a spray of gravel, lights flashing. The booth was empty, the mall deserted.

"Goddamn it!" Paul shouted. His hands tightened furiously on the back of Jeannie's chair.

Muledeer's voice crackled. "Can't see a soul. You want us to go off on foot or in the cars?"

The operator looked up at Paul, who angrily grabbed a headset and put it on. "Secure the booth until Stines can get there and dust it. Who's with you?"

"Avila and Lockheart."

"Leave Avila. You and Lockheart get in your units and canvas the area. You see anyone who looks suspicious, pull him over."

LaSalle hurried into the room. Paul threw him an irritated glance before continuing to Muledeer. "You're looking for a male, Bobby. Probably Anglo from the sound of his voice, most likely by himself. You'll need probable cause, so use a traffic violation. If you don't like his story, haul his ass in here. And make sure you use caution approaching the vehicle. You done searching your sector of the city yet?"

"Not quite, boss. Maybe another half-hour."

"If you don't come up with anything in the next ten minutes, go back on patrol. We gotta keep looking for the bus." Paul ripped the headset off and said, "We lost him. He's not going to be out on the street. Goddamn it!"

LaSalle said, "He'd set up an escape before making the call. He's a planner."

Paul turned to Ellen. "Call Howard, tell him to get down and dust that phone booth for prints. But there ain't a chance in hell he'll find anything."

"Don't dust it," LaSalle said. "Cut it off and bring it in here."

"What?"

"Bring the whole phone in. I'll send it to D.C. for laser analysis. Sometimes we can pick up prints that have been wiped off."

Paul turned again to Ellen. "All right. Christ! Have Howard bring it in. I don't know how the hell he's going to cut it off though." He paused, his features softening. "You might as well go on home, Ellen. Denise is probably missing you. Nothing else's going to happen until he calls tomorrow."

Ellen shook her head. "Forget it, Paul. We're short-handed as it is." She smiled abruptly. "Besides, it'll be twenty years before something else exciting happens in Las Cruces. I might as well be here."

LaSalle said, "I want to hear the tape. We're going to want to send it to D.C., too."

Clearly annoyed, Paul said, "Wouldn't it be easier to bring the whole damn lab to Las Cruces?"

"I know it's a hassle," LaSalle told him. "Can't be helped."

Exley came hurriedly into the room, looking tense, Ellen thought. It seemed strangely reassuring. After a lifetime of dealing with the psychotic as well as the merely dangerous, he still had the capacity to feel.

Paul dropped to one knee and flipped open a drawer beneath the dispatch operator's phone console, exposing the reel-to-reel recorder. Working quickly, he removed the tape and replaced it with the spare reel. By the time he was finished, Ellen had plugged another recorder into a receptacle next to the operator. Paul threaded the tape, fast-forwarded to the proper counter number, then punched the Play button.

"Monica Ochoa's wearing red and white tennis shoes, and she has a four-inch scar on her neck . . ."

A pall fell on the room as time slowed to the cadence of the kidnapper's voice. Ellen said, "I'll call her mother just to make sure. This might be an opportunist."

" . . . twenty-four hours to get $20 million. I'll tell you later what to do with it."

LaSalle said, "If you do pick someone up, we can get a voice print." He smiled thinly at Paul. "We won't have to go to D.C. I can have the equipment sent in from L.A."

While Jeannie continued conversing with patrol cars, they listened as the kidnapper made his demands.

"He definitely knows what he's doing," Exley said. "The only place to get thirty thousand hundred-dollar bills is a federal reserve bank."

Of course he knows what he's doing, Ellen thought. Remember the knife? He's been planning this for years. And with a sad reluctance she recalled Exley's, "someone local, someone you know."

"He seems to be familiar with the diamond trade, too," Exley went on. "Think he might be a jeweler?"

LaSalle, pacing back and forth in front of the table, shook his head irritably. "He wants to travel light. He could put the cash in a suitcase and seventeen million in diamonds in a pouch. He's planning on running the second he gets the pay-off. We'll have to alert the border patrol as well as nearby police departments."

"Next time he calls," Exley said to Paul, "put the call through to the conference room. Let me talk to him. I don't think we'll hear from him again until tomorrow though. He's a cautious man. He'll stay off the phone and away from phone booths."

Paul hit the Stop button and reversed the tape. Then he punched Play and they listened again. When it was over, LaSalle stopped his pacing and glanced at everyone. "What do you think?" His voice was abrupt.

"No accent," Ellen said. "He's obviously trying to disguise it." And something moved in the back of her mind, something she couldn't put her finger on but that would continue to tug at her consciousness.

"Age?" LaSalle asked at once.

"Thirties or forties," Paul guessed and Exley agreed. "Kidnappers tend to be older than most felons. I'd guess around forty."

LaSalle said, "I'll call Washington. We'll have to do what he says and get the money and diamonds."

"Think there'll be any problem?" Ellen asked.

"Not with the money. The diamonds? Who knows? I guess the bureau will have to buy them. Can't ask for a seventeen million dollar contribution."

Exley said, "After what he did, we obviously have to take his threat to kill the children seriously. He sounds completely affectless to me. There's no emotion, no feeling at all. Those kids are virtually inanimate to him. Like dolls."

"I think some of them are already dead," Ellen said, surprising herself as though it were an admission of defeat. She added, "Those that needed medicine. Just a feeling I have." She turned suddenly to Exley. "What did you turn up with your sex offenders?"

"The computer gave us a bit more than two thousand names within eighty miles of here. Most of them weren't violent offenders—uncles or grandfathers fondling relatives, indecent exposure, possession of child pornography. We'll start checking them out, but it'll take a great deal of time. We're unlikely to have anything by the time he calls tomorrow." He turned to LaSalle. "I've asked for help on this, Matthew. I don't want you to think I'm going behind your back. But since we seem determined to rule out anyone in the department—"

Jeannie interrupted, shouting over her shoulder, "Marcus Cox on three, Chief," as she took another call.

Paul grabbed a phone from a desk. "Just wanted to let you know, Chief Whitehorse. We turned up a kid's tennis shoe about a half-mile north of where that lunch box was found. We've got a car bringing it in to you so you can check with the parents. If it turns out to belong to one of the missing kids, we'll bring our dogs in."

"Get the dogs, anyway," Paul said irritably. "I want them ready to go."

"Four hundred and thirty dollars an hour, Chief."

"For Christ's sake, Marcus, we'll pay it! Jesus! Stay out there on the damn road. We'll let you know as soon as we can."

He told the others what the sheriff's department had found. LaSalle looked hopeful. "The momentum's changed. We're narrowing it down now. He's heading toward the mines."

"Still a lot of territory," Paul said.

LaSalle shook his head. "We'll find him. It's like a snowball rolling downhill. Now we have some data to work with. Each time he calls, we'll add a little bit more, then a little bit more, until we have him."

Ellen felt uneasy. Again, everyone was focusing on the kidnapper rather than the victims. It didn't necessarily follow that catching the one would free the others or that finding the children even depended on apprehending the kidnapper. LaSalle's "a little bit more, then a little bit more" didn't bode well for a quick resolution. What had she told herself this morning? If you don't get the hostages back within six to twelve hours, you won't get them back alive. It was almost twelve hours now. She turned to Paul. "We need to get some doctors in. They'll have to get to the children as soon as we do."

"Check with the National Guard headquarters. They can fly in a team of medics with their own chopper."

Ellen reached for the phone. "I'm going to try to get some cots sent over, too, so the parents can stay together. If we don't find their children, it's going to be a long twenty-four hours." And again something struggled to work its way loose in her mind and failed, leaving her with a rising frustration.

7:42 P.M.

Manny Rios hadn't completed his questioning of potential witnesses along the bus route until well after seven, when he realized he hadn't eaten since breakfast. Better stop before getting back to the station, he decided; there was no telling what Whitehorse had planned for tonight. Probably more driving around, looking for an invisible bus. Damn waste of time. It was in Mexico by now. Along with the clown, if there ever was one. A clown, for Christ's sake! Bozo with a bazooka.

So what's it to be, Burger King or Jack in the Box? Flame-broiled animal fat or fried animal fat? Decisions, decisions. Life as a gourmet was tougher than people thought. He decided finally on Burger King since there was one coming up on Stapleton and Jack in the Box was way the hell over on Main. Two minutes later, Manny was pulling his squad car into the line at the drive-thru, and setting himself to wait.

After leisurely finishing his dinner—crab enchiladas (surely a gringo concoction), two home-made tamales, and refried beans, which, as always, he left untouched—DeVries was not quite ready to appear on the street. Let things cool down a bit more, he decided. Every cop in Las Cruces was probably within a mile of him this very instant, but in another fifteen minutes they'd give it up. No one would expect the anonymous caller to hang around longer than he had to. The key to success lay in keeping the opposition off guard, never doing what experience has taught them you will do. Introduce a little ambiguity into their lives, a little chaos.

"Chaos," he whispered aloud, smiling, letting the word roll slowly off his tongue. His new religion.

Picking up his margarita, still untouched, he carried it

into the bar. The room was crowded with men in their twenties and thirties watching a baseball game on the large-
screen TV. DeVries chose a table along the brick wall in the
rear and sipped at his drink, waving off the short-skirted waitress who came by and smiled at him. One of the teams was
evidently from Atlanta, the other from Los Angeles. Baseball,
with its odd uniforms and odder rituals, bored him, and he
watched the men in the bar with amused contempt. Losers,
nothing better to do with their lives than sit around with
strangers, drinking beer out of bottles and yelling at men
playing boys' games. It was pathetic. But there would be little need to endure this sort of childish machismo much
longer. In two months, he would be relaxing in Costa Rica,
where he owned beach-front property under the name of
Harold Nichols. Mr. Nichols was a long-time visitor to the ver-
dant and amiable Central American country, a well-to-do
Canadian known as a stylish dresser, an aficionado of fine
food, and a man who greatly enjoyed the favor of young girls.
There had been, he knew, a few tut-tuts about this last indulgence, but as long as he kept his life-style low-key, no one
would make any real trouble. Especially for such a wealthy
and generous *patrón*. And the world was, after far too long
a time, finally developing a more reasonable attitude toward
sex with the young. Those who thought of it as exploitive just
didn't see that it could be beneficial, as well as enjoyable, to
both parties. And wasn't it true anyway that some of the
world's great civilizations considered child-love a crucial
component of a fulfilled life? Look at the British, with their
long if somewhat secretive, history of upper-class pederasty.
Or the Dutch of today, to say nothing of the Turks, Thais,
and Japanese. Or the marvelously successful ancient Greeks,
who made it not merely acceptable but official policy.

Or, he thought, with a smile, look at Joseph R. MacAllister, serving his third term on the city council and who Lowell had noticed one hot summer evening quietly slipping
into Miss Violet's. Some gentle probing of Violet herself—
along with $500—had brought the news that ol' round-
belly Joey was enjoying himself on the boys' side of the

house. He wondered what the councilman's frizzy-haired wife would think of that. It was a tiny tidbit of information that DeVries had gleefully filed away to use someday, but the occasion would never arise now. Perhaps when he was in Costa Rica he would call the newspaper and let them know about the sanctimonious MacAllister's hobby.

He looked again at his watch. Seven forty-five. Time to give the police another little shove. Do you feel it, Ellen? The wind at your back? Do you feel it pushing you along? With that phone call, you became my plaything.

He left his drink, still largely untouched, and strolled out to the parking lot in the early evening heat.

Easing slowly out of the drive-thru with a Whopper, fries, and chocolate shake balanced precariously on his lap, Manny Rios watched as the purple Buick Park Avenue slid out of the El Matador parking lot across the street and casually went through a red light on Stapleton. Well, maybe a yellow light but it turned red almost immediately, right in front of him. Assholes in their fancy cars think they can do anything they want, he thought. Coming out of the El Mat alone like that, probably been sitting in the fuckin' bar all night watching the game and sucking up margaritas.

Rios felt it like a personal affront, a slap in the face, and thought, You're mine, asshole.

DeVries was listening with growing annoyance to the nearby public radio station on his car radio. "The New Sound of Classical Music" they were calling it now as they tried to broaden their listenership with vapid show tunes and folk music from around the world. More of the pandering to the "common man" that had become endemic in America. Common indeed. Maybe he'd blow the station up so Las Cruces could once again have a real classical station. Wouldn't it be nice to hear some Wagner or Mahler or . . . . Suddenly his heart skipped a beat as a burst of red and blue police lights appeared in the rearview mirror, partially illuminating the interior of his car with their anxious, pulsing intensity. It can't be for me, he thought. It can't. Any second now the squad car would swerve to the left and shoot past, probably on the way to an accident. But it didn't, it stayed right behind, not more than ten feet separating the two vehicles.

No! Lowell shouted silently to himself. No! There was no way anyone could have seen him make that phone call. There had been no one around. And if someone had seen the car, the police would be looking for a Ford Taurus. His fingers tightened painfully on the steering wheel. It's not going to end like this, he swore. It's not! I've spent too much time and energy planning everything. Three years, goddamn it! Three fucking years! It's not going to end because some bastard saw me at the phone booth.

The police car's siren wailed for two seconds like a child's feverish cry for help. Don't panic, he told himself. Don't blow it. Take a breath, let it out slowly. Now, do what he wants, pull over, do it gently. There's a long-deserted Exxon station coming up. Yes. That'd be perfect—off the street, no one would see . . .

He hit the turn signal, slowed, and reached his hand under the seat, extracting his .38 revolver. Drifting up the drive leading to the gas pumps, his shoulders straight, he slipped the gun into his waistband and promised himself: It's not going to end here. I've put too much thought into this. It is not going to end.

Rios hissed his breath out in a long, angry sigh. It took the asshole almost a block to pull over, he thought. Probably so fuckin' drunk he didn't see the lights. He took a bite of his Whopper, then tossed it on the passenger seat. If the guy is drunk, he thought, it'll take twenty minutes to give him a field test, cuff him, and get him to the station. What's a twenty-minute-old burger and fries going to taste like? Christ, maybe I should've let him go. I have more important things to do tonight than run in one more drunk. But how would I feel if the dude runs into someone down the block?

The Buick's front door eased open, and the driver stepped out. Good-looking middle-aged guy, wearing an expensive suit, looked like it cost more than Rios made in two weeks. Businessman from Palm Springs, probably. Or an attorney. How Rios loved busting attorneys! Guy was standing still, staring at the police car with his arms crossed, trying like hell not to appear drunk.

Rios grabbed his baton from the front seat, slipping it onto his belt as he stepped from the car. The asshole hasn't moved, he thought. Frozen, like he's waiting to be beamed up to the fuckin' Starship Enterprise. Rios unsnapped his holster flap as he walked up to him.

The man smiled, looking curious, not belligerent, trying to be Mr. Nice Guy. "What'd I do, officer?"

Christ, they never know what they did, he thought. Nothing, asshole, I pulled you over for the hell of it, because I got nothin' better to do with my life. "May I see your driver's license, please?"

"Of course." DeVries put his right hand into the inside pocket of his suit coat and drew out his wallet. His heart was pounding, but he felt under control. No need for panic, he told himself. Relax. See what he wants. But his mind was already made up: If he tries to search me, he dies.

Still smiling, DeVries flipped open the wallet and removed his license. The cop glanced cursorily at it, then stared hard into DeVries's face. He knows! DeVries thought at once and had to force his body to remain still while his mind was screaming: Run, run. But he saw it in the cop's eyes: He knows. Someone must have seen me. Act fast. Step up to him so the muzzle of the gun is pressed against his heart. Shoot twice. He'll be dead in seconds. Pull the body into the patrol car and—

"You been drinking, Mr. DeVries?" The cop was looking again at the driver's license, turning it over and glancing at the back.

"Drinking?" Jesus, is that what it was? Drinking? There was probably a trace of alcohol on his breath from the margarita, but he hadn't taken more than two or three sips. The cop was staring into his eyes, looking at the pupils like he could read something there.

"No, no," he said with a relaxed smile. He began to feel giddy with relief and gave a chuckle. "I had dinner at the El Matador. A bunch of us from work. One of my friends had a margarita and I took a sip. That was it. Don't like alcohol, actually. Did I do something wrong? Was I going too fast? It didn't seem so."

"You went through a red light back there."

DeVries was genuinely startled. "It was yellow!" *Wrong answer! My God, don't argue! Don't start anything.*

The cop was staring at him again with interest, like he was trying to work something out in his mind. *I haven't got time for this,* Lowell decided suddenly. *Damn it, I've got to get rid of the other shoe and take one of the kids—*

"Would you step over here, please, Mr. DeVries."

The policeman had moved away from the car to the front of the locked office. DeVries hesitated, his anxiety mounting, but with no time to make up his mind. Finally, he smoothed his suit coat over his revolver and crossed to the building. His heart pounded against his chest and his nerve endings seemed on fire.

"Put your feet together, head back, and close your eyes. When I tell you to, I want you to touch your nose with the index finger of your right hand."

Don't argue. Do as he says. Get it over with.

DeVries took a deep, silent breath to steady his nerves, then did as instructed, but as he stretched out his arm he sensed his suit coat riding up on his waist, and his spine grew cold. *Oh God, the gun!* He opened his eyes, but Rios was staring at his face. He quickly dropped his arm.

"All right, Mr. DeVries, I'd like you to walk from here over to the gas pumps there in a straight line, heel to toe. Like this. See?" Rios demonstrated for him. "Heel touching toe. Do you understand?"

"Of course."

Trying desperately to remain relaxed, DeVries walked

heel to toe to the gas pumps, stopped, and without turning around, said, "Okay?"

"Step over to your car, please."

"What for? I—"

"Step over to the car and put your hands on the hood."

DeVries's heart began to jump. Something's wrong, he thought, something's desperately wrong. He did as he was told but walked the long way around the car so his back would be to the road. As he bent over the hood, he felt the .38 in his waistband and thought: Stay calm.

Rios moved to the opposite side of the car and opened the door. He knew the man had been drinking even if he had passed the field test. Some guys were just like that, no matter how much they'd had. Like fat Artie Torres, the pitcher on his softball team. Guy could guzzle two six-packs and still do the heel-to-toe, touch-the-nose business. He probably practiced at home every night. It didn't matter. They could do a blood test at the station. He couldn't fake that. Of course, it'd be nice to find an open container. That'd take Mr. Yuppie Scum's license for a mandatory six months. Let him walk home from work in the middle of summer in that $1800 suit.

Hoping to find a bottle, Rios ran his hand under the front seat. Nothing but a rag of some sort. He pulled it out. Lipstick or makeup all over it. And some white crap, looked like makeup, too. Guy's girlfriend liked to pretty up in the car before spreading out in the back seat, evidently. Or maybe the dude likes dressing up like a woman. Hey, they're going to love you in jail tonight, Sweetie, he laughed to himself.

He stuffed the rag back and opened the glove compartment. Nothing but a small Kleenex box. Mr. Neat. He pushed the trunk release and walked around to the back of the car. Dude's got that nervous look again, he noticed. Fuck's wrong with him, eyes darting, mouth all tensed? Jesus, look at him. You hiding something, Mr. Neat?

Rios turned to the trunk, expecting to find it as spotless as the glove compartment but surprised to see it full of crap: work boots, beat-up old fifty-foot tape measure, three gray loose-leaf binders, two pairs of gloves, tool box. Did the guy work out of his car? Also a kid's tennis shoe, looked pretty new. Mama's going to be looking for that, pal. No booze, no dope, no weapons. He slammed the trunk shut.

Something wasn't right. Still standing at the rear of the car, Rios casually rested his hand on the butt of his 9 mm automatic.

The guy was still staring at him with that weird look. Christ, forget it, he thought. I'm just antsy because of that damn ransom call. Even though it hadn't come from his part of the city, he'd heard all the excitement on the radio, Whitehorse screaming at Muledeer and Lockheart to find the guy, like he was going to sit in front of the phone booth and wait to be arrested. Everything's getting crazy, he thought. It makes you see things that aren't there. Even the chief was acting edgy. Rios had never seen that before, hadn't thought the man had a nervous bone in his body.

He looked back at DeVries. So do I run the dude in or let him go? he wondered.

"Officer," DeVries lifted his hands from the hood and straightened, "if you're done, I really do have a date." Trying a little smile now, Mr. Nice Guy again.

His mind still not made up, Rios walked to the front of the car. DeVries pointedly looked at his watch. Something ain't right here, Manny thought again. Goddamn it, I can feel it. A cop's sixth sense. What do they tell you when you're a rookie? "Everyone lies." Everyone! He was staring into DeVries's face, moving it around in his mind and wondering if he should run the license for wants and warrants, when his mind drew up the image of that messy rag under the front seat. Makeup. Why did that suddenly bother him so much? And a single tennis shoe in the trunk.

DeVries was staring back at him with dead gray eyes, calmly unbuttoning his suit coat with his right hand, when the confusion in Rios's mind suddenly clarified, like a movie projector coming abruptly into focus, and a sick feeling rose in his stomach as he thought, *Oh, shit!*

8:09 P.M.

Ellen stood in the crowded conference room, the phone to one ear, her finger pressed to the other, trying to talk to Monica Ochoa's mother downstairs, while around her everyone seemed to be shouting. The woman didn't speak English, and Ellen's Spanish was rapidly evaporating in the noisy confusion. Finally, she made herself understood. "Yes, yes," Mrs. Ochoa said excitedly. "Monica has a small scar on her neck from where she fell down on a toy truck last year, and she was wearing brand new red tennis shoes." They'd just bought them at Kmart last Sunday.

Ellen put the phone down and turned at once to Paul. "It's her."

Paul nodded but said nothing, his eyes focused on the city map hanging on the wall. It's getting to him, Ellen thought as she stared at his face, and she could feel what he was going through. Everyone was feeling it. They'd been so close to the kidnapper, within seconds; if only they had been quicker.

A yellow pin in the map indicated the phone booth on Palm, not more than a mile from the Civic Center. LaSalle had been right, of course: the kidnapper was a thinker, he'd have had an escape route planned out ahead of time. Ellen stared at the map. Or would he? Maybe escape would mean not escaping, hiding in plain sight. Where could he have disappeared to within two minutes? There was a Wal-Mart, a Price Cutters, a Catholic Church.

Deep in thought, she didn't hear someone come up from behind, touching her elbow, and she whirled around to see Matthew LaSalle. There was a tenseness to his features, a straining around the eyes and mouth, she hadn't seen before. "The cash is coming in from Federal Reserve Banks in San Francisco and Dallas," he said at once. "They're flying it to March Air Force Base. Our L.A. field office is working on the diamonds. They'll be at March early tomorrow afternoon. We should have everything here by two or three."

"Cutting it pretty close," Ellen said. "What if there's a foul-up somewhere?"

LaSalle frowned and nodded. "I know, but it can't be helped. The diamonds have to be rounded up. He knew what he was doing. Bigger diamonds would have been harder for us to find. And harder for him to sell—"

Maggie stuck her head in the door, interrupting. "Your photo experts just came in, Mr. LaSalle. They said they'd need a quiet room to work in."

LaSalle looked at Paul, who turned from the map with annoyance. "Put them in with Howard, Maggie. We've only got so much space here."

Ellen said, "Let me know if there's any problem with the diamonds. I still have to get on the phone and round up some cots for the parents downstairs. Most of them are spending the night."

"Have some sent up here, too. Exley needs to stay by the phone in case he calls again. And we'll need sleeping arrangements for my people. I guess I'll be here, also."

Ellen went back to the phone and called the Red Cross. They agreed to send over a hundred cots and some volunteer counselors for the parents. As she hung up, the National Guard called on the other line. They were setting up a field hospital in the parking lot of Los Coyotes Medical Center and wanted to know what kind of medication the kids needed. Ellen transferred the call to Dr. Sanderson downstairs, then turned around and saw Howard Stines talking to Paul and hurried over to them. Stines smiled thinly when he saw her. "We dusted the entire booth before we cut off the phone. There were a hundred-and-twelve partial and complete prints. None of them are likely to be the bad guy's, but I'm hoping one will be the governor's. The phone's already on the way to Washington with the tape of the ransom call."

"Send the prints to Sacramento anyway," Paul told him. "Something might turn up. He might have been in the booth last week for a rehearsal. Let the computer sort things out."

Exley's annoyed voice came loudly from across the room. "Can someone please shut that door? We need to listen to the tape again. We've got to get a feel for this person if we're going to negotiate with him."

Everyone was on edge, even Exley, Ellen thought. We're all trying not to show it, but we feel the panic now, see it in each other's eyes.

Stines hurried off to the lab, and Paul shut the door behind him. The room seemed eerily quiet. Everyone but Ellen sat at the table as Exley threaded the duplicated tape, then pushed the button.

"Monica Ochoa's wearing red and white tennis shoes . . ."

They listened, then listened again.

Ellen felt an iciness creep along her spine as the disembodied voice casually threatened to kill twenty-six children. Her eyes focused on the laminated tabletop, the empty stained Styrofoam coffee cups, the three boxes of half-eaten pizza the F.B.I. had had sent up earlier. And she wondered: What are they doing right now, this very minute? What are those children feeling and thinking? Can they even comprehend what's going on? There were both mentally and physically handicapped kids on the bus, the teachers said. So perhaps some of them aren't aware of what has happened. But some would be.

"No inflection, no affect." Exley's voice hung darkly in the strained silence as he leaned back and gazed up at the ceiling. "A thinker, for sure, though. He asked for a ransom that, while large, is both high in liquidity and easy to transport. And not all that difficult for us to procure in twenty-four hours. Unusual, isn't it? The first demand is typically for something completely out of the question, a bargaining ploy so we'll feel more comfortable with the later demands. Of course, money needn't be the issue here. Perhaps if he hasn't a gripe against your department, he's angry with the city." He turned and looked at Ellen and Paul.

"Like the Pied Piper?" Ellen suggested. Odd, she thought,

that's the second time I've thought of that today. But she said, "I can't think of anyone," though again something nudged her unconscious, something almost familiar in the kidnapper's voice.

"I think he just wants to be rich," Paul said, annoyed at the psychologist's continual theorizing. "Don't make this into something it isn't. He wants twenty million, and this is the only way to get it."

"Probably correct," Exley conceded. "Nevertheless, we must consider all possibilities. That's why I asked about people in your department and why we're checking sex offenders. It might—"

The phone rang and Ellen grabbed it, losing track of the conversation as she listened to a sheriff's deputy downstairs. A minute later she put the receiver down and turned to Paul. "One of the mothers identified the shoe. It belongs to the same child who lost the lunch box." The boy must have thrown them out the window, she thought. Was he leaving a trail or was it just random hijinks?

Paul pushed to his feet and went to the map on the wall. "A half-mile north of the lunch box."

LaSalle joined him, and Ellen watched from behind as the two men studied the map, the taller, older Whitehorse somehow less assured and confident than his well-dressed F.B.I. counterpart. LaSalle said, "They could be anywhere in those hills. Or even that abandoned airfield. But I think he's up in those mines somewhere."

"I don't know," Paul replied. "He could have gone west from there." He pointed to a road leading off the highway. "Didn't have to go north or east. Could even be over by the Salton Sea. Lots of places to hide."

LaSalle jabbed his finger at a half-dozen locations marked "KEEP OUT." "There are more bombing and gunnery areas than I thought. Looks like half the county's off limits."

Paul turned to Ellen. "Let Marcus Cox know. He's got dogs waiting. I want them moving."

As Ellen called Jeannie downstairs and told her to con-

tact the sheriff's department, Exley said, "If we don't locate
the hostages, we'll have to deal with the kidnapper. As I said,
we already have a procedure for that. Our strategy is to bar-
gain with him, appeal to his reason, show him why we can't
possibly come up with the ransom he expects. We drag it
out over a period of days if we can. It makes him antsy and
more likely he'll make a mistake, give us an idea where he's
holding the victims. This time . . ." he fluttered a hand
in the air and let it drop to the tabletop, "this time I think
he won't be put off. He knows we can get what he
demands. As I said before, I have a feeling he even knows
how we operate."

"We've been through that," Paul said, wheeling around
from the map. "We haven't had any personnel problems."

"Then he may be an ex-policeman. From a different lo-
cality, perhaps. Or maybe he took criminology courses in
college. Or came across training manuals. The information is there for anyone determined to get it. From the
sound of his voice, I'd say he's supremely confident about
his ability to pull this off. I wouldn't be surprised if, when
we arrest him, you discover it's someone you know, probably someone quite intelligent. Perhaps a true sociopath,
though that's extremely rare. If he is not an ex-, or current,
police officer, I would guess he has a record of juvenile of-
fenses, run-ins with teachers, parents, police. As an adult,
he would have become sufficiently sophisticated to stay out
of jail and probably out of trouble. But still, a failure who
blames everyone but himself. Frustrated. Angry. Striking
back at society."

"Dangerous?" Ellen asked. "Would he kill those children?
All of them?"

Surprised, Exley turned his wide, bespectacled face in her
direction. "Oh, yes. Dangerous, indeed. He would have no
real sense of right and wrong where his own behavior is concerned. It would be literally irrelevant to someone like him
if those children lived or died. Or if any of us lived or died.
I don't want to overdramatize, but it's almost as though
people like this belong to a species that evolved separately

from *homo sapiens*. There's a gap, an absolute hole, where the rest of us have a conscience. Peoples' lives or deaths would be of no more significance to him than it would be to you to walk out the back door and step on a dozen ants. Nevertheless, I believe we should try an appeal. Perhaps it'll have some effect."

"What kind of appeal?" Ellen asked at once, her alarm mounting as the psychologist calmly described the mental state of the man holding twenty-six innocent children's lives in his hands.

Exley said, "We've had parents or relatives make a public appeal in previous kidnappings. It's worth a shot. Have them go on television, speak directly to the kidnapper, see if they can find something human in his soul to touch."

"We've got less than twenty-four hours until he starts killing them," Paul said. "We'd better hurry."

Ellen got quickly to her feet. "We can do it from the high school. I'll set things up."

"I suggest you arrange it for as soon as possible," Exley said. "I'm not sure we do have twenty-four hours. Someone like this, walking a line as it were between intense self-control and madness is liable to snap at any time. When he does, when the pressures that build up become too much, that's when he's going to kill those children. No matter what we do."

7. Choose One

Linda Sowell was on her knees, frantically trying to loosen the screws in the interior door handle when the exit door up the ramp banged loudly open. Gasping for breath, her heart racing wildly, she spun around and almost collapsed on the floor as she saw him. The room erupted in a wail as the children noticed him at the same time and shrieked in fright. Instinctively, they shrank back from the ramp toward her, seeking protection.

The man, huge and terrifying as he stood outlined in the uncertain light of the doorway, stared down into the underground chamber. His eyes went at once to Tiffany, the mute girl, lingered, seemed to tremble, then shifted abruptly to Linda. His voice boomed out, further frightening the children. "You! I want you."

Terrified, Linda pressed her back against the wall and forced herself to speak. "Why? What do you want?" She had to scream to be heard over the children.

"Up here," he said. "Now!"

DeVries felt more confident than ever. After leaving the gas station, he had driven back without incident. He'd heard no sirens and seen no patrol cars. It would all come out sooner or later, of course, but that was okay. He could not be implicated in any way. And if they tied it to the kidnapper, so much the better. It would give everyone something to think about for the next—he looked at his watch—twenty-eight hours.

Lowell closed the trapdoor as Linda came through, and slipped a padlock on the clasp without locking it. He sat calmly on one of the lawn chairs and casually motioned Linda to the other. "Sit."

"What did you do with Emilio?" Linda demanded without moving. Her eyes burned with fear, but she remained defiant. "Where is he? I want to know what you did with him!"

DeVries's voice was weary. "Sit."

"Is he hurt? Where'd you take him?" She was screaming, waving her arms, but staying out of the man's reach.

"Sit down, damn it." He raised his arm as if to hit her.

Linda stepped back at once and lowered herself into the chair, staring fearfully at the building she was in. A barn or large garage, bare cement floor, rotting wooden plank walls, smell of age and decay. The bus was still there along with a large American car. The building's windows were boarded up with plywood, but a partially open door beyond showed that it was dark outside. The heat was stifling.

DeVries watched her darting eyes as though he could read her mind. "Don't even think about running. You'd never make it."

Her gaze shifted to his face. He looked no different from this morning, a business executive, maybe. Good-looking, well-dressed, hair neatly combed, wearing cologne, perhaps even freshly shaved. But dead blue eyes in a blank face, as if he were hiding behind a wax mask. She shuddered and went slack in the shoulders. "What do you want with me?"

He gazed at her with open curiosity but still didn't smile. "You needn't be afraid. I'm not going to harm you."

"I don't believe you!" Linda said forcefully. She sensed that she shouldn't argue with him but didn't care now. He was insane, a madman; she could see it in those eyes, crazy eyes, crazy face, the way he stared at her. He was going to kill them all, everyone. "The children . . ." she began, and trembled up and down her body; her voice was sore and raspy from crying and trying to comfort the kids, and she knew she was filthy, her clothes fouled with sweat and dirt and smelling of urine and vomit. With an effort, she made herself go on. "The children need their medicine. Why are you keeping us here? What do you want from us?"

This time he did smile at her, completely at ease, as he considered the question. "What do I want? Fair enough. I want what I deserve, the reward for my years of effort. And, with your assistance, I will get it. We have become partners, you see, you and I. You are vital, Linda. And tomorrow you will become famous. I offer you immortality."

"Immortality?" She flew from her chair, fists clenched, barely able to control herself. But DeVries merely moved a hand as if he were urging away a fly, and she sank down and hung her head in her hands. Unexpectedly, he came to his feet. "On second thought, come with me. I will show you. Then you will believe."

Linda looked up at him.

"Come," he said again, like a parent to a child, and stepped toward the doorway.

Watching him fearfully, Linda stood and moved tentatively toward the door, her feet dragging on the ground as if they were too heavy to lift. DeVries remained in front, unwilling to come too close to her. As they stepped outside into the evening heat, she quickly scanned the surrounding area for signs of life but found none. A small dilapidated house that she had briefly noticed yesterday, a rusted pickup truck, a few scattered yucca trees. Desert. Darkness. Isolation.

"Quickly," DeVries said and led her up a rotted wooden step and into the unlit house. Enough starlight drifted through the broken windows to show that it was deserted and probably had been for years. The odor of dust and cat urine hung in the air.

"This way," he said, smiling pleasantly as she stepped slowly into what had once been the kitchen but had long ago been vandalized beyond repair. A small black-and-white television was playing with the sound off. DeVries turned up the volume:

". . . the F.B.I. agents in Las Cruces haven't been clear about their role in the investigation, but an official spokesperson in Washington said the team is being headed by Matthew LaSalle, an expert on kidnappings and terrorism. Assisting him . . ."

"Matthew LaSalle," DeVries said and smiled knowingly. "One of their kidnapping gurus. A master of the hunt and all that, a sign of how important they view your rescue. Or the children's rescue, to be quite honest about it. I'm afraid you're pretty small fish at this point. Don't worry though. We'll change that tomorrow." He flipped the dial. "I'm afraid we can only get three channels here. This is Palm Springs."

". . . the similar crime almost twenty years ago lasted only a few hours. We've already gone beyond that."

DeVries switched channels again. A man's voice:

"What did the school district say, Diane?"

"We talked to the superintendent. He said he couldn't imagine . . ."

DeVries switched off the television and looked at Linda.

"Immortality." The word floated gently from him like a half-whispered song, and he added, "You, me, the children. The whole world is watching. It is the ultimate media event, a synecdoche for *fin de siècle* America, and something that will never be topped. England, Japan, Russia, Africa—everyone waits, everyone hopes. Churches stay open, politicians appeal, millions, billions, pray. Buddhists, Christians, Jews, Moslems implore God. For you, Linda. You and the children, innocent victims of a mad kidnapper, a killer of infants. Such a sense of shared community it has created, drawing the world together. Now everyone knows Linda Sowell. Everyone cares. You needn't worry that your time on earth will pass unnoticed. You are already famous; tomorrow, as I said, we will merely take things a level higher."

Linda stared uncomprehendingly at the mute television. What was he talking about? This was crazy! It was insane! She needed to say something, to ask something, but her mind wouldn't work. Her heart raced and her fingers clenched and her head felt as though it would burst. But all she could say was, "You can't get away with it. You can't possibly. . . . Everyone is looking. So many people . . ."

DeVries rested his seat against the drain board and crossed his arms. "So many people indeed. That is part of the fun, don't you see? All these law-enforcement types. The more the merrier. If only one agency were involved, perhaps I'd have something to worry about. But I stirred the pot for them. I muddied their precious jurisdictional territories, forced them into new ways of thinking. 'Shifting the paradigm,' their textbooks will term it someday; disturbing the universe with my handful of dust. Is this a local crime? State? Federal? Is the reservation involved? Perhaps Interpol should jump in alongside the local police, the sheriff, the F.B.I., and the military. All these lines in the sand, these departments; they can't possibly work together. Especially when a little confusion, a little chaos, suddenly sprouts up in their lives."

"They'll catch you," Linda said angrily and stared at his face, burning its lines and contours into her memory. "They'll catch you. You'll die in the gas chamber."

He shook his head. "Statistically, you're quite right, of course. The F.B.I. claims a ninety-seven percent capture rate for kidnappings. Very impressive, no? They want us to concentrate on their successes, naturally. But for those who got away, the F.B.I.'s failures, they got one hundred percent away, didn't they? That is what I choose to focus on, the ones who were not caught.

"I've given this a great deal of thought, dear Linda. I've planned it out in more detail than the Pentagon plans World War III. Did you know that the F.B.I. publishes a handbook, a very thick handbook at that, on how they deal with kidnappings? And that it's available at libraries? What madness. A sort of how-to guide for villains. Very handy for me, naturally.

"As were numerous accounts of past kidnappings. Lindbergh, Patty Hearst, the school bus up north, the Exxon executive in New Jersey, the I.R.A., Red Brigade, P.L.O., Shining Path, Baader-Meinhof. Dozens more. Kidnapping was quite the crime of the seventies and eighties. There were some classic cases in Europe and South America. Remember the Sinatra child, or the Getty boy and his ear that came in the mail, as it were? It was all very instructive.

"More than anything, it showed me that kidnapping contains a fatal flaw that keeps it from being more common, the transfer of the ransom money. How to pick up several million dollars without being caught? Most commonly, of course, kidnappers rely on what the F.B.I. calls the 'treasure hunt approach.' The person delivering the money is instructed to drive to point A, where a message will be found instructing him to point B, and so on. All of this to see if anyone is following. Well, of course, they needn't follow at all nowadays, given the state of electronic surveillance. Merely put a bug on the person and the police can sit in their air-conditioned cars miles away and watch on a video screen. Or put special infrared lights on the package, 'fireflies' they call them, and observe from a distance. This makes it very difficult to effect a safe getaway, as you can imagine.

"But, as I say, I have given it a lot of thought, and the method I have come up with is foolproof. I am not in the least worried. Nor am I concerned about their countermeasures. As I said, everything is laid out in the F.B.I.'s manuals; a 'Kidnap Plan' they actually call it in their dull bureaucratic manner." He smiled at her. "I can tell you exactly what they're doing right now—again, there's a finite number of responses, and creativity is frowned upon. The F.B.I. assumes that what worked in the past will work in the future, so they'll bring in dozens of agents and technical people in the hope that numbers alone will triumph. They'll have their computers at the N.C.I.C. humming all night with the names of everyone who's had any connection to the school or the victims. They'll stake out both the school and kidnap site and note down the license plate of everyone who drives by. They'll tap phones, bring in behavioral science experts, send dogs chasing after the scents I so conveniently left for them, create an air force to search the desert. Above all, they will be cautious because no one wants to be responsible for another F.B.I. disaster like Waco or Ruby Ridge.

"It's all predictable, you see, and as formulaic as an algebraic proof. I know what their response to every step in the game will be. And to push them along I left a few little clues, as well as the slightest whiff of madness, to excite their interest and whisk them on to the next decision point. For the remaining twenty-eight hours of our game, they will imagine they are deducing, reasoning, using information to close in on me. They will think: mines, the desert, the abandoned airfield. They will worry and agonize about the children and try not to upset me. And reassure themselves that it's only a matter of time anyway because kidnappers are always caught.

He hadn't taken his eyes from Linda. His voice remained as gentle as a spring day, his face completely without emotion. Linda was becoming even more panicky watching him, sweat pouring down her sides, and her pulse pounding in her temples. Jesus, he's totally crazy, she thought. He's just barely under control. I saw people in jail like that, forcing away their emotions, pretending to be calm. But he's going to blow any second.

DeVries stepped abruptly away from the drain board and she jumped back, her knees weak with fear. "Why are you telling me all this? What are you going to do?" But she knew: Dear God, he's going to kill me. That's why he told me his plan, let me see him. It doesn't matter if I know who he is. He's going to kill me!

"You worry too much," DeVries said as if reading her thoughts, and reached out to take her elbow, then decided not to. She was filthy and stank, and he didn't want to touch her. "But I have rather let my ego run away with me, haven't I? I suppose I wanted someone to know before. . . . But it doesn't matter." His tone became brusque. "Come. I need your assistance. We have one thing remaining to do tonight."

They left the house, recrossed twenty yards of desert sand, and entered the larger building and its trapped heat and noxious smells. Crossing to the ramp leading underground, he slipped off the lock and pulled up the metal door. Linda stared at him, trembling.

"You first," he said. "I will follow."

The moment the door opened, they heard the wailing from inside, like howls drifting from the center of the earth. Terrified at what he intended, Linda stepped slowly toward the opening, DeVries watching intently. Her skin was filthy, hair scraggly, clothes ripped and soiled. Rather pretty, though, he thought suddenly, the moist shirt molding her body, her legs long and thin. Firm and healthy. He began to feel a familiar stirring. Maybe he'd—but no. Don't improvise, Lowell, he told himself. You know better. There are plans for Linda. She's crucial. Tomorrow. Tomorrow would be Linda's day.

She began down the ramp, DeVries following. The smell of urine and vomit and confinement rose thickly to meet them. DeVries tried to ignore it, but the stench was over-powering and it revolted him. With each step, the children's crying seemed to get louder, more insistent. Linda descended to the floor, DeVries remaining above her on the ramp. A girl in leg braces attached herself to Linda's ankles, he noted with loathing, and the room jumped with groaning, howling, shrieking. He hadn't expected this zoo-like atmosphere and it unnerved him. Noise, yes, of course, that was why isolation was so vital. But this insistent, pulsing moaning and shouting, the heavy scent of sickness and death—it was too much. Despite his effort to stay focused, his mind began to race backward against his will, pulling up moments of similar emotion in the past: as a teenager he had had occasional panic attacks, terrible, terrible times of loss of control when his breathing had become labored and his heart had felt as though it would hammer its way through his body. But that had been years ago. He had conquered that. It wouldn't happen again. Still, he had to get this over with as soon as possible. Glancing rapidly around the room, his eyes settled on a child.

"That boy. What's his name?"

"What boy?" Linda cried in alarm. Her breath caught in her throat, and she could hardly speak.

"The blond. The pretty one."

Oh, dear God, Linda thought in a storm of panic. *Eric! No, no!* Her voice soared despite her attempts to control it. "Why? Why do you want his name?"

Impatient and angry, he took a step down, seized her arm, and demanded, "Tell me!"

"Eric," she managed, but her body was convulsing and she could hardly keep on her feet. Not my baby, she thought. Please, God, not Eric.

His grip tightened painfully. "Why doesn't he look disabled?"

"He's brain-damaged."

"I want him."

"Want him? Want him?" She tried twisting out of his grip, but he merely squeezed tighter and forced her to her knees. Please, dear God, she prayed. Please don't let him . . .

But DeVries's eyes suddenly darted away as his attention was drawn to eleven-year-old Tiffany, and he felt a moment of run-away excitement. But it passed quickly. A mute child wouldn't work. Not for this. But she did appeal to him. So pretty. He could come back later. But now, a *girl*, yes, a girl, and his gaze quickly swept the faces of the children. "That one," he demanded. "Her name." He yanked again, viciously twisting Linda's arm.

She looked at him through her tears. "Sara. Please don't—"

"How old?"

"Six."

DeVries dropped Linda's hand and took two hurried steps toward the little girl. "I'm taking you," he said and seized her by the upper arm, pulling her roughly to his body.

The girl blanched, whimpered, but didn't scream as DeVries yanked her toward the ramp.

"Please!" Linda pleaded. "Please don't hurt her."

But DeVries had dragged the girl up the ramp. At the last moment, he turned back. "Remember those cases I told you about—Sinatra, Getty, the Exxon executive, and so forth? Famous for the victims, you see. But can you name a single kidnapper? Even one?" His voice edged up in range and began to race wildly in a way Linda had not heard before. "You can't, can you? No one can because they were ciphers. They did nothing to ensure their immortality." The door thudded shut. Linda collapsed on the floor, the children, terrified and screaming loudly, swarming around her, while upstairs DeVries's mind whirled and whirled as he began quickly to undress the girl, and he thought: Chaos, and felt something in his mind slip, like a bottle falling from a shelf.

Chaos!

8:25 P.M.

Hurrying up the narrow back stairs to the third floor, people she'd never seen before moving quickly aside as she squeezed past, Ellen found her resentment mounting by the second. Why had she agreed to take care of the arrangements for the press conference when one of the F.B.I. people could have done it? Notifying reporters, finding parents to take part, rounding up transportation, having Louie Sharperson set things up at the high school—and making sure it was all ready to go at 9:00 P.M. A pain in the ass! Especially dealing with reporters. While talking to Sharperson in the squad room, Ellen had automatically reached for the phone on her desk when it rang. The BBC from London; they had two film teams flying into Las Cruces. Worldwide coverage. Essential to have a videotaped interview with Sergeant Camacho. She'd slammed the receiver down. Why hadn't LaSalle, with all his experience with TV people, been put in charge of the press conference? Or Middleton? She laughed out loud as she reached the second-floor landing and started up the next flight. *Charley Meets the Press*. That should do wonders for the F.B.I.'s image.

And what was that song and dance of LaSalle's about dinner? The movie-star cop's well-polished come-on line? *Hey, Baby, let's do dinner at the Hilton*. Right! At least it was better than *What's your sign?* or *Aren't you in films?* Maybe he hadn't been in L.A. long enough to pick those up yet. She should have said no at once, instead of playing around with him. Why'd she do that? It wasn't like her. Normally, she'd turn so icy no one would think of asking again. So why not this time?

Because I was caught off-guard, she told herself. Because I didn't want to hurt his feelings. Because I want the F.B.I. to cooperate with us. Because . . . . Oh, hell, I don't know. Because. But it's not going to happen. No way, pal. I'm too old to fall for the dazzling smile and confident manner again. Been there. Done that. It would be like escaping from a burning house only to run back to see what you'd left behind. It just ain't going to happen.

There was no way she'd do anything to hurt Paul. For too many years she had felt condemned to a life of betrayals and deceptions repeated over and over in an endless pattern. From her father's disappearance before she was born to her mother's incessant lying to Pete's infidelities, nothing had changed, except that she had gotten older. But that was all in the past now. Like she had told Denise again and again: Honesty is the most important thing we have in life. Being true to yourself and true to those you love. Complete honesty in everything. It had been the cause of the only fight she and Paul had ever had. Two months earlier, with Paul watching Denise while Ellen worked a night shift, he had let the little girl ride on the back of one of his horses. Ellen had been livid. Denise was never to be allowed on a horse because of her head injury. He knew that. He'd promised.

"She was on Denver," Paul explained calmly. "He's so old he can't do anything but a slow walk. I was right next to her all the time, holding on."

"I don't care!" Ellen screamed. "I told you never—"

"Ellen, you can't protect her from everything."

"Why not?" she cried. "Why can't I?" But that was not the point. The point was absolute honesty in all things. Honesty above expediency, intelligence, even love. She wouldn't stand for another betrayal of her trust. Paul at least understood. Someone like LaSalle wouldn't. So why waste time thinking about him? Especially now with twenty-six children missing.

Besides, there had already been too many changes in her life to invite another one. Not now. Not ever. She was tired. She was thirty-four years old. She didn't want the moon and the stars. She just wanted to be happy. And Paul could give her that.

She hit the third-floor stairwell door with her fist. Damn

Matthew LaSalle with his pale blue eyes and perfect teeth and confident manner.

Hurrying along the hallway to Paul's office, she sensed with another flash of annoyance that it, too, was crowded with unfamiliar people: a well-dressed, middle-aged man she recognized instinctively as an F.B.I. press officer, along with two young female assistants; three civilians from the C.I.A. who had come in to interpret the aerial photographs; a half-dozen agents from Los Angeles wearing blue windbreakers with a huge yellow "F.B.I." logo plastered on the back so the TV cameras couldn't miss it. Everyone bustling around with an air of self-importance.

Someone shouted her name, and she turned to see LaSalle hastening down the corridor in her direction, a young black woman holding a metal briefcase hurrying to keep up.

"Classified files on terrorism suspects," LaSalle told her, indicating the attaché case. He seemed flustered, the muscles around his eyes tight and his voice straining with impatience. "The director wants me to review them with someone local by ten o'clock and get back to him. Is Paul—"

Ellen immediately shook her head. "I think he's still on the phone with the sheriff."

"Zach Harris?"

"Not a chance. He's the only one left down there."

"Looks like you, then."

Ellen looked at him with exasperation. "I haven't got the time, Matt. I've got to get over to Kennedy. The parents' press conference is in half an hour."

He glanced hurriedly at his watch. "How long a drive is it?"

"Five minutes."

"We'll do the files in twenty. You'll be there in time."

Ellen started to argue, then gave in. Just get it over with, she thought. "All right." Her eyes darted along the crowded hallway. "We'll have to use the Xerox room, though. Every other place is taken up by your people."

The woman with the attaché case frowned as though disappointed her role was over. "You'll both have to sign," she said and shoved a receipt book at them.

Without reading it, Ellen scribbled her name, then hurried down the corridor to the Xerox room. "In there," she yelled over her shoulder to LaSalle and ducked just far enough into an adjacent office to grab two chairs. In addition to the huge floor model copier, there was a metal work table with a paper cutter and three-hole punch in the closet-sized area. When Ellen shoved the chairs inside, they just about consumed the remaining space. She and LaSalle sat at the table, shoulders touching, and he quickly spread out two dozen files.

"This is everyone D.C. could come up with who might have a connection to southern California. We'll take them one at a time and see if any ring a bell."

"I don't understand why we're wasting time on this. Political terrorists don't usually ask for money." Why was she being so argumentative? She tried to soften her tone. "Aren't they usually after something less tangible, a change in U.S. foreign policy or getting people released from prison? Something like that?"

"In Italy and South America, terrorists finance their operations with bank robberies and kidnappings. There's a certain symmetry to it that appeals to them, the establishment participating in its own destruction." As LaSalle leaned forward to flip open a folder, his thigh pressed against hers, sending a shiver through her, but he seemed not to notice. "Adolpho Cisneros, from Peru. A *Sindero Luminoso,* Shining Path, bomb expert and certified psychopath. He entered the country illegally three months ago. An informant claims he's in Hollywood, supposedly planning to stage an attack on a movie studio. They see Hollywood as a particularly egregious example of mindless cultural exploitation." He smiled unexpectedly and leaned back. "Sounds like pretty good thinking to me. Maybe I'll join up with him if we ever find where he's hiding." He drew out two pictures of an intense, bearded young man, one a grainy full-length shot evidently taken with a long-range surveillance camera. "Familiar?"

Ellen looked closely at it. "No. I'm sure not."

He flipped open another folder and read from the stapled dossier. "Mohammed Razar, a.k.a. Mo Salami. U.S.C. engineering grad, secretly runs a group he calls the Ninth Battalion. As far as we know his battalion has three people . . ."

Fifteen minutes later they were done. Ellen had recognized none of them. Wasted time. "Sorry," she said, looking at her watch and pushing her chair back. "I wish I could have identified someone. Not that it would have solved anything. We still wouldn't know where he is."

LaSalle stacked the folders in a neat pile. "It's not a waste of time. I think we can eliminate terrorism once and for all, which gets the director off my back, and concentrate on the alternative."

"Which is?"

"A nut."

"But you don't believe that either."

"I guess not. I guess I think we've got a very bright guy here who knows exactly what he's doing. I think he likes playing with us. And killing children. I'm going to enjoy seeing him in prison."

"Let's not forget our main priority, Matt: I want the kids back, safe and sound. I don't really care that much what happens to him."

LaSalle smiled ruefully. "My dad would have a fit if he heard you say that."

"Is he a cop?"

"Was. In Seattle. An old school homicide dick. A local legend. Had the highest apprehension rate in the city. He was like an old-time bounty hunter. He'd come home after one of his goofs was sentenced and slap a little decal of a skull on his closet door. Did his thirty-and-out and retired at fifty-two, the door and half the bedroom wall covered with skulls. Now he takes it easy, fishes a lot, watches TV, listens to his short-wave. It's a good life."

Something made Ellen say, "But not what you want for yourself."

He shook his head. "He was happy being on the street, running down villains. I've been at this twelve years now. I think it's time to move on."

Ellen smiled again, aware of his closeness, breathing in his cologne, not the cold musky odor so many men seemed to think enhanced their sexuality but a clean, ice-like fragrance, the way emeralds would smell if they had a scent. She felt surprised at how comfortable she was with him, even pressed together in this warm claustrophobic room, as though she'd known him for years. She looked into his face. "What exactly does 'moving on' mean? Getting a promotion? Leaving the Bureau?"

He remained silent, staring at her from startlingly clear eyes, then without warning bent over, his lips touching hers. Seemingly against her will, her mouth opened, her body tensed, and her tongue darted against his as she leaned into him, timidly at first, then with a sudden fierceness, as though trying to inhale every atom of his being. She felt his hand on the back of her neck as the breath rushed out of her, his fingers warm and hard on her flesh, before he drew back. Her palms pressed against his shirtfront, and she could feel his heart beating on her fingertips. Smiling, his face surprising in its unexpected gentleness, he said, "Does that mean you'll have dinner with me?"

She felt a rising of alarm and confusion and a warm tingle on her skin that made the hairs on her forearm come erect as she pulled her hands from his chest. A voice that must have been hers said, "I guess so," but all the time warning bells were going off in her mind, and she thought, My God, what am I doing, what's happening? She wanted to run as a wonderfully terrifying loss of control took possession of her. She wanted him to put his arms around her, hold her against his body and kiss her. For the first time in years she was truly scared. Knowing she sounded strange, she said, "I feel stupid." A tremor of hysteria rang in her voice. "I mean. . . . I don't know. . . . I don't know what I'm saying."

He laughed as he stared at her, but there seemed to be confusion in his voice also. "You're saying you'll have dinner with me."

Ellen shook her head back and forth like someone climbing out of a swimming pool. "I just met you. I don't even know you." And I don't want to have dinner with you, she thought but didn't say.

"But you can trust my extraordinarily high moral character or I'd have long ago been drummed out of the corps," he joked. "You know how the Bureau is. Only straight shooters—"

"But—"

"I've never been married. I like soul food and sixties rock and Agatha Christie. Want more? How about, Loves long walks on the beach, art museums, and candlelight dinners?"

She shook her head and laughed. A cop with a sense of humor. How long had it been since she had seen that? If ever. But she liked it, liked it a lot. Still laughing, she said, "I think you're being more creative than honest."

"You're right. But it sounds good. Actually, I hate the beach and want to see what I'm eating. The Agatha Christie part was true."

Ellen sat back and gazed at him, her heart returning to normal. "Give me the thirty-second story, then, the one that got you through the first round of F.B.I. interviews."

"Okay. Degree in public administration, B plus average, meaning I'm moderately but not excessively bright. Third-string tight end on the football team, with a total of fourteen minutes playing time in four years. Meaning I'm big but not too fast. Want to go as far as I can in the agency, meaning assistant director, and willing to do the dirty jobs if it means I can do the sexy ones later."

"Is this one of the dirty jobs?"

"This is definitely high risk. I'm here because of my experience, but no one else in the office wanted to join me. Charley came up from San Diego because he's a friend and because he doesn't give a shit about his reputation. But if this thing blows up, more of the kids die or the kidnapper gets away with twenty million, it's going to damage some reps for a long time. Mine especially. Screw up in a public way, make the Bureau look bad, and you get sent to Idaho or Mississippi or, if they really don't like you, Detroit. I'm willing to risk it."

"Every hour that goes by, the more likely it is more kids are going to die," Ellen said.

"That's why I want to concentrate on the mines. Everything points north. The mines or that abandoned airfield."

The door suddenly popped open, and Vince Garibaldi stuck his head in. He looked at them in turn, his face surprised, then going red with embarrassment. Finally, his voice strained, he said, "D.C.'s on the phone, Matt. They said it's urgent."

Ellen was already on her feet, pulse racing, feeling almost guilty, as though she had been caught in some horrible act. "I've got to get to the high school. I don't want to be late." Brushing past Garibaldi, she hurried out of the room, her legs feeling as though they couldn't support her body.

LaSalle sank back in his chair and stared at the younger man, who stiffened perceptibly under the hard gaze; after a moment, he stood up and gave Garibaldi a pat on the shoulder as he left the room.

> **"A moment's insight is sometimes worth a life's experiences."**
>
> —*Oliver Wendell Holmes, 1859*

Chaos! The word hummed with manic intensity in DeVries's consciousness. He was still holding the girl from below, her clothes strewn on the floor at his feet, but his mind had begun rapidly abstracting from the concrete.

If ever he came to write the history of his life (and almost certainly he would, people would want to know), pride of place would have to be given to the day, so clearly remembered, that Chaos came rushing like an epiphany into his life. It had been in Riverside, in the drearily modern university library reserve book room, DeVries taking a break from his inquiries into F.B.I. tactics by seeking out undiscovered aphorisms. In a text on Greek history, he stumbled across white-bearded Hesiod, that most ancient of philosophers ("Often an entire city has suffered because of the evil of one man." Yes!).

But it was Hesiod's cosmology and not his philosophy that had given Lowell the heart-leaping thrill of discovery.

Chaos, the Greek wrote, was the oldest of the gods.

Chaos existed before anything.

Yes, DeVries had thought. And the idea had begun to take form, building and building in his mind.

Chaos.

Disorder.

Dis–order.

His mind had begun to sing, and he'd bent forward excitedly, knowing that he was on the verge of something crucial, and read further. Before anything there was not nothing but a disorganized something.

First, chaos.

Wasn't that also what Genesis said?

He'd pushed from his chair, hurriedly found a Bible on the shelves, and, still standing, read:

"And the earth was without form, and void; and darkness was upon the face of the deep."

Only then did God create heaven and earth.

First chaos, the void, then structure. Order. Things.

Scientists, too—physicists, cosmologists, astronomers—saw order as resulting from the creation of the universe, recognized that there was a cosmic skeleton-like foundation of meaning that underlay the seeming randomness of space and time. With the "big bang" (God, he loved that phrase), time began, and with time, order. But until then . . .

Until then, time and order made no sense.

That was the inexorable progression of the world, of everything: from uncertainty to certainty, from chaos to structure. Only then could the slow, seemingly inevitable dissolution of entropy, the immutable second law, begin. It was as though God had drawn a steel curtain across the formless, meaningless, prehistory of time, pushing chaos behind it and proclaiming: All on this side is Order.

And the world moved in that instant, in that immeasurably tiny speck of time, from disorder to order, from formlessness and chaos to organization and thing-ness.

But behind the curtain Chaos raged.

Our lives, the lives of every thing that has ever lived, have existed only within this realm, the realm of meaning, of time and structure. All we know and can know lies on this, our, side of the curtain.

His excitement had mounted so quickly it had been difficult to remain still. So many things had suddenly become explicable, burst into a bright, blinding clarity that had made him weak with knowledge. He'd sat again in his chair, feeling his heart racing, remembering Weir droning on endlessly about ordered, authoritarian personalities, those people who demand a disproportionate certainty in their lives. They were the backbone of Fascist and other totalitarian regimes, he'd said. They resisted newness, change, difference, ambiguity. Police officers are often like this. And judges and accountants and architects and . . .

"Psychologists?" he'd wondered aloud and smiled.

"Frequently," Weir had admitted.

Weir had thought that Lowell, too, had fit this, "description" was what he'd said but DeVries had known he meant, "pathology." DeVries was, Weir had felt certain, an overly structured personality, an authoritarian. And this would make life more difficult for him as an adult in an increasingly ambiguous world.

But, DeVries had seen with instant and complete understanding, we all are authoritarian, bound by natural law to structure and order. God drew the curtain: order on one side, confusion on the other. And not just in the outside world, the world of observable matter, but in our minds, too, this same terrible division existed, the same absolute curtaining off that only a few seers and shamans and lunatics have grasped. Just below consciousness lies the roiling turbulence of disorder and meaninglessness and un-thingness. It takes all our psychic energy to keep it there, to not allow it to bubble to the surface. We tire ourselves, relentlessly but unconsciously, throwing on layer upon layer of defenses, building the ramparts ever higher, hoping to keep our aware world, the real, separate from the unaware and unawarable because we know if we slip just once and allow the chaos below to seep through, we will go mad.

This is the great secret we are born with, the single, horrible kernel of absolute truth that was stamped with burning brands into our primeval DNA the day life began. There is a curtain beyond which disorder is all *(and darkness was upon the face of the deep)* and where we can know and understand nothing.

God's curtain.

All I need do, he'd thought with a thrill he felt even now in his toes and arms and to the depths of his soul, a thrill he knew he could never fully explain in his memoirs, a thrill that gave him an erection like he had never experienced, is rip a tiny hole in the curtain, loosen the fabric of time, and Chaos will rush in.

He'd sunk back into his chair and smiled up at the tubular white lights stretching across the library ceiling. Chaos.

And now, months later, for the first time in a long, long, time, as he stared down at the soft nude form of six-year-old Sara trying to twist out of his grasp and felt the storm of passion in his mind, he wondered at the cost of his knowledge.

8:55 P.M.

Trying desperately not to think of Matthew LaSalle, trying to force away the lingering sense of his lips and tongue, the taste of him, Ellen stared at the assembled reporters in front of her. "You're going to have to quiet down or we'll forget the whole thing." She had steeled herself for an angry outburst, so when it rose at once from the crowd packed into the high school cafeteria, she was ready. She stood silently, not moving, waiting for quiet. But again her mind wouldn't allow her to relax, taunting her instead with visions drawn from that dangerous corner of memory where she tried to bury everything threatening or uncomfortable. Why do I act so strangely around him? she thought. Just being in the same room made her stupid. But she felt so different when he was near, felt an awakening of passion that she hadn't experienced since first meeting Pete. God, she realized: More than ten years ago. Remember that? Remember how you ached so for him? Has it been there all these years, this flame waiting to be rekindled? Halfway through my thirties is that spark still alive? Then why do I feel so embarrassed just thinking about it?

The noise from the reporters brought her back to the present, and she repeated her earlier warning, this time adding a threat. "Local TV and print reporters, the networks, and CNN. That's all we have room for. The rest of you can watch from TVs out here. Anyone gives me any trouble, I'll have him thrown out." Again the moans and shouts rose. Without another word, Ellen turned and walked directly to the library, where Louie Sharperson was standing guard. "I mean it," she told the overweight policeman. "The networks and the locals. Anyone else tries to get in, you kick them out. They give you any trouble, arrest them. I'll back you up."

Sharperson sighed and pushed back the cap on his huge round head. "I'm supposed to be going home, Ellen. I've done two full shifts. Come on, give me a break."

"Don't fight me, Louie. Thirty minutes. Then maybe you can take off until morning. Here they come. Start checking I.D.s. I want you to write down the name and affiliation of everyone in this room."

"What am I supposed to write it on?" he asked with sarcasm.

She put a hand on his shoulder and looked into his eyes. "Louie, this is a school. Find a piece of paper."

Reporters and technicians were noisily funneling toward them down a corridor from the cafeteria beyond. Like the last day of school in reverse, Ellen thought with a twist of irony and guessed the building had never witnessed a rush into the library before.

She turned and crossed hurriedly through the empty, booklined room, past the circulation desk, and into the librarian's small, cluttered office, where she had earlier deposited the parents; they were sitting stiffly and silently in folding metal chairs, hands on thighs, and looked up sharply as she came in. There were four of them: Mrs. Torres, the young Mexican woman she had seen at the school earlier; Willard Scranton, a huge, unkempt man in his fifties; and two women she didn't know, both crying softly.

Ellen closed the door quietly behind her. "When the cameras are set up, I'll take you out," she said and tried to sound soothing. Don't give them any instructions, Exley had cautioned her. It has to be spontaneous, from the heart. She smiled wanly at them and kept her voice soft. "Just say whatever you feel, let the kidnapper know you want your children back."

"Emily's going to go into convulsions without her medication," Mr. Scranton said with a catch to his voice. "He has to let her go."

"Then let him know that. Maybe it'll help."

Holding a crucifix to her breast, Mrs. Torres began to pray in Spanish, her body swaying from side to side on the chair. Ellen felt suddenly overwhelmed. These people were looking to her for help, desperate for some solace, some hint that everything would be all right. How can I give them advice? she thought. There was nothing she could say. Nothing at all. All at once, she felt an urge to flee; she didn't want to feel their pain, to be a part of their suffering. There's nothing I can do to make it better for you.

Feeling guilty and a little upset with herself, she hurried back to the library. "How much longer?" she asked, and a technician glanced up from the microphone he was adjusting. "Ten minutes."

But it was twenty before everyone was ready. Ellen returned to the office and brought out the parents. A lectern had been set on a wooden table in front of a bookcase stuffed haphazardly with books. Before approaching the table and its aggressive, thrusting microphones, Ellen said to the reporters, "This is not a press conference. It's an opportunity for the parents to make a direct appeal to the person who has their children. Please let them do it their way, in their own words. And let them take as much time as they need. Do not ask any questions."

A few scattered grumbles came from the three or four dozen reporters and technicians crowded among the tables and chairs in the room. *They don't believe it will do any good,* Ellen realized suddenly. *This is just an opportunity to amass twenty seconds of tape for the eleven o'clock news. They're going through the motions; they think the kids are dead.*

The nuts don't though. The weirdos and crazies, loved so by the California media, had converged on Las Cruces like grasshoppers in August. Psychics "saw" the children alive in a "white place" or near water or wandering alone in a large house. A man calling himself Xylan-8 said the children were taken as objects of study by extraterrestrials and would soon be released. An L.A. TV station hired a channeler to search the netherworld for information on their whereabouts; they would have the results at eleven.

The world gone mad, Ellen thought. *A Gresham's law of sanity.*

The appeal was being broadcast live on a Palm Springs station, then by satellite to the world, so they had to wait for a countdown given by the station's field reporter. Ellen led Emily Scranton's father to the lectern, then moved to the side. When the countdown reached "one," she nodded at him.

Willard Scranton opened his mouth but said nothing. He had masses of wild, unruly red hair jutting out from his head, a face with seemingly dozens of planes and angles and shadows, and large dark eyes sunk deep within cavernous sockets. He looked, Ellen thought, like a television version of a mad scientist. Again, his mouth dropped open and his eyes misted. When finally he spoke, the words trailed out haltingly:

"I want to ask whoever took my daughter to please, please let her go. She has severe epilepsy and she needs to be given daily doses of Tegrotol. If you don't release her, she'll die. If there's something you want from me, something you want me to do, please call and tell me. But let my little girl go. Please—"

He couldn't go on and turned and stepped rapidly from the lectern. Ellen nodded to one of the mothers, who walked up to the microphones. "I want my baby back," the woman said in a weak voice, and Ellen suddenly sensed Willard Scranton standing next to her, a vague, silent presence trembling with emotion. A chill shot through her when his huge hand took hers and pressed, and he began to cry. She was overwhelmed with emotion and angry with Willard Scranton for forcing his grief on her and with herself for reacting this way. Again, she felt like fleeing, running from here as fast as she could.

The woman at the lectern was making an eloquent appeal for the release of the children. They were burdened with unusual and often debilitating handicaps to begin with, she said. Life was already a constant struggle for them, one they were just beginning to master. It was cruel to add to their problems another, perhaps insurmountable, difficulty. They weren't like other children, they wouldn't bounce back easily. Whatever it was the kidnapper wanted, it wasn't worth twenty-seven lives.

Every parent in the world must be saying that now, Ellen thought. It's not worth twenty-seven lives. Or one. When the woman finished, Ellen indicated to Mrs. Torres that it was her turn. The young woman looked at her with frightened eyes, looked at the reporters, then stepped rapidly to the lectern. As she was speaking in Spanish, Louie Sharperson came up behind Ellen. "Bobby Muledeer's out in the hall. He needs to see you. Says it's urgent."

With a sense of relief, Ellen dropped Willard Scranton's hand and hurried out with Sharperson. Bobby Muledeer, in a rumpled, sweat-stained uniform, was standing with his hands on his hips, looking impatient as he shuffled from foot to foot. Sharperson shut the door, abruptly blocking out the noise from the library.

"The Chief sent me," Muledeer said. "One of the kids has been released. She's at the hospital. I'll take you there in the unit."

In the patrol car, siren screaming as they raced through town, Muledeer said loudly, "Somebody called the radio station twenty minutes ago and said we could find one of the kidnapped kids at the 7-Eleven on Baseline. They called us instead of going public with it. Lockheart went over, and sure enough, there she was, nude, in the field behind the store."

"Nude? Was she raped?"

"Doesn't appear to be. Doesn't appear to be hurt at all."

"Who called? The kidnapper? Or someone who recognized the child?"

"The kidnapper. He said it was a gift. 'A gift to the city.' Some kind of gift, huh? Kill one, release one."

"What's the child's name?"

Muledeer slowed as he neared an intersection, twisting his head rapidly back and forth as cars jerked to the side of the road, then gunned the black-and-white through. "She's not talking, but they think it's the Torres kid, Sara Torres."

"Jesus," Ellen said to herself. Even before the mother made her appeal the child had been released. So the kidnapper let her go for some other reason. Just one child. Why? And why that one?

Rounding a corner at high speed, Muledeer said, "We also got the lab results on the dead kid's clothes. They picked up traces of a cheap synthetic carpet fiber, dirt, grease, and motor oil."

"He was transported in the killer's trunk, then."

"Right. No surprise, I guess. But they also picked up slight traces of red chalk and drywall dust."

Ellen's head snapped in his direction. "A construction worker! They use red chalk to mark plumb lines and cut-marks."

"Right. Jesus Christ!" He pulled across the double yellow line to pass a silver BMW that refused to move over. "Idiots! No one respects sirens anymore. Fuckin' BMW drivers! Anyway, Paul's pretty excited about it. How much construction can there be in Las Cruces right now? Kinda narrows things down."

"Doesn't have to be someone local though. Could be someone from L.A. or anywhere else." But it was a start, Ellen thought, something to work with, and she could feel her excitement mounting.

Muledeer reached over and switched off the siren as he approached the medical center at the edge of Old Town. As they passed the parking lot, Ellen could see the army medical team setting up its mobile hospital in two huge olive drab tents. The green-clad soldiers looked like ghosts as they moved swiftly in and out of the vague circles of light thrown by the mercury-vapor street lamps. Muledeer whipped the Chevy Caprice into the Emergency entrance, screeching to a halt next to an orange and white ambulance backed up to the door. As Ellen reached for the door handle, he said, "Hold on a minute."

Something in his voice made her feel uneasy as she turned back to him.

He looked torn as he twisted in his seat and held the steering wheel with both hands. The car seemed suddenly very quiet. "Look, Ellen, I've known you and Paul almost all my life, right? I mean since you and me was little. And Paul and me have been buddies since I used to go snake hunting with him. Remember how we used to come home with a sack full of rattlers and cook 'em up and all the little kids would come by and stare?"

Ellen's hands felt sticky. "What's your point, Bobby?"

Muledeer's eyes shifted away from her face as he stared

out the windshield. "Well, it's none of my business, but I don't want Paul getting hurt. You either."

Ellen's voice hardened. "I don't think I like where you're going with this."

He looked back at her. "Well, someone said they saw you and the F.B.I. guy . . ." He raced on, a note of belligerence in his voice as he saw her face go red. "Look, I'm not saying it's true. I'm just telling you what I heard. I figured you'd want to know. If it was me, I would."

Ellen swore and jerked on the door handle, stepping onto the asphalt just as a panel truck from a San Diego television station raced in behind them. "Damn it," she muttered and slammed her door furiously. She wheeled on Muledeer, who was climbing out of his side of the cruiser. "How'd they find out?"

The patrolman threw the truck a dismissive glance. "It's what they do, Ellen. Find things out. Probably bribed someone in hospital admissions or heard it on a scanner."

Ellen swore to herself as she strode rapidly toward the automatic doors which flew open noisily in front of her, and into the refrigerated air of the hospital with its heavy overlay of death and disease. Already angry, she felt the skin on her arms grow cold with rage. She hated hospitals—the stench of medicine and disinfectant, the wheeled carts and gurneys clattering noisily down tiled hallways, the edgy disembodied pagings and announcements that filled the air from hidden speakers. Mostly, though, she loathed the stupefying artificiality of everything—the childishly bright colors of the walls, the starched smiles of the nurses, the determined cheerfulness of the flowers and stuffed animals and balloons that seemed to be everywhere, as though appearances alone could convince people they weren't sick. Irrational, stupid fears, she lectured herself, childish phobias; but the feeling never went away—a tightness clutching at her heart and a knot as big as a fist in the back of her neck. It was foolish, she knew, ridiculous. If it hadn't been for doctors, Denise would certainly have died. But if it hadn't been for doctors and nurses and hospitals and the

maddening way in which care had been wrenched from
humans and handed to machines, Denise wouldn't have
hovered so near death in the first place. Ellen's mother had
been in a hospital just once in her life, when Ellen's younger
sister had been born, and her grandfather had refused to
return after his stroke. Maybe it's a genetic aversion then,
Ellen thought half-seriously, an inherited trait handed down
from generation to generation like a family totem. Since
coming back to Las Cruces, she had been in here exactly
twice, both times to interview people who had been in automobile accidents. Both of them had died.

Quickening her pace, she glanced over her shoulder at
Muledeer hurrying to keep up with her. "Goddamn it, stay
at the door, Bobby." Her voice was angrier than it should
have been, but she could do nothing about it. "I don't care
how you do it, but keep the reporters outside. I'll decide
what to do about them later."

Muledeer nodded glumly and Ellen half-sprinted to the
admissions desk and flashed her I.D. "Where's the little girl
that was brought in?"

Hearing her voice, Paul stepped from a curtained area off
to the side. "Ellen." He held the curtain back as she hurriedly entered, then replaced it. The girl was in a bed, talking to a Spanish-speaking nurse as a man, evidently a doctor,
stood by, waiting for her comments to be translated into
English. Even in Spanish her voice sounded unclear, and
the nurse had to bend near her mouth to hear.

"Drugged?" Ellen asked.

The man reached across the bed to shake hands. "Dr.
Powers," he said, introducing himself. "She doesn't appear
to be drugged or harmed at all. I take it she doesn't speak
much anyway. But I don't think she's at all the worse for
wear. It's a miracle. Especially since she was nude. We naturally assumed . . ."

"He let her go? Just like that?"

"A gift," Paul said; by habit, it seemed, he had taken her
hand, and she could feel tension transfer like electricity
from his body to hers. It's the lab results, she thought; they

had something to work with finally, and Paul wanted to move on it as soon as possible.

Ellen asked, "What's she said about the person who took her or where she was kept?"

Paul's hand moved to her shoulder and began to rub. "She told us she was scared by a clown and put in a dark place. The teacher was there, and it was very noisy."

"What teacher?"

"That's what the kids call the bus driver, the Sowell woman."

Ellen said to the nurse, "Ask her how she got to the 7-Eleven."

The nurse looked up at her and shook her head. "I tried. All she says is 'a man.' A man took her clothes away, then drove her in a big car." She looked at the girl a moment and then back at Ellen. "She's very, very frightened. Her heart's going like crazy."

"Does she know what the man looks like?"

The nurse shrugged. "A man. An Anglo."

Ellen said to Paul, "Are you sure it's the Torres child?"

"She says her name is Sara. We'll have the mom come in, but I figured we'd better let her finish her TV appeal."

Ellen said, "I'll radio Louie and have him bring her over here. Maybe she can get something out of the girl."

An orderly came in with a plate of food, but the little girl looked frightened and shrank back as he placed it on the tray next to the bed.

Paul stepped toward the curtain, maneuvering Ellen with him, and lowered his voice so the others couldn't hear. "Bobby tell you about the lab report?"

She nodded without looking at him, thinking of what else Bobby had had to say. "A construction worker. Carpenter or painter, maybe."

"We're going to move on this as fast as we can. I called Helen Jorgenson as soon as I heard. She's in charge of issuing building permits. She said there's not much going on in town, the economy the way it is. But she's coming in to her office to make me a list of projects. Should be done in an hour or so. I told her to contact the county, too, have them work their side. I'll organize everything in the city. We'll check out each site, get a list of everyone who's worked on it. Then find out where the hell they were this morning at seven-thirty."

"You have the manpower for that?"

"We'll find it. Bring in more feds if necessary. You know how I look forward to that. But we've got to move fast. It's the only thing we have."

"No need to visit the sites, Paul. Just find out who the general contractor is on each one. It'll be listed on the building permit. Have someone call him at home, wake him up, get him to fax us a list of everyone who's worked on the project. Tell them to get down to their office if they need to. We can't wait until morning. You can even narrow it down more than that. They have to have an inspector sign off for each phase of the work. We know this guy was there during drywall installation, so you can ignore any project not to that point yet. That should eliminate at least half the work going on in town."

Paul's face was tense. "Let me see how many Helen comes up with. If there's not too many, maybe Zach can handle it. Where's that F.B.I. guy?"

"Who? LaSalle?" Her voice was abrupt.

Paul nodded, and Ellen said, "How would I know? Probably the Civic Center."

Muledeer hurried up to them from the corridor. "Half the reporters in town are outside, Ellen. The kidnapper called the TV station and newspapers and told them what he'd done."

Ellen's face flushed with anger. "Damn it! Don't let 'em in, Bobby. We'll issue a written statement later." She turned at once to Paul, her voice trembling. "What the hell's he doing, calling the press like that?"

"Having fun," Paul guessed. "Making life interesting for us. Can't figure any other reason."

8. *Showtime*

DeVries banged the door open and hurried down the ramp, a video camera held loosely in his right hand. The noise in the underground room, muted until then, rose again in a sudden cacophonous wail that made his nerves jump.

His eyes darted around at the children. Most of them were sprawled on the floor, trying to sleep; a girl had slipped from a wheelchair and appeared to be comatose; a boy was beating his right hand against the floor. Linda was on the other side of the room. She spun around, her face going white with fear.

"I told you to keep some order in here," he said loudly.

Linda fell to her knees, hurriedly dropping the nail file behind Eric who had fallen asleep. "What do you want? Where's Sara? What did you do to her?"

DeVries glanced up the ramp to make sure the door was closed, then said, "Get over here. Now!"

"No!" The word blurted out, defiant though unplanned. But it gave her courage and she added, "I'm not going to do it. I'm not going to do anything you want!"

Still holding the camera, DeVries reached down for the nearest child, a boy about seven, and yanked him to his feet. Then with a furious fling of his arm, he slammed the boy face-first into the wall. The child howled with pain and sank to the floor; blood surged from his nose, and his forehead turned red and purple.

Linda leapt to her feet. "Stop it, stop it!" Her hands flailed the air, as if she could halt him from twenty feet away.

"Get over here," he said again, his face calm and his voice without emotion.

Stepping uneasily around the children on the floor, Linda came slowly up to him. He was smiling at her, looking unperturbed, still dressed in a suit, and she thought, Oh, God, he's going to kill me now.

His gaze left her face, wandered around the room, briefly studying the children.

"Where's Sara?" Linda demanded again. "What did you do to her?"

DeVries turned in Linda's direction and again a smile came to his face. "I let her go."

"I don't believe you."

DeVries ignored her, staring around the room. Then he said, "We'll do it right here. Push that wheelchair near the bottom of the ramp. Then stand next to it."

"Why?"

"Just do it!" he snapped, tired of being asked to explain himself. He reached down and yanked up the boy he'd slammed into the wall; the child was whimpering, and his face was covered in tears and blood. Effortlessly, DeVries dragged him over to Linda. Dropping the boy at her feet, he slapped her hard across the face. "Get the kid in the wheelchair!"

"No!" she said and managed to keep from crying although her face burned with pain.

DeVries raised his arm to hit her again, then said, "Would you rather I get him?"

Linda opened her mouth, started to say something, but changed her mind. Stifling a sob, she stepped over to the wheelchair.

DeVries again stared around the room, thinking, looking at their faces, making up his mind. "Ah, Tiffany." He went over to where the mute girl was standing, knelt to one knee, and said, "You remember me, don't you, your new friend?" While talking, he quickly untied her shoes and pulled them off, then pulled off her shorts and T-shirt. The girl stared at him but didn't object.

Pushing the wheelchair, Linda saw what he had done and screamed. "What are you doing?"

DeVries slipped the girl's panties off. Leaving the camera on the floor, he took her by the hand and led her to the wheelchair. "Lie down, Tiffany, here—" He turned to Linda. "Don't move," he warned her and quickly grabbed three more children, including the girl who had suffered a seizure, arranging them on the floor in front of the wheelchair. Most of them were trembling with fear and moaning and crying.

DeVries picked up the camera, retreated halfway up the ramp, then stopped. "It's time to further channel their thinking," he said and grinned. "In case their minds begin to wander, we want them to remember where they've seen this sort of thing before. Would you like to sing for all the nice folks watching? Let me start: *Ring around the rosie, pocket full of posies . . .*"

He held the camera to his eye, humming silently to himself, *"Ashes, ashes,"* as he began taping the small group: Linda, the boy in the wheelchair, Tiffany, the other children. Almost everyone in the room was wailing and moaning, and Linda was pleading with him, "Please don't do this. Let us out of here." He smiled and thought brightly, *All fall down!*

After two minutes, he swung the camera lens away from the group to the comatose girl who had slipped from her wheelchair, and let it linger. There was an oozing of vomit near her mouth.

"Perfect," he said after several seconds, snapping the camera off. "Perfect, perfect, perfect!"

Linda and the children hadn't moved from where they were. DeVries cast one final dismissive glance at them, then hurried up the ramp without a word.

"Don't go!" Linda screamed and rushed toward him. But the door slammed shut.

Linda sank to the floor at the bottom of the ramp and let her back sag against the wall. After a moment, she drew her knees up and hung her head. She was so tired. This shouldn't be happening, she thought. I tried so hard, so hard. I built my life day by day, layer by layer, making something of myself, and now he's taking it all away.

I'm not going to let him do it, she told herself determinedly. I'm not going to let him take my life away.

But she sat without moving.

DeVries slipped the lock onto the clasp and snapped it shut. Now to deliver the tape. He wondered what Ellen Camacho would think of it. Will she see an intimation of her future in its three minutes of *cinema verité*? Is she perceptive enough to sense the truth? No, no, no. She couldn't. No one could. Not even you, Dr. Walter Exley, expert on criminal behavior. In your excitement, you'll take every wrong turn I offer, including this one. He smiled, his anticipation mounting rapidly, rushing almost out of control. You're going to love it, Doctor, something to cast your theories over as these next twenty-five hours tick away. But your mind works with such predictable linearity that you needn't agonize over meaning: Who has done this sort of thing before? What precedents, what past cases, do we have? Nothing is new, nothing at all. History is prologue, the seeds of present behavior are sown in the past, every crime is like some other crime. Punch in the details, search the data base. What have we?

They have, DeVries thought with a smile, Charles Singleton II.

10:45 P.M.

Feeling tense and expectant, anxious for Whitehorse to finish the list of building projects so they could start questioning workers, Matthew LaSalle strode nervously around the unfamiliar Civic Center building, through the squad room and tiny jail, across the eerily empty two-story lobby to the civilian side with its warren of overly neat, overly small offices, all closed and dark for the night, then back to the police department and its crowded corridors and ringing phones. Finally, after twenty minutes, he pushed on the heavy back door and found himself in the abrupt silence of the employee parking lot. It was still stifling hot, probably over ninety, he thought, but a barely perceptible breeze was rising out of the west.

Rubbing at the knot of tension tightening painfully in his neck, he looked up at the sky through the clear desert air and blinked in surprise. There were more stars than he'd seen since he was a child, an unexpected bright, glitter-rich blanket that burned with the same sort of intensity he remembered seeing on summer nights so many years ago in eastern Washington. Closing his eyes, he took in a deep breath and felt an odd calmness flow through his body as a distant memory shook loose—eight years old, standing alone in the huge empty field behind Grandma Lynn's house, hands jammed in pockets, staring into the star-filled night as crickets chirped at his feet. But the memory and the calm faded as he felt Ellen's kiss as real as if it were happening now, felt the way she responded to him, smelled again the faint whiff of perfume she was wearing. Damn it! he told himself angrily, snap out of it. He didn't want to get mixed up with this woman, now or ever. He couldn't afford that sort of involvement. Especially with a high-profile, high-intensity investigation swirling around their heads. Nothing good could come from it. Nothing! But even if this case were not going on, he wasn't looking to get involved with someone, not at thirty-three, especially not while stationed in Los Angeles, working out of the Federal Building on Wilshire Boulevard, right in the center of the city's rich and beautiful. He hadn't believed his luck when he started working there. All he had to do was walk outside at lunchtime and stare in amazement at the legions of women passing by: aspiring actresses, *real* actresses, U.C.L.A. students, Beverly Hills housewives . . .

So what was he doing falling for a cop he'd just met? Hormones, Charley said; thinking with your crotch. Hell, yeah, partly. She's pretty, more than pretty, in an exotic, un-L.A. sort of way: glossy black hair, huge dark eyes, high cheekbones, but not the thin Audrey Hepburn cheekbones; these were round and prominent and smooth as polished flint. Marvelous full red lips with a touch of electricity that made the blood race all the way to his toes. But five minutes on Wilshire and he'd see twenty just as good.

So what the hell's the big deal?

This just wasn't the time for a blossoming romance. It didn't look right; even Vinnie Garibaldi was giving him odd looks. And especially not with Ellen's boyfriend or fiancé or whatever he was, working with them both. It would be better to wait until he was back in Los Angeles. But how would that work out? Not very well, not with Whitehorse here while he was away.

He wondered what she was doing right now, if she was thinking about him.

Christ, forget it! Get back to the kidnapping. Stop dreaming.

A helicopter appeared unexpectedly overhead, a massive spotlight snapping on and splashing the parking lot with a sudden circle of illumination that washed rapidly over the cars and asphalt and up the side of the building. A TV station, he thought with a burst of irritation and flattened back against the door, out of sight. The copter circled noisily for a minute, not more than eighty feet off the ground, its spotlight racing through the lot, hoping for something, anything, to film, before abruptly taking off, probably for the high school.

Hell, drop it! Drop it! Matthew again warned himself. Use your brain. Don't let anything develop. You can't jeopardize your career. Young Matt LaSalle was one of the Bureau's golden boys, on the "fast track" as they called it in D.C., a "comer," due for a promotion any time now. The Assistant S.A.C. in L.A., a fifty-year-old careerist who had long ago topped out, called him Johnny Rocket, on his way up, up, up, and wondered if he'd been born with a silver G-Man badge in his mouth. It was the sort of petty resentment Matt had learned to accept without complaint or comment. Do your job well, get a reputation, and the mediocrities are going to feel threatened and start clawing at your back. It wouldn't be any different at General Motors or the Miami

P.D. or the post office. But he *was* on his way up and he liked it, liked being thought of as a star. And he knew—and knew he wasn't supposed to—that his next assignment was to be an administrative job in D.C. to give him management and budgetary experience. Somehow they'd gotten it into their heads that if he wasn't brought into headquarters soon, he'd quit and go to one of the big industrial security agencies, where he could double his salary overnight. But it had never occurred to him to leave. He had committed to the F.B.I. and would stick to it. Besides, he loved what he was doing and didn't want to spend the rest of his life trying to find out who was stealing Corn Flake data from Kelloggs.

What's Ellen doing? he wondered.

He felt someone pushing the door on the other side and moved to see Vince Garibaldi standing in the light.

Garibaldi's face was as expressionless as a Noh mask. Poor Vinnie, he thought, just a year out of college and already unhappy with what he's seeing of the bureau and his mentors and probably the world in general. Real life ain't what it's cracked up to be, is it my young friend?

Garibaldi hesitated just a second, then half-smiled, perhaps relieved that LaSalle was alone. "Charley's looking for you, Matt."

He smiled back and put his hand on the young man's shoulder as though to reassure him that truth and beauty and goodness and the other eternal verities he had learned about in school, though rarely glimpsed, indeed still existed, even in the F.B.I., and followed him inside.

10:46 P.M.

Paul Whitehorse felt a growing excitement as he sat at his desk, going through the mass of information Helen Jorgenson had ready for him when he returned from the hospital. Not only the location of all ninety-seven current building projects in town but the original permits, cost estimates, blueprints, and signed inspector slips for each phase of the project. By going through the inspections, he was able to eliminate fifty-four that had not progressed to the drywall stage. Eleven more were not planning to use drywall. That left thirty-two projects—all single-family homes—that had reached that point and been signed off. Of these, only twenty-one general contractors were involved. Helen had jotted their home phone numbers on the permits. He glanced at his watch. Not quite eleven. He'd have to find some people to call the contractors as soon as possible and get a list of employees, then get to work checking them out. He could sense the adrenaline pulsing in his veins. They were onto something, finally. He could feel it, the excitement licking at his flesh like flames. Thirty-two single-family homes, he thought. How many workers could that possibly be? Two or three hundred, maybe; hell, could be half that many. So, now to call the contractors. He wanted a list of employees by sun-up. Suddenly he felt a need to be moving about, exercising his muscles. He pushed to his feet and began to stretch when the phone rang.

"I hate to tell you this, boss," Zachary Harris said, "but Manny hasn't returned from his sector and isn't responding to radio calls. We've completely lost contact. I sent two cars to where he was working, but they haven't seen anything. What do you want we should do?"

Paul felt as though he had been struck; his mind went blank, then filled with a sad inevitability that made his skin turn cold. After several seconds, he asked, "What part of town was he checking?"

"Northwest, between Slater and Yuma. But he could've been coming in. He was finishing his second shift. Or maybe he went north on Yuma into the desert. You know Manny. No telling what he was up to."

Paul felt suddenly impotent, unable to act. A pain began pulsing slowly on the left side of his body and working its way up his arm to the back of his head. Sinking into his chair he put his elbows on the desk and began to rub his neck. His voice was weak. "We can't stop looking for the bus, Zach. Keep the two cars you have in his sector. They can search for both Manny and the bus. Where was he the last time he checked in?"

"He'd gone northward from Clay to Lassen, hadn't seen anything suspicious."

"Okay, confine the search to the area north of Lassen and between Slater and Yuma. If you don't come up with anything by midnight, transfer two more cars and recheck his whole area building by building. Manny must've come across something out there. I hate to think what happened to him."

"Doesn't have to be the kidnappers, boss. Could've been drug smugglers coming in from Mexico, armed robbers, anything. Bad guys are going crazy knowing we can't take the time to respond."

Paul tried to reply but couldn't formulate the words, sinking instead into a silence that lengthened uneasily and gave no sign of ending.

"I hate to mention it, boss," Harris went on at last, his voice uncharacteristically tentative, "but I ain't been home since last night. Isn't there someone you can—"

Paul roused himself. "Damn it, Zach, there isn't anyone. Get a cot from over where the parents are. You're going to have to sleep in the squad room. There's no other way." He suddenly remembered the construction workers. "And find three bodies you can send up here to do some telephoning. F.B.I. guys if there's no one else. What do you hear from Exley's people on their sex offenders?"

"Hear? Me? Fuckin' feds don't tell me diddly."

"All right, Christ! But get some people up here as soon as you can. We might be able to save some lives."

Putting the receiver down, Paul winced as another pain shot up his arm. Goddamn it! he screamed inwardly. What else can go wrong? He pushed to his feet and crossed over to the window. He could see LaSalle down in the parking lot, standing alone in the darkness, hands in pockets. What the hell's he thinking about down there? he wondered. Goddamn F.B.I. Hot shot outsiders with their college degrees and computers and fucking laser analysis. Paul's eyes shifted to the lights in the distance: cars moving about, buildings, trailer parks, junkyards. More and more often lately he'd catch himself standing here for minutes at a time, staring out at the desert and imagining what it must have been like a hundred years ago, before Las Cruces had been founded as a railroad stop, and wishing the whole thing would disappear.

He crossed back to his desk and lowered himself to the leather chair. He felt tired and unsettled and suddenly desperately sad. A helicopter appeared from somewhere and began buzzing loudly overhead. Its spotlight flashed on, sending a sudden circle of illumination racing along the far wall like prison yard searchlights. Didn't the F.A.A. shut down this area? Goddamn reporters, turning the Civic Center into a one-ring circus.

Where the hell was Manny? He didn't want to think about it. The answer was obvious. But why? He must have come across something and tried to check it out himself. How many times had he told Manny not to be so impetuous, to use a little more caution? But Manny wasn't the sort to listen. He had the personality of someone fated to end up either a hero or a victim. There was no middle way.

Coming to his feet, Paul stared without thought at his littered desktop, then turned once more toward the window. LaSalle was still down there in the parking lot. Odd how things happen, chance bringing people together who would never have met. Most of life is chance, randomness. Or magic, the old people would say. Like when, shortly after getting out of the army, he'd gone up to Palm Springs to see about buying a used car and run into Rosa in a Denny's restaurant. He'd gone up and introduced himself and six months later they were married. If he hadn't dropped into that restaurant . . .

Chance. Magic.

Like the kidnapping bringing the F.B.I. to Las Cruces.

He rubbed his eyes and moved from the window. He felt like a kid who'd seen his girlfriend with another boy and rushed home crying. Except that Paul couldn't remember the last time he'd cried. Christ, he swore at himself, stop acting like an idiot! Ellen wasn't interested in LaSalle. She wasn't about to leave Las Cruces, anyway. She'd been away— they both had—and didn't like it, didn't fit in. This was home, and home can't be duplicated. A pain was building behind his eyes and he rubbed at them again with his knuckles.

He wondered how the children were doing. And where the three guys he'd asked Zach to send up were. He reached angrily for the phone. *Goddamn it, we've got to get moving on this,* he thought. A chill went suddenly all the way through his body, and he stared again toward the window. *I have to be very careful how I handle things.*

11:50 P.M.

Even though it was clear that nothing was going to happen until morning, Ellen had resisted going home. She was being foolish, she knew, but still it seemed to be letting everyone down; what if Paul turned up something from his list of construction projects or the air or ground search found the bus? But Paul had insisted, using guilt where logic had failed: Denise and her grandfather would be worried about her; if anything happened during the night, he'd call at once. Then, capping the offer with what he knew was an irrefutable inducement, he reminded her that she'd have a chance to relax in the tub as she enjoyed doing before going to sleep every night. Her "sanity time," she called it, an opportunity to unwind and think. Paul said he'd drop by and have a drink with her before she went to bed, but he was going to stop at his own place first for his electric razor and a change of clothes. He'd be sleeping at the station until this was over.

So after Julie Garcia left, Ellen, as she usually did, poured herself a glass of Gallo Chablis from the already opened bottle in the refrigerator and stepped gingerly into the steaming tub. The soapy, raspberry-scented water rose up comfortingly, gathering around her like an embrace, and almost immediately she could feel her muscles begin to relax. Setting her wineglass on the tile floor, she stared out the window she'd recently had installed high up on the wall above her feet so the moon and stars would be visible from the tub. The entire bathroom had been remodeled last year. At first, she had only intended to put in the window, but then she'd gotten carried away and added the huge spa-style bathtub that was elevated and surrounded by a magenta tile seating area. That was going to make the sink look trashy, so out it came, along with the old overhead lighting and cheap mirrors. Now she was paying $180 a month to take care of the loan, but it was worth it. This was the nicest room in the house.

When she had gotten home, Denise and Julie Garcia were asleep on the couch in front of the television. When Ellen flicked it off, they both woke up, and Mrs. Garcia looked at her with embarrassment. "We were watching the news all night. I guess we dozed off."

"That's fine," Ellen told her. "Denise doesn't get to see Mommy on TV every day. But she better get to bed now."

Denise had scurried off to brush her teeth, and Ellen and Julie talked about the kidnapping for a minute before the baby-sitter left for her own home. Ellen escorted her daughter to the girl's room, tucking her in the bed, a frilly "country" concoction that Ellen had designed herself, another extravagance perhaps, but there were so many fancy boys' beds in the stores—race cars and football helmets and so on—and little for girls. She had used fabric from the spread for the headboard and to cover two picture frames, and yards of white lace and rayon to create an elaborate princess-like canopy overhead.

Denise was wearing Winnie the Pooh pajamas, the ones with a lugubrious-looking Eeyore on the chest, and she pulled the bedspread up to her chin as Ellen bent to kiss her good night.

"Read, Mommy?" she asked automatically.

"Not tonight, hon. I'm tired." And upset, she thought but didn't say, and very, very worried about twenty-five children.

But Denise drew *Green Eggs and Ham* from under the sheets, where she had stashed it, and looked at her expectantly. "Just one?"

Ellen relented, smiling and sitting on the bed and reading the book aloud for probably the two-hundredth time. The girl delighted in the odd phrasing and familiar refrains, squealing with joy as Ellen read with exaggerated seriousness. "Do you like green eggs and ham? I do not like them, Sam I am. I do not like green eggs and ham."

When Ellen finished, she felt a familiar surge of warmth toward her daughter. She reached over and touched the side of the girl's face with the back of her fingers, enjoying the feel: skin to skin, mother to daughter, the generations joined. There was something special about the time they spent reading together, a closeness that Ellen had never experienced with her own mother, and it strengthened her resolve to make their years together something they would both look back on with joy, rather than regret or indifference. Standing up, she bent to give Denise a hug and yawned unexpectedly. Denise quickly slipped the book back under her covers and smiled excitedly. "I've got a secret."

"What secret?" Ellen asked, already thinking with pleasure about her warm tub.

"Mrs. Garcia told me."

Denise wanted to be coaxed. Ellen smiled and tried to sound anxious to hear whatever it was. "Okay, what did Mrs. Garcia tell you?"

"I'm going to have a daddy."

"What?" She looked at Denise as though not sure she had heard correctly.

"Paul! Paul's going to be my daddy."

Ellen caught her breath as a mix of feelings she couldn't separate crowded suddenly together in her mind: irritation, definitely, at this intrusion of the baby-sitter in her personal life, and . . . pleasure? concern? Uneasily, not knowing how to proceed, she said, "Well, I don't know." How did Julie find out about her and Paul? She assumed some people knew by now—Bobby Muledeer, Maggie. If Julie knew, though, it must be general knowledge.

But she and Paul hadn't been considering marriage. Not seriously, anyway. The notion had hovered around the back of her mind—Paul's too, probably—the past few months, of course, but they had been content to leave it there, something to think about more carefully in the future. There wasn't a need to rush into anything, especially after her last marriage.

She smiled at her daughter and began to leave. "Don't believe everything you hear, Denise. It's just a story. Like *Green Eggs and Ham.*"

"Does that mean you're not going to get married?" Denise frowned at her in a way that seemed definitely manipulative, as though to say, You have to marry him!

"We'll see," Ellen told her, closing the door and wondering if Denise would realize that she hadn't answered the question. Probably so: children can be harder than adults to fool. On the way to her own bedroom she had checked her grandfather's door. Shut. She waited for a moment and listened. Not a sound inside. Julie said she hadn't seen him all day.

In the tub, Ellen sipped again at her wine, then put the glass on the floor and peered into the darkness beyond the window. Only a sliver of moon tonight. A thousand stars though. The night comes so quickly here, she thought. Not like L.A., where the sun seems to creep interminably across the broad, flat basin to the ocean, where it sometimes turns the sky red for up to an hour, giving up its light reluctantly. Out here the mountains fade to blue, then black, then suddenly disappear. On nights like this, you can walk out into the desert and sense the immense timelessness of life, experience the world as it was before humankind: calm and balanced, everything in equilibrium. The world of Mukat the Creator, where coyotes howl and crickets chirp and lizards and snakes, unchanged in a million years, scurry from the darkness, seeking the warmth of the earth. And the air stands completely still, waiting for morning, waiting to start the cycle again.

Ellen put her hand down, brought the wineglass once more to her lips, and closed her eyes as she took a sip. The cold liquid raced through her body, and she shivered and, as though the wine had knocked something vital loose, saw a hole opening suddenly and rapidly in her being, growing larger and larger like a balloon being inflated too quickly. She sat up, a terrible loneliness searing her, and thought: Grandfather is going to die! She saw it, within days. Days. Grandfather. Mother. A father she never knew also probably dead. All that would remain was Denise. Her heart thudded, then slowed to a crawl at the thought: I stretch back into the darkness when Mukat created the earth and sky and animals, giving life to everything. But in a few days, all that will remain for the future is Denise.

She felt at once vulnerable and threatened in some fierce but ill-defined way, felt like dashing from the tub, fleeing an invisible adversary snapping like a coyote at her heels.

What is it? she wondered. What are you afraid of? Is that what the parents of those children are feeling right now? Do they see that great black hole opening up in their lives? He's taking their blood away, this kidnapper; like an evil *pul*, or shaman, he's ripping part of their being away, exposing this hole, this terrible core of loneliness we spend our lives trying to plaster over to protect ourselves.

She stirred uncomfortably, water falling from her breasts, splashing into the tub. Don't get maudlin, she warned herself as she put her glass down. It's time's cycle: death, life, death. The way things are and must be.

But the mood wouldn't go away and she thought: If I had lost Denise in the hospital, there would be nothing now. Except Paul.

Still, she wasn't at all sure she wanted to marry. She took pride in independence, in managing her family and career by herself. She didn't need to get married. Anyway, as well as she knew Paul, there were strange gaps in his history, holes that ran through his life like arroyos in the desert, things she would want to find out about if they were to get married. His father had come from Gallup, New Mexico. A handsome, romantic sort of guy, people said, who traveled around working in oil fields—Texas, Oklahoma, California. Then he'd lost three fingers of his right hand in a drilling-bit accident in Bakersfield and had had to go in for something simpler. So he'd started working on road crews around Indio, driving an asphalt truck. That's where he'd met Paul's mother. They'd moved back to Gallup shortly after Paul was born. Two years later, his mother pregnant with his sister, his father had died of lung cancer. Almost immediately, he and his mother had returned to the reservation at Las Cruces.

Paul and Ellen had known each other as kids, though he was almost nine years older. Marriage had always been a possibility, of course, but they'd just never connected that way. Funny how those things happen, Ellen thought. We were always brother–sister and never wanted to be anything else.

Then Paul had gone into the army and more or less disappeared from her life. Later, Ellen had left for college and subsequently moved to Los Angeles.

When she'd come back to Las Cruces three years ago, she'd been overjoyed to see him again; it had been like reclaiming a lost part of her past. A year later, they'd become lovers.

Funny how things happen.

And it wasn't just "old friends," despite what LaSalle had said. She and Paul had something deeper, more meaningful, than that. She understood what love was now, and it sure wasn't what she had felt for Pete. That had been—lust? escape? An excitement that had burned at first like a fire just beneath the surface of her skin. But not love. This was different. Her soul joined Paul's in ways she couldn't explain, couldn't begin to understand, but knew.

Not just "old friends," then, the words suddenly stinging her. What would Paul have said if LaSalle had made the same comment to him? Maybe Paul *was* thinking of marriage. She'd never asked him. Or did he have secret fantasies about other women, women at work perhaps? Maybe sexy little Jeannie Wheatley, twirling her fingers through that long blonde hair.

Ellen's eyes closed and her face eased into a smile as she sank lower into the warm, perfumed water. Paul and Jeannie. Come on! She ought to be concentrating on that missing bus, not creating soap-opera fantasies out of her own neurotic musings. The bus . . . somewhere within fifty miles . . . somewhere . . . a huge yellow school bus with twenty-five handicapped children.

But a bubble of anger appeared suddenly in her mind as Bobby Muledeer's "Someone said they saw you" came back to her. What the hell was that all about? she wondered. Someone? Maggie again. Why do people act like that? Jealousy? Bitchiness? "You and the F.B.I. guy." God, all I've done is kiss him once and people act like we're having sex in the squad room. Which was maybe not a bad idea after all . . .

Oh, hell, grow up, Ellen! You're just excited by his interest in you. But what's wrong with that? It's nice to be admired, nice to get your ego stroked once in a while. Especially since Paul isn't the type to give a lot of compliments. But that was just the sort of superficial attraction that had drawn her and Pete together, wasn't it? When she got married again—*if* she got married again—it would go beyond the obvious appeal of good looks and the allure of sex.

Not that there was anything wrong with the allure and excitement of sex. It was there with Paul, too. He was a good-looking guy. When they'd go out to dinner, women would turn and stare at him as if she wasn't there, inviting him with their eyes. Stretched out in the tub, she could almost feel his large hands moving over the contours of her body, his fingertips tracing a path along the soft skin of her belly, moving gently between her thighs (making her wait, wait, anticipate, thinking about it), cupping her buttocks, his lips reaching to gently take a nipple.

Where was Paul? He was supposed to shave and shower and then drop by. Probably on the phone to Jane, his daughter at school in Berkeley. On the rare occasions she called, it was invariably late, having little consideration for anyone else's need for sleep. And it was always to complain about something: money, school, her father's lack of a "social conscience." Going through her know-it-all stage, Paul said mildly and refused to get upset. Going through her bitch stage, Ellen had thought silently and wondered what it would be like to be Jane's stepmother. If she and Paul married, Jane and Denise would become sisters. Something to be endured rather than enjoyed. At least Jane wouldn't be living with them.

Why wasn't LaSalle married? she wondered, her thoughts careening off again. Weren't all F.B.I. agents married? Didn't they all live in perfect Brady Bunch houses and have perfect Brady Bunch families? Probably not; there was nothing Brady-like about Middleton. Thinking of Middleton made her uneasy. There was something troubling about him, dangerous almost. But there was also a strange vitality, an intensity about life, that in someone else would have been attractive. But with him nothing was attractive, only menacing. It was obvious to her even if LaSalle couldn't see it.

She sighed and put her head back against the wall. Her hands began to move under the perfumed bubbles, sliding along the edge of the tub before dropping abruptly to her sides. Closing her eyes, she didn't move as the water lapped gently at her chin.

"Police officer drowns in home spa," Paul said and smiled at her. "Very interesting film at eleven." He was holding the bottle of wine and another glass, and he lowered himself to the tile step next to the tub. Reaching over, he refilled her glass, then moved aside some wet hair to kiss her forehead. A clump of white foam dangled from her chin, and she smelled fresh and wonderful, like wild raspberries.

Ellen's eyes opened onto the black square of window above her feet and focused on the scattering of stars. After a moment she said, "Grandfather is going to die."

He said, "Yes."

She picked up her glass and took a drink. "No one knows

how old he is. Eighty-eight, ninety. There were no records back then. He used to tell me stories. He wanted me to have a son, I think. He never said it. But that's what he wanted." She turned and smiled at Paul. "An anthropologist came out from the University of California and wanted Grandfather to record his memories of childhood. He wouldn't do it, wouldn't become an object of study."

"I don't blame him. They look at you like you're a Martian. Screw 'em." He stared at her skin, glistening with moisture and reflecting light as if it were glass. He could feel himself becoming aroused and looked away. Sounding more gruff than he wanted, he asked, "How's Denise?"

Ellen started to tell him what her daughter had said, then changed her mind. "Asleep, I hope. She and Julie got a glimpse of me on TV at the parents' press conference. Mom's a star now. Denise is pretty excited, I guess." She sighed and flicked the water with her toes, watching as a spray of white foam shot onto the tile wall and slid slowly back into the tub. "Tomorrow's a preschool day. Maybe I won't have her go."

"Kidnapper's holed up somewhere, Ellen. He's already got more than enough hostages if that's what you're thinking."

"Oh, I know. But I think I'll have her stay home anyway." She again flicked the water with her feet and smiled at him. "I just feel like being a neurotic mother today."

Paul shifted his body and stared out the window. "I've got three guys calling contractors at home. By daybreak we should have a list of everyone who's worked on a building project recently. County's doing the same thing. Then we put as many people as we can on it and start to narrow things down: who was not at work at seven-thirty? Contractors won't necessarily know, so we'll have to talk to foremen, maybe even some of the workers themselves. Who wasn't at work, who came late? We'll move as fast and hard as we can. Shouldn't take too long."

Ellen glanced at the side of his face. He seemed drawn and tired, and she wondered if he had heard the same rumors Bobby Muledeer had. Probably not. She said, "You don't sound too excited about it, Paul. This is what we've been waiting for. This—"

"Ellen, Manny's missing," he said, interrupting. He turned back toward her.

"What?" She sat bolt upright and stared at him in disbelief.

"He was in his unit searching the north side of town. Never reported in. Just disappeared. Like the kids. We're looking for him now."

"My God!" What else could go wrong? she wondered as shock and fear merged in her mind. She felt a tremor go through her body.

"No telling what happened. But I guess I know." Paul stood up suddenly, his muscles tight with tension, swallowed what was left in his wine glass, then abruptly sat down again.

Ellen asked, "Do you think he came across the kids?"

"The kids. The kidnapper. An accomplice. Christ. Probably tried to be a hero and got himself killed."

"We need to put more people in his sector, Paul. We need to focus on it."

"If he doesn't turn up by morning, we will. But I don't want to forget the rest of town yet. This guy's pretty sharp. He could've killed Manny just to divert our attention from where he really is. There's just no way to figure him. Look how he released the Torres girl. What was the point? It's like he's playing a game with us. But I think she's the last kid we'll see alive."

Ellen looked at him. "Why do you say that?"

"Once he gets his twenty million, he's planning to live it up, not go to jail. Some of the kids on that bus are bright enough to be able to identify him. The driver sure as hell can. He's going to figure he has no choice, he has to kill them. If they're in one of those mines up in the hills, we might not ever find them. Manny, too, Ellen. We gotta figure he's either dead or with the kids."

Ellen sank lower in the tub, only her head above water. "And to think I came back to Las Cruces for the quiet life."

She pushed up again with a sigh and shook the hair from her neck as water flowed over her shoulders to her breasts, splitting into two streams as it rushed past her erect nipples and back into the tub between her legs. Suddenly uncomfortable, Paul stared at the side of her face, trying to gauge her thoughts—what's going on? what's she thinking?—and finally gave up.

With an abrupt gesture, he grabbed the bottle and splashed more wine in his glass. "Bobby Jasper and his brother stopped by the house when I was picking up my clothes. Bobby said he had enough votes to get me off the tribal council. Him, Jessy, Hek Gomez, Ennis Cooper, that bunch. They're talking to some guy from Chicago about running the bingo. Guy with a big cigar, wears dark glasses inside."

"Bobby's blowing smoke. The old folks won't go for it." Ellen stirred, moved around restlessly, the water lapping.

"Old folks are dying," Paul said and nodded toward her grandfather's room. "Bobby told me maybe they'd work on the city council next, get Art Peña made police chief here in the city. Of course, if I went along with them, stopped fighting, they'd back off. I told them to get the hell out of my house or I'd arrest them for trespassing."

Ellen shook her head. "They used to be your friends. You used to go to the sweat hut with them."

"The old days. Before they saw dollar signs everywhere."

"Do you think Art really searched the reservation for the kids? They could be back in the hills somewhere and it'd be hard to spot them."

"Art's no dummy. If something like that happened, he'd look like an idiot. Or an accomplice. Anyway, I don't think there's any way that damn bus could have been driven through the reservation without someone seeing it."

Ellen looked at him. "Then where is it, Paul? There's no way it could have been taken anywhere without someone noticing."

"Remember that magician who made the Statue of Liberty disappear on TV? It's like that. Gone!"

But the Statue of Liberty hadn't disappeared, she thought to herself. He just made us think so. After a moment she said, "I wonder how the driver's faring? Linda something—"

"Sowell. She's been in tough spots before, you know. I think she's probably doing okay. If she's alive."

"She's alive. The kids, too. I don't think he'll kill any more as long as they might be of some use to him. But after . . ." She sighed and drew her arm from under the water, letting it dangle over the side of the tub onto the tile step. "We'd better turn up something with those building contractors. It's the only hope we have now."

Paul said, "Getting hectic downtown. F.B.I.'s bringing in more people again. I asked LaSalle where he's going to put them, and he said don't worry about it. I said I'm not worried, I just want to know where the hell you're going to put them. He just gave me a look, an F.B.I. look. Getting real used to that. Pretty soon it's going to be like that siege they had down in Waco. Remember that? Lasted six or seven weeks, and they must've had a hundred agents tripping over each other trying to figure out what the hell to do. And they still fucked up. It's how they deal with a problem though: keep throwing more and more people at it. They never run out."

Ellen shifted around, waves lapping against the side of the tub. "I don't think we'll have any trouble with them. They're pretty sharp. They know what they're doing."

"Maybe so, but I wouldn't trust a one of them for a minute. Always on the phone to D.C. or faxing things back and forth, and when I try to find out what they're doing, they either clam up or lie to me. Hell, every police department in the country hates them."

"Matt's not like that," Ellen said. "He wants those kids back as much as we do. He'll be straight with us." And she thought, but did not add, He's not the type to lie. Especially to me. He's got too much honor.

Paul stared at her a minute and started to say something, then changed his mind and looked out the window and the stars overhead. After a moment, he turned back and tried a smile. "Thinking maybe I'd join you in the tub. Didn't get a chance to take a shower when Bobby Jasper showed up. I'm going to have to do some serious soaking." He began to unbutton his shirt.

Ellen shook her head. "I've got to get some sleep, Paul. Both of us do." An odd feeling started to move within her, almost like guilt. But over what? Then she sat up suddenly, splashing water on the floor, and fixed an intent look on him. "There's something I wanted to ask you about though. How often do you fantasize about Jeannie Wheatley?"

An hour later, lying stiffly on her back and staring into the darkness of the bedroom, Ellen knew sleep was never going to come. Rolling onto her side, she thought: Something I don't like is happening to me, something bad.

A mild dizziness went through her, as though the earth were shifting under her bed. Events were suddenly taking on their own momentum and moving beyond anyone's ability to control them. Endings and beginnings. Fate. Destiny. Her mother thought you couldn't change the future, only accept it. Ellen had never believed that. I control my life through every decision I make, she thought. The sense that other people could intrude on this process, insert themselves unasked into the dynamics of her existence, frightened and annoyed her.

She and Paul had been happy together, were happy together, and would continue to be.

Goddamn it, why did Matt have to show up, especially now? It's all part of the plan, her mother would have said. It's the way things were meant to be.

No, mother. You're wrong!

Maybe he wasn't serious anyway. Maybe it was just the sort of casual interest she had seen in men most of her life. They were always staring at her, doing double-takes, coming up and introducing themselves, smiling, talking, touching her. Almost without exception they'd been jerks, guys ten years older than herself, driving Corvette convertibles and wearing gold chains and diamond pinkie rings. Even while making arrests, she'd get the stupid comments. Once on Hill Street in L.A., across from Pershing Square, she and her partner had been questioning a guy about a purse snatching when he'd casually begun to rub his huge filthy hand on her butt. Ellen had instantly slammed his head into the patrol car; they had had to make up a story about resisting arrest to explain the bruises on his face.

Throwing off the sheet, she turned over. Hot tonight, hotter than normal. She was wearing a nightgown Paul had given her, sheer pink that fell to mid-thigh. Sitting up, she pulled it off. Still too hot. Almost as bad as the trip she and Paul had taken last year to the Yucatan. For eleven days they had trekked through the jungle with a dozen others, studying the more remote Mayan ruins, taking pictures, listening to lectures. "Strenuous hiking" the brochure had said, neglecting to mention the hundred percent humidity that left you drained and amazed that anyone could have built a civilization out there. Afterward, instead of going home as planned, they'd flown to Puerto Vallarta and lay on the beach for three days to recuperate and talked and talked. If she'd been there with Pete, she'd thought at the time, they'd never have left the hotel. And never talked. Vacation, for Pete, was drinking and screwing, not necessarily in that order. Pete had seen less of more cities than anyone she knew.

Why had Mrs. Garcia told Denise that she and Paul were going to get married? What made her think so? Ellen had never even talked to her about Paul. Anyway, it was none of her business.

Matt had said he'd never been married. Someone that good-looking probably had girlfriends all over the place. Like Pete. Why pick on her, then? Or was he one of those guys who collects women everywhere he goes, keeping score like his dad kept count of murder convictions?

Pushing abruptly out of bed, she walked naked into the hallway where the thermostat was located and turned on the air conditioner. She hated having it on at night, hated the way it made the air smell artificial, but it was too hot to sleep. Going back in the bedroom she shut the window, then dropped again on top of the sheets. The air conditioner hummed, and cool air breezed gently over her bare body, chilling the thin layer of sweat that had collected on her breasts and thighs. She could feel her nipples stiffen and a muscle in the small of her back tighten and release.

Why did I let him kiss me? she thought. God, I can't believe I did that. I should have left the room, but I moved into it, as though I wanted him to, and I could feel my whole body responding, going tense, then shuddering from something that came from deep inside. And I knew he was going to do it. The minute I chose the Xerox room to meet in, I knew what was going to happen. Why hadn't the F.B.I. sent someone else?

She started feeling angry with herself; she needed sleep, had been up too long. She never thought clearly when up too long. Tomorrow was going to be worse.

Those poor children, she thought again. Things weren't going right. Not at all. This wasn't how kidnappings were supposed to go down. Too much confusion, everything being pushed in too many directions.

She'd reacted so guiltily when Vince Garibaldi had opened the door and seen her and Matt sitting together, not even touching, but her face instantly coloring, and her temperature flaring. She'd felt as though she'd been caught in adultery.

A tremor went through her body, and she realized she must have fallen asleep, though it couldn't have been for more than a few minutes. But she had already been dreaming. Strange how quickly dreams come. And how weird they are, the mind playing tricks. It was like watching herself in a movie: she was thrashing about in a body of water (the Salton Sea?), beginning to drown, when someone offered her a hand. She grasped it thankfully, managed to right herself, and was pulled to safety. But something made her let go, and she began to flail fearfully again. Then her feet touched bottom, and the camera pulled back to show that she was only five feet from shore. A lizard, resting on a rock, was laughing at her and sticking out its tongue.

She wished she could ask Grandfather about it. Maybe in a couple of days she'd go out to the reservation and talk to Henry Salas. He always knew what dreams meant.

The air conditioner hummed in the darkness. She listened to it, matching her heartbeat to its rhythms. Such soft expressive eyes Matt has, she thought, the pupils pale and blue within deep-set sockets. His face was completely without lines, like a child's. Ellen had crinkles around her eyes that deepened like caverns when she smiled, and tiny (almost invisible, she hoped) triangular dents on either side of her mouth. It wasn't fair. Men shouldn't have such perfect skin. They don't deserve it.

Paul knows, doesn't he? He's seen me staring at Matt, heard it in Matt's voice. Why doesn't he say something? Why doesn't he ask me about it?

What can Paul be feeling? What I felt when I found out about Pete.

The phone rang on the night stand and Ellen grabbed it.

"Did I wake you?"

A ripple of sadness and excitement raced through her, and at once she wanted to hang up but instead asked, "How'd you get my number?"

"I'm an investigator. It's what I do."

She didn't know what to say and began to feel both apprehensive and incredibly stupid, while a part of her mind repeated over and over, Don't talk to him.

LaSalle said, "I was thinking about you, so I decided to call."

Ellen heard herself breathe in and out, the sound deafening in the silent room. The receiver was cool against her skin. She shifted on her back, drew up her knees, and closed her eyes as she again felt the spasm along her spine.

LaSalle's tone became more neutral, and he said, "I just got off the phone with the director. Twelve years I've been with the F.B.I., and I've never talked to the director before.

I told him to forget the terrorism angle. He's interested in those old mines, though, and has a bunch of people in D.C. going over the records to see what's happened to them."

"Matt," she said, "I don't think this is a good idea. You and me—"

"Of course not," he replied quickly. His voice was almost light, but she could hear a new note of tension also, though he was trying to mask it. She wondered where he was, if anyone could hear him. "It never is," he went on. "But let's give it a try. Don't end it before it begins. You'll always wonder."

"Paul and I are going to get married," she blurted out and wondered at once why she said it.

"And you and I are going to have dinner. The two events aren't mutually exclusive. Anyway, I'm a federal agent. You have to do what I say. It's the law."

Still on her back, she smiled against her will into the hot, empty room. "You're infringing on my civil rights."

"Of course. It's part of our training. So, dinner."

"All right," she heard herself say, heard the smile in her voice. "Dinner."

"And let's have breakfast this morning, say about six-thirty. There must be a decent place for pancakes in Las Cruces."

"Not a chance. I told Paul I'd be in at six. But I'll bring you some donuts. Now I'm going to sleep. You should, too."

She quickly hung up. Embarrassment rose as she felt a rush of physical desire come over her. Sweat covered her body again, and she lay on her back in the darkness and let the air conditioner slowly blow it off.

1:05 A.M.

I'll go up to my office and get some sleep in a few minutes, Paul thought, but first I want to take one final walk through the Civic Center. Normally, the building was pretty well shut down by nine o'clock, except for the jail. Tonight, though, it pulsed with excitement, F.B.I. and sheriff's "experts" of one sort or another, most of whom he had never even been introduced to, hurrying through hallways and crowding offices. Everywhere phones ringing, fax machines beeping, people rushing about, shouting at one another; it was as though the building's nervous system had gone haywire and was in the throes of a breakdown.

Down in Records and Fines he saw several huge black plastic bags, evidently filled with garbage, resting on desktops. "What the hell is this?" he asked one of the two young women slapping labels on the bags.

"Contents of trash bins within two miles of the kidnap site. Who are you?"

"Trash bins? Who the hell told you to do that?"

"The special agent in charge of the investigation. It's going to Quantico for analysis. Are you supposed to be in here?"

"Jesus," Paul muttered and walked away.

In another office, three Las Cruces patrolmen who normally worked the early shift were sitting on the floor, playing cards. "Shouldn't you guys get some sleep?"

"Coffee," one of them said and pointed at a mass of Styrofoam cups and smiled. "Too much caffeine. Everyone's wired. Got to be back at seven anyway. Why are you up?"

Paul shook his head. "Hell, I don't know."

"Any news on Manny?"

"We've got four cars out there now. We'll turn up something soon." Nobody believed it.

Five minutes later he found himself outside, in front of the Civic Center by the fountain, which had turned off automatically at midnight. Facing him on the other side of the shallow reflecting pool was the city council's newest folly. "Public art," they called it, insisting that Las Cruces needed some large-scale statuary in front of its primary municipal building. So they'd authorized $185,000 for what appeared to be brass boxes impaled on three twenty-foot nails hammered into the ground. They liked it, they said, these art experts.

Shoving his hands in his pockets, he walked slowly to the opposite side of the fountain. Goddamn F.B.I., with its com-

puters and psychologists and lab techs and encrypted communications, he thought. They talked to him as if he were
an idiot, as though every small-town cop was Barney Fife.

Before going to Ellen's tonight he had called a friend of
his in the Dallas P.D., who used to be with the F.B.I. "What
do you know about a guy called Matt LaSalle?"

"Good man. You're lucky to have him. They could have
sent you an asshole. They have enough to spare."

"Good how?"

"He's got a rep as an organizer, a guy who can get things
done. D.C. loves him—'new-breed F.B.I.' and all that. He'll
be a mover-and-shaker someday."

"He married? Divorced? What?"

"How the hell would I know? What difference does it
make? You want to go out with him?"

"What about Charles Middleton?"

His friend laughed. "Crazy Charley? A wild man, hanging
on by a thread."

"To his job?"

"Reality! My opinion only, of course. Other people like
him, I guess. Even Attila had friends."

Paul dipped a hand into the pool and dabbed some of
the cool water onto his eyelids. What are those poor kids
doing right now? Screaming, crying, hiding their faces and
hoping it's all a dream? He felt a burden of sympathy for
them. Children shouldn't have to suffer. They can't comprehend it, the motivelessness and evil of the world is too
vast to grasp. And slowly forcing its way out of the back of
his mind, where it had lain hidden because it was too
painful to face, was the certainty that they'd never be seen
alive again. Someone who would do this is not the type to
let them go. He winced as a stab of anger at Manny rose,
and he thought, Goddamn it, why'd you have to go and
screw up just when things were starting to get better? Now
he'd have to take people away from checking the construction workers.

What's Ellen thinking? he wondered abruptly, his body

stiffening uncomfortably. I know you're not asleep, Ellen. What are you thinking about?

Ellen, the adult Ellen, had come into his life like a surprise, like an unexpected gift, after years of separation and while he still felt the grief of his wife's death. Maybe its abruptness and timing was why he'd always sensed he didn't deserve her, wasn't entitled to such sudden happiness, that it would all come to an end someday because happiness always comes to an end.

Several times he had almost asked her to marry him but in the end had held back. It hadn't been the right time or right mood or . . . something. That he loved her he was certain, though it was the sort of thing that made him uncomfortable to give much conscious thought to. But he knew also that a huge imbalance existed in their relationship, his love so much more than hers. There is no greater sadness than this, he thought, when love lies more heavily on one than another. Maybe that was Peter's legacy, that she could never give herself fully again. He recalled for the first time in years his high school English teacher saying that in tragedy we learn about ourselves. How smug that sounded, how much like the middle-class Anglo world of comfort and opportunity, where tragedy seldom visited, except in books.

So, Paul, what have you learned about yourself today?

That only a few things in life truly matter: the missing children, all children, Ellen . . .

What else?

Family, community, the land, ancient things, things that endure.

He wished Ellen was here to talk to. Or her grandfather or Henry Salas. He wanted to go out in the desert and walk and walk until his legs were sore, feel the ground crunch under his shoes, stare at the peaks. Maybe he'd call Henry tomorrow. Someone to be with. When Paul had told Ellen about Bobby Jasper and his brother coming out to his house tonight he hadn't mentioned that they'd been madder than hell. Paul had been out back with the horses when they'd shown up. Bobby, Jess, Hek Gomez, all the others who wanted gambling, were ratcheting things up a notch. Bobby had said he already had more than enough votes to get Paul off the council, and if Paul wouldn't drop his opposition he wouldn't have a friend left on the reservation, except for the old folk. Ellen, too, Bobby had told him, working himself into a lather. People wouldn't have anything to do with her, seeing her as Paul's partner in all of this. Maybe so. Already, people he'd known all his life weren't talking to him.

Folks were getting worked up, no doubt about it. Every once in a while, some of the younger guys would get tanked up and come by Paul's house at two or three in the morning and yell at him. Hey, *White*horse, they'd shout, their voices loud and angry in the thin desert air. Hey, *Whitey*. You belong to Rotary yet, Whitey? How come you play poker at Desertview or the Elks and we can't get Bingo? How come, Whitey?

Last April someone had put a live rattler in his mailbox. Had to have been a kid; the older ones would have remembered, would have known better. Paul had gone to the garage for a shovel, grabbed the snake behind the eyes, and thrown it to the ground, where he'd calmly cut off its head. Then he'd draped the snake over the fence out by the road so everyone could see it.

How incompetent human beings are, he thought. We come into the world as infants without the skills to deal with one another and leave the same way. We stumble through life with our eyes closed.

JUNE 12

After Chaos, next appeared Earth . . . then
Eros, most beautiful of the gods.

—Hesiod

5:58 A.M.

An early morning chill in the air, Ellen stood tensely by her desk and stared at the dozen long-stemmed yellow roses. There was no one in the squad room but Zachary Harris. She said, "Who—"

Harris, in his shirtsleeves, tie already loosened, tilted noisily back in his chair and looked at her through his rimless glasses. "Your S.A., I guess."

"What?" Her head snapped in his direction. She had been only half listening; she was anxious to see how far Paul had gotten with the construction workers and had been hurrying upstairs when she'd been startled to see the huge bouquet of flowers on her desk.

Harris peered up at her. "Your secret admirer. Didn't know you had one." He smiled. "Someone I know? Maybe an Indian guy with a cute little ponytail? Hey, there's something different about you today, isn't there? What is it, new hairstyle? You look, I don't know, sexier. I like it."

"There's nothing different, Zach."

"Sure there is. What is it? New clothes? Change your lipstick? Come on, Ellen. I'm not very good at this stuff."

"Nothing, Zach. Forget it." She had spent a little more time than usual on her hair and makeup this morning, but that, she insisted to herself, was so she wouldn't look like a zombie after a sleepless night. "Wasn't there a card with the flowers? And who delivered it? No one can get within two blocks of the Civic Center."

"Love conquers all. Or so I hear. I never got beyond lust with my first two wives."

Ellen picked up the vase. It was cut crystal rather than the cheap glass that florists generally used. Instinctively, her face eased toward the flowers; she sniffed and smiled at the fragrance, feeling a gentle tingling run all the way to her toes.

"That stuff's an aphrodisiac, isn't it?" Harris said, picking up a report and beginning to read. "Maybe I should try it sometime. You think Jeannie Wheatley likes flowers?"

Ellen loved things that grew, maybe roses most of all since they were so rare in the desert. She felt an urge to take one out and carry it all day so that she could keep its beauty and fragrance with her. But she put the vase back on her desk. Harris, not looking up from his papers, said, "Never would've thought Paul was the type. Flowers. Christ, what next? Little balloon bouquets? Sunday brunch at the Red Lion? Guy's turning into a yuppie. It's an ugly thing to see."

Ellen looked at the wall clock, five after six, and her pulse quickened. "Anything on Manny yet?"

"I just put another car in that part of the city. We're going door to door now, waking people up. But that means five cars I've pulled from looking for the bus."

"Well, we had to do it." But despite herself, Ellen felt a tiny surge of irritation at Manny for diverting resources from the children, then a twist of shame for feeling so. Abruptly she shoved the box she was carrying at Zach. "Have a donut. I've got to get upstairs. We were supposed to meet at six. Maybe food will take your mind off Jeannie."

Harris flipped up the lid and quickly took two. "Better my mind than my hands, I guess. She'd probably sue for harassment if I even looked at her sideways. Everyone else does today. The Land of the Litigants, right? Anyway, your meeting started half an hour ago. Everyone's worked up about those construction workers. Maybe I'll get to go home tonight."

"Half an hour ago? Why didn't someone call me?"

"I did. You were gone. Probably at Winchell's. Hey, you

think we could get Denny's to send over bacon and eggs? I'm about to O.D. on sugar."

Swearing under her breath, Ellen took the stairs two at a time to the third floor, walking angrily into the conference room and an obvious argument. Everyone stopped talking at once as she halted in the doorway and looked at them in turn: Paul, pacing rapidly in front of the floor-to-ceiling window, head down, hands clenched at his sides; LaSalle, bent over the table, his finger running down some papers in front of him; Exley hovering next to LaSalle, looking agitated. They stared at her dumbly, as though she wasn't supposed to be there. Feeling suddenly uneasy, she walked in and dropped the donuts on the near end of the table. "Sorry I'm late. I wanted to bring breakfast."

Ignoring her, Paul wheeled around toward LaSalle as though he was going to hit him. "It's not either-or, damn it!" he shouted. "We're going to do both!"

LaSalle's face flushed as he snatched up the papers he had been studying. "If we find the kids, we find your officer."

Ellen felt an instant of alarm. What were they talking about? She'd never seen Paul this worked up before; he started to say something to LaSalle, but Exley interrupted, stepping away from the table. "We have to be realistic about this, Chief. Your man's almost certainly dead—"

"Almost isn't certainly!" Paul snapped. "What if he were an F.B.I. agent?"

"Even so—"

"Bullshit! He's my officer. We're looking for him and checking the construction workers."

LaSalle, trying to rein in his anger, shook his head. "We haven't got the personnel. And there's only so much time. We've got to prioritize."

Paul stalked back to the table. "Then we'll get more people," he said, sounding almost as though he were pleading. "Look, I know how important it is to check out the construction workers. I know it's the only lead we have. Damn it, I agree with you—"

"It's more than a lead," Exley said. "It's a breakthrough, the sort of thing that can solve a case in minutes. This person doesn't know we're on to him, so there'll be no need for him to devise an alibi by showing up at work today. Do you see what I mean? We won't have to check all those names. Just find out who's been unavailable for work the past two days. How many people can that be?"

Paul and LaSalle both started to say something, but Ellen quickly asked, "How many names are on the list?" Exley was right, she sensed with excitement. She empathized with Paul's desire to look for Manny and understood the pain he felt at being unable to help one of his officers. But since last night it had become obvious that this was the lead they'd been praying for; they couldn't go at it half-heartedly when it was conceivable they could have the children back by noon.

LaSalle glanced at the papers. "One hundred and sixteen."

Her heart skipped a beat. That was twice as many as she had expected. "Can you get more agents?"

He looked at her uncertainly. "If I have to."

"You have to. How long would it take to get twenty people here?"

"From L.A.?" He looked at his watch. "Maybe ten o'clock."

She turned to Paul. "How about sheriffs?"

He waved his arm, looking suddenly tired and dispirited. "You know how tied up they are."

"They've put most of their uniformed people in this part of the county searching for the bus. Maybe they could send up half a dozen from South County, traffic officers or jailers."

"Maybe—"

"Until then we can use civilian employees to start checking by phone with contractors and foremen. All they have to do at this point is find out who wasn't at the job site today or yesterday, or at least who wasn't there at the time of the kidnapping. We can get them on it right away. When

the F.B.I. agents show up, we can put them in the field trying to locate any names we come up with. We'll put everyone on it we can. If we can't find someone, we'll talk to their
friends, relatives. We'll give every officer a list of questions:
Has this person been spending time in the desert or the
mountains or talking about the school or kids? Or doing
anything strange? We can get court orders and search their
houses if we have to. While the F.B.I.'s hitting this, we can
put the sheriff's deputies in the streets to search for Manny."
She looked at Paul, who spread his arms in resignation,
though he didn't seem happy with the compromise.

LaSalle reached at once for the phone and began punch-
ing out a number, relieved that a decision had been made.
"If we find those kids alive, it's going to be because of this.
It's the only mistake he's made. We can't expect—"

LaSalle began barking into the phone, and Ellen turned
to Paul. "I'll get Zach to round up some civilian employees
for phone duty. When he's got them ready, I'll direct it until
the F.B.I. people get here. You can call the sheriff and try
to get some officers sent up from South County."

She hurried down to the squad room, where Harris was
finishing his second donut. "It'll probably take twenty minutes," he said when she explained what she wanted. "Civilians are just dribbling in to work." But even the normally
unflappable Zach was excited.

"See if you can hurry it up. Grab anyone who comes
through the door. I don't care if they're custodians or council members. We've got to hustle on this. We're going to be
on this guy's doorstep by lunchtime."

She returned to the conference room just as LaSalle was
hanging up the phone. "I've got a dozen agents coming in
from Los Angeles and Santa Ana and another six from San
Diego. They should all be here by ten, if not sooner."

Paul said, "We've still got to set things up for tonight in
case this turns out to be a bust."

"It won't be a bust," Ellen said with confidence. "I can feel
it. All we needed was one mistake and we got it. But," she
looked around the room where everyone was still standing

and impatiently waved them to chairs, "I've already decided how I want to handle things if we do go to a ransom exchange. I don't think we'll get to that point, but we might as well run through it." Unable to sleep, she had risen at 4:15 and settled herself at the kitchen table, thinking through various scenarios. Regardless of what happened, she was determined not to be caught unprepared and not to screw up. She had worked through everything, then gone over it again and again until she was certain nothing had been left out. Glancing around the table, she said, "Once he calls, things are going to move quickly and we won't have time to improvise. So I want us to be prepared for whatever happens. We'll start with the ransom. The diamonds probably can't be marked in any way. Is that right?" She turned to LaSalle, and as he met her gaze all the turmoil and emotion of last night flooded back in an instant. She sensed her worry for the children being pushed aside by more private concerns. A wave of unworthiness and shame came over her, and she cursed herself for her pettiness. Still, she couldn't shake the feeling that shuddered through her when she looked into his face, then turned to see Paul staring at the two of them, eyes intent but face resolute, without emotion. Stop acting like a fool, she warned herself furiously. Lying in bed last night she had relived LaSalle's touch, kiss, words, gentleness a hundred times in the same obsessive but unwilling way she'd used to relive Peter's betrayals, replaying his lies and excuses endlessly until she'd thought she'd go mad. But how different was she from Pete, she wondered, as in her mind (she knew for certain only in this instant) she had decided to betray Paul with a man she had known less than twenty-four hours?

LaSalle, seemingly unaware of her emotion, leaned back in his chair. "We could probably mark the diamonds somehow. But there's no point. We'll have photos and exact descriptions we can distribute to the trade. It won't do any good though. He could recut them if he had to. Anyway, he's not going to have any trouble selling them. Diamonds are like cash."

"What about the money?"

"He said no infrared, so we won't. There's a dozen people at the Federal Reserve Bank reading serial numbers into tape recorders. There'll be a record of every bill he gets. We'll know if the money turns up somewhere. As it will, of course. And we'll be there within hours when it does."

"But all that is after the fact. Are we going to bug the money when we drop it?"

LaSalle leaned forward, glancing at Exley. "I think we have to. He'll have us drop the package somewhere remote, probably out in the desert, and then drive away." He paused a moment, and Ellen watched as his eyes moved to Paul, who was staring at him from the other end of the table. In that instant, something seemed to pass between the two men, and she felt a sudden flaring of anger, as though they were having a private conversation about her. But the moment quickly passed as she saw its origin in her own murky feelings. That's what guilt can do, she thought; even if you haven't done anything, it sears your conscience like a fire. Paul's gaze shifted from LaSalle to her. He knows, doesn't he?

LaSalle turned in his chair as he continued to look at Paul. "Shouldn't we have Marcus Cox here? He's our liaison with the sheriff. If a pay-off comes, it's likely to be in their territory."

Paul regarded him a minute, his face blank, as everyone waited. After a few seconds, he shifted uncomfortably and waved a stiff hand as he tried to keep the annoyance out of his voice. "I suppose I should have asked for him when I had the sheriff on the line. I just forgot."

"You're going to have to let him know what's happening in case we end up out there," LaSalle said, then looked around the table. "We don't want a patrol car stumbling onto the pay-off and scaring off our bad guy. We've got to figure he'll set it up for someplace where he can watch and see if we follow his directions. When he's sure there's no one around, he'll grab the money. If we slip a bug in the package, we won't have to risk trying to watch him. We'll be able to track it."

Obviously annoyed with himself for forgetting to call Cox, Paul snapped, "What's to keep him from finding the bug? He'll be expecting it."

"We'll use two just to be sure." LaSalle reached into his briefcase and removed a small brown envelope, spilling a half-dozen silver objects about half the size of a dime on the tabletop. "We can glue one inside a bundle of bills. He won't take the time to look, he'll want to get the hell out of there. The other we'll put in the suitcase we deliver the money in. All we have to do is slit the lining and slip it in."

"I think he's pretty sharp," Ellen said. "I think he'll be expecting a bug. He'll look for it."

"He won't be ready for these. They're brand new. They don't transmit on normal frequencies. He can be out there with a scanner and never pick up a signal. He'd need the base station."

"All right," Ellen said, yanking out a chair at the end of the table and sitting heavily. She could feel her earlier enthusiasm begin to drain as a pain started to build in the back of her head. She winced unintentionally and rubbed at her eyes.

"You feeling okay?" Paul asked with concern.

She smiled weakly and tried to make her voice flat. "Not enough sleep. Like everyone else, I guess." She turned to LaSalle. "We'll try the bugs unless he specifically tells us not to. I'm not willing to fool with this guy. If we do get to the point of a ransom transfer, I want to do exactly what he says. I want the kids freed a hell of a lot more than I want him captured."

There was a small silence until Exley said, "Of course. We all want the children freed. That goes without saying. But this device, if we in fact put it with the ransom, would be impossible to discover. Impossible!"

Surprised at the psychologist's tone, Ellen said, "Nothing is impossible, Doctor. We'll wait. If he doesn't say anything, the bugs stay. If he warns us against it, they go."

Exley frowned, spread his large hands slowly across the polished tabletop as though inspecting its grain, and seemed reluctant to go on. But finally, his voice cautious, he murmured, "In less than ninety minutes, it will be twenty-four hours since the abduction. It will no longer be your problem."

Paul's face instantly flushed, but before he could say anything LaSalle snapped, "This is a case for the Las Cruces police, Doctor. We're not going to get bogged down fighting turf wars. We're here to help." He looked at Ellen. "If you decide it's too risky to use the bugs, we won't. Your decision."

Exley started to say something, but Ellen said, "Let's wait until he calls again." Wanting to move on, she added quickly, "That takes care of the ransom. Next question: Who delivers it?"

LaSalle said, "I think that's an area where we can help. I suggest we take advantage of the expertise we have here and use Dr. Exley. There's always the possibility that kidnapper and courier will meet, and Walt has the experience to deal with him where none of us would."

Ellen wasn't sure. Exley didn't seem like the sort of person to send on a law-enforcement mission where more than two dozen lives were at stake. She looked over at Paul, who also seemed dubious. He asked Exley, "Armed?"

"I think not," the psychologist said, leaning forward. His voice sounded tense as he added, "But again, let's wait and see what the kidnapper says. Almost certainly he will instruct us to send an unarmed courier, even if he intends not to meet him. If that's what he wants, that's what we'll do. A gun cannot be hidden as easily as a bug."

It passed momentarily through Ellen's mind that the F.B.I. would be credited with the kidnapper's capture if it occurred while one of their men was making the pay-off. But she quickly dismissed the thought. Utilizing Exley made sense. Especially if the kidnapper was mentally ill, which she felt was almost a certainty. "All right," she said. "Dr. Exley delivers the ransom. That brings us to the big question: If we don't use a tracking device, do we follow him? If the kidnapper sends the courier on a treasure hunt can we afford to have him lead a parade of unmarked cars? Or do we set the courier free on his own?" Trying to keep her eyes from LaSalle, she focused on Paul.

"He'll position himself to see if anyone's following," Paul mused. "He'll be expecting it."

"We could have civilian cars all over town," Ellen suggested. "No matter where Dr. Exley is directed, a car could pick him up for a while, then have another one take over, then another, and so forth."

Paul gave an irritated shake of his head. "Even if we had that many cars and that many bodies, they'd have to communicate by radio. He'll be listening."

LaSalle agreed. "We've done it like that in the past. Hell, I used thirty-five vehicles once, including a lunch wagon and fire truck. But the bad guys are pretty sophisticated now. You gotta figure they'll have a radio."

"Exley could have a car phone," Paul said. "One of those you put in the sun visor and don't have to hold. No one would see him talking. He could tell us where he's going as he gets instructions from the kidnapper. We could even get a car to the next stop before he arrives there and stake out the place."

"Again, it's not secure," LaSalle said. "Cellular phones can be monitored on scanners. You have to figure any sort of voice communication, even eight hundred megahertz transmissions and scrambled radios, can be picked up by anyone moderately sophisticated with electronics. It's just too risky."

"All right," Ellen said. She was beginning to feel uneasy again, though she was unable to tell why. "Dr. Exley will have to be on his own then if we don't bug the money." She turned to him. "Are you sure you don't mind that? You could be somewhere in the mountains or the desert by yourself, no weapon, no transmitter."

Exley shrugged and tried to appear unaffected. "It doesn't make me happy. But if it has to be . . ."

Ellen studied him a moment, unable to read his emotion, then turned away. "Okay, then what about manpower? We've got to have some support for Dr. Exley. He'll be out there alone. How do you usually handle this sort of situation?" She turned to LaSalle, expecting to find him staring at her, but he was looking at his notes. He glanced up quickly.

"The key is to stay flexible and mobile. How we handle it depends on where the pay-off is. Do you have an assault team in the department?"

Ellen shook her head. Twenty-four sworn officers—what did he expect?

"Then set one up. You'll need four to six people. Have all your gear ready—flack jackets, weapons, tear gas, stun grenades. You have equipment, don't you?"

"Yes."

"Maybe you could arrange with the Sheriff's Department," he started to glance at Paul but thought better of it, "for a helicopter and pilot. Then sit and wait. And hope you're not needed."

"And if it's in the county?" Paul asked.

"You'll have to coordinate with the sheriff but—"

"They'll want to go in by themselves," Ellen interrupted. "You saw how they are."

"All right, I'll call the sheriff personally," LaSalle said, a hint of annoyance in his voice. "But it's vital to have a single team ready no matter where the pay-off is. It might be more acceptable to them if the idea comes from me. I'll want some of my people going, too."

With a recurrence of his earlier ire, Paul asked, "What about the extra agents you were going to bring in to hold Exley's hand? They here yet?"

LaSalle paused a moment as an annoyed look flashed across his face. "They arrived late last night. They're out at the kidnap site right now, getting oriented. I had to bunk them in the locker room when they arrived. It was the only place left."

Paul's jaw tightened as he looked at the other man. "You

should have checked with me first. If you take over the locker room, where the hell are my people going? They're already feeling pressed. I could've got you some room on the city side of the building last night. Too damn late now; city workers are already coming in."

"I looked for you," LaSalle said without emotion. "You weren't here. I guess you went home."

"I've got a phone."

LaSalle didn't respond.

"And you want these agents of yours going on the rescue?" Paul went on. His irritation was growing again, and Ellen looked at him with concern. It wasn't like him to get so agitated, and she found herself becoming annoyed with his persistence. He continued to stare angrily at LaSalle. "Seems kinda like overkill, doesn't it? Us, the sheriff, all you federal guys. It's going to look like World War III."

LaSalle remained calm. "I want my people ready. You or Ellen can decide whether you need them. I'm not going to make that decision. Getting your own team together is more important."

Paul looked over at Ellen and sighed heavily. "Christ! You take care of it. Brooks is our so-called weapons expert. Have him take five guys who've been through the county SWAT course, if we've got five." He was still clearly upset, whether at LaSalle's use of the locker room or the size of the rescue team or something else Ellen couldn't tell. He said, "Tell them they'll be bunking with federal agents, so they ought to make sure they have clean underwear on." He reached over and snatched a donut from the box. "What about the army? They going to be moving in with us, too?"

"They're still set up at the edge of town," LaSalle said. "They won't make a move unless you or I ask for it. I'm liaison officer, and I'll stay here. I'm not going to tell you how to handle things, Chief. If you want the army, I'll give the go-ahead. They can be airborne in three minutes. But it's your decision. Yours and Ellen's. Let's wait and see what our bad guy is planning."

As LaSalle was talking, Ellen started pacing. This morn-

ng she had felt confident. The carpenter's chalk was going
to lead them to the kidnapper. Even if it didn't and they had
to go along with his ransom demands, everyone would be
working together today, marching in step toward the same
goal. But something she couldn't identify had happened in
the past few minutes, and a vague unease, a darkening of
emotion as though all their planning would be in vain, settled over her. When the phone rang, she jumped, seizing
it, then relaxing a moment later and handing the receiver
to Paul. "Sheriff's Department," she said and turned to
LaSalle, another thought in her mind. "What do we do if
he arranges for the pay-off in the city and we're able to visually track the car? Do you want to move in when he picks
up the money or wait until he returns to where the children
are?"

"If the pay-off location is away from civilians, we'll saturate the area with cars and move in the instant he picks it
up. It's too risky to let him return to the hostages. We can
send in two helicopter teams if need be, yours and the army.
When he sees two choppers coming at him, especially one
of those army gunships, he'll give it up right there. I'll have
the army stay in the air and let you make the arrest. If he
tries to run, they can set down on the road and box him in."

Ellen said, "The worst thing would be if he leaves a partner with the kids and the guy panics when his buddy doesn't
return."

"The worst thing," Dr. Exley corrected, straightening papers in front of him, "would be if he's running this game
by himself and some trigger-happy law-enforcement officer
shoots and kills him. We might not ever find the hostages.
It's happened."

Paul put the phone down. "The sheriff's dogs followed
Ridge Road for three miles from where that kid's shoe was
found before they picked up the scent again near where a
county road intersects it. The other shoe was there. They
tried going another five miles north, but that was it—no
scent. They finally took the dogs home. I told Marcus to get
his butt in here so we can coordinate with his people."

Exley pushed out of his chair and hurried over to the map. "Show me where this is."

Paul crossed over and ran his finger along a dotted line that intersected the highway. "It's a dirt road, washes out in the winter. In the best of times only a four-wheeler could do it. A bus would bog down. Going west it dead ends at a gunnery range."

"And east?"

"Up in the old mines."

"We can't ignore it," LaSalle said, getting up to look at the map. "We'll redirect our aircraft up there. Maybe with a smaller area to patrol they can spot something."

"And hope to hell it doesn't spook the guy," Paul said. He walked to where Ellen had sat down at the table and stood behind her, massaging her neck and shoulders. But instead of releasing her tension, his large hands seemed only to heighten it. She turned suddenly, moving from his touch, and said to LaSalle, "It's too easy. Finding that shoe, I mean. It's like he's leading us into the mines."

"You think he left it on purpose?" he asked with surprise.

"I don't know. But I don't like it. Remember whose fingerprints were on the knife. Does that sound like someone who'd allow a kid to throw things out a window?"

The room fell silent. After a moment LaSalle said, "We won't commit ourselves. But we've got to check it out."

Ellen looked at her watch. "We're not going to have anything definite on the construction workers for a while. We've got to keep looking for the kids. Manny, too."

LaSalle said, "This close to the ransom exchange we don't want to press the guy too much with a public search. Ninety percent of the time we're able to make an arrest the day of the pay-off. But, yeah, we want to find those kids alive. We'll keep looking."

Suddenly remembering something she'd forgotten in the excitement of the carpenter's chalk, Ellen said to Exley, "What about your sex offenders? Any possibles?"

"We've got people on it right now. Don't expect anything soon though. It's more than two thousand names." He looked down at his watch. "Twelve and a half hours until he calls. I wonder what other surprises he has for us."

6:44 A.M.

Linda Sowell had been awake for twenty minutes, but she lay without moving on the cement floor, the moans of the children rising on all sides, sapping what little energy she retained. Her fingers were torn and bloody from hours and hours of trying to loosen the screws in the door handle. Finally, late in the night, she had given up; the nail file was too thick and too flimsy to make even the slightest progress. The screws were probably frozen in place from lack of use; only power tools would be able to dislodge them. Sinking to the floor, she had thought: We'll never get out of here, never. She'd fallen asleep weeping.

The moaning around her began to get louder, more insistent. Most of the children were awake now, and their sobbing became infectious as fear bred fear in a spiraling cycle of emotion. Slowly her eyes opened.

"Mommy, I hungry." Eric had crawled onto her shoulder and was speaking directly into her ear, his hands pulling painfully at her hair. "I want something to eat."

Linda reached out and hugged her son. I can't let them see me cry again, she warned herself over and over. It frightens them so much; I'm all they have.

Her eyes went to Eric's face, and she could see him try to smile through the fear as he drew comfort from her. She hugged him closer, feeling his warmth. How small you are, she thought. But he had been such a tiny baby, and she had worried so about him. Even when she was pregnant, she was concerned that because of the drugs he might not have all his fingers or toes. She'd heard so many stories about that sort of thing. But you were beautiful, she thought. I was so happy I cried for hours. Then later when the doctor said you weren't right—he said "right"—but it was not my fault, not anyone's, he said it was just one of those things, and I was going to kill myself because I thought it was my fault, but I didn't because I couldn't stand the thought of not being with you and I can't stand the thought now.

Eric's foot gave an involuntary twitch against her midsection. She released her grip, letting him slide away, and pushed unsteadily to her feet. A wave of nausea rose at once, and her head spun. Taking her son by the hand, she said, "Come on, Eric. Everyone's hungry."

On a table by the television were the two cartons with a half-dozen boxes of breakfast cereal. They'd eaten most of it last night and less than two complete boxes remained. Just a handful for each child. She shook some corn flakes into the palm of her hand and offered it to Eric.

He began to wail. "I want Lucky Charms. And milk, Mommy, milk."

"Please, Eric. I told you last night. This is all the cereal there is. And there is no milk."

But his crying got louder and took on a fierce, strained quality. Despite her effort at control, Linda's temper shot up and she screamed, "Goddamn it, Eric, I told you that's all there is. Now shut up!"

Everyone in the room started crying now, sounding like a thousand devils screeching in her ears, and Linda angrily threw the cereal on the floor. *"Shut up! Shut up! Goddamn it, shut up!"*

In a rage, she yanked the wheelchair nearest her and spun it around, almost throwing the comatose boy in it to the floor. One of the retractable metal flaps that held his feet swung back violently and banged on the cement floor. A boy about twelve, almost as tall as Linda, howled in terror and raced fearfully to the far end of the room. Linda screamed, "Shut up, shut up, all of you!"

But it was clear they weren't going to quiet. Her hands clenched at her sides and she started to scream, then suddenly realized what she was doing. If she lost control now, if she gave into the madness she felt clamping so furiously onto her mind, she'd never be able to calm them again. Their hold on "normal" behavior was fragile enough as it was; she had to ensure they didn't lose it.

Her fingers unclenched, and she tried to catch her breath. But she couldn't, her heart wouldn't slow down, and she bent forward at the waist, her head hanging down, and heaved and heaved, gulping for air. Stay quiet, she told herself, calm yourself . . . relax . . .

Her legs unexpectedly gave way, and she sank to her knees and tumbled forward, her forehead touching the cement floor like a distance runner at the end of a race. Breathe slowly . . . relax . . . . And gradually it came back to her: I have to feed the children. They need something to eat. I have to feed them.

But it was another minute before she could act. Struggling uncertainly to her feet, she picked up one of the half-empty cereal boxes and went up to Lisa, the four-year-old schizophrenic. Vaguely, her mind registered the fact that the normally exquisite-looking girl was filthy and wild-looking, like a child raised by wolves. She was crying and shouting at the same time, and pounding her fists on the wall.

"Look, Lisa. Food."

But the girl wouldn't stop screaming. Her hands were red and bruised from the repeated banging and some of her fingers looked broken. Linda showed her the cereal, tipping the box in her direction. "Food. Do you want to eat, Lisa?"

The girl spun around, and her hand shot out greedily, seizing the flakes of dry cereal and shoving them in her mouth.

"More!" the girl demanded, her mouth still full.

"That's all, Lisa. The other children have to eat."

The girl's hands latched furiously onto Linda's wrist and when Linda tried to retrieve her arm Lisa hung on as if it were a tow rope and began to kick violently at Linda's shins. "That's all, Lisa! There isn't enough—"

"I want more, I want more, I want more." The girl had lost control and was screaming and kicking and crying. Her eyes seemed dilated, dark, and feral. Abruptly she let go of Linda's wrist and attacked her thighs with her hands, clawing and scratching and pounding. Frightened, Linda stepped hurriedly back, banging painfully into an empty wheelchair. The intensity of the girl's attack terrified her, and she began to feel sick and panicky again. "Stop it, Lisa. Stop! Here," She tipped the cereal box in the child's direction and two tiny cupped palms flew up quickly. Linda filled the hands with corn flakes and, when Lisa began to eat, hurriedly turned away and started to feed the others. She quickly began to run out of cereal, though, and there was scarcely any remaining for the last few children.

Arturo, an eight-year-old who she thought was sleeping, hadn't awoken. She bent and shook him by the shoulder, but he didn't even groan. Was Arturo diabetic? She couldn't remember. Putting her hand on his neck, she sought a pulse and felt a faint irregular throbbing under the cold skin. She filled with despair. Why hadn't they trained her to deal with a child in a coma? "Drive to the hospital" was all she had been told. Arturo's body gave a twitch, and his left foot twisted suddenly on the concrete floor. She clambered up and hurried to the water bottle, thinking without reason that that was what he needed. But there were no cups! She quickly poured water into a cereal box and hurried back, dropping to the floor again. Propping the boy up with one hand, she put the box to his lips. The water spilled out of his mouth onto his shirt. "Drink it, Arturo, drink—"

But he couldn't. Linda put the box down. The little girl who had fallen from her wheelchair also appeared to be unconscious. Linda stared at the girl's glassy, unseeing eyes as panic again began to run away with her: I've got to get us out of here. We're all going to die.

Oh my God, where's Roni? she wondered suddenly. She couldn't remember the girl clamoring for cereal with the other children.

"Eric, where's Roni?" Hysteria tore at her voice and she clenched her jaw until it hurt as she tried to maintain control.

"Sleeping, Mommy. I want Lucky Charms."

"Sleeping where, Eric? Where?"

He turned her around and pointed behind the wheelchairs. Roni was sprawled on the floor, her arm splayed under her head.

Oh God, Linda thought, Roni's had another seizure. She hurried over, dropping to her knees and feeling the girl's forehead. Clammy. No! Linda pressed her palm tightly against the child's heart. Nothing. Nothing. Nothing.

My God, no. I can't say anything, I can't tell them.

She scrambled to her feet, eyes darting wildly around the room. But there was nothing she could use for a tool or a weapon.

Her pulse throbbed so loudly she had to put her hand against the wall to steady herself. Her eyes lit on the empty wheelchair and hope flooded back; she took two hurried steps toward it, knowing at once what she could do. Jerking on the vinyl seat, the chair folded together. I'm getting us out of here, she thought! She picked it up and hurried over to the door she had been working on. With a mighty effort, she lifted the heavy chair over her head with both hands and swung down on the door handle. The handle shook but didn't detach. Again she lifted the chair and slammed it violently down on the handle, then again and again as the children stopped their crying to look at her. Suddenly the handle shifted slightly. She screamed when she saw it move, hefted the chair once more above her head and crashed it down on the handle as hard as she could; this time it broke completely but still didn't fall away. Her body trembled with excitement. "Look! Look! It broke! We're getting out of here! We're getting out!" She was screaming more to herself than the children, but they began to scream, too, feeding off her hysteria and crowding noisily around her. Gasping for breath and sweating with exertion, Linda dropped the chair to the floor, pulled furiously on the handle, and it immediately slipped off, exposing the lock assembly. Her pulse throbbed so wildly she knew she was about to lose control. But it didn't matter. She'd done it! She'd gotten it open! Oblivious to the pain in her fingers, she jabbed them in the small opening, pulled back on the latch, and yanked on the door with her left hand.

It swung open. The children crowded forward, shouting with excitement, crying, pushing each other to hurry past her. Linda, sobbing with relief, leapt to her feet and saw empty shelves. A pantry.

Screaming, howling, everywhere, everywhere.

"To the man who is afraid, everything rustles."

—*Sophocles, 5th Century* B.C.

"Aren't we supposed to talk about dreams?" Lowell DeVries had asked Dr. Weir one day.

"Okay, let's talk about dreams."

"No, I mean, isn't that what shrinks do? Ask people what they're dreaming and then tell them what the dreams mean?"

"Not 'tell' them but perhaps help them see the origin of the dream. Anxieties they might be having, for example. But it's not like reading pictographs. No one can say for certain what meaning any dream has, or even if meaning in fact exists."

"So if I dream of a cigar or a telephone pole I'm not thinking of cocks. It doesn't mean I'm a fag. Is that what you're telling me?"

Weir had leaned back in his chair, resting his hands in his lap, the boy giving him his aggressive don't-fuck-with-me look, a look the psychologist had seen on virtually every inmate he had talked to in his eight years at the institution. It was a sort of a psychoanalytic rite of passage, a deliberate provocation that had to be silently weathered if a fruitful relationship was to be forged. Weir had smiled, hoping to diffuse the emotion and ease them both over this ritualistic hump. "It might mean you want a smoke, or perhaps you have an overwhelming desire to work for the phone company. But, no, it probably wouldn't have anything to do with sexual orientation. Dreams typically have meaning only within the context of a larger life experience. So if a sixteen-year-old on the outside dreamed of chains, for example, I'd say it was probably without significance, but if you did, while incarcerated here, I'd think it bespoke some deeper anxiety you were feeling. Which would be understandable, of course. No one likes being locked up and . . ."

As Weir had rattled on Lowell's eyes had blinked involuntarily several times, like venetian blinds being rapidly opened and closed, and the psychologist's form had seemed suddenly to magnify in front of him, gaining both definition and clarity. It was a trick of the senses, he knew, a dysfunction of the brain that sometimes came to him at times of stress, at other times for no apparent reason. All at once he would begin to notice things previously hidden, things he was certain no one else was able to see. Weir's entire being had appeared to him hugely, moving through his field of vision as though it were a specimen viewed under a magnifying glass. Wiry black hairs had sprung into view between the knuckles of the man's massive hand as it gently tapped on the arm of the chair; crow's feet had seemed to deepen into huge caverns as they ran in a complex pattern from the side of Weir's face toward his squinty, almond-colored eyes; faint hints of gray and red had shown almost luminously within the mass of unruly black hair on his head. Lowell had liked this, had liked it a lot, the way his senses had intensified almost magically, like a zoom lens on a video camera, and he'd wished that he could will it. But he couldn't; it was magical and always unexpected.

His perception already returning to normal, he'd relaxed and given the smile adults always seemed to fall for, lots of white teeth flashing and eyes going wide: baby-face Lowell, the Eagle Scout. "Well, thanks, Doc. I just wondered."

"Why don't we talk about it, then?" Weir had suggested, not willing to be put off. "What have you been dreaming about? Maybe we can put it in a more meaningful context."

Lowell's grin didn't alter as he let his body go loose in the chair. Already he'd learned how easy it was to co-opt and confound those in authority by affecting the behaviors they expected to see. "Girls," he said. "I dream about getting laid."

And he'd spun out an elaborate fantasy, making it up as

he went along, because there was no way he was going to tell Dr. Weir that he woke up in a sweat every night as the last vestiges of the same dream fled raucously from his consciousness: Lowell tied naked to a bed—or was it the floor? and was he tied or nailed?—while being attacked by dozens of absurdly small children and babies, some of them nude, others wearing diapers. It was like pictures he had seen of Gulliver being tortured in Lilliput except the children had knives and swords and straight razors and huge pins, and they stabbed and slashed and cut until he sat up with a start, stifling a scream. His heart would be pounding wildly, his eyes flash open in the darkness, and in that instant of semi-sleep as he suddenly snapped awake, in his mind's most secret eye, he saw the children—they were so tiny, no larger than a baby's fist—flying from his body and rushing away down a dark corridor to hide in his unconscious until the next time he slept.

Instead, he'd told Weir a banal adolescent boy's tale about this blonde with tits as big as August watermelons, who came to his dreams each night and lavished his body with kisses because Weir seemed to enjoy it and because Lowell didn't want to know what lay hidden in that distant corner of his psyche where tiny naked children retreated, laughing, each night.

Weir had nodded and said that that type of sexual wish fulfillment was to be expected, given Lowell's incarceration, but that he should try to guide his unconscious by directing it toward safer visions. Sex was normally an acceptable fantasy, of course, but it would do him little good to hope for the unattainable while in juvenile hall and it would be better if . . .

But Lowell's attention had wandered, and his eyes had begun to drift lazily around the room. Weir's office had been the only one in the entire facility with a carpet, and he'd liked that. Deep, deep red, the color of the absurdly expensive wine his folks drank, and he drank when they weren't around. Weir had told him that he bought the carpet himself, the state would never pay for such extravagances, and Lowell had thought, Big fucking deal, you want a commendation? Framed pictures on the wall of country-sides and mountains. He'd liked those, too. Supposed to make us feel all warm and fuzzy inside, he'd thought. Big old-fashioned brown leather swivel chair for Weir. The state didn't pay for that, either. An upholstered chair and couch for patients. Weir had told him he never had anyone lie down, and Lowell had said, "Sure, you just ask them to bend over." Weir had smiled knowingly: "I'll give you a D for orig-inality. Maybe we can work on your creativity while you're here." That was before they'd started getting along.

Still, Weir had gone on about sex dreams. Lowell, hiding his annoyance, had turned his attention to him again. "Hey, Doc, calm down. I made it up. The whole thing. I don't dream at night. Nothing. That's why I asked you. Wanted to see what you'd say."

6:55 A.M.

Ellen was sitting behind Paul's desk when he strode in and gave her a look of mock anger. "You got a warrant to make that search?" His tone made him sound more upset than he intended.

"Calling Zach. I want to make sure he's got those civilians working on the phones. They might have turned up some-thing by now."

He turned to look at the clock. "Jesus, Ellen, it's only been twenty minutes."

"I know how long it's been, Paul. I can tell time."

"Sheriff's deputies won't be here until—" But Ellen was already talking into the phone. Paul left, taking the eleva-tor down to the cafeteria. It wasn't scheduled to open for another five minutes, and the white-clad workers were scur-rying around, slapping at the tables with wet cloths and slipping trays of food under the heat lamps. Already, though, a half-dozen F.B.I. lab and computer people sat hunched over coffee at a table in the corner, talking loudly, laughing. They were everywhere he looked lately. Paul walked over to the coffeemaker, poured two cups full, and carried them to the empty check-out station. Leaving a dollar on the register, he went back upstairs, entering his office in time to hear Ellen on the phone to her daughter now. "Well, what does Mrs. Garcia think, Denise?"

Paul put a cup in front of her and sat in one of the visitor's chairs, a dull pain springing up suddenly in the small of his back as he hit the seat. Age, he thought with irritation. Only forty-three and already he had a bad back and high blood pressure. Not to mention at least one stroke. There had been another weird pain a couple of months ago, but he hadn't told anyone, even Ellen. No sense worrying people. So what other surprises were lurking in the wings, ready to strike? He was starting to become one of the Old People. But it beat the alternative; his father didn't even make it to forty.

Ellen was saying, "Uh-huh . . ." Sounding wary, maybe even a little irritated, Paul thought, remembering the tone from his own parenting days. It made him feel close to Ellen again, though, as if they were sharing something private, something they both valued. He placed his cup on the glass-topped table and wondered if there were any donuts left next door. Better not, he decided, starting to put on weight; anyway, he was supposed to be watching his cholesterol and fat in-take. Christ, what a way to live!

Ellen sighed, trying not to show her irritation. "I think I better talk to Mrs. Garcia, honey." She shot Paul a look as she waited for the baby-sitter to get back on the line, then said into the phone, "I don't think today is a very good day for that, Julie."

A yawn came unexpectedly as Paul sat back and stretched out his legs. He had spent the night on the couch, getting at best three hours sleep. He didn't feel too bad now, but it would catch up to him by evening, he knew. He wondered how much sleep Ellen had gotten. She'd said she was going to bed as soon as she got out of the tub. That would have been around midnight. She hadn't, though, he knew. She was tired and tense, squeezing the phone with her left hand while the fingers of her right hand tapped impatiently on the desktop.

One of the Old People, Paul repeated to himself. That wouldn't be so bad. Even if young folk didn't have the respect they used to, the Old People knew that the years had given them in wisdom what they had taken in physical prowess. Paul himself was proof of that. Even the eight years he'd done in the army had been sufficient to change him in ways that were easy to see, if difficult sometimes to understand. But he'd definitely come back calmer, more at peace with the world. The Wild Man tamed, people had said at the time, the old ones nodding sagely and the teenagers scratching their heads.

Ellen was still talking to Mrs. Garcia, a battle of wills with Ellen's voice becoming increasingly strained as she tried to maintain her composure. After a moment, Denise was evidently again on the line and Ellen said, "I just don't think it would be a good idea, hon. I want you to stay home and watch TV. We'll go another day, maybe Saturday."

A few minutes later, Ellen hung up and shook her head as the knot of tension tightened painfully again in her neck. She squeezed her eyes shut, resting her forehead in her hand. "Denise wanted to go to the swimming pool at the park. I just don't want her doing it. I'm going to be a hysterical mom until we catch this guy. Julie thinks I'm overprotective. What do you think?"

"Julie's right. And so are you. Sometimes it's okay to be a little weird. This guy's not going to be running around snatching more kids, but why give yourself something else to worry about? Hell, yes, keep her home."

"I guess I still feel bad about her being with a sitter all day. Children should be brought up by their parents, not paid help."

"Couldn't prove it by your mother," Paul said and immediately regretted it. "Sorry—"

Ellen gave him a look he couldn't read, but her voice was tight with emotion. "Maybe you could say I went from broken home to broken home. From verbal abuse to physical abuse in one generation. Not much of an improvement, was it?" She came suddenly to her feet again. "Are there any donuts left? I'm hungry."

"Didn't you have breakfast?" He was staring at her face. She looked different today, prettier almost, despite the obvious tension, though he wasn't sure exactly why. Maybe it was just his imagination.

"I didn't have time." She sounded annoyed. "Or I wasn't in the mood. I don't know. What difference does it make?"

"I'll look next door. What'd Zach have to say?"

"They haven't got anything—" The phone buzzed and Ellen snatched the receiver, shoving it over the desk to Paul before he could leave. It was Bobby Muledeer in the squad room.

"Our boy just called, Chief. He asked for Robbery and no one was here so I picked it up. He said we got twelve more hours. Just wanted to remind us. Like we'd forget, right?"

LaSalle sat next to Ellen on the leather couch in Paul's office and said, "Did you get a recording?"

Pacing behind his desk, Paul shook his head. "Only calls to reception or nine one one are recorded."

LaSalle frowned and sank back against the cushions, seeming to retreat within his mind. "Then we can't be certain of the exact wording."

"No."

"It had to be him though," LaSalle said as if to himself. "No one outside this building knew of the seven P.M. deadline. There's been no leak, no mention of it on TV. I wonder if he called the squad room knowing that it wouldn't be recorded?"

"He may have been expecting to get me," Ellen said. "Assuming that's who called me in the squad room yesterday. Or more likely he's just trying to shake us up, doing the unexpected." Ellen wasn't sure she believed it. Grasping at straws, she told herself, watching LaSalle as he thought things out. Like Paul, he seemed to have the ability to channel his thoughts along an unusually narrow path when he wanted to, allowing nothing to anger or excite him. She didn't know if she would want to be like that, using her will to impose rationality on a situation that had none; it distanced you from what people were feeling, altering the reality of events too much by changing victims into things and crimes into puzzles. Her own nerves were stretched ever tighter as she worried about the sanity of the kidnapper and wondered what the children must be going through; twenty-four hours they had been held captive by this madman dressed as a clown, and every hour had to be harder to endure than every previous hour. Harder on the parents, too. Matt doesn't know what it's like, she thought. Only a parent would understand.

Paul halted his pacing and sounded angry. "He's pretty damn good at doing the unexpected, isn't he? Like with the Torres girl."

"You get anything useful from her yet?" LaSalle asked.

"Fragments," Ellen said and waved a hand. "Clown, man, big car, noise. We'll talk to her again this morning, maybe have her teacher try, too. But I don't think she'll be able to tell us much."

"Is she mentally retarded?"

"Down syndrome. She has an I.Q. of about 60, I guess."

A young civilian employee from downstairs appeared at the door. "Chief?"

He handed Paul a piece of paper. "Fax from El Centro."

As Paul took it, the man said, "Any news on Rios?"

"No, there's no news. Goddamn it, you think I'd keep it a secret if there was?" The other man blanched, and Paul said, "Sorry, Ken. No. We don't know anything."

The young man hurried away and Paul stalked back to his desk and read the fax without sitting down. "Autopsy on the boy. Shot twice, probably with a handgun, but both bullets exited the body. Would have died almost instantly. The clown hat and makeup were sent to D.C. for analysis." He darted a hostile look at LaSalle. "The body had been neatly arranged in that woman's house, as though watching television." He tossed the report on the desktop. "That's it. Not a goddamn thing to help us."

"You'll need to tell the press," LaSalle said. "No point in keeping it quiet. Do they know about Rios yet?"

"I put out a statement this morning. Figured someone might've seen his car." He walked over to the window and stared across the street. "Gonna have to talk to them anyway," he muttered. "Christ!"

Ellen turned toward the window. "Reporters?"

"Like army ants," he said with his back to them. "One of them spots food and they all jump in line. Except ants are more disciplined."

LaSalle said, "I'll come along if you want. Give them two targets to shoot at."

Paul turned around and looked at Ellen, his face without expression. "What do you think? You want to see Matt and me perform together? Kinda compare our techniques?"

There was something new in his tone, a sarcasm Ellen hadn't encountered before, and it startled her. Carefully, she said, "Not if you don't want to, Paul."

He stared at her a moment, then made an impatient gesture with his hand. "Hell, let's do it. Dog and pony show." He turned toward the window again. "God, I wish I knew what happened to Manny."

"I got a call from Los Angeles this morning," LaSalle said. "The ransom's going to be here around two. It'll come in on an armed army chopper. We sure as hell don't want people to know there's twenty million dollars in here. So let's arrange the press conference for two o'clock at the high school. That'll get the reporters away. We can put the chopper down in the parking lot out back and hustle the money inside in a couple of duffel bags and hope no one hanging around figures it out."

Paul looked at his watch. "Six and a half hours. Maybe we'll actually have something to tell them."

"Our planes will be up soon," LaSalle said. "Or something might turn up with the construction workers. It could all be over by then."

"You don't believe that," Paul said with annoyance as the phone rang. He crossed back to the desk and pushed the speaker-phone button.

"The Palm Springs TV station." Maggie's voice came clearly into the room. "They said it's important."

Paul glanced at Ellen, then dropped down in his swivel chair and said wearily, "Chief Whitehorse."

"Elton Neville, Station Manager, Chief. I'm contacting you out of courtesy. Someone called our reception desk this morning and said there was a videotape of the kidnapped kids in the trash dumpster in back of the studio. One of our reporters went out and looked, and sure as hell, there it was in a plastic trash bag."

Ellen felt a shiver along her spine; she straightened and threw a glance at LaSalle, who didn't move, his eyes riveted on the phone. Paul leaned toward the speaker. "You know for sure it's the kids?"

"Hell, yes, it's the kids! The guy made a tape—the kids, the bus driver, everyone screaming. Pretty gruesome. But I guess he wants you to know he has them."

"Jesus," Paul muttered.

"It's not very long," the station manager said. "Maybe three or four minutes. But dramatic stuff. I've got a guy on his way to you now with the original."

"The original?"

"We made a copy. We're going to broadcast it. That's why I called you. I wanted you to hear it from us first. We're going to break into our regular programming in ten minutes and show it. You might want to watch. You should get the original in half an hour or so."

"Now wait a minute—"

"We're showing the film, Chief. It's our responsibility. I didn't even have to call you. I did it out of courtesy. If you want to see it before it gets there, turn on the TV."

The lunchroom was packed solid: police, F.B.I., clerical staff. So many people had heard about it that twenty or thirty were left standing in the hallway, hoping to hear if they couldn't watch. Paul and Ellen stood stiffly in front of the television, waiting for what the kidnapper wanted them to see.

A talk show was on, a woman standing in the studio audience with a microphone. Without warning, she vanished and the local news anchor appeared.

"We interrupt our regularly scheduled programming to show you a dramatic piece of videotape that was evidently delivered to this station by the kidnapper of twenty-seven Las Cruces school children. An anonymous caller to the station this morning asked us to check a trash dumpster in the rear of the building for a video cassette. When we did, this is what we found. I should warn you, this is not for the faint of heart. If the sight of these children held as hostages, some of them apparently quite ill or hurt, might upset you, please turn off your TV. Now here it is."

Images unsteadily captured by a hand-held camera danced abruptly onto the screen.

A group of five children, Ellen quickly noted, her pulse beginning to thump. One of them nude. Noise everywhere, it seemed: moaning, wailing, crying. Why is that girl nude? My God, is he raping them? The bus driver in filthy shorts. A boy with a battered and bloody face. Jesus, what's he doing to them? A boy in a wheelchair who looks catatonic.

"Christ," Paul said softly, and Ellen could feel his body tense with emotion.

The camera zoomed in close on the nude girl, lingered. Why are they broadcasting this? Ellen wondered as her flesh grew cold. The parents of these children must be going crazy right now. The poor mother of that little girl.

The camera shifted to Linda Sowell's face, zoomed in as close as it could—filthy, eyes red, hair unkempt. Where are her glasses? She normally wore glasses, didn't she? Almost in slow motion, Linda's head fell to her chest, and she begged softly, "Please don't do this. Let us out of here."

"Goddamn it!" Paul said. "I'm going to call a federal judge. I'm going to confiscate that film. I don't want it shown anywhere in the country until we catch this guy."

"It won't do any good," Ellen replied softly. "Every TV station in the country will have copied it by now."

The camera had gone on to a girl who appeared to be unconscious, sprawled on the floor amid her own waste. Then abruptly it was over.

"I'm going to do it anyway," Paul snapped. "Don't these people have a conscience?"

Ellen glanced at him. "Rhetorical question?"

The newscaster said, "In case you missed any of that the first time, we're going to show it in its entirety again."

The film started anew.

"I'm calling a judge," Paul said and hurriedly left.

Ellen stayed and watched again. A largish room, it appeared this time as her gaze was drawn to the background details. A bare cement floor. What kind of place would have a cement floor? A warehouse, maybe. She couldn't see the walls; the kidnapper had contrived to keep them out of view. The nude girl wasn't moving. Was she alive? The bus driver's hands appeared to be bloody.

Ellen could feel a tenseness moving about the room. The men and women around her were muttering angrily to one another. Dr. Exley squeezed in next to her. "This, of course, is a ploy," he said without emotion. "He is trying to engage your sympathy for these children."

"Then he's been successful," Ellen said, her eyes riveted on the television.

"This is not the first time I've encountered something like this. He's exposing a little bit of himself for us, showing us what he's like. To make sure the ransom is delivered."

Ellen looked at him, blank-faced. "Was there ever any doubt?"

He shrugged. "Not to us perhaps. But to him, of course. They always worry about it."

"And what would happen if we didn't find enough diamonds of the sort he wanted in the time he gave us?"

"He would kill these children. Or, more correctly, some of them. Some must be kept as bargaining chips."

The film ended.

The small lunchroom was hot and smelled of confinement, as though the air had stopped moving.

The newscaster stared dully into the camera. "So far we have no reaction from the F.B.I. or the Las Cruces Police Department. When we do—"

Ellen stepped to the TV and angrily flipped it off. Just then a uniformed officer forced her way in from the hallway. "All hell's breaking loose out on the street, Ellen. The reporters won't stay at the high school anymore. They're going crazy. They want a statement from Paul. They want to know what we're doing."

Ellen swore quietly to herself. "How many are there?"

The woman shook her head nervously. "Couple of hundred, maybe. But Ferguson called from Kennedy. He couldn't keep them there. He said there'll be a thousand people out front in ten minutes."

"Goddamn it!" Ellen snapped. "The Sheriff's Department only sent two patrolmen for crowd control. We can't use our people. We won't have anyone left for the investigation."

"Maybe we could call the sheriff's again, see if they can send more."

Ellen hurried out of the room toward the front door, the officer striding along beside her, a dozen civilians following to see what the excitement was. They passed out of the police side of the building and into the lobby. On the other side of the double glass doors they could see Ricky Price, the youngest of Las Cruces' police officers, standing in front of a crowd of angry reporters. Ellen said at once, "Find Paul. Get him down here quick."

The woman took off at a run, and Ellen pushed on the doors, stepping out into the early morning heat. Ricky turned his boyish face in her direction and tried without success to appear calm. "Shucks, don't need but one Texas Ranger, ma'am. Ain't but one riot."

Ellen smiled grimly at the probably apocryphal line. "Ricky, there isn't a cop in the world who can stand up to an enraged anchorperson in the wild. They'll have you for lunch."

Price had managed to keep the reporters in the street and off the steps. They began yelling at Ellen the moment she appeared. She put her hand on Ricky's arm. "Cover me, pal. I'm going out there. If I'm not back in ten minutes, notify my next of kin."

She walked down the marble steps to the sidewalk and the mushrooming crowd of reporters and camera operators and photographers. They swarmed at once around her, shouting. She held up a hand. "I'm not going to say a word until you quiet down and move away from the building."

Suddenly Paul was at her side. "We're not going to say a word, period," he announced in a loud voice. Three uniformed patrolmen, probably all that were available, had followed him outside. Paul's face had gone red, and it was all he could do to maintain control, Ellen thought, feeling rage rise like heat from his body.

"You people are going to go back to the high school or to jail. I'm tired of this interference. I told you, when we have something to say, we'll say it. Until—"

"What about the videotape?" someone yelled, and another shouted, "What were you feeling when you saw those children?"

"You've got sixty seconds," Paul said, noticing the red lights on the cameras and realizing that they weren't being taped; it was going out live; the world was watching this instant as it happened. He was beyond caring though. "Start dispersing or I'll lock you up. We've got two dozen kids to look for." The white minivan the department used to transport prisoners turned a corner onto the street and began to slowly force its way into the crowd.

The man who had yelled earlier said, "You got no right to do this, Chief. You can't tell us how to cover a story."

"Forty-five seconds," Paul yelled. "I've called the governor. He's sending the National Guard in from San Diego for crowd control. Since you don't like dealing with me, you can talk to the army."

The minivan had managed to ease into the middle of the crowd and was completely surrounded by people. The driver shut off the engine and waited. Ellen wondered who had been left to drive it.

"I mean it," Paul said, moving forward aggressively, and yelling at the top of his voice. "You folks get out of here now. Get the hell back to Kennedy. I'll come down there later and give a press conference."

Ellen had never seen him so angry. It wasn't just the reporters leaving the high school that disturbed him but the way the TV station had broadcast the tape without considering how it might affect the parents or disrupt the investigation. Paul had crossed in front of her and she could see his shoulder muscles tensed and the skin of his neck, under the black, pulled-back hair, stretched tight with rage.

A middle-aged reporter stepped from the crowd and began to wave his fist in Paul's face. "You can't do this. We have the right—"

"You have five seconds to turn around and walk out of here," Paul said so softly that Ellen wasn't sure the man could hear it. It's going to blow up, she thought in a panic. She had to do something. Quickly stepping forward, she grabbed the reporter's elbow to usher him away, but he angrily shook her off and yelled, "Bullshit! You can't—"

With a single motion Paul seized the man's forearm and twisted him to his knees, snapping a handcuff on one wrist; the man howled in pain and began to thrash about madly as the crowd exploded in yelling. One of the other patrolmen had seized the writhing reporter's free hand and held it while Paul snapped the other cuff.

All at once dozens of reporters surged toward them, shouting angrily. Ellen felt her pulse rush, adrenaline pumping wildly through her veins. TV cameras were being jerked aloft everywhere, over the heads of the crowd, pointing like periscopes from every direction. People shouted, jostled, pushed ahead. The whole of the crowd jolted at once forward, as if it were a single living thing, engulfing them with its rage. Reporters on all sides were thrusting microphones and cameras in their direction. A woman screamed as someone's elbow caught her in the face, breaking her nose, spewing blood on those next to her. Paul grabbed the handcuffed reporter and tried to lead him up the stairs but the crowd wouldn't let him through. Ellen couldn't tell if they were attempting to keep the man from jail or just trying to record what was happening. But a sense of panic and shared hysteria animated everyone now, and she was jostled and shoved and knocked off balance as reporters pushed past her.

The three patrolmen had grabbed their batons and were holding them in the two-handed stance they had learned in their crowd control class at the academy. Stepping in front of Paul, they cleared a path. Ellen quickly moved the other way and let the crowd flow past her like a huge wave, then suddenly found herself free. Standing on the sidewalk, she watched as Paul pushed the prisoner in front of him up the steps and into the Civic Center behind the three patrolmen. Then the glass doors slammed and locked behind them. The crowd roared its anger.

A horn honked behind her, and Ellen turned to see the police van. Howard Stines stuck his head out the window. "Better come with me, Ellen. We can slip in the back way through the booking entrance."

Ellen hurried toward him and slid into the passenger seat. Stines said, "Christ, he blew it, Ellen. That's not like Paul at all. What the hell was he trying to do, start a riot? The press is going to crucify him."

She didn't say anything but thought, Yeah, he blew it. This is going to be trouble.

"I teach that all men are crazy."

—*Horace, ca. 25 B.C.*

What are the police and F.B.I. thinking as they watch this? DeVries wondered as he stared with rapt attention at the television. The station was running his tape for the third time, evidently for the slow learners.

Not very good camera technique, he decided as the lens zoomed in for a close-up, but adequate . . . adequate. Ah, yes, the girl. Sexy little thing, sprawled on her back without any clothes on. Such soft, soft skin, warm as a bath, legs splayed just so. His eyes fixed intently on her nude body, and he began to feel an erection, blood rushing pleasurably into his penis and throbbing in tune to his accelerated pulse.

He'd only killed one child and that was—what?—ten, twelve years ago? The daughter of that woman in Calixeco he'd gone out with for a while, Gabriela something. The kid's name was Maria. Six, seven, something like that, so not exactly a baby. She'd deserved to die anyway, the way she'd made eyes at him, touching him, snuggling against his body, knowing full well what was on his mind, wanting it, begging for it (he could hear it in his mind even if she hadn't spoken the words), then panicking when he'd picked her up one afternoon after school and taken her out in the desert. By the time he'd got her panties off, she was screaming so loudly what could he do? From then on, though, he decided he'd better make the drive down to Miss Violet's rather than risk going to jail again. Nothing was worth going to jail for again.

It was too bad he and Gabriela had broken up shortly after. She'd had a wild, sensual playfulness about her and would laugh out loud in her lusty Latin voice and call him crazy because of some of the things he liked to do with her. God, how he had loved her youthful good looks, her pouty baby face with its round, fleshy cheeks and full lips, which she always kept covered—smeared really, like a little girl— in thick dabs of fiery-red lipstick that left traces all over his body like the stigmata of sex. He wanted her to call him Daddy and talk baby talk and say bad things so he would have to spank her until welts sprang up on her skin. She cried and fought and scratched when he did, but oh, she liked it, too. Loved it. That was before Maria had died; afterward, Gabriela hadn't been much fun.

But as hard as he tried to obliterate it from his memory,

he couldn't help thinking about what she'd said. Still thought about it, sometimes couldn't manage to drive it from his mind, the word repeating over and over until he'd want to scream. "Crazy." He'd heard it before Gabriela, of course. Everyone had. *Cra-zeee! Crazy Lowell!* When he was younger, the thought used to bother him a lot, coming unbidden and ruffling the surface of his mind like the wind on a lake. Surely it was a result of spending too much time with Weir. How could anyone be in "counseling" and not worry about their sanity? Even psychologists, he had heard, agonized over their own mental well-being.

Weir had tried to set his mind at ease. Lowell was not crazy, by any means. Unusually "detached" might be a more accurate description. Lowell seemed to believe that society's collectively agreed upon rules of behavior—don't force yourself on others, as perhaps the most obvious example—did not apply to him. Maybe, Weir had speculated, as a result of constantly moving around as a child and his parents' inability to function pragmatically in the world, Lowell did not view himself as properly integrated into the larger community of mankind, and if he would only make an effort, join some clubs, blah, blah, blah . . .

Fuck it, Lowell had told himself and tuned out. So I'm not crazy.

But he wondered.

The difficulty was in defining the term. Weir had seemed to be saying it was those who functioned outside the norm. ("Three or more standard deviations from the mean," he'd said with a smile.) Hell, if that were the case, we'd have to include Einstein, say, or da Vinci, or Lowell's mother's obsession, J.S. Bach. So if he were mad, and he most definitely was not, he would be in good company, wouldn't he?

Still, he wondered. And worried.

Oh, how he worried.

Again DeVries's eyes focused on the television and the videotape of the children. People all over the world were watching it this very minute. All . . . over . . . the . . . *world!*

And wondering what the hell it meant.

Exley thinks he has me figured out, but you're not sure, are you, Agent LaSalle? You're trying to stay ahead of me, to get into my brain. I can feel it. You're trying so hard to understand me.

So what do I plan next?

You have no idea.

No fucking idea.

Still, it might be best to check in and see what was happening. He had resisted the temptation until now.

Hell, it might be fun, Lowell.

Do it.

"Las Cruces Police," Jeannie Wheatley said, knowing her voice showed more than a trace of ill humor but not really caring since Whitehorse refused to get anyone in to help her despite the fact that her workload had tripled or quadrupled or whatever.

"Hi, babe. What's up?"

"Lowell!" Jeannie's heart did a little tumble, and her annoyance quickly vanished. "I'm so glad you called. All I've been getting since yesterday are those rude reporters. They just won't take no for an answer."

He laughed softly. "Neither will I, babe. That's why we get along so well. I turn your 'no' into *'ahhh'.* "

Jeannie giggled and wondered if she was blushing. "So what happened to you last night, Superman?"

"Must be the flu. Got a fever. Makes me so-o-o hot, the way you like me. Just lying here on my big new waterbed now, feeling the waves going in and out, in and out, in and out—"

"Lowell, stop it. I told you these calls are recorded."

"Yeah, but who's going to listen? They're only interested in the kidnapper. Tell you what, I'll call your home answering machine and leave a nice long message about what

I'm going to do to your luscious body once I get over the flu."

"I'd rather you do it than talk about it. Hold on, let me get this call."

There was a short silence until she came back on the line. "A Mexico City newspaper. Can you believe it? But 'no' means 'no' in Spanish, too."

"So what's going on with your boss, Sweetie? Going nutso looking for the kids?"

"Remember that old movie we saw last month about the insane asylum? All those people running around, acting crazy? That's what it's like. The chief seems to be a little pissed at all the F.B.I. people here. I don't blame him. Don't tell anyone, but the F.B.I. has a lot of airplanes up, looking for the bus. Hold on."

A minute later she came back on the line.

"Where'd they send the planes?" he asked with elaborate casualness.

"Up north, I guess. I think they're checking out all those old mines."

"Do tell."

"Don't you say anything about this, Lowell DeVries! I'm serious. It'd mean my job."

"Don't worry, babe. Did you see that video the kidnapper made?"

"On my break. I couldn't believe it. How could anyone be so cruel?"

"Dysfunctional childhood, I imagine. How's that woman cop doing? Ellen something. You know, the foxy one."

"Pissy, short-tempered. Like everyone else. And what do you mean, foxy? She's ten years older than me. She could be a grandmother."

"And the shrink? Is he pissy, too?"

"Everyone, Lowell. We've got a bunch more F.B.I. people coming in, too. Something about checking out construction workers."

DeVries felt a sudden chill along his spine. "Construction workers? What does that have to do with anything?"

"I don't know, but it must be important. Everyone's worked up about it. Kinda weird, huh? You don't think of those guys being the type to do something like this. I thought all they wanted to do was drink beer and whistle at girls. Oops, another call, two calls! I gotta go. Call me later."

But his mind was already churning. Construction workers. What the hell did that mean? He didn't know. But he felt certain that something was wrong. Terribly, terribly wrong. He would have to fix it. But he couldn't for the life of him figure out what it was.

8:44 A.M.

Ellen stood stiffly at Paul's floor-to-ceiling window, staring in disbelief at the reporters below as they moved in an eerily silent, unchoreographed mob. Like metal filings shifted by an invisible magnet, they surged in clumps from place to place, exercising their anger. A weariness spread through her limbs. How had it come to this? What had gone wrong? The door behind her slammed loudly, and she spun around to see Paul striding rapidly toward his desk. "Booked him," he said without looking at her. "Threw his ass in jail." He grabbed the phone off his desk, punched a button, waited until it was answered, then said, "Round up your troops, LaSalle. We're going to meet. My office. Now!" He slammed the receiver down. "Goddamn it!" His hand shook as he removed it from the phone.

Ellen moved around to the front of the desk. "What'd you charge him with?"

"Obstructing justice, inciting a riot, disturbing the peace. I told him to wait, I'd think of a few more."

The door opened and LaSalle came in. Ellen felt a flush as he smiled uneasily at her, then a sudden piercing of hostility as Middleton walked in a second later. She hadn't seen Middleton since yesterday, when he'd been interviewing the parents, and had half-forgotten about him. But his rudeness returned at once, like a flame that wouldn't stay extinguished. He was dressed in faded Levi's today, cowboy boots, and a ratty brown corduroy sportcoat. He thinks he's an Old West marshall, she thought. He thinks he's in Dodge City bringing law and order to the frontier. Middleton ignored them both and crossed to the window, where he stood with his hands jammed on his hips, staring down at the reporters. "Bastards," he muttered, his low voice filling the room with a cold menace. "Like buzzards after carrion." Exley came in seconds later, silent and worried looking, and everyone but Paul moved toward the chairs and couch.

Ellen watched the federal agents sitting stiffly, waiting, not looking at each other, and thought: They don't like the way events are unfolding. Too much confusion, too many unforeseen things happening. Especially the trouble between the police and the press, and now the National Guard being called in to maintain order. Kidnappings usually aren't so chaotic, so public, and it's unnerving them.

Exley especially appeared concerned. Like Middleton, he thought the Las Cruces police were screwing up and wanted the investigation taken away before it was too late but was unwilling to make an issue of it. Only LaSalle seemed to side with Paul and the department, and she wondered how long that would last.

Paul stepped aggressively from behind the desk, like a boxer leaving his corner, and advanced around to the other side, where he stood with his seat resting against the desktop. His face was flushed, and he folded his arms and looked directly at LaSalle, holding his gaze. "I fucked up. I lost control and arrested the bastard. I shouldn't have done it. But now that he's in jail, I'm not letting him out until he makes bail. Fuck him. If you guys or the D.A. want to fight me over this, fine. But I'm trying to find two dozen kidnapped kids before they're dead, and those people outside don't give a damn about anything but their stories."

Unexpectedly, Middleton waved dismissively toward the window as though it weren't worth talking about. "Don't be so hard on yourself. You warned them to stay away and they didn't."

LaSalle's face was blank, his eyes on Paul, as he asked, "When's the National Guard going to be here?" Ellen was unable to read his mood. He seemed to be willing his body into a stony impassivity so as not to betray his feelings. He also seemed to be consciously not looking in her direction. Or was she imagining it, her spiraling anxiety conjuring up things that did not exist?

Paul gave his watch a quick glance. "Another two hours or so. The governor said he'd send riot troops. He sure as hell better because there's no reporters left at the high school. They're all out front. The troops are going to have to get them back."

"Or we leave and go to Kennedy," Middleton said. "Let them watch the wrong building. No reason we have to stay here."

Paul stepped from the desk, his self-control at the breaking point, and began to pace around the room. "Why the hell did he call the TV stations last night and tell them he released that girl? Why send that video out? I thought kidnappers want to stay hidden. How the hell does it help him to have the goddamn press involved?"

Exley sat with his eyes determinedly fixed straight ahead as LaSalle shifted on the couch, and an image came suddenly to Ellen's mind: boats being tossed about by a storm as their mooring lines were slipped one by one. We're drifting, she thought. We've lost control. Everyone sees it. We don't know what we're doing.

"Dr. Exley and I have been talking about that," LaSalle finally said, glancing briefly at the psychologist sitting next to him. "Our best guess is he's trying to make the reporters players rather than observers. He's set up an adversary relationship between us and them. Nothing happens now without news people instantly showing up and creating problems. That was the point of the video. He's got us so worked up about the press we're turning our attention from finding the kids to dealing with the media."

"Which, of course, we are doing this very instant," the psychologist said, moving about in his chair. His eyes darted toward Ellen. "Meanwhile, the children are still missing."

"Every goddamn patrol car we have is out looking for that bus," Paul said as though being accused of something. Continuing to pace, he ran his hand down the back of his head to his neck before turning toward the others. "Plus eight officers in civilian vehicles, sheriff's deputies, planes up. There's no place left to look." He sounded both bewildered and angry. "Maybe he's close by after all. Everyone in California knows about that damn bus, but no one saw it. Maybe it's because it never left town."

The door opened without knocking and Zachary Harris came in. He seemed both excited and agitated as he crossed over to Paul and handed him a sheet of paper. "We've finally got a list of missing construction workers. But it might not be what you want."

Paul glanced at it, his head snapping up almost at once. "Sixty-five names?" He had expected ten or twenty at most.

Zach looked around at the others. "People who weren't on the job site yesterday at seven-thirty," he explained. "But most of them weren't scheduled to be. They're day workers. They might work two days one week and six days the next. Carpenters, electricians, plumbers, roofers, a few laborers from Mexico. It ain't going to be easy to check out all these guys by tonight."

"Sheriffs here yet?"

"Dribbling in. I sent 'em out to the north area like you said."

"Any F.B.I.?"

He shook his head.

LaSalle, an edge to his voice, said, "I told you it'll be another hour or so."

Paul looked exasperated as he stared at the list, then at the F.B.I. agent. "Who's going to be in charge of this? Zach can't do everything."

LaSalle glanced at Middleton but was unwilling to volunteer his friend after saddling him with the parent interviews yesterday. But Middleton sighed and reached out his hand. "Hell, I'll do it. Can't start until the bodies get here though."

Paul handed him the list as Harris hurried back to the squad room.

LaSalle asked, "Do you still want to hold a press conference?" He had made his face go blank again—his F.B.I. mask, Ellen thought. She wondered what he was thinking and why he still wouldn't look at her.

Paul glared at the man as if he were mad. "Hell, no! I'm through with the goddamn reporters." The ringing phone seemed to startle everyone, and Paul snatched at it furiously. It was one of the federal agents in the conference room for LaSalle. Paul shoved the phone almost angrily across the desk, then turned and began to wander around the room, running his left hand through his hair and down the back of his neck, occasionally shaking his left arm as though it were stiff. An uneasy feeling grew in Ellen as everyone waited, watching LaSalle as he held the receiver, listened, nodded, stared silently at the floor. She glanced at Exley, whose eyes—pale, cautious, intense—had shifted to Middleton at the other end of the couch, sitting with his legs jammed out in front of him, gazing at his boots. After a moment, LaSalle carefully lowered the receiver to the desk. "An L.A. radio station is reporting that the fingerprints on that knife you found belong to the governor. Evidently, they're getting quite a laugh out of it."

LaSalle's tone had been unaccusing, but Paul stopped his pacing and his face flushed instantly with rage. "It didn't come from my people. Goddamn it, it could've been someone in Sacramento or one of yours."

Middleton grunted, twisted in his seat, and swore softly.

Ellen shook her head. "The bad guy," she said in a low voice. "Having a little fun." A sense of alarm, of events careening faster and faster out of control, began to take over her mind. The kidnapper's making us look like idiots, she thought. He's toying with us.

"What the hell's he up to?" Paul asked, echoing her feelings. There was a plaintive quality to his voice as he looked at the F.B.I. agents. "What's he get out of this?"

"Confusion," Dr. Exley said gently. "Turmoil." He rubbed at his chin with his thumb. "Mythos."

Paul had come back to his desk and stood in front of it, staring aggressively at the psychologist. "What the hell's that supposed to mean?"

Exley looked at him benignly. "He's creating a legend, a mythology, so he won't be forgotten. It's his way of defeating death and gaining immortality, living forever in people's minds. I think we can expect him to do something big today, something dramatic to ensure he's never forgotten."

Middleton exhaled a derisive "Jesus!" and jerked to his feet, stalking away from the couch with his hands rammed in his back pockets. Ellen's eyes followed him as he crossed to the far end of the room; his constant pacing and moving about continued to unnerve her, and she felt like screaming at him to stay put.

For a long moment, no one spoke, then Exley said softly, "We had a case similar to this some years ago." Ellen turned to watch him; he seemed unsure whether to go on, nervous even, his fingers laced tightly in his lap. Making up his mind, he eased back in his chair and stared up at the ceiling with his glasses off. "A man by the name of Charles Singleton II." His gaze slid down from the ceiling to the wall, ignoring Middleton and LaSalle and coming to rest finally on Ellen's face, his eyes startling her with their intensity. He wants something from me, she thought at once. He's trying to get me on his side for some reason.

"A young man in West Virginia," Exley continued, trying to make his tone conversational. "A 'survivalist,' an antigovernment, antitax sort. An outcast. He kidnapped a number of school children, just like this person, and like this person he made a video of his victims and sent it to a TV station with his list of demands. When the local police finally found him, he was holed up in a nearby mine with the children."

"A mine—" Paul looked at Ellen, then LaSalle.

Exley nodded. "Exactly what I've been thinking," and Ellen saw at once why he wanted her support.

Exley's gaze moved around the room, taking in each face in turn. "I think that is where we need to turn our attention now. We should be looking for someone, probably someone local, who's familiar with the mines out in the desert. A prospector, ranger, survivalist. Or even an off-road enthusiast. Perhaps an outcast or loner, or a person who's had trouble with taxes or child support, something like that." He turned again to Ellen, his voice edging up in volume. "You need to get your officers checking with local judges, going over tax records, and so on. And direct your search efforts away from the city to the desert and mountains, especially those abandoned mines."

Ellen was feeling increasingly uneasy as Exley focused on her, his gaze intent and demanding. Almost immediately though, LaSalle shattered the mood. "Wait a minute!" he snapped, and everyone turned in his direction. He continued, a surprising edge to his voice, staring at the psychologist. "Are you telling us now we should forget about the sex offenders?"

"We have sufficient people for that." Exley said at once. "Of course, we will continue to check them out. We must follow all leads. But the link with Singleton is just too compelling to ignore. And those mines—"

"Why the mines?" LaSalle interrupted. "He could just as well be out in the bombing range. Or, as Chief Whitehorse says, here in town since no one saw the bus. Or any place else, for that matter. This is one hell of a leap of faith you're attempting, Doctor. Just because this man made a videotape of his victims doesn't mean he's following the same M.O. as Charles Singleton."

"It fits both the M.O. and the pathology," Exley said, turning all the way around in his chair and looking LaSalle full in the face. "Cold-blooded, sociopathic, determined. Like Singleton, he's a thinker, a planner. It's what we call an authoritarian personality. These people are unusually structured, they plan everything ahead of time, including what they're going to wear the next day and where they'll eat. They also have what we term an external locus of control, meaning nothing is ever their fault, society is to blame for their troubles, or their boss is to blame or their ex-wife. Always someone else, you see. Conspiracy theorists—"

"Still . . ." LaSalle said, clearly unconvinced. He began to fidget in his chair. "Are you saying we should forget about the construction workers, then?"

"No, not at all. It, too, is worth a chance. Every lead needs to be followed up. But you're using Bureau personnel for that. I'm suggesting that the local authorities redirect their personnel from a search that has proven futile since yesterday and put them to work in a more productive field."

On the other side of the room, Middleton had stopped his roving and was standing still, staring intently at the psychologist, and Ellen wondered what had caught his attention.

"He's going to call again in ten hours," Exley continued forcefully. "Chief Whitehorse must pull his cars from the street. They're doing no good and it's a waste of manpower. There is very little time left; we must use it wisely. We must put people to work digging up information. There are two things you're after at this point, Matthew. One: Who's had trouble with the system in the last few years, perhaps gone to jail and just gotten out? Two: How many abandoned mines are there out there? Where are they? Could they hold a school bus without being seen? Could a school bus even get there, or are the roads too difficult?"

"Jesus Christ!" Middleton said with derision and began to pace again. His anger seemed out of proportion, and Ellen watched him in a sort of alarmed fascination, a wild man, loosely tethered to the world, too big, too much energy, too much emotion. He waved his arms. "Yesterday you were telling us it was someone in this building. Then it was a sex offender. Now it's some nut hiding in a mine!"

"We use the evidence that's available," Exley said with a mixture of contempt and superior knowledge. "Should we ignore the obvious parallels between the two cases simply because you can't see them?"

LaSalle was also increasingly ill at ease, but he tried to keep his voice calm. "I'm not sure this is the approach we want—" His eyes focused on Ellen for the first time since the meeting began, and she felt a pinprick of emotion that was quickly crowded out by Exley's emphatic voice.

"We have just ten hours until he kills these children! Don't you understand that? If we can identify a suspect or possible location in the mines, we might be able to get to those children before the pay-off. It would be far safer, before some grand gesture of his—"

Ellen shifted uncomfortably in her chair and started to say something, but Exley didn't let up. "From what we know I'd say it's almost certainly a single kidnapper. When he makes his seven o'clock call, he'll not do it from where the children are because he knows we can trace it within seconds. So he'll come to town, leaving the children locked up. If we can identify some likely mines, we can use helicopters and Chief Whitehorse's officers and check them out. Start at, say, 6:30 or 6:45. Half a dozen helicopters hitting selected locations. Bang, bang, bang." He pounded his knuckles three times on the coffee table. "In and out. We could check twenty sites in fifteen minutes."

"I don't know," Paul said, and the psychologist turned to him in surprise as if he had forgotten, or was irritated, that he was still there. Sounding unsure of himself in the face of expert opinion, Paul added, "I don't like the idea of pulling my cars off the street. I still think he might be here in the city. Anyway, I've got a missing officer to look for. I'm not about to stop that."

"You have sheriff's deputies for that—" Exley began, but Ellen cut him off: "We can't risk it. What if they're needed—"

"Not likely," Exley shot back, obviously annoyed. He slipped his glasses back on his head and looked around the room as though astonished at their reluctance to accept his diagnosis. "This man's an anti-urban type. Believe me, he's out there." He waved toward the windows and the mountains beyond.

LaSalle frowned and shook his head. "I don't agree at all." His voice was full of emotion, his eyes narrowed and his jaw set as he stared at the man. "What are we basing this decision on? Suddenly we have a whole mental history on someone we can't even name, for Christ's sake! It's—"

"Psychological research," Exley said as though invoking a deity. He was clearly angry, his face reddening and his voice rising. He strained forward in his chair. "Behaviors—particularly such manifestly deviant behaviors—don't just happen. They're caused. This person we're looking for has had a succession of problems. Count on it. He will have a string of court and police encounters. He almost certainly will have had a particularly crushing blow, such as Singleton's loss of his business. That is where your effort needs to be expended, not in driving aimlessly around looking for an obviously well-hidden bus. What has that gotten you to this point?"

"You're not answering the question, Doctor," LaSalle said hotly. "What are you basing this conclusion of yours *on*? We have no information at all to point us in that direction. Nothing. This is just guesswork."

Her alarm beginning to soar out of control, Ellen glanced at Paul. He was staring fixedly at LaSalle, and she wondered at once what he was thinking. His face was blank but his eyes intense, the muscles in his neck taut with emotion. Then his gaze shifted and met hers, and she felt her chest tighten; the room seemed suddenly dry and warm, as though the heat had been switched on.

"My conclusion is based on my professional expertise," Exley snapped. "This is what I do, just as you make decisions on tactics based on your expertise. The final decision is up to you, naturally—"

"It's up to Chief Whitehorse," LaSalle shot back, coming to his feet and staring at the psychologist. "This is a local investigation. We're advisors. Goddamn it, you know that. We're not going to tell them—"

"Then it's up to Chief Whitehorse," Exley said, lifting his hands and looking at Paul, and Ellen thought: There are layers of meaning here I don't think anyone truly understands—politics, pride, past successes and failures, and who knows what else—and it's frightening because we're going to make a decision that could affect the lives of dozens of people while we're pulled about by forces we don't even recognize.

Exley's voice filled the room again. "We have just hours left to us." With an effort he made his face soften into a smile, but his body denied the emotion by tensing perceptibly. "If we want to send out helicopters near the time the kidnapper calls, we need to stop this arguing and identify possible locations." His eyes swept around to Ellen. "And if we want to identify suspects, people with arguments against the authorities—"

"It's not practical." Paul interrupted forcefully. He jerked away from the desk and shoved his hands in his pockets. "Goddamn it, I'm not taking my cars off the street, especially when I have a missing officer. And how the hell do you expect me to identify everyone with a gripe against the city?"

"Not everyone," Exley replied. He was clearly frustrated as he stared at the others. "That's the whole point. Don't you see? I'm telling you who to look for: a middle-aged male who's suffered some significant loss, probably in the past five years. Probably a survivalist or gun nut—"

"Anal-retentive types," Middleton explained helpfully from the other end of the room. "Poor potty trainers. Victims of childhood trauma."

Paul shot Middleton an angry look, then turned again to the psychologist. "There's probably a hundred thousand people in southern California who've suffered some sort of loss, who are gun nuts—"

"I think it unlikely. But even granting there may be many, your local judges surely would know who around here might be a likely suspect." He appealed to LaSalle, a soothing look on his face that Ellen didn't buy for a second. "I simply do not understand your reluctance, Matthew. We've worked together on these sorts of problems before. I have been right before—"

"Before we had some reason for making whatever assumptions we did. This time you've got nothing but a very tenuous comparison to a kidnapper who died five years ago."

"Then I feel I must remind you," Exley announced, sitting heavily back in his chair and staring at his colleague, "that your refusal to take my professional advice will, if things turn out as badly as I suspect, follow you for years to come. It is unfortunate but true as you—"

"I understand what you're saying, Doctor," Matthew replied at once, glaring angrily at the man. "Perfectly."

Ellen's frustration suddenly boiled over, and she bolted to her feet. "I don't know what the hell's going on between all you guys, but for the past two days you've acted like a bunch of school kids who can't get along. Is there something here I should know about? If there is, maybe we should get it out on the table and talk about it because none of this is helping us find the children."

There was a strained silence for a moment as she stared from the psychologist to LaSalle and Middleton. Then Exley twisted in his chair to look at her. "Group decision-making sometimes sounds more confrontational than it actually is. Often it takes a while for people to find their proper working relationships."

"Christ," Ellen muttered and let out a sigh. Her head sank onto her chest and she closed her eyes.

LaSalle said, "I guess the different departments of the Bureau don't always work together the way they should." He sounded apologetic. "It won't stop us from finding the kids."

"This isn't going anywhere," Paul snapped and went around his desk and dropped into the chair. "I can't take my officers off patrol and put them to work talking to people. And Matt needs his people checking out sixty-five construction workers, one of whom is our man." He turned his dark eyes on Exley. "If you think there's reason to look for some sort of outcast with a mad-on against the city, you do it. I'll give you one officer to help out. He can take you around to the local judges. When you get done with that, you can deal with the Bureau of Land Management. Find a bad guy or find a hiding spot. But until then, I'm keeping my people in the streets." He grabbed the phone and punched a button. "Send Muñoz up here," he barked, then slammed the receiver down and glared at Exley. "Do what you want with him. You've got ten hours."

9. Bang

It's coming together, DeVries thought as he bent to unlock the ramp. God, it's beautiful. It's happening; it's happening.

His fingers moved quickly as he slipped off the lock, mind and body together crackling with excitement, feeling as good as he had twenty-five years ago with that bitch from the projects—Annie or whatever her name was—the marvelous anticipation of waiting for her to leave school, waiting, waiting, sensing the stirring in his groin and the heightened awareness of his body as he and Rudy Ayala grabbed her and took her out to the Flats in Rudy's '65 Chevy, watching her struggle and scream and scream and scream as she writhed naked on the desert floor. Except that then, just a teenager, his body had been in charge, not his mind, and his body had been—*was!* Christ, yes!—a machine out of control. That's what happens when you give in to your emotions and allow hormonal urgings that nature programmed for madness make decisions. (After all, Eros—the most beautiful, most alluring, of the immortals, according to Hesiod—"in every man and every god softens the sinews and overpowers the prudent purpose of the mind.") But this time it would be different; this time his mind was in charge. So much so that when he concentrated with all his might and looked into a mirror, he could see the willpower rise from the surface of his body like a fog, actually see it, a pale purple aura that completely surrounded him the way a golden glow surrounded saints in medieval paintings. His body was conquered.

But still his heart beat and beat with excitement.

Slapping the trapdoor open, he listened to the sad susurrations drifting up from below, sensed the smells, noxious and nauseating, as he took a hurried step down. So excited, nerve endings alive and jumping with anticipation! Then a pain exploded suddenly and massively in his head, a terrible noise hammered in his ears, and the room went black as the light was extinguished.

"Run!" he heard darkly through the screaming of his pain, the word as distant as a whisper but feverish with excitement as it was repeated over and over, swirling around the horrible throbbing in his ears. *"Run, run, run!"*

He could see nothing in the blackness but felt himself roughly jostled, tiny hands pushing and shoving angrily against his legs and torso. His head swam with nausea and confusion, and he sensed himself losing his balance on the ramp, his legs weakly giving way as he lurched forward, took a confused step, tripped on something, tried to right himself, and fell to one knee. What's happening? he thought. What's happening? Then another horrible blow crashed down on the back of his head, and he blacked out completely for a fraction of a second before his mind angrily rebelled at the attack and forced a return to consciousness. Lunging forward instinctively, lashing out with his fists, he struck Linda Sowell in the chest as she was again lifting something heavy over her head. He couldn't see in the darkness but knew that whatever it was it had crashed noisily to the floor. Screaming in rage, he kicked out repeatedly with his foot, striking the collapsed wheelchair—the weapon! Yes! As well as two or three children who erupted at once in wails. A child was trying to slip by him up the ramp, but he leaped furiously at the shadowy form as it moved past, knocking the boy to his knees and kicking as hard as he could at his stomach and face.

Where's Sowell?

Enough light slanted down the ramp from above that he saw her body flash suddenly in front of him, and he jerked aside just as she sprang in his direction. Howling like an animal, the sound filling the small room with her rage and hatred, Linda's hands flew to his face, bloodied fingers outstretched like eagle's talons, clawing, scratching, trying to gouge his eyes out. He grabbed her wrists, but oddly she seemed to be expecting it, allowing her body to be propelled forward as though it were weightless. Then pain seared his midsection as her knee slammed into his groin. He screamed and staggered backward as she shrieked in triumph.

"Bitch!" he roared but didn't let go, and she rammed him again with her knee and this time he sank to the floor, the pain excruciating, but he managed still to hold onto her wrists.

"Bitch! Bitch! Bitch! I'll kill you!"

His grip tightened, and, using his arm strength, he twisted Linda viciously onto the floor of the ramp, face-first, where he could climb onto her back.

Dropping her wrists, both of his hands flew to her neck and he squeezed as tight as he could, harder, harder, harder, until his fingers and biceps rebelled in pain, and he felt the fight seep at last out of her. Still in a rage, he seized the back of Linda's head and slammed her face repeatedly into the cement floor, shrieking at the top of his voice, "Bitch, bitch, bitch," until he remembered, the children! Oh, Christ, the door's open.

Leaping to his feet, heart pounding with fear, he raced up the ramp, slamming the door shut behind him. Did anyone get out? He looked around, his eyes darting wildly. There was no way of knowing without going back down and counting, but he didn't want to do that. Not yet. Wait a second! Think, damn it! Think!

Panting for breath, he sank to the floor.

Take a minute and work it out.

Pushing onto his knees, he breathed deeply. His hands were sore from choking the Sowell woman, and the pain in his groin made him want to vomit. That goddamn bitch, he thought. She deserves exactly what she's going to get.

Move! he commanded himself. No time to be sick. Have to find out if a kid's escaped. Looking around, eyes darting again, he saw no one, no sign that anyone had gotten away. But he couldn't take a chance. He'd have to go underground and count them.

She still had the wheelchair. She'd be waiting for him.

He'd hurt her, though; she wouldn't have much fight left. But every second he put it off, she was getting stronger, getting ready for him, maybe getting the kids ready to attack him with their knives and swords and straight razors. His head went light and a chill ran all the way through his bones. He wanted nothing so much as to go down there and put a .38 slug in the bitch's forehead. But he couldn't do it. She was needed; he couldn't change the plan now. That's why you have plans.

Get down there. You have to count the kids.

He needed a weapon. But not the gun. He might lose his temper and shoot her. Vaguely, he recalled seeing a pile of lumber outside. Struggling to his feet, a wave of nausea rose at once and his legs began to buckle. Goddamn her! Goddamn her! Damn, damn, damn.

Moving slowly, feeling he would vomit any second, he forced himself to walk outside, the bright sun blinding him for a few seconds. Around back he found a four-foot length of weathered two-by-four pine and carried it back inside. For a moment, he stood by the underground entrance, catching his breath. Then he flipped up the trapdoor.

Darkness. Soft wailing. A child coughing.

"Turn on the light," he screamed.

Nothing happened.

"Turn it on! Now, goddamn it."

Still nothing.

She was waiting for him. They all were.

His heart began to race and he heard the catch in his voice; surely, they could hear it, too. "Goddamn it, turn it on."

Movement. Someone whispering urgently. What the hell was the bitch doing?

More whispering, bodies shifting in the darkness.

Angry, frightened, he stepped away and slammed the door shut.

We'll do it my way then.

Straw, probably several years old, lay on the ground everywhere. Using his foot he made a pile next to the door, then went to the Buick, where there were matches in the trunk. He struck a match, dropped it into the straw, and smiled with pleasure when it *whooshed* suddenly into flame. Beautiful! Bending down, he flipped the door up and kicked the flaming pile into the underground room.

Screams erupted from below as the burning pieces of straw scattered fire into the darkness. "Turn on the goddamn light or I'll burn you all right here."

The light snapped on, and he saw Linda and two of the children stamping out the flames. Smoke rose and spread, and some of the children began choking. "You're going to die for this, you stupid bitch," DeVries screamed. "Give me any more trouble and I'll kill the kids, too. You understand me, goddamn it?"

Linda said nothing, stomping on the last piece of burning straw. Her neck was bruised from DeVries's hands, her face bled from a half-dozen open abrasions, and her nose was horribly swollen.

"Goddamn her," he mumbled and then remembered the children and began quickly to count. It took a minute because some of them were moving about, but he came up with only twenty-three. That meant two had escaped. It couldn't be.

"Everybody stand still," he screamed, but they didn't seem to hear him so he stepped all the way down the ramp, the two-by-four held in his hand like a baseball bat. He banged the stick angrily against the wall, then screamed again, "Stand still. Don't move."

Within a minute most of the children had stopped what they were doing sufficiently for him to again count. Twenty-four! Goddamn it! Once again he counted, slowly, slowly, looking at each face. Twenty-four. One of them was loose!

He turned and raced up the ramp, slamming and locking the door behind him.

He stared around, huge drops of sweat falling from his forehead to the ground. He wasn't going to let it end here. He'd put in too much effort, planned too carefully. It wasn't fair! He had to find the kid.

Maybe the bastard hadn't escaped after all. Maybe he was still here, still in the building, hiding under the bus or the Buick. Lowell quickly looked, but there was no one under either vehicle. Inside? He stepped into the bus, raced down the aisle. Empty. The car also was empty.

Outside then. The kid could be a mile away by now. It didn't matter. He had to find him. He took the .38 from the Buick, jammed it in his waistband, and hurried outside. Try the house first.

Running, he glanced into each of the vacant rooms, found nothing, went outside again. Where the hell would he go? It couldn't be a physically handicapped kid, obviously, so a nut case, a psycho. No telling where the hell he'd be.

Would he leave footprints in the dirt? DeVries hurriedly looked, saw nothing. He stared around, felt his chest heaving with fear, his body tremble. Where?

Get the car, damn it! Find him! Now!

He ran back to the Buick. The highway. That's the most logical place. He gunned the car out to the road and stopped, foot jammed on the brake, looking in both directions, deciding. The sun was already strong enough to make heat waves shimmer off the asphalt. No sign of life anywhere. A pickup truck appeared suddenly over the rise, coming from the right. He waited, waited, angry and impatient, watching it approach, seeming to take forever, then pass. Would the kid know which way town was? Maybe he'd been out here with his parents.

Move, goddamn it! Do something!

He spun the wheel to the left, aiming the Buick toward town, calming himself: Slowly, Lowell, slowly, take your time, look. It's just a kid. He can't be too far.

Traveling at fifteen miles an hour, he drifted down the road, staring out at the desert. It was flat and featureless, barren as a moonscape. Some rocks and tumbleweeds big enough to hide behind, but the kid probably wouldn't; he'd run and run and run. A nut case.

A car was coming up from behind. He pulled onto the shoulder and let it shoot past, the air waves rocking him back and forth and whipping up clouds of dust as his eyes scanned the desert on both sides of the highway. The kid might not have even registered the fact that the Buick was next to the bus, wouldn't recognize it on the road.

The highway was clear.

He moved off again, staring.

Nothing out there was moving, not even the air.

There wasn't enough time for the kid to be more than a mile away. If nothing turned up in the next couple of minutes, he'd have to try the other direction. But what if the bastard wasn't on the road and had struck off into the desert? Or been picked up by someone? It won't happen. He's out here. He is! I'll find him.

Then he saw the culvert ahead, a three-foot diameter storm drain about forty feet long where the road ran over a normally dry river bed.

He pulled off the road before the earthen bridge and quickly stepped out into the barren desert heat. No time to waste. Hurrying, he half-slid down the embankment and looked into the corrugated metal pipe.

"Get out," he yelled at the girl cowering inside. She was five or six years old.

The child said nothing, hugged her knees, trembled.

"Get out, goddamn it!"

The girl turned her head in the other direction, as if it would make him disappear.

He would have to crawl on his stomach if he went inside to get her and he didn't want to do that. He tried another tack. "Your mother wants you. Come here and I'll take you home."

But the girl was having none of it, and all at once she screamed hideously and began to scramble on her hands and knees toward the other end of the pipe.

"Goddamn it," he howled and raced up the embankment and across the road. As he began scurrying down the slope the girl emerged as if shot from a gun and took off across the desert, still screaming with fear. Slipping on the steep incline, he hurried down to the desert floor and ran after her.

"Come back here, you little bitch," he shouted, but the girl didn't slow. His longer legs soon closed the distance, and he could hear the child gasping for breath and crying as she tried to stay out of his reach. He managed to grab the girl's arm, and she slowed jerkily, shoulders heaving as she attempted to keep air in her lungs. He slowed also, but the girl suddenly pulled from his grasp and headed back toward the highway. DeVries made a desperate lunge at the child, knocking her off her feet, and the two of them went sprawling on the rocky terrain. The girl was bawling loudly and struggling for breath. He reached into his waistband, pulled out the .38 and jammed it into the back of the girl's neck. "Goddamn you! Goddamn you! You little bitch!" His entire body was shaking with emotion as he yelled again, "You little bitch!" and pulled the trigger, the sound booming along the desert floor as Emily Scranton died instantly.

The Buick braked to a sudden stop next to the school bus. Going around to the passenger door, DeVries pulled out the child's body and carried it to the trapdoor. Grunting with exhaustion and still trembling violently with rage, he jerked the door up, threw the body inside, and slammed it shut without a word.

Get in the house, he warned himself. Relax! Don't do anything while you're upset. Need to think clearly.

Inside, he slumped down in the lawn chair and, breathing heavily, flicked on the television. More inane yak, yak, yak from newscasters trying to fill time. It suddenly infuriated him. Speculation, guesses, theories. "You people don't know shit! You don't have any idea!" He came to his feet and began to pace around the vacant house. No one knows anything! You're all guessing, guessing. Like that crap about construction workers. What the hell was that supposed to mean? Construction workers! Do they think a fucking plumber pulled this off? "None of you people know a goddamn thing. Do you, Dr. Exley?" The expert on criminal behavior. Well, we'll see, won't we? So many neat little boxes you construct for yourself, Herr Doktor Expert. Just like friend Weir used to, finding a label for everything because it negated the need for further thought. I've read your reports over and over, *Doktor.* I'm inside your brain. I know exactly how you proceed. So which little box have you shoved me in? Psychotic? Paranoid-schizophrenic? Sociopath? I know! Let's build a new box, just you and me, lay the planks and nail them down together.

"The DeVries Box, Dr. Exley." His voice soared. "Each one unique, no deposit, no return. We can start with the Conscience plank. Play along now. First question: What is it the kidnapper feels about his victims? Ah!" He stopped his pacing. "I see you don't need any time at all: Clearly, he cares nothing about them, they are valueless." He began to walk quickly again, back and forth, back and forth, speaking rapidly. "But you're not playing fair; you're trying to use one of your old boxes rather than labor on a new one. So like a civil servant! Indeed I do care. I care a great deal, a very great deal. Some I value more than others, of course, though I have plans for all. But we needn't belabor that point now.

"Let's pull out the Sociopath plank, then. It's always useful in situations like this since it absolves the 'authorities' (such a stupid word) of responsibility for quickly catching the culprit. After all, he is a cunning and cautious villain with such a hatred of society that he's willing to go to great lengths to wreak his carnage and—Well, you know the drill. But that plank's cut far too long, Doctor. I don't hate society at all, not at all. In fact, I quite enjoy life in its rich and infinite variety."

His pace increased. "Pattern crimes, then? Perhaps you should check your computers for someone who has done something of this sort before. Yes, that's it. Shall we try? Let's do, the two of us. Check your files. Punch in your key words. Maybe we can nail something down.

"But no, that won't help, I'm afraid. There are no precedents for a crime of this sort, Doctor. None! Even those idiots in Northern California are no guide to what I have planned."

He came to a stop. His heart was beating so rapidly he had to catch his breath.

He spoke aloud to the wall. "Maybe I better point you in the right direction."

Jeannie Wheatley hadn't had a moment's rest. Why didn't they just tape record her responses? No, the chief can't be bothered. No, we haven't found the missing police officer. No, there are no new developments. So when the call came in from creepy-voiced Dr. Sanderson wanting to speak to one of the parents in the conference room, it was understandable that she was a little sharp with him.

"Sorry, Doctor. No calls. Chief's orders." Getting ready to hang up.

"Mr. Eric Gunderson is one of my patients. It's imperative I talk to him at once."

Jeannie wavered just a little. Sanderson was a sort of bigshot, wasn't he? "I don't know, Doctor. Chief Whitehorse said not to put through any calls. I don't think I better."

"Young lady, I work for the department. I must speak to

Mr. Gunderson. Call the chief if you wish, but do it now."

"Hold on, Dr. Sanderson. I'll connect you with the conference room." She had only spoken to Sanderson a couple of times but was surprised at the psychologist's temper. Jeez, she thought, weren't they supposed to be as mellow as Bob Newhart on that old TV show? I mean, who would want to tell her life story to this jerk?

When the phone rang in the conference room, one of the parents picked it up, then said, "Is there an Eric Gunderson here?"

A large, slightly unkempt man in a three-piece suit came forward tentatively and took the receiver. "Yes?"

"I have your child," DeVries whispered urgently into the man's ear. "Do you understand what I'm saying? I have the little bastard."

Gunderson paled and clutched the phone. "Yes" was all he could bring himself to say, but he felt as though he had been kicked as disbelief and fear joined in his mind.

"Your kid, all the kids," the horrible, hate-filled voice continued in rapid-fire speech. "They are pissing me off. The parents are pissing me off. The goddamn F.B.I. is pissing me off. I am very, very angry." He was screaming and whispering at the same time. "So I killed one. One of the lucky twenty-five. How does that sound to you, Eric? A bullet to the back of the head. Bang! Pieces of brain everywhere. Picture it in your mind, Eric. Picture it!"

Gunderson's legs started to give way. He put his hand out to steady himself against the wall as he heard the voice say, "Tell the parents, all those goddamn middle-class chicken shit assholes. Tell them! Let them wonder which child I killed. Which mommy and daddy are free to go home now?"

The line went dead.

12:40 P.M.

"Christ, this is going to take all fucking day!" Middleton clicked off his pocket phone and slammed it down on the conference table. He stared at the wall, where he had taped fourteen pieces of paper, one for each of the two-person F.B.I. teams he had searching for the sixty-five unaccounted for construction workers. Finding what he was looking for, he crossed off a name. It was only the third one. "Hell, some of these guys are on vacation, two of them went fishing off San Diego, one's supposedly visiting his mama in Mexico City. Even the ones here in town we can't eliminate until we check their alibis."

The phone rang again. LaSalle closed his eyes, tried to block out Charley's voice, and thought, We're drowning in a sea of data. And it's going to get worse. As a precaution, he had put a van near the school and another at the kidnap site, agents inside with binoculars and headsets reading the license number of every car that passed to clerks at the Civic Center, who simultaneously typed them into computers, where they were run through both Sacramento and F.B.I. records. He didn't expect anything to come from it, but it was part of the kidnap plan and had to be done. He had another group of agents running down leads generated from the parent interviews. And Exley's people were searching out sex offenders, while Exley continued to follow his own weird trail of Singleton look-alikes.

He glanced at his watch. Twenty-nine hours. How many children are dead now? How many has he dressed up in a clown suit and shot? How many die each hour without their medicine? While we waste time arguing about what to do next. The nation's most sophisticated police agency making an ass of itself moment by moment on live TV. He's showing us how powerless we are, all of us. The world held hostage by a single madman.

What could motivate a person like that? Ego? Narcissism? (Look at me! Look at me! Look at me!) Merely kidnapping the children wasn't enough. Like Exley said, he needs to be famous. That means some sort of grand, megalomaniacal gesture, something to ensure the world will never forget. But what?

LaSalle glanced down at the notes he had been jotting and would later expand and dictate into a tape recorder and even later have typed up by a secretary. It was a sign of life at the end of the twentieth century, he thought, that at this very minute agents all over the country, instead of working in the field, doing what the public thought they were doing and paid them for doing, were hunched tensely at their desks, minutely documenting their every action and thought in case things blew up and explanations were called for. And things here were definitely going to blow up. Exley had begun already to disengage himself from LaSalle, hoping to further isolate him on his little stretch of desert when the explosion came. "Be sure to mention my dissent to your decision," the psychologist said as he stopped by on his way to interview local judges. Then, with a smile that spread like an oil slick across his wide, cherubic face, he added ritualistically, "No offense."

Of course no offense, LaSalle thought as he started to write again. Just human nature, as automatic to the chronically insecure time-servers of the F.B.I. as drawing their next breath. It's probably lesson one at the academy now: First erect your defenses, protect yourself from blame because if things go wrong blame is sure to follow. Only then worry about doing your job. A sign of the times, indeed. More than that: a sign of terminally ill organizations and decaying institutions.

The phone rang, and Middleton grabbed it at once. LaSalle could tell it was Colonel Streeter, the commander of the California National Guard unit sent in to control the crowds; evidently, the press was more intractable than Streeter had expected. Welcome to the real world, he thought wryly, where the pen is mightier than shoe salesmen and bookkeepers dressed up as soldiers. And how, he wondered with an inward smile, did the militarily correct colonel like dealing with Charley? Middleton was the antithesis of the Streeters and Exleys of the world, an *agent provocateur*, roaming the corridors of the Bureau with a basket full of bombs, which he genially tossed into one office after another.

What's Ellen doing? he suddenly wondered, his mind reeling off into an area he had tried to push aside with busy work. Forget it, he warned himself. Don't start. But an intense urge to see her rose in him, filling him with a nervous anticipation. Maybe he'd go next door and strike up a conversation, ask about the mines or desert or. . . . No, better not. Let things cool down a bit. He'd sort of made a fool of himself last night. Nerves. First-date jitters. How many times had he gone over their conversation? Thirty? Fifty? And it always came back the same way. Dumb. Dumber than dumb. Maybe the flowers would help smooth things over.

Probably not though. He was moving too fast. It was making Ellen uncomfortable, and he didn't want that, didn't want to alarm her. But he'd definitely said something supremely stupid last night. Wanted to be a big-shot with that Palm Springs shit.

Funny, he'd never had trouble before talking to someone he was interested in. But this was all so sudden and weird and so damn improbable. Yet it delighted also, its improbability itself pleasing and exciting, while at the same time, in some tense, obscure way, frightening, too, because he wasn't sure about any of it. He never should have kissed her. That had been another stupid mistake. Too pushy and not what she wanted. But she could have slapped him or walked away, and she didn't. She held her ground. He liked that, liked the way she held her ground with Charley, too, challenging him, arguing, making her point. Most people back off as soon as Charley pushed a little. But Ellen wasn't afraid to push back. He liked how she'd look you in the eye, making sure she was being understood without having to raise her voice. And the way her face turned soft and her eyes lit up when she talked about her daughter.

Then, as though some submerged core of rationality in his mind was determined that he give up his fantasies, a wave of disappointment shot through him, and he thought, Ellen's not interested in me, not really. He was fooling himself, his subconscious having a little fun, mentally sticking his toes in the fire to teach him a lesson. His ego gone wild. Whom the gods would destroy they first make mad. With love? Was that how? With love? So get back to earth.

He stared at his notes. Cover your ass, Special Agent. His dad would have a fit if he knew how political things had become. His father had lived, still lived, by a litany of now quaint-sounding strictures: Do your job well and you'll get ahead. Ambition is good but loyalty paramount. Arm yourself with facts but wield them judiciously. Aim for respect first, then friendship. Bad guys are bad guys and belong in jail.

Pop, your stomach would turn if you saw what I'm doing now.

But the world had changed since his father joined the Seattle P.D. What would his parents say if he told them about Ellen? Hey, I'm in love with an Indian cop! They'd be tickled pink. Damn right they would because they wanted whatever he wanted. And what would they say at Quantico, those faceless, Brooks Brothers-suited bureaucrats who made and destroyed careers? Sitting in the dining room at lunch, would they wonder aloud about Agent LaSalle? As they passed the warm sourdough rolls and poked at their endive-and-prosciutto salad would they mumble about his "judgment," this year's code word for screwing up?

He pushed aside an empty pizza box and began to write:

Procedures followed by Temp. S.A.C. in above-referenced case are those stipulated in most recent policy manual . . .

His eyes went to the far wall. How serious are Ellen and Whitehorse? The guy must be ten or fifteen years older than her. It can't be real.

"Pussy," Middleton grunted from across the room as he put the phone back.

LaSalle swiveled around. Despite his reputation and his sometimes grating personality, he liked Charley in a way that he did not like most agents, liked the edgy unpredictability he brought to a case and his almost perfect intuition about criminal behavior. Mostly, though, he liked, envied even, Charley's icy courage, the way he would walk open-eyed to the edge of a precipice and look straight down without flinching, even though he knew people were lining up behind him to push. He'd been a bit harder than usual to get along with lately, but that was just the case, LaSalle knew. It had been making everyone jumpy. Still, LaSalle felt a sudden tenseness. "What the hell are you talking about, Charley?"

Middleton rested his butt against the windowsill and folded his heavy arms. "You're going spacey, thinking about pussy. Been away from West L.A. too long. Forget it. We'll be outta here in a few days, and you can go back to your Hollywood bimbos. But don't let it interfere with the case."

"Is it?" As he asked, in a part of his mind he wondered uneasily if Charley was still angry about having to interview the parents yesterday. It had been a stupid thing to do, a bit of grandstanding for Ellen that accomplished nothing but embarrassing his friend, and he felt a little ashamed of himself. Whitehorse had been right about not leaving any wounded: your enemies always come back to do you harm, no matter how long it takes. But Charley wasn't an enemy.

Middleton pushed off the windowsill and began to wander around the office, shaking his large head, his voice loud, almost angry, surprising LaSalle with its vehemence. "Of course it's interfering with the case. You wouldn't be asking if you weren't worried about it."

LaSalle smiled and tried to keep things light. "So what are my chances?"

Middleton stopped and looked at him. "With the girl or the kidnapper?"

"Either. Both."

Middleton laughed without humor. "Christ, can you see this mutt getting away? Not a chance. Kids are dead though. Count on it. There's no way he's going to bother with two dozen screaming crazies. Bang, bang, bang and he's got nothing more to worry about. The squaw? Not a prayer, my son, not with her Indian boss dickin' her in his office at lunch. You've got two strikes against you already. Just like Whitehorse would have in L.A. or any other civilized place. Go downstairs, take a cold shower, relax. Take in the matinee at the porno theater, if they've got one. Maybe we'll be outta here by tomorrow."

The cellular phone rang, and Middleton answered it while striding over to the lists taped on the wall. He studied one for a moment, then crossed off a name and put the phone in his pocket. Just then one of the agents who had arrived last night walked past the room and did a double-take when he saw Middleton. "Hey, it's the Cisco Kid!" he said, coming inside. "You down here to practice your quick draw, Cisco?" He dropped into a crouch and made a shooting motion with his hand.

"Fuck you, Beasley. Still spending your time peering under toilet stalls looking for child molesters? I hear little boys got to be sort of a hobby with you."

The other man looked at LaSalle with a smile as he turned to leave. "Something about a reprimand he got for using his piece 'precipitously.' Isn't that right, Cisco?"

LaSalle got up to pour himself some coffee from a coffeemaker that had mysteriously appeared in the conference room, then sat down again. "I've got to finish my notes."

"Yeah, yeah," Middleton muttered, moving off again. "Cover your ass, Special Agent LaSalle. Join the modern world of law enforcement with all the other fucking Bureaucrats. I guess you've enlisted with them, huh, buddy? You've gone over to the enemy."

LaSalle sat back and sighed. "Look, I'm sorry about yesterday, Charley. I mean it. I shouldn't have sent you down to interview the parents. I could have used Vinnie or asked for more help."

Middleton slid his hands into the back pockets of his Levi's and stared down at LaSalle without emotion. "You're sorry you embarrassed me in front of these rube cops after I volunteered to come up here to this fucking dry hole to help you? That's good, Matt. Good. I feel lots better now."

LaSalle went back to his writing, but Middleton wasn't through. He came over and sat across from him at the table. "You know what it is, you and Pocahontas?" He began to tap a pen on the table—*tap, tap, tap*—the noise unsettling LaSalle, but he tried to ignore it.

"It's a white man's sexual fantasy," Middleton went on, unaffected by the other man's silence. He ducked his head and leaned forward so LaSalle would have to look at him. "You're hooked on her differentness. You think she's exotic—that long black hair and dark skin and—"

"Charley, shut up!"

"It's not anything special, believe me. Different is different, not better. Central America, China, India—it's just pussy, my friend, believe me. Three months from now you'll be bored and want out. Of course," he straightened and smiled, "there's the abduction factor, also. You stealing the lovely Ellen from Whitehorse, I mean. Kinda kidnapping her publicly like that, right in front of her lover. Interesting, isn't it? Our little Freudian would be fascinated." His eyes widened inquisitively. "So what's your layman's opinion, Matt? What makes a man try to take another man's woman? Envy? Excitement?" He made a face and wagged his finger. "Tut, tut, my young friend. Let us not be naive. It's ego. Ego, narcissism, self-love, *amour propre*, with maybe a touch of our kidnapper's megalomania thrown in. You think you're better than Whitehorse, better than this dumb, aged, hick-town cop. But maybe you're not, Matt. You ever consider that?"

"Fuck you, Charley," LaSalle said, suddenly furious, then immediately embarrassed by the feebleness of his reply. He could feel his heart beating loudly in shame and anger, and his whole body was warm with passion.

Middleton grinned unexpectedly as though at a minor victory, but his voice sounded almost disappointed. "Hey, you're just like everyone else, aren't you, Matt? You ain't nothing special. Old Johnny Rocket's got a dark side just like the rest of us."

Ignoring the comment, LaSalle came to his feet and handed his notes to Middleton. "Dig up someone around here to type this. I've got to find Whitehorse and get to the high school. He decided to go ahead with the press conference after all. He figures it'll take some pressure off us."

Middleton pushed his chair back from the table and clasped his hands behind his head. "You might want to hold off. We got a fax from D.C. half an hour ago. They're rushing their two top press officers out here on an air force jet. I guess they're not happy with the way we're coming across to the media as just a teensy bit confused. They want a more professional approach."

"Screw 'em. We canceled it once already. I'm not going to cancel again."

The other man smiled. "Very ballsy of you, my friend. Congratulations on a minor rebellion. There's hope yet. But you better wear my tie." He indicated the string tie and turquoise and silver clasp at his neck. "It'll set you apart from all the other dickhead F.B.I. guys on TV. Maybe you'll get some fan mail from lonely ladies."

LaSalle smiled and shook his head as he pulled on his suit coat. "I think that's something I'm not going to be interested in anymore."

Middleton's cellular phone rang, and he sighed as he got to his feet. "It's like talking to a wall. You're about to fuck up, aren't you, Matt? You're about to make the biggest mistake of your life."

LaSalle looked at him a moment as he considered. "I reckon so."

"It is a sin peculiar to man to hate his victim."

—*Tacitus, 2nd Century* A.D.

How much better DeVries felt after his phone call to the parents. Almost like a purgative, it drained his system of the poison of rage. He could relax now, again in control.

Drawing a breath so he wouldn't have to take in the fetid air below, he stepped down the ramp. No mass outpouring of grief this time, no howling and crying, only a gentle wafting of soft, undulating moans that stiffened the hairs on his neck and arms the deeper he went.

Children lay sprawled everywhere on the floor. The dead girl's body was next to the wall, on her stomach as though asleep, her hair caked with blood. Where's the Sowell bitch? There she is, sleeping, unconscious maybe, a boy lying next to her, his face in a pool of his own waste.

"You!" he shouted.

Several children raised their heads or popped open their eyes but said nothing. The bus driver didn't move.

DeVries again shouted. *"You! Linda Sowell!"*

She didn't respond.

He glanced back at the open door, looked at the children to ensure none could get behind him, then walked briskly into the center of the room and kicked at Linda's body. She moaned, turned her bloody head, and opened her eyes. Then closed them again.

"Up!" DeVries ordered.

"Go away," a whisper only.

Again DeVries kicked her, harder this time, in the shoulder. "Get up! Now!"

As though warding off blows, Linda wrapped her arms around her head. "No." But there was no fight in her voice, no defiance, only defeat and resignation.

DeVries felt an escalation of anger, then, sensing himself about to lose control, tamped it down. The boy next to her, was that her son? She was supposed to have a kid on the bus. He reached down and grabbed the child, pulling him roughly to his feet. "You want me to take the boy instead?"

Linda sat up suddenly. "Take him? Take him where?"

"Get up," DeVries told her. "Come with me. I'll leave him alone."

Linda blanched, and her face turned from apathy to fear. Her voice faltered. "What are you going to do?"

"I told you not to ask questions. Now get up or I'll take the kid."

She struggled to her feet. She was filthy, her clothes covered with sweat and dirt and urine and vomit, her hair straggly, eyes puffy and red. The sight of her revolted him; still, he needed her: Linda Sowell was chaos in the making. And shortly to be immortal. He said, "Follow me," and headed toward the ramp.

Bending down, Linda hugged the boy, who had already begun to cry. He's going to kill me now, she thought suddenly. Oh God, please don't let him. Eric needs me so much.

Eric was sobbing uncontrollably, and he grasped onto her tightly, as though sensing he would never see her again. "Don't go, Mommy. I scared."

Her son indeed, DeVries thought and congratulated himself on that minor feat of deduction. "Hurry up, damn it."

Linda pushed Eric away and moved quickly toward the ramp. When she was up to DeVries she said, "What are you going to do with me?"

He noted the catch in her voice, the fear animating her eyes. She hadn't given up. The will to live, surely the most primal of all urges, stronger even than that of sex, had triumphed. Let's see how long it lasts, he thought.

At the top of the ramp, he seized her by the wrist, dragged her quickly out, then let go. "I'm going to concentrate the attention of the universe on a single, insignificant bus driver. Do not move." He slammed the door shut, locked it, and looked up to see Linda staring fearfully at the Dodge minivan parked next to the Buick. "For you," he said and smiled broadly like a father with an unexpected gift. "The joy of confusion. You don't mind taking your clothes off, do you? Then we'll look in the back and see what the future holds."

1:20 P.M.

Howard Stines sat in his cramped lab and stared into his electron microscope with a growing excitement. Most lab work in Las Cruces, unless it was routine like fingerprinting or blood typing, had to be sent out, usually to El Centro or Sacramento, though occasionally back to F.B.I. headquarters.

That was why the feds flew the carpet samples to Quantico. Howard had never tried to match fibers before, though he figured it couldn't be very difficult. The problem was in the time and tedium of going through thousands of examples, looking for a match. It was like trying to find a license plate when you only had three or four numbers; it could take weeks to check out all the possibles.

But when the F.B.I. turned up fibers on the dead boy, Howard asked for a couple so he could play around with them. Their lab techs had even used his equipment so they could immediately rule out the carpet from the house where the victim had been found.

So what Howard was doing wasn't official. More in the line of training or "continuing education." Even if he turned up something, he had been on the witness stand enough to know that a defense attorney would crucify him: "And Mr. Stines, exactly how many times have you served as an expert witness on carpet fibers?"

He'd had the samples since yesterday, but there hadn't been time until this afternoon to look at them. But now, as he sat in his office and stared through the microscope, his heart missed a beat and he thought: No, I must be doing something wrong.

He turned to one of the aerial surveillance guys sharing his office and said, "Hey, look at this and tell me if I'm nuts." But he knew he wasn't, and he was suddenly very, very frightened.

1:30 P.M.

Walking to the chief's office, LaSalle nodded at Maggie, who threw him a dour, silent look over her glasses as he passed by her desk and into the room beyond, where he found Ellen pacing agitatedly back and forth in front of the window. "Did you hear about the call from the kidnapper?" she asked the instant she saw him. Her face was tight with emotion as if she was about to explode, and her hands clenched and unclenched at her sides.

When he said no, she told him, the words spilling out

rapidly and angrily. "The parents are going crazy down there, wondering if it's their child. I can't believe he'd do something like this." Turning abruptly, she crossed to the couch and sank down as if all her energy had drained away at once. "Paul's trying to calm them but—" She left it hanging. What could anyone say to the parents now? And Paul was on edge himself anyway from talking to Manny's wife on the phone. She had been near hysterical, demanding to know why they couldn't find her husband more than fifteen hours after he'd disappeared. The police weren't seriously looking because no one liked Manny, his wife had screamed through tears; all anyone cared about was those damn children. The TV people never even mentioned her husband. Paul had tried to reassure her. But there had been no words with which to console her. The moment he'd hung up, he'd called her parents in Calexico to come up and be with her, then had asked Dr. Sanderson to hurry over as soon as he could.

LaSalle's spirits plummeted. As the room filled with silence, he pulled out a chair and sat down. After a moment, he said, "I wonder how those poor kids are doing knowing that two of their classmates are dead? They must be terrified." If they're alive, he added to himself, not willing yet to give up hope but too realistic to expect a miracle. He stared at his watch. "Thirty hours."

Ellen's head lifted. "Paul wants to go ahead with the press conference. He doesn't want the call mentioned though."

LaSalle nodded abstractly. "He said he'd take me to the high school with him. I could never find it by myself."

"He'll be back in ten or fifteen minutes. It doesn't take long to get there."

"I'll have to try to put my F.B.I. face on, I guess. We don't want the press to think things are going bad. Ten or fifteen minutes?"

Ellen nodded, looking away from him and rubbing at the knot of tension in her neck.

He stared at her, then without thinking about it said,

"Let's go downstairs and get a Coke. I need a break. We both do."

She looked at him uncertainly. "We don't have that much time."

"Sure we do." He stood and put his hand out to help her up. "You need to get your mind off this for a while. And don't worry about the reporters. They won't mind if they have to wait a few minutes. It'll give them time to sharpen their knives."

"Well . . ." Half against her better judgment, she put her hand in his and allowed herself to be pulled up.

"You can finish telling me your life story," he said as they walked through Maggie's office. "So far I only have the outline."

"I've hit all the high points," she said out in the hallway and smiled at him. "There aren't that many. I'm just a small town girl that—"

"Hold it." They were passing the Xerox room. He took her by the elbow. "Come in here a moment. I want to duplicate something."

Before she could answer, he had maneuvered her into the tiny room and closed the door with his foot.

She knew at once what he was going to do and had an instant of alarm. You can walk away, she told herself immediately. You don't have to stay, he's not forcing you. But before she could think it out their arms were around each other and he was kissing her almost furiously, his fingers racing down her body, pulling her against his midsection. She couldn't breathe, felt a wild stab of panic trying to force itself free from somewhere deep in her brain, jumped back, gasped. "What's happening?" She was dizzy and her knees felt as if they'd give way.

He reached for her again, an urgency in his motions. No, she thought as she kissed him, and then, Yes, God, yes. Her mouth against his, her heart beating on his chest. Oh God, why do I want him so? But I do, I want him so much. And at once she thought, Stop, please. But his hands were holding her to him, and he was kissing her so softly now, so gently she felt like screaming, as if something wonderful were being offered and withheld at the same time, his lips barely touching hers, his tongue tracing a trail of excitement on the inside of her mouth so tenderly that it made her body ache with longing.

He tilted his head back and said so softly she could hardly hear, "I don't usually do this."

"I *never* do this." My God, I sound hysterical, she thought, dropping her hands and stepping back quickly, banging against the work table. "What are we doing?" Her eyes wouldn't focus, seeming to shift to some point between them where the answers might lay. She took a sudden, nervous step toward the door.

"Don't think about it. Don't ask," he said at once, then winced at the banality of his comments. Say something! he told himself angrily. Don't let her get away. She's frightened.

"Please." He maneuvered a chair next to her, and she lowered herself without thought, her face turned to his with questions she was too confused to put into words. He was suddenly abashed. "I didn't mean to do this. I really planned to get a Coke. I saw the door and . . . I don't know. It just happened. I'm sorry."

She brushed some hair from her forehead with shaking fingers. He looked so miserable she tried to ease his pain. "Don't be angry with yourself." Her voice sounded strange even to her—a halting whisper, as though gasping for air after a marathon. "Sometimes things just happen, I guess. They don't usually happen to me though." She shook her head vigorously from side to side. What things? she asked herself sharply, almost angrily, unable to sort out her feelings. Damn it, Ellen, what things happen? What are you talking about?

He yanked the other chair over and sat down, his knees touching hers. "Look, I'm sorry. That's all I can say. Maybe it's the kidnapping, the frustration. Nothing's going right. This has never happened to me before, and it's driving me nuts." He bolted up again, his voice trembling with anger at himself. "I can't keep my hands off you."

She smiled. "I guess I know that."

"What are you thinking? Please tell me." He looked into her eyes without blinking. "Please."

She moved her head slowly back and forth. "That this is all too fast. I didn't expect—I mean, I *never* expected . . . I don't know. I don't know what I'm thinking. Gibberish. I'm thinking gibberish." She looked at his flushed face, smiled, and added, "We're a pair, aren't we?"

Embarrassed, he again came to his feet and started to say something, but she looked up at him, surprising herself as she felt something like pity stir within her. "We have a few minutes. Instead of getting a Coke, let's do our getting to know each other here." She looked at her watch, smiled, and tried to sound calm. "Ten minute time limit, five minutes each. What do you want to know about Ellen Camacho?"

He sat almost eagerly. "How serious are you and Paul?"

He could tell by her face it was the wrong question. For a moment, she didn't answer. Finally, she said, "I'll never hurt him. He's my friend. The best friend I've ever had." She paused a moment, looked at her hands. "Paul went through a lot when his wife died. She suffered quite a bit, was in and out of the hospital for more than a year. He wasn't looking for another relationship. Neither of us were. We had been friends since we were kids and never thought of each other that way. But it just happened." She brushed again at her hair. "Paul's everything Pete wasn't: intelligent, caring, calm—"

"A rock," he said and instantly regretted it. "Sorry. I didn't mean to be flippant."

"But he is." She seized on his phrase as though it was what she had been searching for. "Paul is a rock. That's what I needed." And fleetingly she wondered, Needed? That's what I said? Past tense? Am I beyond that now? Has Paul's stability become a monotonous certainty? "I'm thirty-four," she said aloud, surprising herself with the words. "That's not old, is it? Too young, maybe. Sometimes I wish I was fifty. Life would be calmer."

He smiled and touched her hand with his. "I guess I've never heard anyone say that before. But it wouldn't change things. Love doesn't have an age limit. And life doesn't come to an end just because you've settled down."

As he squeezed her hand, she turned away. Something was happening; he could feel her body tense as she struggled with an emotion she wanted, but was unable, to hide. It hurt him to see her like this, and he tried to move to a safer topic. "Tell me about your daughter."

"The proud mamma bit?" She looked back at him. Her eyes were red but she was smiling. "I overdo that sometimes, don't I?"

"It looks good on you. Parents shouldn't be embarrassed to show their love. Hell, my dad's as proud of me as if I were president of the United States."

"Do you want kids?" Ellen asked at once, then shook her head. "Dumb question. What are you going to say? 'No, I hate the little bastards?' I hope you do though. Kids change you. If nothing else, they teach you humility." She looked suddenly at her watch. "I guess we'd better—"

"No, please. There's time."

She began to laugh. "What else do you want to know? What my favorite color is? My lucky number? Most admired American?"

"You haven't asked me anything."

"I guess I figure it'll all come in time. No need to force it."

"I wish I had your calm. Look at you. You could be writing a traffic ticket for all the emotion you show. And my heart's going at about a hundred and fifty beats a minute."

Ellen stood up. "If you only knew. Grab a few pieces of paper. You were supposed to be duplicating something."

He smiled and kissed her quickly on the forehead.

He turned to leave, but she murmured, "Uh-uh," and put her arms around his neck, softly adding "More" and giving him a long, passionate kiss. He smiled beautifully as he slid his hands along her hips. "I'm looking forward to this case ending."

As they entered Paul's outer office, Maggie looked up from her keyboard and said, "The chief's looking for you, Mr. LaSalle. I told him I thought I saw the two of you going into the Xerox room about fifteen minutes ago. Did he find you?" Her dull gaze shifted from LaSalle to Ellen.

His voice was calm. "Where is he now?"

"You about ready?" Paul asked, walking in from the corridor behind them.

Ellen turned quickly and wondered what her expression showed. Her hand started to go to her face, where she was sure her lipstick was disarranged, but she lowered it and, keeping her voice calm, asked, "When do you think you'll be back?"

"Not long." He looked at them both. "I want to get this over with as soon as possible. What about you, Matt? Hoping for a quickie?"

LaSalle stared at him without emotion. "Let's do it," he said, but Maggie suddenly interrupted: "Howard Stines, Chief," and handed him the phone.

"Better be important, Howard. I'm late—"

"Paul, goddamn it, it is. It's the carpet fibers."

Paul glanced at the clock on the wall. "What about them?"

"Well, there were these two types, you know, like I told you. Both synthetic. Ten samples in all. Ellsworth, the F.B.I. tech, brought them into my lab for a look-see before sending them back to D.C.; so I helped him out a little. I was interested because I never get to do that sort of thing. We always have to send it to El Centro because we haven't got enough experience since nothing ever happens around here—"

"Howard, Christ!"

"So Ellsworth lets me look along with him. Ten samples, eight and two. The two he knows off the bat, he's seen them enough: automobile trunk carpeting, 'Mafia shrouds' he calls 'em, cheap shit, sheds like a collie. The other eight he doesn't know, so he's got to send 'em back to D.C. I told him to hold back a couple, let me play with them, maybe I'll do this sort of thing again someday. If I get some experience, we won't have to go to El Centro, save the city a few bucks—"

Paul's eyes went to LaSalle waiting for him by the door. "Howard, if you don't get to the point, I'm going to hang up."

"So he says sure, leaves me two, what does he need 'em for? Right? He's got six more. And this synthetic stuff, every fiber is exactly like every other fiber in the carpet. So a few minutes ago, I finally had some time to play around with them, stuck one under the electron microscope, looked at its structure, how it's put together. Pretty interesting stuff, geometric, you know. But these are the first fibers I've looked at since college, so I don't know how they compare to other carpets. It's like fingerprints—what good's one set? You gotta compare them. So I thought okay, let's see how these fibers compare to, say, the fibers in my office carpet. So I got my scissors out and snipped a piece and stuck it under the other side of the microscope—"

"Jesus Christ, Howard—"

"They matched."

"What?"

"They matched. The fibers in my office and the fibers found on the dead kid."

"Are you telling me the kidnapper was in your office?"

"My office, your office, the lobby. The carpet's all over the building, Paul."

Paul's fingers tightened on the receiver. He didn't know what to say.

"So is that the good news or bad news?" Stines raced on. "Who knows? This carpet, commercial-quality gray, it's probably in a dozen buildings around town. Doesn't have to be the Civic Center. I could call the folks down at Carpetown. They probably supplied it. Or they'd know who did."

For a moment, Paul was silent, immobile with disbelief; then he roused himself. "All right. Call them." His heart was thumping, not from the excitement of closing in on the kidnapper but with an undefined fear, a vague sense that this was the worst sort of news he could have heard. "Tell them we'll hire everyone that works there. Send them out to every large commercial building in town to see who has a carpet like ours. Maybe the kidnapper wasn't here after all. Get them moving, Howard. Now!" He hung up and quickly told Ellen and LaSalle what Stines had found.

Ellen shook her head in disbelief. "That's what Dr. Exley said yesterday: someone in the department." The thought of it made her ill—someone she worked with, someone she saw every day, perhaps. A friend.

"Goddamn it, Ellen, it doesn't mean someone in the department. Even if the fibers are from here, all it means is he was in the building. He could've come in to check things out for some reason. Or could be a delivery person. Hell, it could still be a construction worker. Someone could be having the same type of carpet installed and a worker picked up fibers when he was at the job site. You know how new carpets shed."

LaSalle was silent, staring at his feet. For some reason, this seemed to incense Paul. "Goddamn it, it's not someone from here!"

Ellen sat down in a visitor's chair and tried to reason it out. "I don't know how long carpet fibers would stay attached to someone's shoes or slacks." She looked up at Paul, holding his gaze while thinking out loud. "Carpenter's chalk, drywall dust, commercial carpet. . . . If it is this building—"

"A repairman," Paul said at once. "Electrician. Air conditioning. Remember the air conditioner went down last month? How many people did we have in to fix it?"

Ellen came to her feet. "I'll have someone check the sign-in log downstairs for the past month, see who's been here."

"Not the past month, damn it, the past six months. Give it to one of the goddamn feds sitting around down there playing with himself. Every repairperson who's been in this building this year. Get a list, then send the feds out to talk to every one of them."

Paul hadn't asked for LaSalle's opinion or permission to use his people, but the F.B.I. agent said nothing. Glancing at the clock again, Paul said, "Christ, we're late already. If we don't get down there, we'll have another riot. Let's get the hell going."

As the two men left, Ellen thought: And maybe it's not a repairman or a construction worker. Maybe he's playing with us again. Maybe he's had those fibers as long as he's had the knife.

2:04 P.M.

What the hell am I doing here? LaSalle wondered, staring out the window of Paul's Jeep Cherokee as they sped through the city to the high school, already late for the press conference. He should have canceled after hearing about the carpet fibers and taken over that part of the investigation, but Paul was determined to meet the reporters, almost as though he wanted to get LaSalle out of the building. So here he was. It was awkward for both of them, it seemed, and for a time neither spoke. Finally, an edge to his voice, Paul said, "So what are we going to do?"

"About what?"

Paul looked over at him. "The press conference. You want to take the lead?"

"Yeah, sure. If you want."

"Don't mention the fibers. No sense letting the bad guy know we're on to something."

LaSalle stared again at the landscape flashing by at seventy miles an hour. Other than the Civic Center, there didn't seem to be another building over two stories tall anywhere in the city. Dust. Cactus. Snakes. Air without a hint of moisture in it. What a place.

After a minute, Paul said, "Had to do the worst two things I've ever done as a cop this afternoon: talking to Manny's wife and trying to reassure the parents everything's going to be all right. The parents really got to me. Most of them are convinced it's their kid that was killed. They don't say it, but they think it. I don't want to go through another experience like that." He turned to LaSalle, a new thought in his mind. "You folks seem to be having a problem getting along."

"What do you mean?" A boarded-up Exxon station flew past outside.

"You, Exley, Middleton. Having a problem getting along. Surprises me, I guess. All you up-to-date, touchy-feely types."

"Yeah, well. People disagree about policy. I'm sure it happens in your department."

Paul shook his head. "I am the policy." He turned his dark eyes on LaSalle. "Reckon you city guys wouldn't like working in a little department like mine. It's not a democracy, we don't sit around debating. No psychologist to tell us what to think or press officers telling us what to say. But I guess our people would have trouble in the city. Like Ellen did."

He didn't reply, so Paul said, "Ellen tell you about her ex?"

"Just to mention him."

"Peter Camacho. Family came from Mexico. A third-generation American. Ellen's a three-hundredth generation American. Anybody could have told her it wouldn't work out. You can't expect people to listen, of course. Love's blind. And stupid. You plan on going back to D.C. someday, working at a desk with all the pencil pushers?"

"I haven't given it a lot of thought." A lie, but he felt no compulsion to share his life plans. He was also becoming increasingly irked at the man's probing. Where was he headed with this?

"Tell me about this Singleton fellow, the one you guys lost. How'd it happen?"

"What do you mean 'we'?" LaSalle asked with annoyance. "I wasn't involved."

"The F.B.I., the *Bureau.*" Paul drew the word out, as if it were a magic incantation. "That kind of 'we.' How'd you guys screw up so badly? Sounds like another Branch Davidians case."

"The Branch Davidians was an Alcohol, Tobacco, and Firearms operation. F.B.I. was there but A.T.F. was in charge.

They screwed up. Send your letters of complaint to them."

"And Singleton?"

"Some dumb-ass, trigger-happy local cops who didn't know what the hell they were doing opened up on him, scared him into the mine. We had a negotiator on the way when it happened. Five more minutes was all we needed, but these hick-town Wyatt Earps tried to take him out with thirty-year-old deer rifles."

"Is that what you F.B.I. fellas think of small-town cops? Hick-town Wyatt Earps?"

"Of course not." He could have expanded on his answer but didn't; he wished Whitehorse would just shut up. Why hadn't Ellen come along? Whitehorse wouldn't be doing this, whatever the hell it was he was doing, if she were here.

He heard Paul let out a sigh and glanced over as his hands tightened on the steering wheel. "We're not getting anywhere," Paul said without taking his eyes from the road. His voice sounded both angry and frustrated. "We're no closer than yesterday morning. F.B.I., sheriff, police. Nothing's happening. And everyone knows it. It's goddamn demoralizing. Kids are dying—"

"Maybe Charley'll turn up something with those construction workers. He's narrowing it down."

"Yeah, maybe. Or maybe Exley will turn up something with the sex offenders, or the carpet fibers will lead to something. We keep saying that, don't we? We keep hoping." He nodded suddenly off to the right. "See that little park out there? That's George S. Patton Park. Old Blood and Guts used to train tank battalions not far from here. You can still see tank tracks out in the desert. Me and Ellen come out to the park with her daughter sometimes. They got a swimming pool. Denise can't really swim, just sort of splashes around. You got any kids?"

"I'm not married."

"Not what I asked."

"No. No kids."

Going too fast, Paul swung sharply onto a side street, throwing LaSalle against the door. "When I was in the military police, I had to work with the F.B.I. a few times. Drug cases, mostly. I'm trying to remember the guys' names. Otten, out of New York, I remember. Garrido, something like that, and Boselli in New Jersey. You know them?"

"No." LaSalle turned again toward the side window. They were moving through a tract of newer middle-class homes— brownish grass competing with dirt and rocks, scraggly water-starved trees, minivans baking in driveways.

"You ever notice how movies and TV always make F.B.I. agents look stupid?" Paul went on. "I never understood it. I always thought they were pretty sharp—college degrees, some with graduate degrees, even law degrees. Why do you think screen writers always make them out to be so dumb?"

LaSalle said nothing.

"Funny thing is," Paul went on, "there was always something about F.B.I. guys I didn't like. Never could put my finger on it. An attitude, maybe. You must know what I mean. You work with them every day. It's like they're looking down on everyone else."

"Yeah?" What does he want me to say? LaSalle wondered. Am I supposed to argue with him? Holding his head steady, he moved his eyes to the other man's face, and for a startling instant it seemed as if a veil had unexpectedly lifted and he saw Whitehorse as he was, without the blustering talk or trappings of office: old and weak and horribly vulnerable. And he longed suddenly to help him as he would help anyone who found himself threatened and unable to fight back. But Paul muttered something he couldn't catch, his hands angrily squeezed the steering wheel, and the veil again fell. The moment had passed and he recognized them both now for what they were in fact: two men who didn't like each other and hoped never to see one another once the case was closed, thrown together by circumstances neither could have foreseen. To hell with it, he decided; his mind turned to Ellen, and he felt an unexpected calm descend. How strange love is, he thought, startling himself with the word he'd determinedly avoided until now, as though it were a snake coiled on the road in front of him.

But he had felt it, even if not consciously admitting it, since the first time they met, when she'd smiled at him in the stairwell and shaken his hand. He knew it then, looking into her eyes, feeling her smile, knew that this was different.

He had recognized it as love, he guessed now, because it struck him so oddly, its oddness in itself thrilling, yet so natural he couldn't believe his good fortune. But good fortune had followed him all his life. He always seemed to have the ability to flourish where others declined, especially in the Bureau, where he was surrounded by people who thrived on guilt and anger and self-doubt. Stalled careers, crummy marriages, alcoholism, gambling—it seemed to be a part of any middle-aged agent's life. But it would never happen to him. He was an achiever, not a survivor, and he was going to succeed, as he had all his life. Succeed in the Bureau, succeed with Ellen, succeed in life.

Thankfully, Paul had turned quiet. LaSalle could see the modern high school looming up ahead. God, what a place, he thought. It looked like a collection of huge cement blocks that had been dropped haphazardly in the sand from above. The parking lot was full, and cars and vans had been left everywhere in the street and on the athletic field to the rear and sides of the gymnasium. Paul drove abruptly over a curb and braked to a stop at the building entrance. They climbed out into the numbing heat and slammed the Jeep's doors.

"You do the talking," Paul said as they walked toward the door. "The media thinks the F.B.I.'s something special. Pretty superficial view, isn't it?"

2:05 P.M.

Alone in the tense quiet of Paul's office, Ellen stopped pacing long enough to look at her watch. The press conference should be under way by now. Both Matthew and Paul had wanted her to take part, but she'd refused, wouldn't even go down and watch on TV. It would mean acquiescing in a farce, allowing the media to control the flow of events. Paul had agreed to talk to the reporters only after the National Guard commander had said he wasn't going to try to herd them back to the high school unless there was a promise of a reward when they got there. "Carrot and stick," Colonel Streeter had said in his gruff don't-argue-with-me manner: "Give them something so they can do their job, too. Make things easier for all of us." Especially you, she thought sourly. The army didn't want to deal with the press any more than the police or the F.B.I. did.

She had watched the soldiers arrive in the city with a mingling of sadness and disbelief. A half-mile-long convoy of troops and green canvas-backed trucks and all-terrain vehicles rumbling down on the Civic Center like an occupation army. The fact that most of them were mechanics and salesmen and schoolteachers made little difference. It was like a revolution in some Third-World country, not something she had ever expected to see here, and it depressed her deeply.

Lowering to the couch, she lifted her feet onto the coffee table and closed her eyes. A pain was building again in the back of her neck and coiling upward into her head. Too much happening in too short a time. An evil *pul* nearby, her grandfather would say. When bad things happen, it's because someone made them happen. There had been an evil *pul* on the reservation when her mother was little, her grandfather had told her many times. No one was certain who it was, but he'd made people get sick, made the rains go away, the wind stop. That was about the time her grandfather had learned that he, too, was a *pul*. Owl came to him in a dream, as sometimes happened to a man in middle age, and told him he had been given the power. He hadn't wanted it, but he'd had no choice but to go to the other *puls* and allow himself to be instructed in the rituals.

No one ever learned who the bad *pul* was, he'd said. But after a year, there was a terrible rumbling of the earth and the evil stopped.

Last year Henry Salas, the father of her only close friend when growing up, had gone to her grandfather, saying that a coyote had spoken to him on the reservation road, telling him he also was to become a *pul,* telling him he had to accept the call. Henry had gone away with the old man and another *pul* to be questioned just as they'd been years earlier.

The changing of the generations. Now her grandfather wouldn't come out of his room, even for Henry.

Waiting to die.

When Julie had come over to baby-sit, she said she'd try to get him to come into the living room today and watch TV. Just ask him, Ellen had warned her; please don't insist. Don't make him do anything he doesn't want to do. Julie had laughed and slapped her on the back and said "Hey, don' worry, no one makes Grandfather do anything he doesn't want to do. You don' gotta baby him." Meaning Ellen babied Denise, which perhaps she did. But she was determined to be a good mother, and there was much to do if your child was to develop correctly. She wanted to teach Denise to be respectful without being servile, to be assertive and to think and act on her own without being pushy, to have a realistic picture of the world without being cynical. Unlike her own mother, who hadn't been able to tear herself away from the TV long enough to even talk to her daughter.

"Stop it!" she said aloud, something she automatically did when she saw herself falling victim to her own imperfectly constructed mythology. And because she knew that nothing was as important as the truth, she repeated to herself: Mother was sick. She couldn't help herself. She was not an ogre. It wasn't as bad as all that.

So stop blaming her.

She looked at her watch again. Ten minutes after two. How was the press conference going? Had Matt calmed down enough to make his typical "We're on top of things" impression on the reporters? She smiled, thinking about him. She wished she had half his composure when dealing with the media. She wished he was here right now.

Maybe she was being too tough on the press. They were just doing their job. How would she react in their shoes?

Ask questions, push, try to get a story.

But they were going beyond that. Especially the TV people, broadcasting that video. They didn't give a damn how the parents of those poor children would feel. Would the station manager have broadcast it if it had been his children? Frighteningly, maybe so.

But why do they hate the police so? she wondered. We're the ones trying to help the children, and they treat us like enemies, like we're the villains.

She shifted her feet on the coffee table, saw something, and picked it up. One of the class pictures the school had sent over. The teachers were posed at either side, and between them the children stood or sat in wheelchairs, everyone smiling or trying to. Ellen looked at it closely for the first time and almost jumped. She knew one of the children! A boy named Louis. He lived on the reservation, and he had been at a birthday party at the preschool with Denise last month. Ellen had talked to his mom for twenty minutes as they'd waited for the party to end. ·

She suddenly felt inexpressibly sad. Someone in the department, maybe someone she knew. No, no one she knew could do this.

Twelve minutes after two. If Matt were here, she could thank him for the flowers. She hadn't wanted to mention it in the meeting and had forgotten when they were alone. What did he think of the way she was handling the case? Ellen found herself wanting to please him. More than please, impress. She smiled to herself. Dinner in Palm Springs. Why not? She'd like that. Maybe get another fifty-dollar lobster. And a room at the Hilton for the night? Was that in confident, young Matthew LaSalle's plan, too? Of course it was.

She'd only met him yesterday.

She grew warm thinking about it. No wonder the F.B.I. was known for moving fast.

No guilt! Ellen lectured herself. No more neurotic musings. You're thirty-four years old. Life is passing by. Or rushing by. So don't waste time second-guessing yourself. Or agonizing about Paul. He's a big boy.

And what was it you wanted above all else to teach Denise, Mother Ellen? To value truth and respect the self? Because even if all else disappears, the self remains.

A dull flapping noise came suddenly from somewhere outside and seemed to be drawing closer. It sounded as though it was directly above the building, beating incessantly and regularly, like Poe's tell-tale heart grown huge. Ellen crossed to the window and looked out. A large olive-drab army helicopter was setting down in the roped-off street. The ransom money. She watched as the chopper hovered a moment like a massive mechanical dragonfly, then lowered itself tentatively to the asphalt, kicking up clouds of dust and sand and dead leaves that spun wildly in the overheated air. The rotors still whirling, three men in desert camouflage uniforms with M-16s in their hands hopped out and ran toward the Civic Center. One of the men was carrying a single duffel bag by a strap. Twenty million dollars doesn't make a very big package, she thought.

The door behind her opened and Maggie stepped in. "Telephone, Ellen."

In the distance, too far away to see, a squadron of F-14s flew close to the ground, setting off sound waves that rocked the windows.

Bobby Muledeer was walking through the Civic Center parking lot, a look of skeptical curiosity on his ruddy face. A Dodge van on the police department side with a naked woman in it, the caller had said. Right! He should be so lucky. Jeannie Wheatley, who had taken the call, had lost her composure momentarily and said, "What?" then had quickly regained her cool and said, "What is your name, sir?"

"Nice-looking babe," the voice went on in what Jeannie took to be a Southern accent. "She's got a big ol' bed in there, been servicin' the office workers on lunch and coffee breaks. Check it out."

"I'll do it!" Bobby said eagerly and figured it was probably the only time he'd volunteered for anything in his whole
life. So here I am, he thought, a hundred and fifteen fuckin'
degrees out here, probably more like a hundred and forty
with the heat radiating up from the asphalt, looking for a
hooker in a minivan. At least I got to watch that army helicopter, same type they used in the Gulf War, setting down
out on the street, three guys looking like fuckin' comman-
dos jumping out with automatic rifles as though they're
going to invade the Civic Center. That'd be something,
wouldn't it? Blow the fuckin' building away like one of them
Schwarzenegger films. No one was saying what they were
doing here, but you gotta figure it's to deliver the ransom.
Did Paul think he could keep something like that secret?
She-it. Now where the hell was that van?

Ellen felt her fingers tighten on the phone as she said,
"What did you say?"
The thin, wispy voice on the other end said, "Can you see
the parking lot from where you are?"
She took the phone to the window. "Yes."
"Watch."
"Watch what?"
"There's a cop out there."
There was, moving among the cars. Bobby Muledeer, it
looked like.
"Watch," the voice whispered.

Muledeer's interest perked up as he saw the van. "No
shit," he muttered aloud, a note of wonder in his voice.
Ratty-looking old thing; must be fifteen, twenty years old.
All the paint had burned off, and rust spots dotted the
sides. He walked up and stared in the passenger window. No
naked ladies there. A curtain hung between the front seat
and the rear of the van, and the side windows behind the
curtain had been painted black, a crappy job, like with a can

of spray paint. He tried the door. Locked. Going around to the rear, Bobby put his hand on the chrome door handle and jumped back. Jesus, it was hot! Like touching a fuckin' stovetop. He took a handkerchief from his rear pocket, draped it on the handle, and tried again. The door opened with a creaking sound.

Muledeer looked at the nude woman staring back at him and said, "Holy Christ."

Ellen felt her spine grow cold. "Who are you?" she asked, still staring into the parking lot.

"Watch," the man said softly. "Do not take your eyes from him."

"Do you have the children? Does this have something to do with the children?"

"What is that officer's name?" the voice whispered. "Is he a friend of yours, Ellen? A friend?"

She put the palm of her hand on the warm window glass, and the hairs on the back of her neck stiffened all at once. Something was wrong out there, terribly, terribly wrong. She had to warn Bobby. But how? And of what? Again she said into the phone, "Who . . . ?"

Bobby Muledeer stared at the woman. She was nude and on her back, tied to a padded black bench like weight lifters use. Her head was bent toward him, attached to the bench with rope, and she was gagged.

"Jesus, what happened to you?" Bobby said, stepping inside the overheated vehicle.

The woman's eyes had grown huge. Nice-looking, he had to admit, though he felt bad thinking so at a time like this. Someone sure as hell wasn't happy with her, though, to do this. Her body was dripping with sweat and she was struggling like mad and trying to say something around the gag. Her eyes blinked and blinked. What the hell was she trying to say? Sounded like pigs grunting. Christ, wait till I get the fuckin' gag off. Bobby took a step toward her, tripping a wire under a newspaper, and the truck exploded.

The voice whispered, "Pretty, wasn't it?"

Ellen felt rooted to the floor. Her hand, still on the window, trembled as the glass shook from the blast. People were streaming from the Civic Center, running into the parking lot, waving their arms. Black smoke rose to the sky in a single, feather-like plume.

"Call home," the man said softly.

"What?" Her mind suddenly refocused. "What did—"

But there was only a dial tone.

Frantically, she punched out her home number.

The phone rang without interruption.

Where could they be? She had told Julie not to take Denise anywhere today, not even to the store.

She must have misdialed. Too nervous. She tried again, taking it slowly. Deep breath . . . do it carefully.

Still no answer.

What's going on? And in the back of her mind a fog, cold and dense, rose and took hold of her, and she thought, No.

The intercom buzzed. Ellen grabbed the receiver. *"What?"*

"Line two for you," Maggie said.

Ellen jabbed at the button. *"Yes?"* She stared down at the parking lot. An ambulance was turning in already, people leaping aside as it hurried toward the twisted remains of the van.

"We have your child."

"What?" Oh God, no, no. It can't be. Her mind seemed to splinter in a million places, sweat washed over her body, and she felt suddenly, horribly dizzy. What did he say? My child—

"And the baby-sitter," the voice went on, and Ellen was thinking, This can't be happening, it can't be. But it was, and he said, "We have them. They're ours. Do as I say and they will not be harmed."

He was speaking with a horribly exaggerated calm, a calm

he couldn't possibly be feeling, but she could scarcely make out the words because her mind was careening so wildly. All the air seemed to leave her lungs in a rush, and she had to force herself to say, "What do you want? Why did you do this?"

"Do you doubt I will do as I say?" His voice had gone slightly wondering, as if he really wanted an answer. "Do you doubt we will kill your daughter and the Mexican woman?"

"No," she managed, and put her hand on the desk to steady herself as her legs began to give way. "No." And she thought: That voice! My God, I've heard that voice before.

"I will contact you later. We have something for you to do. Tell no one. We are quite expert with electronics, Ellen. If you try to trace these calls, we will know instantly. We will kill pretty little Denise, slowly and painfully and as surely as we killed the other children and Linda Sowell and that unfortunate policeman in the parking lot. You do believe me."

Ellen's mind turned over a thousand times. "Yes," she whispered. "Yes. I believe you."

"Then wait for my call. It will come this afternoon. And Ellen," he paused a moment before continuing, "you are very pretty. I may want you, too."

2:33 P.M.

"Goddamn it!" Paul exploded into the first-floor stairwell from the parking lot, LaSalle and Middleton hurrying behind him. "Goddamn it!" He was charging up the stairs two at a time, his voice echoing in the three-story vertical shaft. He felt like breaking something; he felt like taking his fist and ramming it into the wall. "Why'd he do it? What's the goddamn point?"

Two people needlessly dead: Bobby Muledeer, his closest friend on the force, and an unidentified woman, her body so charred they couldn't even estimate her age.

"Christ, he's a psychopath," Middleton said, breathing heavily as they started up the next flight. "He'd kill anybody."

The explosion had been heard at the press conference, rattling walls of the high school and of buildings all over town. Instantly, everything dissolved into madness as reporters raced for their cars, Paul and LaSalle arriving at the Civic Center in less than five minutes. Several hundred National Guard troops kept the reporters a block away. Paul briefly wondered how the van had been allowed past the soldiers and onto the lot, unless it had had a Civic Center parking sticker. It must have arrived before the troops had deployed around the building and parking lots. The bodies had already been removed by an ambulance and part of the lot was cordoned off awaiting the F.B.I. bomb experts LaSalle had called in.

"But why?" Paul again demanded. He was venting emotion more than expecting an answer. "Why kill them? What was the goddamn reason?"

"He doesn't need a reason," Middleton grunted through deep breaths. "He's psycho. That's enough."

"He probably is crazy," LaSalle agreed. They came out into the third-floor corridor and turned toward Paul's office, ignoring the stares of half a dozen curious clerical workers who had been peering down at the parking lot through a hallway window. "But I think he killed those people for the same reason he made that videotape. He's trying to keep us off balance. He wants us to spend our time worrying about what he'll do next rather than looking for the kids."

"Jesus Christ!" Paul's fury filled the air as they crossed quickly past Maggie's desk and into the office beyond. He slammed the door the second the F.B.I. agents were inside. Vaguely, in the turmoil that his mind had become, he sensed that he hadn't seen Ellen since getting back to the Civic Center. Where the hell was she? he thought. He went to the window and stared out at the confusion below. The National Guard troops were ringed around the building, and again the press had massed with angry insistence just outside the line; there must have been ten times as many reporters as soldiers. But he'd told Streeter to get them back to Kennedy. He didn't care how they did it as long as the reporters were gone. He spun around and started toward his desk. "I'm calling the Guard commander. We can't get anything done with that circus down there. Every move we make will be filmed and criticized on TV—"

"Forget the press for a minute," LaSalle interrupted, still standing. "We'll deal with them. But we've got more important things to worry about first. We need to rethink our strategy before anyone else is killed. What is it we want to do next?"

Paul stopped suddenly, his hand inches from the phone. He didn't like what sounded like paternalism in LaSalle's voice but wondered if his own anxiety was making him overly sensitive. He bit back a sarcastic reply and said, "Number one, we step up our search for the kids. Forget wasting time on sex offenders and construction workers. We've got to get more people out on the streets looking. He's liable to kill all of them."

"Of course he is," LaSalle answered. "But that's exactly why we don't want to overreact. Those killings were a warning to us. We have to back off now, show him we're doing what he says."

"But he's a maniac! He just killed two innocent people." Paul looked at the F.B.I. agents with a growing sense of frustration and anger.

LaSalle's voice was infuriatingly calm as he stared into Paul's face. "We can't provoke him."

"Provoke him?" Paul couldn't believe what he was hearing. "He's holding the lives of two dozen disabled children in the palm of his hand. He's already killed four people. He might decide to kill a few more this afternoon just to make a point. I'm not waiting for that. I'm putting everyone I've got out in the city. And calling the sheriff and the governor. We've got to find him." He reached again for the phone and began to punch out the number.

"Chief." LaSalle's voice was brusque but calm. "Hold off. We, all of us, need to agree on the direction and management of the investigation. Right now. Before any other decisions are made."

Paul held the receiver in his hand and looked at LaSalle hotly. "Direction and management? What the hell are you talking about, direction and management?" A sense of events spinning rapidly out of control clamped itself on his mind, and he looked at the F.B.I. agent as if suddenly recognizing that further trouble lay just ahead.

"We have to be realistic about this, Paul—" LaSalle began, but the use of his first name, with its obvious manipulativeness, instantly infuriated him. He slammed the telephone back on its base and glared at the man.

"Just what the hell do we have to be realistic *about?*"

"Look out there," LaSalle said, waving his arm as he crossed rapidly to the window. His voice began to rise as he found it impossible to maintain the facade of professional composure that had become such a part of him. "It's madness. I've never seen anything like it. It's as bad as a riot."

"That's why the army's here, *Matt!* To bring some calm."

LaSalle turned toward Paul and shook his head. "It's gotten out of hand. It's not your fault, but a city this size isn't set up to deal with a situation as complex as this. You can't keep order in town, go about the normal police duties all communities need, and also look for the kids and deal with the kidnapper. You simply don't have the people."

"The troops are keeping order. And I am looking for the kids and will continue to."

Middleton relaxed back on the couch, his cowboy boots on the coffee table, and stared calmly up at Paul. "Your expertise is the city and its problems, Chief. Ours is kidnapping. The way things have been going the last couple of hours it'd be wisest if we each do what we do best."

Paul boiled over with anger. They had prepared this little talk between them, two suit-coated city boys telling their country cousin what was wrong with his department. He wished Ellen was there; he needed an ally. Or would she be an ally? He couldn't tell anymore, and it made him even angrier to think about it. He glared at Middleton, then LaSalle. "Go ahead and say it. What are you getting at?"

Feeling increasingly uncomfortable, not even certain of

his own motives, LaSalle said, "We're taking over the kidnapping investigation. I'm sorry it's come to this, Paul. You can still do what you want in the city, of course—"

"Bullshit! My investigation!" Sweat broke out under his arms and he could feel himself, despite a deeply ingrained sense that emotion was weakness, losing control of himself.

"The kidnapping at this point is a federal crime," LaSalle went on as he too wondered where Ellen was. He had wanted to explain himself before talking to Whitehorse but hadn't been able to find her. "The two murders are within your purview, of course," he continued. "We won't interfere, unless asked to assist. We'll continue checking out the construction workers, and Exley can follow up on his sex offenders. But when the kidnapper calls, he's ours."

Paul swore angrily and took a step in their direction when Middleton came quickly to his feet. "If we pick him up anywhere around here, we'll give your department credit for the collar if that's what's worrying you."

Paul's voice boomed angrily around the room. "This is my goddamn investigation! The Las Cruces police! We'll handle it!"

LaSalle was suddenly fuming. "Like you've handled things so far? Like you've handled the press and the missing bus and the explosion? Like you've handled the disappearance of your own officer?"

"What the hell could you have done any better?" Paul shouted.

"Brought some professionalism to the investigation," LaSalle shot back.

"Professionalism?" Paul was beside himself. He began to stalk around the room. "Is that what you call it? Professionalism?" His heart was pounding. "Is that what you call chasing after Ellen when two dozen children are missing?" he shouted and immediately wished he hadn't. It was a stupid thing to say, small and petty. He went back to his desk and dropped furiously into the leather chair.

LaSalle seemed startled by the words. He looked at Paul

and muttered, "I don't believe this. I don't believe I'm really having this discussion with a chief of police."

Middleton again tried conciliation. "We don't mean any criticism of you, Chief. Your department's just too small to—"

But Paul, more angry than ever now that he had publicly humiliated himself, interrupted, calling upon whatever remained of his willpower to keep his voice calm: "I told you the conference room's yours as long as you need it. I'll stick to that. But both of you get the hell out of my office. And if you interfere at all in my investigation, one goddamn bit, I'll throw you in jail just like I did that reporter."

Outside, in the silence of the hallway, Middleton turned his heavy, dark face to LaSalle. "Feel better now, Matt? You think you've put this rube cop in his place?"

2:37 P.M.

Fear so strong that it almost made thought impossible seared through Ellen as she raced along Garfield. Her head throbbed, her neck and back were sore and stiff, and she felt as though she would vomit as the words echoed endlessly in her consciousness:

We have your child . . .

Her body trembled horribly, and the world around her, until minutes ago so calm and confident, shattered into a million pieces.

Do you doubt now we will kill your daughter and the Mexican woman?

They won't, they won't, they won't, Ellen told herself. They won't kill her.

Her hands squeezed the steering wheel until her knuckles were wracked with pain. At Sherman, she shot through a red light, oblivious to the honking horns and screeching tires. It's all a mistake, a wild mistake, or a dream. When she got home everything would be okay because it had to be okay. Moments later, she sped into the short driveway, slammed the gear shift into Park, and jumped out, leaving the door open and engine running.

Up the steps, panting, feeling as if she were going to be sick.

The front door wasn't locked.

"Denise? Julie?"

Heart pounding out of control, she stepped into the living room, eyes darting, her mind quickly registering the surroundings: television on, air conditioner humming . . .

"Julie! Denise! Where are you?"

She raced into the kitchen. No one. Bathroom . . . Denise's room . . . her own bedroom.

The backyard. Her legs weakening, she ran to the rear door, hurrying into the yard, the heat, staring, staring wildly. Nothing.

Grandfather.

She turned, rushed back inside. His door was shut. She tried the handle and it opened.

"Grandfather!"

He was sitting stiffly on the side of the bed, eating a bowl of cereal without milk.

"Grandfather!"

The old man—lean, almost emaciated, his face webbed with deep wrinkles, gray hair to his shoulders—looked up at her without expression. Ellen hurried into the room.

"Grandfather. Where's Denise? Where did she go?"

He looked at her blankly, then continued to eat, feet on the floor, the bowl balanced on his lap.

She dropped to one knee next to him and put her hand on his right arm. "Where's Denise, Grandfather? Where is she? Did someone come and get her?"

But he merely looked at her with uncomprehending eyes and continued to eat.

She felt a surge of anger and frustration; she jumped to her feet, clenching her fists and wanting to hit the old man. But it passed quickly, and she hurriedly left the room, leaving the door open.

In the living room, she sank onto the couch and began to weep. It can't be, it can't! Her eyes opened, and she saw Denise's play things strewn on the floor: Bert and Ernie dolls, a soccer ball Paul had given her, picture books, Lego blocks. The toys grew suddenly to fill Ellen's field of vision, pounding at her as though the walls of her world were crashing down and she had just seconds to live.

2:39 P.M.

An office job, Kim Zeigler thought wryly as she maneuvered the Edison panel truck down Vandenberg toward Baseline. What I wanted was to sit in a nice air-conditioned office and shuffle papers back and forth and talk to people on the phone all day. That had been four years ago, when she had graduated from Kennedy and gone knocking on doors, looking for a job. Edison had an opening, not in the office but as a line-worker trainee, part of a program to put more women in the field. And at a pretty good wage, too.

After some thought, and no other job offers, she took it. So instead of an air-conditioned office and a padded chair, she got snakes and scorpions and searing heat and blistered hands and parched skin that was probably going to lead straight to skin cancer someday. But she was making more than most of the kids she graduated with, except Joey Marshall, of course, whose dad owned Marshall's Furniture and made Joey the Dipshit a vice president at age twenty. Maybe she'd get to do some repair work at Marshall's someday. She could fix things so that every time fat Joey picked up his vice presidential phone he'd get three hundred volts through the receiver.

Snakes and scorpions. She'd been in the crawl space under a house in Old Town one day and seen a nest of baby rattlers, along with their mama. Or mamas. See Kim crawl. See Kim crawl backward. See Kim crawl backward very quickly.

How hot was it today? More than a hundred and ten degrees. Easy. And no air-conditioned office. At least she got to spend an hour or so a day in the truck, which meant seven hours in the heat. Or the cold. Deserts have winters, too.

She liked working out here on the edge of town the best. It was sure more interesting than the new tracts with their cookie-cutter "Mediterranean" houses. The local folks seemed to be moving to the tracts, though, and the refugees from the city buying up these places, especially the old farmhouses because you could still get a few acres. The old-timers, the real old-timers from the forties and fifties, were making out just dandy, cutting up their no-account farms and ranches into five-acre parcels and taking the money to the bank in wheelbarrows.

Of course, the wiring out here's pretty primitive some-times, she thought, glancing up at the poles and wires fly-ing past at sixty miles an hour. Some of these installations can be tricky, dangerous even. You had to know what you were doing. On the other hand, if she were back in the city, she could watch all the excitement: cops and reporters everywhere, satellite TV trucks, dish antennas, local people being interviewed on foreign news shows. Who'd have thunk it, here in Las Cruces?

Suddenly she hit the brakes. What the hell is that? An abandoned farmhouse. Someone's run a wire from the pole to a side window. An illegal tap. Damn, right out in the open like he doesn't give a hoot who sees it! Squatters, probably. But, hell, you can't go stealing electricity, and that tap they have is dangerous as hell. Someone could get electrocuted. I'd better go and take a look and then tell the boss.

2:40 P.M.

The phone rang in Ellen's living room. She jumped from the couch, seized it. "Yes."

"Good afternoon, Ellen."

Her heart tumbled out of control, and she shrieked, "I want my daughter back! Please—"

"An interesting thought, my love. What's the twenty-four-hour record for murder? Fifteen? Twenty? Does the Guin-ness book keep count? Maybe the World Almanac."

"Please—"

"Calm yourself, Ellen. Your daughter and the baby-sitter and the other children will be all right. But only if you do as I say."

"Do what?" she asked. Her breathing was uneven as she gasped for air, and again in the recesses of her mind she thought, I've heard that voice before. I know him.

"Go back to work," he said. "Act as if none of this has happened. One of us will call you."

"Act as if nothing has happened? How can I act as if my daughter hasn't been kidnapped?"

"Again, you're getting carried away. It will be all right."

"How did you know I was home?" she asked abruptly. She hadn't told anyone she'd be here. "Why did you call me?"

"We know all about you, Ellen. All about you. We chose you from among many."

Panic again took hold of her. "Chose me? Chose me how? What do you mean?"

"We have been studying you for years, Ellen. We know everything there is to know about you. We know Denise wants to be an airline pilot when she grows up and that she was once very near death. We know your grandfather is sadly deteriorated and barely able to function. We know of the curiously torrid love affair you are carrying on with Chief Whitehorse. You have been successful in keeping it from the world outside, haven't you? He regains his youth around you, I notice, although two nights ago he was a bit . . . well, off his game. Tired, I suppose. It was all rather perfunctory. I would have been able to entertain you more fully, my dear, but, alas, I was occupied elsewhere. Perhaps we can look forward to a time in the future when I can share your magnificent bathtub with you. We can gaze together out the window and lather each other with that marvelous raspberry-scented soap you so love."

Ellen's body went rigid, and she stumbled on the words. "How do you know all this? Are you spying on me? How long have you been—"

"Ellen, please. You are becoming irrational. Take a few deep breaths, relax. And if you value pretty little Denise's life, as I'm sure you do, get back to the Civic Center and wait for my call."

He hung up.

Ellen dropped the receiver to the floor and began to tremble violently.

He knows all about me! He knows everything I do. How can he? How can he know?

Her eyes began racing wildly over the ceiling, walls, floor. *He knows everything!*

It's more than just watching me! They must have bugged the house. They must have transmitters here.

Her gaze flew past the couch, lamps, carpets, pictures, the kitchen beyond. It all began to swim in front of her. Too many places to look. Too many. She could go back to the station, see if they had any electronic bug detectors. But that would take too much time. He was listening to her, listening to her right now, right now!

Unthinkingly, knowing only she had to end it, she raced to the nearest wall, pulled a picture off, looked at its back, dropped it to the floor. Running, she went from lamp to lamp, yanking off shades, throwing them down. Falling to her knees, she peered under the couch, then leapt to her feet and pulled it over. Pushed chairs on their sides, tipped up end tables. Breathing heavily, she ran into the kitchen and pulled out drawers, letting them fall to the tile. But there was nothing. Back in the living room, her eyes lit on the ceiling fan. She grabbed a chair, jumped on it, put her hand on top of the brass motor mechanism and closed her fingers around a small metal object. Prying it off, she drew the microphone to her, then screamed in rage and terror, screamed again and again, and threw it against the wall.

2:41 P.M.

Still furious with LaSalle, Paul snatched the phone off his desk and said, "Maggie, you call downstairs, have someone go out and find Streeter and tell him to get his ass up here. Something's got to be done about these reporters."

"Don't hang up, Chief," Maggie said hurriedly. "The governor's on line four."

He groaned. "Jesus, what does he want?"

"Your recipe for chocolate chip cookies," Maggie said sourly, then quickly changed her tone. "Sorry, Paul. But this is getting to me, too. Just tell him you control all the votes in this part of the county, and maybe he'll leave you alone."

He punched the button on his phone and said, "Chief Whitehorse."

It was indeed the governor. How were things going? he wondered. Any progress? What about that bombing thing? Was this the work of an urban terrorist group? Maybe the state could send in some investigators from Sacramento . . .

Paul listened to the preternaturally smooth and silky voice, thanked him, but said, no, no more help. There were enough people "helping" as it was. Maybe what they needed was a little room to maneuver around in.

Well, if you're quite sure, the governor told him, but he was going to send the attorney general down anyway. A case like this, the state's chief law-enforcement officer should be there.

Fine, fine, Paul told him. The attorney general would be just fine. A minute later he slammed the phone down and said, "Christ!"

A knock sounded on the door and he said, "What?"

LaSalle opened the door and took two steps inside. "When the call comes in, I want Dr. Exley to take it. He knows how to deal with people like this. He's an expert. He's even written a textbook on criminal behavior."

Paul stared at LaSalle a moment, biting back his anger. Finally, forcing himself to speak, he said, "We don't even know he's going to call here. For all we know he'll phone the mayor. Hell, maybe even the TV station."

"He's called here twice already. We're his contact. And we've got the ransom."

"Well, tell you what, *Matt*, if he calls here and asks to speak to the F.B.I. expert on criminal behavior, we'll put your Dr. Exley on the line. Otherwise, I guess we'll just answer our own phones. How's that sound to you?"

LaSalle's expression didn't change. "I just heard from D.C. Ellis Whitfield's flying in on an air force jet. He should be here in two hours. I'm sure he'll want to personally take over the investigation."

The director of the F.B.I. The president's golfing buddy and old school chum.

Paul smiled at LaSalle. "That'll be just dandy, Matt. He can get together with the attorney general and talk crime, maybe hold one of those press conferences you people like so much. But they'll have to go down to the Yucca Cafe because I don't think I've got room in this building for either of them."

The phone rang and Paul said, "Shut the door on the way out," as he picked it up.

"It's Howard, Chief. Preliminary look at the bomb mechanism, or what's left of it, makes me think it was not very sophisticated. Looks like T.N.T., maybe something from one of those old mining operations outside of town. Some sort of igniter and a tripping mechanism. Sorry about Bobby. He was a nice guy. Hate to see anyone go like that. At least he never knew what hit him."

"Doesn't make it any easier, Howard. What about that list of buildings you were going to get me from Carpetown?"

"Working on it. And an F.B.I. dude's handling the sign-in sheets. But it's only been about thirty minutes. Give it another hour. Can't work miracles."

"All right. Christ! Call me as soon as you have something." He hung up and looked furiously around the office. Where the hell's Ellen? he thought. And why can't we find even a trace of Manny Rios?

2:42 P.M.

Kim Zeigler pulled her Edison panel truck off the highway and onto the unpaved drive leading to the abandoned farm. Leaving the engine idling and air conditioner on high, she looked around. The house was a small, clapboard, ranch-style affair, not more than a thousand square feet, she thought. Built before the war by someone with more hope than common sense; probably a half-century's worth of dead snakes and rodents decaying in the crawl space. It looked as though it had been vacant for years, a faded Century 21 "For Sale" sign permanently painted on the front of the building.

Off to the side, a barn slowly rotted in the sun. A chain-link fence, incongruous in its shiny newness, stretched around the back and sides of both buildings, separating them from nonexistent neighbors. Another subdivided farm but no one had built on any of the plots yet; probably hadn't even been sold.

And an illegal power tap running from the pole down to the house and, she could see now, to the barn. Jeez, she thought, talk about flagrant theft. But the wire to the barn meant it wasn't the homeless. Illegal marijuana growers, almost certainly. She glanced apprehensively around as her pulse speeded up. Indoor pot farmers were legendary for their paranoia and violence, usually booby-trapping their buildings to keep hijackers away. Thank God they generally didn't stay at their "farms"—typically commercial buildings rented under phony names. That way, if the cops showed up, they couldn't be connected to it. From what she'd heard, they used a drip irrigation system on a timer; the whole set-up was automatic once the seedlings sprouted. They'd drive by every day or so to make sure no one was nosing around; anyone who even accidentally stumbled onto the pot would be killed without the slightest compunction. One of these farms could be worth millions.

Ironic that a line worker would spot it, she thought. Usually the billing office noticed a sudden increase in someone's electric usage. But these guys were smart enough not to be billed.

She'd have to tell her supervisor. Better make sure it is a pot farm first, she thought. Don't need a dozen cops descending on the place if it's just electricity theft. She put the truck in gear and drifted up to the front of the house on the gravel drive. No vehicles, no one visible. Might as well get out and have a look-see.

She stepped into the wilting afternoon heat. Her heart began to race even faster, her senses sharpen. Don't spend all day thinking about it, she told herself, just take a quick look and get the hell out. Sweat beaded on her forehead and underarms. Kind of spooky, two empty buildings like this. Where did the growers live? Not close, she hoped. Of course, this was only about three miles from the edge of town; if they had some kind of sensing mechanism, like an electric eye, they could be here in minutes. You're starting to fantasize, Kim scolded herself. Electric eyes! Cut it out. Just go over, look, and beat it.

Walking rapidly across the baked ground, she crossed to the barn. The faded doors were locked, but she knew they would be. A new clasp and shiny new padlock. She walked around to the side, where there was a window. Plywood nailed inside, evidently. Couldn't see a thing. Same for the window on the other side.

Well, that pretty well sealed things. These people wouldn't go to all that trouble for nothing. There was some funny farming in there.

She wondered if the same thing was going on in the house. They could set growing lights up in there, too, and hook a hose to a bathroom faucet. She crossed over to the front door and tried it. Locked tight. Walking out to the rear of the home she noticed tire tracks in the dust. Feeling a little like Sherlock Holmes or Columbo, she dropped to one knee and studied them. Two or three vehicles, she guessed. One with pretty good sized tires. Probably a truck for harvest time. And a lot of tracks belonging to a car. They all looked fresh. Maybe even today, she thought.

She straightened and went over to the back door. The wooden screen door was off its hinges and leaning against the wall. Looked just as ratty as the one in her folk's house twenty years ago. The back door was locked, too, but from the outside with a clasp and combination lock, just like the garage. At least she wouldn't have to go inside now, she thought with a smile. But she could at least peek in the windows; she'd already noticed that they weren't boarded up. Going around to the side, she peered through a bedroom window. The room was completely empty. Same for the living room. A small bathroom window was painted over. That left the kitchen. She put her hands to her eyes and looked through. Empty. Except . . . except for a lawn chair and a small television on the drain board. Interesting. Maybe the pot farmer didn't want to miss "General Hospital." She could empathize with that.

No doubt about what was going on though. Someone was using this place.

She hurried back to her truck and turned the key, letting the air conditioner cool her off for a minute before putting the gear shift in reverse. She backed out onto the road and thought, You're dead meat, buddy. Cops'll have your ass in jail in twenty-four hours. But she couldn't shake the feeling that snooping around had been a grave mistake. Live and let live, her mom was always saying. Don't go looking for trouble. Well, shit, this was trouble. No doubt about that.

DeVries let his Buick Park Avenue slow to a crawl as he saw the Edison panel truck pull out of the drive and accelerate down the highway. What the hell was that all about?

He swung quickly onto the shoulder of the road near the farmhouse and looked around. No one seemed to be nearby. What had the repair truck been doing there, then? Nobody would have called to have the service turned on; the place had been vacant for years.

Then his eyes came to rest on the wire he had used to tap into the power lines. Could that be it? Had the driver seen the tap and decided to investigate?

He'd have to check the barn, see if the repairman had been inside. But if he did, he'd never catch up with the truck again. Act fast, then. Assume the worst: the repairman's figured out where the kids are. Something has to be done about it. Now! Don't think, don't lose him. Move! Move!

He slammed the car into Drive and took off quickly down Baseline. He had to find that truck.

2:45 P.M.

Paul walked down to the squad room where Zach Harris was coordinating the search for Manny. Even with the extra sheriff's deputies, it was taking longer than expected because they had to stop and personally check each possible location. Harris, on the phone, nodded a greeting as Paul strode nervously around the room, waiting for him to hang up, then dropped into the visitor's chair as Harris put the receiver down and said, "How's the F.B.I.?"

"Like an albatross around my neck."

"Don't know what that means, but I guess it's something bad."

"We're having a little jurisdictional tussle. If they ask for so much as the time of day, you check with me first. Where's Ellen?"

"Haven't seen her since about lunchtime."

"Goddamn it. Does she want to be in charge of the investigation or not? You'd think she'd let me know where the hell she is." He twisted his head to glance at the wall clock, then turned back to Harris. "What's going on with your people?"

Harris took off his glasses and rubbed his eyes. "Haven't turned up anything on Manny or the kids but didn't much expect to. Don't understand about that bus, though, Paul. Little town like this, we should have something by now."

"County's still got their chopper up, F.B.I.'s flying their own goddamn air force. Maybe someone'll turn up something." He grabbed a letter opener off the desk and began to tap it against his knee. "Running out of time with the kids though. They're going to be dying."

"Kids are dead," Harris said flatly. "Got to be realistic about it. Guy's a nut case. He's not going to leave two dozen witnesses. Who you got to deliver the ransom when he calls?"

"LaSalle thinks his people are going to do it. They're 'experts.' Wrote a book. I kinda thought I'd do it."

Harris's expression turned uneasy. "Probably not a good idea, boss. Looks like showboating. Better let me handle it."

"Let's wait till six or so to make up our minds. Maybe something'll come up by then. Feds are still checking out construction workers." Paul glanced irritably around the room. "Who's working on the sign-in sheets?"

"F.B.I. guy, looks like he's about sixteen. He took a chair out to the hallway. It's the only place he could find where the phones aren't ringing all the time."

Paul threw the letter opener onto the desk and went to the squad room door. A young man in gray slacks and a long-sleeved white shirt was sitting with a tablet on his lap as he ran down the loose-leaf sign-in binders, line by line. He squinted up at Paul. "Getting there, Chief. Hard to read some of the names though. Got eighteen so far."

"Let me have what you've got. I'll get some people on it."

He took the list back to the squad room and sat down. "Get a civilian to find phone numbers on these guys and give 'em a call. Don't identify yourself as a cop. Just find out if they're home. Anyone who's not, we'll get the F.B.I. to follow up on."

Harris took the list. "You talk to Bobby's wife yet?"

Paul shook his head slowly and tried not to think about it, tried not to think about the shame it made him feel. "Just couldn't face her, Zach. Not today. I've had enough grief. Father Raul's talking to her now. I'll stop by tomorrow." He sighed with annoyance, came to his feet again, and began to stalk around the small squad room. Like the rest of the Civic Center, it was a modern, featureless, bureaucratic, gray-on-gray area of the sort so appealing to government builders and designers. It depressed him. Couldn't these people build anything a normal person would want to work in? Why hadn't they hired a local architect, someone who knew the desert and had the sense of Las Cruces as a community? An idea suddenly occurred to him, and he turned to Harris. "Maybe someone from the building inspector's office could help us."

"Help us what?"

"Tell us where the hell to hide a bus and two dozen people." His interest quickened as he thought about it. "Who knows the city better than they do? They've probably got the plans for most buildings in Las Cruces, anything built since World War II anyway. Give them a call. They'd be happy to help."

Harris reached for the phone. "Good idea. Christ, any idea is a good idea."

Paul again looked at the clock. "Goddamn it, where the hell's Ellen?"

2:50 P.M.

Heat radiated up from the asphalt in front of her as Kim Zeigler hurtled down Old Ranch Road toward Independence. Hot enough to fry an egg, she thought automatically, and laughed out loud. Every summer the weather dweeb on the Palm Springs station went outside with a raw egg to show that you could actually do it. One of life's imponderables: why are weather reporters such geeks?

Her next job was seven or eight minutes away. Someone had finally bought The Egg House, an abandoned chicken farm, and wanted the power turned on. She wondered if they were planning to go back into the egg business. Or maybe fry a thousand eggs on the sidewalk. The place had been there since before she was born, with a huge white and red fiberglass chicken out front that was now cracked and pitted and covered with graffiti and bird droppings. Maybe they'll want to fix it up and run power to it so they can light it up at night, a neon Rhode Island Red, visible for miles. The F-14s could use it for target practice.

At Independence she swung west and in another four minutes was there. Still deserted. Well, that made sense.

They needed power before they could begin to rehabilitate the dump. Might as well see if anyone's here.

She rolled up the long driveway to the farmhouse and stopped. It looked as vacant as that last place. Didn't matter none. She didn't need to get inside. Grabbing her toolbox, she stepped into the heat and stared around. Off to the side was a large, low-slung wooden building that had evidently been the hatchery. They'd need power out there, too. It must smell like hell once they were operating at capacity, especially in the summer. She wiped at the sweat on her brow and wondered if the water had been turned on yet. She could use a drink.

There was a faucet next to the house. She tried it and was pleased to see water gush out and splash into the dry soil at her feet. She stuck her hands under the flow, washed them off, then took a drink. Man, that was good! There was no way you could run a chicken ranch out here without a lot of water. Couldn't run anything in the desert without a lot of water.

She started walking toward the house when it suddenly struck her: there hadn't been any evidence of water at that last place, had there? No hoses anywhere, no pipes, or sprinklers. How could they be pot farmers without tons of water? Then maybe it wasn't farming going on out there. So what else could it have been? They were sure as hell doing something weird. That place had been like a damn fortress. Or jail.

She felt a sudden instant of terror and excitement. *Oh my God, no!* Her hands began to shake uncontrollably. *I've got to get to a phone. I've got to call the police.*

Dropping her toolbox to the ground, she ran to the truck. *It must be! It must! Why else all the secrecy?* Fingers trembling so she could hardly control them, she turned the key and stepped on the accelerator. *My God, all the time, right outside of town, right next—*A sound somewhere startled her and her eyes flew to the rearview mirror. A car had pulled off the road and was coming up quickly and noisily on the gravel drive behind her. Must be the property owner. Sorry, buddy,

I haven't time for you, she thought. Gears gnashing as she jammed into reverse, the vehicle shot backward.

The car coming down the long drive must have been doing seventy miles an hour. Dude's going to be pissed, but I can't help it. Those kids are more important than your damn chickens.

Kim's truck spun around on the loose gravel and pointed toward the highway. The guy was coming right at her like he didn't want her to leave. Sorry, pal, I'm outta here. Slamming the gear shift forward, the truck hesitated a moment, then accelerated suddenly down the driveway.

Christ, the idiot's coming right at me! What the hell's he doing?

She swerved to the right on the narrow road, but the car jerked in the same direction as though trying to run head-first into her. Her body began to shake. My God, he's crazy! At the last minute, she swung all the way to the right, pulling off the pavement and onto the desert floor, losing control as the truck hit the soft ground and fish-tailed dangerously.

The car shot past her on the road and slammed on its brakes, screeching to a halt in a cloud of dust and smoking rubber. Without hesitation, it spun around, aiming at her again. She twisted the wheel sharply to the left to get back on the road, but the car was racing again in her direction. Panicking, she turned hard right instead, away from the driveway and into the desert, her foot pounding the gas pedal to the floor. Jesus, what's he doing? He's going to kill us both!

Her panel truck bounced roughly over the uneven terrain as she kept both hands on the steering wheel and her foot pressed hard on the accelerator. Gripped by fear, she didn't know what to do. If she kept going into the desert, she'd come across another road in a mile or so but her truck would never make it. She'd blow the tires out by then. The car was gaining on her.

What does he want? But her mind could make no sense of it. The right front tire hit a hole and the truck shuddered violently, almost throwing her from the driver's seat. I'll never make it, I'll have a blow out.

She couldn't keep going into the desert. Her only hope was to get back to Old Ranch Road. She spun the wheel hard left. The car was already behind her, gaining quickly. Oh, God, he's going to ram me, she thought. Please don't let him. I don't want to die! Please! She turned sharply again. As the car pulled adjacent to her on the left, she slammed the brakes and it flew past in a storm of sand and dust. Aiming the truck again toward Old Ranch Road she pushed on the gas pedal as hard as she could. But in seconds he was up to her again. The driver turned sharply, ramming his bumper into her door. She screamed as the truck trembled on two wheels and veered out of control. Frantically, she spun the wheel, but before she could regain control the truck ran into a dry creek bed and thudded to a sudden stop as steam and coolant gushed from the radiator.

She looked out the window as the car skidded to a halt ten feet behind her and the door flew open. The driver leaped out screaming and began running in her direction, a gun in his hand. Sobbing hysterically, she tried the door, but it wouldn't open. She yanked and yanked on the handle, then pounded her fists on the window. She could see the man's sweaty face through the glass as he rushed up to the passenger side. Why is he after me? she wondered. Dear God, what did I do? She lunged frantically over to lock the door, but he hit the window with the barrel of his gun and the glass exploded as she screamed and screamed.

2:52 P.M.

I've got to tell someone, Ellen thought desperately as her world spun out of control. I've got to tell Paul or Matthew. I can't deal with a madman by myself. I need help.

But it was more than that, she knew. She had nobody to share her fear with, and its weight was too much to bear alone. At least the parents had each other and the police and Dr. Sanderson. She had no one, and it was like being slowly crushed by a huge rock lowered onto her chest.

She thought suddenly of Pete. Bolting to her feet, she began to pace rapidly back and forth in the living room. Pete has to know! He's Denise's father. He has a right to know what's happening to his own daughter. Where's he living now? I haven't even talked to him in two years. Where is it? Pasadena? Somewhere in Pasadena? Or had her attorney said he'd moved back to El Monte? When he was on the L.A.P.D., he'd never had a listed number, of course, but he might now.

Hurrying to the kitchen, she seized the phone. Directory Assistance might have a number. If not, she'd call her lawyer. Fingers trembling, she started to dial, then suddenly drew back, horrified at what she was doing, the phone clattering noisily to the tile floor. She couldn't do it. The man said tell no one. *We will kill your daughter* . . .

Her knees weakened, and she put a hand on the kitchen table to steady herself. What good would come from telling Pete, anyway? There was nothing he could do. Except worry. And he wasn't much good at that. He couldn't even remember Denise's birthday. Or wouldn't remember. It was exactly that sort of deliberate neglect that had made her overcompensate, she knew, made her sometimes try too hard with her daughter. That, and her own childhood. Growing up, she had felt a terrible loneliness, with few children her age on the reservation and no one but her grandfather to confide in or draw strength from; it had left her feeling empty and fearful, left her with a horrible core of vulnerability that remained even now, she knew, just below the surface, though she tried desperately not to show it.

Maybe that was why she had been so quick to take up with Pete in the first place. He had offered something she'd craved deeply: an escape from the pain and disarray of the past and an abrupt, almost fierce closeness, a shared soul to cling to and merge with. It had struck her with the sudden impact of driving into a wall, and never having experienced it, not knowing what it was, she had called it love.

Perhaps it really had been on her part. Certain then that it was—her heart soaring with the complete unexpectedness of joy—she had been that much more hurt by his lies and betrayals. They hadn't been married a month, she knew now, *a month,* before he was screwing any female that came his way. And working patrol in Hollywood he was never without willing partners—from fourteen- and fifteen-year-old runaways to forty-five-year-old nickel-bag streetwalkers.

Perhaps it was best it worked out the way it did. There is a reason for everything that happens. Their worlds had been too different, she now understood. Had anyone tried to tell her that when they got engaged? Probably not, though she knew her grandfather had disapproved. She wouldn't have listened anyway. She was too sure of her love. But she saw now there was a gulf ten thousand years wide that had and always would separate them. Pete had grown up in El Monte, a rundown suburb in the San Gabriel Valley, the ragged eastern edge of L.A.'s tense urban sprawl. His life had been a featureless drifting existence of movies and malls and cruising Whittier Boulevard and asphalt and crumbling earthquake-damaged buildings and graffiti-marred freeways that were forever clogged with cars and trucks spewing out tons of effusions. He had graduated from high school only because everyone in California who stuck it out graduated, yet had only the vaguest notion of, and not a scintilla of curiosity about, the world fifty miles or twenty years away. History began the day he was born, and World War II and the Great Depression and Little Bighorn and John Kennedy held no more meaning in his mind than non-Euclidean geometry.

Pete's whole life was devoted to gratifying Pete. He didn't deserve to know a thing about Denise. He wasn't going to come rushing back into her life because of a tragedy. Ellen was Denise's father and mother. She would take care of everything herself. Herself!

But she felt the ground tilt beneath her feet, the floor rise up to meet the ceiling.

10. Demand

DeVries sat in his car in front of the 7-Eleven and felt his pulse. Eighty. Not good. Not good at all. Relax, Lowell, he told himself.

He had already been home, frantically washed the blood from his hands, scrubbing and scrubbing and scrubbing like Lady Macbeth, and changed into clean clothes. I didn't expect the bitch to bleed so much, he thought. Must have hit a goddamn artery, the way it gushed like a faucet all over her shirt and pants. At least she'd been inside the truck.

He hadn't been forced to lift her body with the heart pumping blood through three chest wounds. He'd shot point blank from the passenger side, then yanked her down on the seat. And left the truck where it was. If someone spotted it, they wouldn't necessarily think anything was seriously wrong, just a traffic mishap. Of course, she'd be missed once her shift was over. That was not a problem though. The chicken ranch was in county territory and the Las Cruces police wouldn't be involved. Anyway, both the police and sheriff's department had their manpower tied up elsewhere.

He smiled. Felt his pulse again. Seventy-five.

Think about the money. Think what you're going to do with twenty million dollars. Twenty mil-lion dollars, Lowell! My God. Paradise. Or *paraiso*. Yes! Think of the three Costa Rican girls you're buying. "Housekeepers," you have to call them to keep the authorities happy. Bunch of goddamn hypocrites. Everyone knows what they're doing and it isn't vacuuming. Maybe a couple of preteens and an eighteen- or nineteen-year-old for variety. He still had a catalog he'd picked up when he was down there last year. Fifty pages of pictures and descriptions. *Maria is nine and likes to please* . . .

Yes! Yes, yes, *yesssss!*

Too bad there wouldn't be time tonight to enjoy the marvelous Ellen. Older than he liked but a nice, lithe body. Good definition. And such a lively sex partner! Likes to squeal and moan and bite and tickle. He could tell from the tapes. Unfortunate that she had to die, but it was necessary, of course; the plan couldn't be altered, not even a little, not even for—

But maybe it could work out. Sure! Do her, then kill her. Or vice versa.

Again, he smiled and felt an erection beginning, throbbing, warm feel . . . heartbeat increasing. . . . He loved this, loved becoming aware of his body, feeling it, sensing the parts spring alive, the silky feel of his underwear . . .

Enough, enough! Enjoy your fantasies later, he told himself.

There were two pay phones outside the 7-Eleven and another at the Shell station next door. Are you ready, Special Agent LaSalle? Of course you are. Of course. But don't blame me for how things turn out in the next few hours. You have become author as well as participant in this little drama of ours and must choose from among the threads I offer those you wish to weave.

He grabbed a quarter from the glove compartment and walked over to the gas station. Took a breath. Shook the visions and dreams from his consciousness. *Chaos. Confusion* . . . Dropped the coin. Dialed.

"Las Cruces Police Department."

"Monica Ochoa has a four-inch scar on her neck." A rough, gravelly voice, oddly inflected.

Jeannie Wheatley gasped. "What?" Oh my God, it's him, she thought. She almost cried and her body began to tremble. She didn't want him to call again on her shift; she didn't want to do anything wrong and screw things up. "Yes." was all she could think of to say as blood pounded loudly in her ears. "Who do you want to talk to?"

"Listen to me, bitch! The little people of America have suffered too long. Taxation is confiscation. We are merely recovering what is rightfully ours. Be ready to make the delivery at two A.M. If there's any screw-up, any delay, any argument, we will kill the children, one by one. I will call with further instructions at exactly seven o'clock."

He hung up.

Her heart racing, Jeannie punched a button on her phone. "Maggie, tell the chief. He just called."

3:44 P.M.

Trying with all her might to pull herself together, Ellen hurried down the Civic Center hallway, through the police department business office, to the squad room. Harris was bent over his desk eating a jelly donut, his left hand cupped under his mouth, catching crumbs as they fell. Country music twanged from a radio on his file cabinet. "Hey, Paul's been looking for you," he said, his mouth full and both hands brushing crumbs off his desk.

She felt herself losing control as hysteria rose dangerously in her mind: My baby's missing and you're sitting here eating a goddamn donut! Dropping into her chair without a word, she stared blankly at the papers strewn on her desk. Out of the corner of her eye, she sensed, more than saw, two or three officers in black shirts and pants pass the doorway as they headed toward the locker room. Vaguely she thought: the rescue team. But it meant nothing. Her heart pounded, and she felt she was going to throw up. With a sudden movement of her arm, she swept everything on her desk to the side.

Harris turned noisily in his chair and raised his voice. "Hey, Earth to Ellen. Paul wants to see you."

She didn't hear, consumed with her own thoughts: Dear God, why is this happening to me? What does he want?

She was warm. Fever. Aspirin somewhere. She began to rummage in her desk drawers, shoving aside reports and files, until she found a bottle, pried off the top, shook out three. Where's the water? Looked around.

"Yo, Ellen! Paul wants to see you. You hear me? The kidnapper called again."

Pushing from her chair, she hurried to the drinking fountain in the hall and swallowed the pills, gagging as they went down. People passed back and forth and nodded at her, smiled; the normalcy, the triviality, of it all made her want to scream. Back at her desk she couldn't keep her body from trembling. Can they see it? Can everyone see me shake? My God, what does he want me to do? Why did he take Denise?

The phone rang and she grabbed it. "Yes?"

"Where the hell you been?" Paul asked.

Despair flooded through her. Trying desperately to make her voice calm, to tamp down the emotion raging inside her head, she made herself say, "I had to go out. I wasn't feeling well. What do you want?"

"What do I want? Jesus, Ellen, we're trying to catch a lunatic who's hidden two dozen people and killed God knows how many more. You want to come up and talk to me about it? Christ!"

She didn't answer.

"You hear me?"

Her voice was soft, as if pulled reluctantly from her soul. "I'll be right there."

Maggie was striding rapidly out of the office as Ellen entered. "He's ready to explode," Maggie whispered and quickly shut the door behind her.

Paul looked up sharply from his desk. "Zach say anything to you about the building inspector?"

Standing in the middle of the room, she shook her head, only half listening. "No. Nothing."

"Jesus! Do I have to do everything?" He snatched up the phone and dialed the squad room. She stepped to the window and stared out. The National Guard had cordoned off the building, moving the horde of reporters three blocks away. Behind her she could hear Paul saying, "Well find him, for Christ's sake. You're a fucking detective. Figure it out!"

He slammed the phone down. "Now the goddamn building inspector's gone!"

It finally struck her what he was saying and she turned around, confused. "The building inspector? Why?"

"I figure if anyone knows where you could hide a bus, he would. Should have thought of it earlier."

She felt a surge of interest, almost of hope. Yes, of course! But at once her spirits fell. What if he did know of such a place? They couldn't possibly do anything about it. They still had to do whatever the kidnappers wanted. The children had to be protected.

Paul tilted back in his leather chair and glanced out the window at the sky. "Guess who's coming to dinner? Ellis Whitfield."

Ellen started. "The F.B.I. Director?"

"And the state attorney general. Cozy, huh? Maybe I can get them a room together at the EconoLodge."

"But—" Again she was confused. Nothing seemed to make sense anymore. "Why? What are they going to do?"

He looked at her as if it were obvious. "Everyone wants to help the dumb local cops. LaSalle's already told me the F.B.I.'s taking over the kidnapping part of the case. He didn't ask; he told me. It's their jurisdiction under federal law. He wants Exley to deal with the kidnapper when he calls, talk to him and deliver the ransom; then they'll collar the bad guys. Whitfield will want his picture in the papers snapping handcuffs on the villains just like old J. Edgar used to. Typical F.B.I. horseshit."

This was too much for her to sort out. Why had Matt taken over the case like that? He'd said the Las Cruces police would handle everything. He'd promised them. And why was Whitfield coming out here?

Paul added, "I told them to fuck off. When the guy calls at seven o'clock, we'll handle it."

Ellen's voice leaped. "Seven? How do you know he'll call at seven?"

"He phoned us, Ellen. If you'd been around, you'd have known."

Her hand went to her forehead, and she began to feel faint. The man had told her to wait for his call. Then why had he called the department, too? It didn't make sense. What was he doing? I've got to tell Paul, she realized at once. I've got to tell him about Denise. It's madness not to. He can help. She stepped quickly from the window, then halted and sank onto the couch, nausea mounting as her stomach tightened in knots. I can't! I can't tell anybody. They'll kill her . . .

He was looking at her oddly. "You okay?"

She said abruptly, "I think you should let Dr. Exley talk to him when he calls."

"What?" His chair rocked forward.

"Let Exley handle it," she said, gaining strength. "He's trained, he's a professional. What do any of us know about kidnappings?" But she was thinking, if the children are in danger Exley will do whatever the kidnappers demand. He's not the type to force a confrontation; he's a conciliator. He'll appease them and get the children out safely.

Paul's voice shot up. "I'm not turning this over to the F.B.I., Ellen. What the hell's gotten into you? This is your case. You should want to handle it."

Quickly, she tried to calm him. "I do want to handle it, Paul. But they're experts. They've done this dozens of times. We haven't." Her voice was pleading.

"If it's in the city, it's ours," Paul said hotly. "Jesus! I didn't expect you to turn on me, too. Can't I trust anybody?"

"I'm going to be sick," Ellen whispered, her hand flying to her mouth. She rushed from the room, through Maggie's office, and down to the women's restroom. The instant she burst through the door to the toilet stall she vomited.

A moment later Maggie hurried in behind her, finding Ellen on her knees in front of a toilet. "Are you okay? Do you want me to call a doctor?"

"No, no," Ellen managed. She reached up and flushed the toilet. "Please. I'll be all right." She didn't want a doctor. She didn't want to be sent home. She had to be here when the kidnapper called.

Maggie squinted at her. "You sure?"

Ellen vomited again and started to choke.

"I'm getting a doctor."

"No!" Ellen screamed and turned around, still on her knees. She tried a smile, forcing it to stay on her face. "Just something I ate. I'm okay now. It's over." She flushed the toilet again. "Just let me wash up. I'll be okay. You better get back to Paul."

Maggie looked at her doubtfully. "If you say so. It's your tummy."

Maggie left as another wave of sickness came over Ellen. She bent over the toilet, her hands holding tightly onto the seat, and gagged as nothing but bile came up. She felt dizzy, light-headed. Putting the toilet lid down, she forced herself to sit, cradling her head in her arms, and began to cry.

Paul was hanging up the phone when Ellen returned to his office. "Ellis Whitfield just flew into March Air Force Base. He'll be here in thirty minutes. You look like shit. Why don't you go home?"

"I'm fine," she said with determination. "I'm staying."

"Then when Whitfield gets here, you back me up. You understand? Or I'll take you off the case and give it to Zach. I want Whitfield to understand that *we're* dealing with the kidnapper when he calls. *We're* handling the ransom. If there's an assault, we're in charge."

She sank down on the couch.

"You understand what I'm telling you, Ellen?"

As her eyes lifted to the wide dark face, anger swept through her in waves. You goddamn petty bastard, worried more about your department than the children. You stupid, narrow-minded ass. But she could say nothing; the words just wouldn't come.

"You hear me, Ellen?"

"Yes, goddamn it, I hear you." Her hands clenched and her face went red. She felt a resurgence of hysteria rushing into her mind. The phone rang and they both jumped. The attorney general had just arrived from Sacramento.

> **"It often happens that, if a lie be believed only for an hour, it has done its work, and there is no further occasion for it."**
>
> —*J. Swift, 1715*

The key, DeVries had realized quite early, almost from the beginning, was not too much chaos. One needed to control confusion.

Too much and the "authorities" would sense its unlikelihood, its anomalous nature. Then the structure that lay beneath would become manifest, and what first appeared as random and diffuse would be seen as planned and deliberate, an attempt to lead everyone astray.

Just enough confusion, then, a tiny hole in God's curtain, a managed disarrangement of their universe.

Thus, disparate bits of data—a shoe, a video, a lunch box, a phone call (and jet fuel, a stroke of genius!)—scattered about, offering the merest hint of a pattern (too subtle for most to see, like the tip of a mast glimpsed through fog that only an experienced ship's officer would notice) but which, when sufficient thought was devoted to it, would bring a sudden rush of excitement and closure and that heady thrill of discovery when you leap to your feet and shout, *I've got it!* while congratulating yourself on your wisdom and perspicuity.

Euphoria lifts us, and off we go
    (like the F-14s that race so beautifully above the
        mountains)
    Into the wild
    blue
      yonder
        . . .

Sitting in the chair in the kitchen, Lowell watched the portable television. A Bill Cosby rerun. He felt suddenly dragged down by its banality, all these so-cheerful people in their bright preppy sweaters and day-glo smiles. But the station had milked the kidnapping dry and had—reluctantly, he was certain—gone back to its regular programming. The news would be on in ten minutes, though, and he could see what the police and F.B.I. were up to.

So far everything had gone, if not exactly as planned, close enough. But that was to be expected. There are, in a simple operation like this—particularly one orchestrated and carried out by a single person, especially a person gifted with foresight—a finite number of things that can go wrong, and preplanning quite naturally negates them all. The Edison worker had been a foul-up, to be sure, as was the nosy policeman, but everything had worked out in the end. Planning, preparing, thinking, staying one step ahead of everyone else—the keys to success in life no matter what one does, even when one worked for a trivial governmental bureau as DeVries had for eighteen years. A bit more time in college would have secured a position that better fit his abilities, of course, but all in all he had been satisfied. The pay was acceptable, if not extravagant, and it gave him the freedom from supervision he so coveted. He wondered what his officemates thought of the events of the past two days, those drone-like civil servants (more servant than civil) living their drone-like civil lives. Bees in a hive, he thought, men and women with nothing to live for but their work, gathering nectar for the commonweal. No hobbies, as he had, no indulgences to lift the soul. They, in fact, had been far and away the most difficult part of the job. How hard it had been to be with such people day after day.

He had, through his own choice, developed no friendships at all among his colleagues. His work took him out of the office most of the day anyway. When forced to share their company, such as at the regular Friday afternoon department meetings, he had carefully feigned the expected interest in them and their lives. But he and they had nothing in com-

mon, nothing at all. Once Follette had made a crack about
a twelve-year-old girl who had come into the office with her
mother, and DeVries had gently probed. It would have been
pleasant to have someone to share his hobby with. They
could drive together to Miss Violet's perhaps. But Follette ignored his hints. It made no difference. They were all of a
type, people with little imagination, the sorts who rushed
home every evening to sink down in front of their TVs,
watching the insipid nonsense that passed for entertainment
today, until crawling off to bed. While Lowell lived, *soared!*

No matter. No matter at all. In two months, he would put
in for early retirement—"My heart, don't you know."—and
disappear. Simply disappear. No one would make the connection between the kidnapping and DeVries's leisurely de-
parture from Las Cruces.

Thinking of the job made his mind slip back to when he'd
called in sick again this morning. Two days in a row. Quite
unusual for so dedicated an employee. He wondered if Jorgenson, the bitch, had phoned his home to see if he really
had been ill. Big deal. I'll just tell her I was asleep and didn't
hear it ring. But maybe it would be wise to check his answering machine anyway, see if there were any messages. No
need to go into town for a pay phone this time; he could
use the one in his car.

He glanced out the kitchen window to ensure that no one
was near, then crossed rapidly to the barn, where his Buick
sat next to the bus. Opening the car door, he slid in,
grabbed the receiver, and dialed his home number. When
the recorded greeting came on, he punched in his three-
digit code and waited for the tape to rewind. A moment
later, he heard, "Mr. DeVries, this is Detective Sergeant Harris at the Las Cruces police department. Would you please
call me at extension three-two-six the first opportunity you
can. It's extremely urgent. It involves the missing children."

The breath went out of him in a rush; he slumped back
against the seat and began to feel warm. His thoughts raced
and collided in mad confusion. *The police. . . .* The missing
children . . .

What the hell could that *mean*? There's no way to connect me to the children. Goddamn it, there isn't!

Urgent . . .

In a daze, he put the phone down. It was dark in the barn and hot and stank horribly. But he sat frozen for several minutes without so much as moving a finger. His mind refused to function. This call, whatever it meant, was inexplicable. Perhaps I wasn't as meticulous in my preparations as I could have been, he suddenly thought. Perhaps I moved too soon, after all. I should have waited, waited and prepared more, given it additional thought. Yes! It needed more thought, more planning. *Three* mistakes now, he realized with a start: that goddamn traffic cop last night, the Edison worker, now this.

His body was covered in sweat.

Three mistakes!

Four! That little bitch who escaped this afternoon.

But the cop, that was inconsequential: he had gunned through a yellow light. Everyone does that. Sometimes you get caught, mostly you don't. Not a mistake in planning though. Not a slip-up. Just one of those things. Same for that Edison worker and that kid. How could I have foreseen those sorts of events? You can't plan away serendipity, the random vicissitudes of life. "These weren't my fault," he screamed aloud.

But this call.

Calm yourself, Lowell. Breathe slowly, through your nose.

Pulse. He put his fingers on his wrist. Will yourself to relax. Slowly . . .

He closed his eyes and brought up the image Dr. Weir had taught him to rely on: a beautiful spring morning in the countryside, blue and yellow wildflowers blowing gently in the warm breeze, a crystal clear pond surrounded by tall, green grass, softly rustling. Softly. . . . Slowly he moved his consciousness into the pond and its cool, transparent, soothing water. Focus on the water, so cool . . . and clear. . . . Let it envelop you like moist fingers . . .

Ten minutes later, his eyes opened.

He could not be suspected of anything. If he were, the police certainly wouldn't be calling, would they? He almost laughed at the thought: Dear Sir, we think you guilty of murder and kidnapping; do come in and see us.

Then *why* did they call?

Perhaps he should check with Jeannie. No, no. Don't give her cause for alarm. She might be needed later.

Think it out.

They called because, because. . . . They need his help?

Of course! That was it. His professional assistance. It must be.

How nice.

Glowing with sudden excitement, he grabbed the phone and dialed the police department. Why in the world would they want a building inspector?

5:42 P.M.

Julie Garcia felt her mind was going to snap any second if the kids didn't stop it. A little girl was crying for food and pulling on her leg, a boy in a wheelchair sobbed uncontrollably, another boy was pounding his tiny bloodied fists into the cement floor and screaming at the top of his voice.

What was she supposed to do? How could she help? Or did it matter? The man was going to kill her anyway. He would have to—she had seen him. They all could identify him: a big, good-looking guy, smooth-looking. Didn't look like no clown. A salesman, she had thought when he'd knocked on the door, although she hadn't seen too many salesmen dressed that nice. A police detective, he'd told her. Giving her a big smile, like everything's just dandy, and saying Ellen wanted him to drive Julie and Denise down to the police station. When Julie had looked at him funny and asked, "Why would she want that?" he'd pulled a gun and said, "Don't say another word and you'll be okay."

But she wasn't going to be okay.

At least Denise wasn't crying. She hadn't left Julie's side, but she hadn't cried at all, even when the bastard had thrown them down the ramp and locked the door. Suddenly Denise yanked Julie's hand. "What's the matter with her?"

She was pointing to a girl without any clothes on. Julie had seen the child on TV that morning. Probably raped, the newscaster had said, and Julie had thought, How can they say that, the poor girl's mamma watching?

She went over to the girl, bent, and felt her forehead. Cold. Dropping to her knees, Julie placed her hand on the girl's heart. It was beating, slowly but regularly. And she hadn't been raped. Not even any bruises.

The girl in the corner was dead though. No doubt about that, blood all over her head and back. Even Denise seemed to know. And another girl on her stomach but without any marks or blood had probably died because she hadn't gotten her medicine.

God, it smells horrible in here. Vomit on the floor everywhere. Urine. Shit. Body smells. We're going to die in a cesspool, in a room full of shit. And not more than three or four miles from town. The old Larchmont place. She'd recognized it at once. When she was a kid, old man Larchmont had tried to grow cotton or something out here. Didn't work out though. Everyone thought he was a little weird. If they had only known what he had underneath his barn. What the hell kind of place was this? A torture chamber? Was he some kind of sex nut?

Denise yanked on Julie's hand again. "I think that boy's sick, Mrs. Garcia."

A wheelchair boy sat immobile, his face paralyzed into a grimace, eyes bulging horribly behind thick glasses that were half off his face. Julie was about to test for a pulse when the door behind her flew open with a crash and the kidnapper took two hurried steps down the ramp. He stood still, his eyes searching the room.

"Ah, Julie," he said. He was smiling, the bastard! And how did he know her name? He took several more quick steps down the ramp and looked around the room. "Making out okay?" he asked.

"Okay?" she snapped. "Get us out of here. Why do you need us here?"

"In fact, I probably won't need you. At this point, however, you're bargaining chips, should I require them."

She dropped Denise's hand and walked right up to him, looking into his face. "You're crazy. You know that? Crazy!"

"If that were so," he replied easily, "I suppose I'd be locked up and you'd be on the outside. As it is, I prefer this."

"Crazy," she repeated, waving her arm around the room. "How can you treat these children like this? What have they ever done to you? Huh? Answer me that. Look at that poor boy." She pointed to the autistic boy who had been pounding his fists on the floor. He was screaming at the top of his voice in pain and fear and who knew what else.

DeVries glanced at the boy for a moment and then at the other children in the room. "A case could be made that we do these kids no service by allowing them to live. What sorts of lives can they lead? Most of them will spend their remaining years in institutions, being maintained at our considerable expense."

His gaze came back to her. "I hasten to add that I do not agree with such an assessment. These children are human beings, after all, and need to be treated with dignity, et cetera, et cetera. Ah, Denise." He smiled and moved quickly to the end of the ramp. "You miss your mother, I suppose."

Denise turned away from him, hiding behind Julie.

DeVries said, "She's not usually so timid." He reached his hand out and caressed her cheek with the back of his fingers. "You normally watch the Disney Channel this time of the day, don't you, Denise? I'm sorry to keep you from it today, but I need you here. There's a TV by the wall and a video if you get bored. And you needn't worry. My plans for you are altogether different from those I have for the others."

Defiance sprang up in Denise and she said, "I want to go home."

"I'm sure you do," he said. "But I'm afraid I need your mother's cooperation for a few hours, and you're the only way I'm going to get it."

Julie felt Denise's hand close on hers, but still the girl didn't cry. DeVries turned and started up the ramp. "I'll be back shortly. I have to make an unexpected trip to the Civic Center." He smiled thinly but obviously in good humor. "As the English say, I have to help the authorities with their inquiries."

6:03 P.M.

Harris tilted back in his swivel chair and smiled at the man seated across the desk from him. "I appreciate your coming in, Mr. DeVries, especially when you're not feeling well."

Lowell waved a hand while glancing quickly at Ellen's vacant desk. "No problem, sergeant. But I guess I still don't see how I can help." All the police had told him when he'd called was that they needed to talk to the chief building inspector. He still couldn't understand, and, although he felt in no danger, sweat had begun to form in tiny beads along his ribs and trickle in an icy line toward his waist.

"Well, it's the bus," Harris said, stretching his arms above his head and yawning. He hadn't slept much since this had started and was exhausted and a little cranky with himself for not turning anything up yet. "We figure it's got to be nearby since no one saw it out on the highway. We've looked pretty damn well everywhere in the city it could be. I figured you'd know what kind of hiding places there are around here. Maybe they're being kept where we can't see 'em. Could even be underground."

"In a cave?" DeVries asked. He was beginning to feel warm, as though the air conditioner had shut down.

"Yeah, maybe," Harris said as Ellen came in and sat stiffly at the adjoining desk. "But, like I say, I think it's more likely to be in the city or close to it. Buildings with storage basements, things like that."

DeVries felt his heart begin to thump. He had a terrible urge to turn and stare at Ellen but determinedly kept his eyes on Harris as he said, "Not much of that out here in the desert. Most people prefer to build out rather than up or down."

Harris took off his glasses and rubbed his eyes with the back of his hands. "What about bomb shelters, fall-out shelters, that sort of thing? I remember my dad talking about folks putting in underground shelters back in the fifties, thinking they'd be okay after an atomic war."

DeVries drew a breath and closed his eyes as he hesitated just a second. "I'm afraid that's before my time."

"But you've got records over there, don't you?" Harris waved toward the opposite side of the Civic Center, where the building inspector's office was located.

"Of course. But for then, back in the fifties, it'd all be on microfilm. And I don't know how it's indexed. I don't think I can just look up 'Bomb Shelter' and get a quick answer."

Ignoring the conversation, Ellen stared dully at the wall clock. How long had it been since she'd taken aspirin? Didn't matter, she couldn't keep anything down anyway. She reached in her bottom drawer, pulled out a Kleenex, and dabbed her forehead and cheeks.

Harris said, "You can come up with something though. Even if you have to go address by address, you can tell us who put in a shelter. There couldn't have been more than three thousand people living here then."

"It's not as simple as that. Not everyone would have gotten a permit for a bomb shelter. The way I heard it, most people didn't want their neighbors to know what they were doing and dug them out under barns or garages so it couldn't be seen. Usually they brought in laborers from Mexico to do the work and then sent them home as soon as it was done. No one ever knew."

Harris got an annoyed look on his face, and DeVries saw that he wasn't handling this correctly. Quickly, he added, "But I'll check the records and tell you what we have. I want those kids found, too. I'm sure it'll turn out all right."

At the sound of his words, Ellen spun around in her chair and stared at him in disbelief.

She began to feel dizzy, gripped the edge of her desk.

Harris relaxed back in his chair and his expression eased.

"Thank you, Mr. DeVries. I guess you're our last hope of finding them before the ransom's delivered."

DeVries could feel Ellen's eyes fixed on him, burning through the side of his face like embers. His heart was pounding wildly now, the adrenaline charging through his veins, and his body drenched in sweat. His mind swam. He couldn't hear Harris droning on behind the desk, blood was pounding so loudly in his ears. Slowly, without planning it, but reacting to a terrible invisible force he couldn't deny, he turned his body toward Ellen and smiled at her.

Smiled!

She looked at him without comprehension, her mind registering a dozen different impressions: sweaty face, voice, clock on the wall, Harris. Unthinkingly, she began to rise from the chair, but DeVries made an almost imperceptible motion with his head and she froze in her seat.

He turned again to Harris and got to his feet. Willing his voice into calmness, he said, "I'll get right to it. The 1950s, you say. It can't take too long. I'll give you a call." His eyes went momentarily back to Ellen, then returned to Harris. "Even if you discover the hiding place, you'll have to be careful. There's certainly more than one kidnapper. They'll probably kill all the children at the first hint of an attack, then come out shooting. They're facing the death penalty as it is. People like that are pretty desperate; they'd rather die fighting than subject themselves to such a fate."

Harris smiled without amusement. "You sound like the F.B.I. bunch, Mr. DeVries. Everyone's a goddamn expert on criminal behavior! You find us a hiding place, and we'll take care of the bad guys."

He nodded at them both. "I'll give you a call."

Ellen sat at her desk, head pounding, stomach knotting painfully. My God, she thought. My God! It's him! He works in this building. Her whole body began to shudder terribly. She had to do something. But what? He had Denise.

"Ellen, for Christ's sake, I'm talking to you."

She looked suddenly at Harris but couldn't focus on him as the world spun wildly out of control.

"I said he's a weird bastard, isn't he? I remember seeing him around here before but never knew what he did. Figured he was a lawyer, the way he dressed. What did you think of the bomb shelter idea?"

I've got to get out of here, she thought desperately. I've got to get out. I'm going nuts.

She rose suddenly from her seat, steadied herself against the desk.

Harris rocked forward in his chair and stared at her. "Ellen?"

She ran out of the room. I've got to get out of here. I've got to . . .

6:08 P.M.

Slumped on a toilet in the locked restroom stall, Ellen was shaking uncontrollably. Dear God, she thought. It's him! Him! All this time someone who knew her, or knew of her, someone who worked in this building and probably saw her every day. His voice! She *had* heard it before, probably in the elevator or cafeteria or hallway. She felt deathly ill and began to hyperventilate. Gasping for air, sobbing, her body wouldn't stop trembling. But she couldn't stay here. She had to do something. She had to stop him.

Suddenly the restroom door swished open, and she heard Maggie enter the adjacent stall. *No,* she thought. I don't want her to see me like this. I don't want to have to explain. If she tells Paul, he'll make me go home and I have to be here.

Summoning up all her strength, she forced her body to stop shaking. Her breathing still came with difficulty, but she managed to dampen the sound.

The toilet seat jiggled next to her. Don't breathe, she warned herself furiously. Don't make a sound.

Silence.

Then a fevered whisper came through, around, and over

the partition, "Ellen," and repeated itself so softly, so intently, that she couldn't bring herself to believe what she was hearing.

"Ellen, say nothing," she heard in the now familiar voice, and she leapt at once to her feet, rage and fear charging through her, but the voice said sharply, "Sit down. Now. Listen to me. If you wish to see your daughter again . . ."

DeVries sprawled on the toilet seat, legs extended stiffly, head thrown back dizzily against the wall behind him, his flushed eyes unseeingly fixed on the ceiling. Sweat swam over his entire body, his head ached, and fear pulsed like a virus through his veins.

"I have her, Ellen," he whispered urgently. "Denise. I have her. So pretty, so pretty. She's mine to do with as I want. You understand, don't you?"

"Yes."

"Do nothing. Say nothing. Remain in the building. Everything will be all right if you do as I say."

"Please don't hurt my baby," Ellen half-whispered, half-cried. "Please."

His body jerked suddenly alive as fear and excitement joined thrillingly in his mind. He bent abruptly forward, aware that he had become sexually aroused, the fact registering unexpectedly but pleasurably in his brain. His hands hurried instinctively to his belt; he yanked his pants down and began to stroke himself. Pleasure rose at once as his mind became crowded with visions: Ellen alone, next to him, mounting him, rising up, leaning forward, breasts falling to his lips. . . . Then, as though losing control of his body, his hands fell suddenly to his sides and his head banged sharply against the wall separating the stalls; his lips opened and pressed against the smooth enameled wood in a soft, wet kiss that left a circle of moisture. *"Ellll-len,"* he whispered, drawing the name into a long, slow sigh as he saw in his mind not Ellen this time but her daughter. "I have Denise, Ellen. I have her."

As if a switch had been thrown, his mind again shifted. He jumped to his feet, dizzy, knowing it was mad to stay here. It was stupid. Dangerous. Get out, Lowell, he told himself. Hurry! Hurry!

Metabolism careening out of control, he adjusted his clothes and unlocked the stall with fumbling fingers. Rushing past the wash basins, he hit the restroom door with both fists and disappeared, leaving a terrible silence.

Ellen sat in a daze of disbelief. My God, she thought as her head twisted back and forth. Oh my God! Blindly, she pushed to her feet, stumbled from the restroom, raced unthinkingly into the hallway on trembling legs. My God, he's going to kill her! She had to do something. Rounding a corner, blood pounding in her ears, her head about to explode, she ran blindly into someone, knocking him backward against the wall. Her eyes lifted to stare into the furious dark face of Charles Middleton, and she screamed.

"Delay is preferable to error."

—Thomas Jefferson

Don't panic! DeVries told himself as he mopped sweat from his brow.

This is not a problem.

It's not.

It's an opportunity.

A contingency, only.

He had foreseen that difficulties might arise, of course. Humankind is simply too variable for unerringly accurate predictions about behavior. If you can't predict, you prepare.

A dozen books on business and military strategy had taught him this: all plans must contain contingency provisions.

If . . . then.

If the enemy advances, then strengthen your lines. If a competitor cuts his price, then cut yours more.

And since you can never be certain what the enemy will do, remain flexible, ready to react.

Ready to strike.

Relax, Lowell. Calm yourself. Take a breath.

Contingency planning. If they get too close, then manufacture confusion.

Confusion.

Rip the curtain just a little more.

So, relax.

I can do it.

His heart slowed, and his eyes began to wander around his vacant office.

Two more months he would be here; two months only, surrounded by the mind-numbing tedium of beige metal desks and filing cabinets, gray industrial carpeting, fluorescent lights recessed in a sea of white acoustic tile. An environment designed for robots. By robots. Two months. Then Costa Rica, the jungle. Yes! Goddamn it, yes! It would be like going from black and white to technicolor, like Judy Garland taking that first magical step into Oz.

What's Ellen doing? he wondered. The question thrilled him, and his body tensed as he straightened in the chair, his mind alive with the possibilities. What's mamma doing? Trying to keep her heart from pounding through her chest as she met the man with her precious little daughter. She knew in the squad room. She heard his voice and knew. That was okay, more than okay; it was fine, just fine. He had Denise. As long as he did, mamma was his. And the instant he had the money, the exact moment it touched his fingers, the curtain would inexorably open, Chaos rushing through. *Rushing!*

So what are the police up to? It wasn't hard to figure. Less than a hundred yards away, this very instant, they were scratching their dull, bureaucratic heads, trying to figure out what to do next. Bomb shelters. Lucky guess. It could have been years before someone stumbled onto that or gave any thought to the Larchmont place situated in a gray area, an area of chaos, on the city line, the boundary between police and sheriff's jurisdictions. If they had been scientists, they would have known: everything interesting takes place on a boundary, where systems meet and rub up against each other. And how perfect a locale it was: only six and a half minutes from the time he'd stepped on the bus to the time they'd pulled into the barn. The kids were underground before anyone even knew they were missing.

So they want to know about bomb shelters? No need to look anything up: he'd personally seen them all. May as well give them a list.

But first, contingency: a little misdirection for those in authority.

He reached for the phone and punched out the number of the Palm Springs TV station. Time to disturb the universe. When a receptionist answered, he said forcefully: "Monica Ochoa has a four-inch scar on her neck."

"Sir?"

"Shut up and listen! We have the kids. Chief Whitehorse refuses to cooperate. He has repeatedly refused every one of our demands. If he doesn't start doing what we say, we will kill the children. Every goddamn one of them."

"Sir, I think—"

His voice flew out of control. "Shut up, goddamn it! I want this statement read on television immediately. Write it down: Either Whitehorse cooperates or the children die. If you don't have it on the air in ten minutes, I will personally kill one of them myself." He hung up.

Not bad. Not bad at all. Grabbing a blank piece of paper, he jotted down three addresses, then hurried to his feet. Time to tell the good sergeant where the city's bomb shelters were located. Then to take care of the kids once and for all.

He smiled as he heard the whispering in his ear, the soft, insistent, urging:

Chaos, Lowell. *Chaos!*

6:10 P.M.

Ellen rocked back and forth on the metal stool in the tiny women's locker room, her head in her hands, trying to force herself to think. But it was no good. Her mind was in a panic.

Dear God, what does he want from me? We've done everything he asked. What more?

There was more than one kidnapper, he said. Was that a lie? What difference did it make? She had to assume he was telling the truth.

They'll probably kill all the kids at the first hint of an attack. He's warning me, telling me what he'll do. Please, please, please don't let it happen. Please.

Denise was all she had, and Ellen loved her so much she sometimes thought her heart must shatter. Paul said Ellen babied her. Maybe she did. But they were all each other had since her grandfather's stroke, and if they clung to each other a little too tightly, so what? Who else was there?

What's Denise doing right now, this very second? She's scared and she's thinking of me and she's wondering why I don't come for her. I will come for you, Denise. I will get you home safely. I will do whatever is necessary.

Her hands gripped the edge of the stool: Hear me, Denise. I will get you home. And if I have not been a good mother, if I have somehow wronged you, I will change. I will do better. I know I don't always make the right decisions. I don't always act quickly enough; I didn't when I saw what was happening to Pete. I should have left him when he started hitting me, when he began using cocaine, but I loved him, Denise, and I wanted to help. I loved him. Do you understand that? Still, I should have seen what was happening. I should have seen it.

But how could she? she thought angrily. She hadn't even been able to see what was happening to her own mother, someone she'd lived with for eighteen years—screaming, throwing things, scaring away friends, talking crazy—until she'd finally fled to Arizona in self-defense.

But Mother hadn't been able to help herself, and I should have understood that. I should have been there for her. Why do we desert those we love just when they so urgently need us? But I won't desert you, Denise. I will get you home.

She felt a desperate need to hold her daughter, as she had when Denise was born—not two minutes in this world, crying and wet, just the two of them, flesh to flesh, sharing each other's warmth. It was still the most magical experience of her life, the only sensation of its kind because, like her mother, Ellen was not a toucher. Even with Paul and her grandfather she wasn't the sort to be constantly hugging, embracing, grabbing. She was too reserved and instinctively drew away from the physical contact of almost everyone. But Denise—touching, feeling, loving her softness, so warm and magical.

It had surprised her, this new emotion, and delighted also because she hadn't known it was within her.

And now Denise was all that was left of her family.

Grandfather dying. Mother dead.

I am part of a lineage, she thought. I stretch back ten thousand years. It is a line unbroken from Denise to me to my mother and grandmother to the beginning of time. I will not let it end. I will do anything I have to for you, Denise. Do you hear me? Anything!

6:20 P.M.

Paul vaguely sensed that his emotions had gone from anger to numbness and back to anger. Ellis Whitfield, the F.B.I. Director, had been in the Civic Center for more than an hour, most of that time meeting privately with LaSalle and the other agents, going over their investigation of the construction workers. Nine of the original hundred and sixteen had not been located and nationwide A.P.B.s were issued for them. Another eighteen with unverifiable alibis had been taken to the county jail in El Centro for questioning by the F.B.I., which was progressing fitfully. When Whitfield discovered that C. Richard Bishop, the state's attorney general, was in Las Cruces, he immediately demanded a meeting between himself, Bishop, and Whitehorse. Two minutes into the meeting, with Whitfield angrily lecturing Bishop about the federal kidnapping statute and

Paul staring at the ceiling to keep from hitting somebody, Harris had called from downstairs. "Better hurry down, Chief. Got us a homicide." Leaving Whitfield and Bishop arguing, Paul came into the squad room a minute later to find a vaguely familiar civilian in Harris's visitor's chair.

"Lowell DeVries," Harris said, introducing the stranger. "City building inspector."

Paul was irritated. "I thought you said there was a one-eighty-seven."

"Ferguson's at the scene with Howard, Chief. I wanted you to hear what Mr. DeVries had to say first so he can get on home. He's not feeling well."

Paul suppressed a sigh and turned to the man. "Okay, shoot." Why did this man's name seem familiar? But it was. He had come across it sometime in the last day or two. At any rate, whatever the man had to say it couldn't be as important as the homicide, and Paul wanted to get it over with.

DeVries straightened in his chair and offered up a small, servile smile. "Well, the sergeant here wanted me to look for bomb shelters. I couldn't think of any myself, but I went through our records and turned up three." He handed a half sheet of paper to the chief.

"Big enough to hide a bus?" Paul asked, his interest growing.

The man shook his head with regret. "Big enough, maybe, but you couldn't get a bus inside. They're accessed by ladders or small ramps."

Paul studied the list. "Two in the city and one out in the desert. But they could hold twenty-seven kids?"

"Sure," DeVries said. "It'd be crowded, but they'd fit."

"Can you think of anywhere else here in Las Cruces someone might hide a bus and that many kids?"

"Not in the city," DeVries replied. "But maybe they could be at that abandoned airfield north of here. Lots of old hangars and so forth. You could hide a hundred buses out there."

"Sounds like something the F.B.I. could investigate," Paul

said with sarcasm. Anything that got the feds out of his hair was fine with him. He stuck out his hand to the visitor. "Thank you, Mr. DeVries. You've been very helpful." It was meant as a dismissal, and DeVries came to his feet and smiled. "Any time, Chief. Give me a call if I can be of more help."

Harris waited until DeVries had left and then said, "I didn't want to go into this with a civilian around. You don't want the press latching on to it."

Paul dropped into the chair DeVries had vacated. He didn't want to hear it. But it couldn't possibly be any worse than the past thirty-six hours. Tilting his head back, he closed his eyes and massaged his temples with his fingertips. "Let's have it."

Harris lowered his gaze to a paper on his desk. "Kim Zeigler, mid-twenties, does repair work for Edison. Found inside her truck out at the old Egg House. Been shot several times in the upper torso sometime this afternoon. And her Edison truck was beat to hell, looked like it'd been rammed. It was off the road, stuck in a dry creek bed."

Paul's eyes blinked open, and he straightened in his chair. "You think this has anything to do with the kidnapping?"

Harris nodded. "Guesswork, but it fits. She wasn't raped. Truck wasn't stolen, doesn't look like any equipment's missing."

"Then she knew something or saw something," Paul said at once. It was the first real lead in hours, and he felt suddenly energized. "Has Ferguson checked out the egg ranch yet?"

"Yeah. Place is abandoned. No sign of recent use. Howard's taking a look, too. But it's probably a dead end."

Paul came quickly to his feet. "Then we'll work backward. She probably has a log book. Have Fergie check out each location she stopped off at today. Leave the crime scene to Howard and get Fergie moving now. Maybe you can pull someone from somewhere else to help him. I need people checking out these three bomb shelters, too."

"No log book. Fergie already looked. And I haven't got anyone to spare anyway, boss. Not for Fergie and not for the shelters. Unless you want to take people from looking for Manny. We gotta keep six guys in the rescue team ready to roll."

"Christ!" Paul could feel his anger and frustration shooting up again. Like a man trying to outrun an avalanche, he was being overwhelmed and there was nothing that could be done about it. He wasn't going to ask the F.B.I. for help. Ellis Whitfield had already informed him and the attorney general that the F.B.I. had officially assumed control of the investigation and would henceforth deal with the kidnapper. Unless the pay-off was in the city or the kids found within the city limits, the Las Cruces police had been squeezed out, and Bishop had hardly put up a whimper.

Harris said, "Feds turn up anything with the construction workers or sex offenders?"

"They're still dickin' around with it. You'd think with ten thousand agents here they'd turn up something by now. How's your list of repair people coming along?"

"Ended up with sixty-eight names. We've been able to locate sixty of them by phone. I haven't got anybody to go out and look for the other eight though."

Paul glanced again at the paper in his hand. "Jesus. All right, find that F.B.I. kid, the one who went through the sign-in sheets. Turn the names over to him. Then call the sheriff, have them check out the bomb shelter in their territory. It must be twenty miles from here. Tell them it's a priority one, we can't afford any delay on this. Take one car out of service and have someone run out to the shelter in Old Town. I'll check the other one myself. Shouldn't take more than fifteen minutes. Goddamn it, where's Ellen?"

The phone rang and Harris listened for a moment, then said, "Maggie, Chief."

He took the receiver as though not wanting to hear whatever she had to say. "The TV just broadcast a statement from the kidnapper, Paul. He says if you don't start cooperating, he'll kill more children."

"What?"

"I know, I know—"

"Get the station manager on the phone," Paul shouted. "Now!" Furious, he waited, the phone grasped tightly in his hand, as Maggie completed the call.

"Now just a minute, Chief—" the voice on the other end of the line began, but Paul cut him off.

"What the hell are you trying to do, broadcasting something like that? Do you know how much trouble you're making for us? Whose side are you on, anyway?"

The station manager suddenly sounded bolder as he responded to a familiar complaint. "We're not on anyone's side. We're neutral. We merely report—"

"Neutral? This man's kidnapped twenty-seven kids, killed four innocent people, and you're *neutral?*"

His hand shaking, Paul slammed down the phone. "Goddamn reporters are going to go nuts wanting to know why we're not cooperating with the kidnapper. What are the parents going to think? Jesus! We spend more time with the press than looking for the kids." He snatched up the phone again and said, "Maggie, put Ellis Whitfield on." A moment later he heard the F.B.I. director's silky, Groton-Yale accented, "Whitfield, here."

"The kidnapper just called the Palm Springs TV station, Whitfield. He said we're not cooperating with him, so he's going to start killing kids. You hear what I'm saying?"

"Yes, I understand." But there was confusion in his voice.

"Well, since this is your investigation now, you and your boy LaSalle can trot across the street and talk to the press and tell them exactly what it is you're not doing. The way I figure it, you have about five minutes before they storm this building." He hung up and turned toward Harris. "You sure you got no one else to check out this last shelter?"

"Not unless you want me to go."

"All right, you go, then, and I'll have Ellen take over in here. Where the hell is she?"

"Sick, I guess. She looked like hell. I thought she might have gone home."

Paul felt himself getting hot again. Why hadn't she told him she was leaving? He grabbed the phone and punched out her home number, but it rang without interruption. Why didn't the baby-sitter answer? He hit the intercom button for the front desk. "You seen Ellen in the last few minutes, Jeannie?"

"Not for about an hour."

"Jesus!" He slammed the phone down again and consulted the paper DeVries had given him. "Hawkins. Out on Pipeline. All those old ranches. Okay, Zach, I'll have to go out there. You stay here, but get someone to check out the house in Old Town and get the sheriff moving on the location in their territory. If you need me, you can get me on the radio. I'll be back before the kidnapper calls at seven. And if you hear anything at all about Manny, let me know."

Harris leaned back and looked at him. "What do I do if the F.B.I. starts giving orders to our people?"

"Tell them to fuck off. This is my goddamn department."

Just then Bishop and Whitfield walked into the squad room.

"Tweedledee and Tweedledum," Harris whispered and sat back to watch the show.

Paul threw them a dismissive glance and began to leave. "I haven't got time for you."

The F.B.I. director said nothing, but Bishop, seemingly a man of infinite patience, said, "Perhaps we could go to your office."

"Got a homicide to investigate." He wasn't about to tell the F.B.I. about the bomb shelters; it was the only link that remained between his department and the kidnapping. The Las Cruces police would handle it.

"It's about the press conference," Bishop added. "We, Mr. Whitfield and I, both think it's a good idea. If we don't talk to them, all hell's going to break loose."

Paul shoved the paper with the address of the Hawkins place into his shirt pocket. "So?"

"So," Bishop went on calmly, "it would be of no value to do it without you. The kidnapper specifically mentioned the chief of police, evidently. You'll have to respond. I'm afraid we can't do it for you."

"Bullshit!" Paul said. "Send some hot-shots from the F.B.I. How about one of their 'experts' on criminal behavior? Or one of the twenty-five press officers they have running around here. I've got work to do."

"I'm afraid I must insist," Bishop said and looked at him steadily.

Paul started to object, then thought better of it. It was easier to acquiesce than stand here arguing. "Five minutes," he said. "That's it."

Bishop smiled happily and nodded. "Five minutes. I guarantee it. Then we'll come back and wait for the call."

Paul looked at his watch. Six-thirty already. "Let's get it over with." He headed toward the door.

Outside, the National Guard had managed to keep the reporters three blocks away, behind a barricade of wooden sawhorses and a phalanx of armed soldiers standing two deep. Amazingly, Paul noticed as they approached the crowd, Ellis Whitfield was carrying a battery-operated bullhorn, as though it were a part of the F.B.I. director's daily wardrobe.

Colonel Joseph Streeter, commander of the unit, met them a hundred yards from the barricades, two younger officers in tow. Whitfield explained that the three of them intended to make a short statement to the press, then return inside. It would not take more than ten minutes at the most, he added, and Paul said, "Five!"

Streeter glanced at the crowd, then back at Whitfield, shaking his head. "If I move my people, I'll never get control again. I'll bring up a flatbed truck and put a crate on the back. You can stand on that and speak over the heads of the troops. The reporters won't like it, but I don't see any other way."

Whitfield, Bishop, and Whitehorse stood alone in the middle of the street while an olive-drab flatbed truck was brought up to the line of soldiers. As they waited, a group of F-14s somewhere beyond their line of sight broke the sound barrier. Whitfield jumped. "What the hell was that?"

Paul told him.

He shook his head and stared out toward the eastern mountains. "You don't think the kidnapper could have brought the kids out there, do you?"

Paul looked at him without expression. "Might be. That's federal territory, your jurisdiction. You want to borrow a car and take a look?"

"Gentlemen," Streeter was back, "we're ready for you."

They walked in the early evening heat to the truck, and Streeter indicated the step at the tailgate. As Paul climbed onto the bed, the scent of motor oil and cosmoline instantly bringing back eight years of military life, he could see the reporters massed behind the line of troops. How many were there? Two thousand? He had no way to judge. They were packed in for more than a block; it looked like the crowd at a rock concert. He could see cameras held aloft and people jostling with their neighbors and heard their angry shouts. There's got to be a better way, he thought. This was madness.

The F.B.I. director had climbed onto the wooden crate, putting him three feet higher than Paul and Bishop. "Ladies and gentlemen," Whitfield said into the bullhorn, and his odd amplified voice drifted away from the truck. "I am Ellis Whitfield. I have with me C. Richard Bishop, the California attorney general, and Paul Whitehorse, the Las Cruces police chief. We are here to make a statement."

A low murmur rumbled uneasily from the crowd. They didn't want a statement. They wanted to ask questions. But Whitfield ignored it and began speaking forcefully about how the F.B.I. was doing all it could to meet the kidnapper's ransom demand. They only wanted the children home safely. . . . Banality followed banality with the predictable regularity of a man who had spent his life in the government. Paul tuned out. It was hot on top of the truck, and noise from the crowd swelled around him. He was thinking of the bomb shelters. What if the kids had been this close all along? One of the shelters was in Old Town, not more than a few

locks away, the other out on Pipeline. The list was still in
his pocket.

"Chief?"

Bishop was on top of the box motioning to him. Had
Bishop already spoken? Paul stared at him.

"They want to know what the kidnapper meant by saying
you're not cooperating. You'll have to tell them something."
He looked at Paul with something like sympathy on his
face.

Taking a breath, Paul hoisted himself on top of the
wooden crate and took the bullhorn the attorney general
passed to him. Get it over with, Paul told himself, and began
to speak: "The Las Cruces Police Department has cooper-
ated fully with the kidnapper. We have done everything
he's asked. We can't explain why he thinks we haven't. If the
kidnapper is listening, I want you to know that your demands have been met. We will do whatever you want. Just
don't harm any more children."

He could feel sweat prickling his neck under his short
ponytail. He flicked off the power on the bullhorn and
jumped from the box as reporters began shouting out questions. He glanced at his watch, then looked at Whitfield.
This had taken longer than he'd expected. He said, "We
need to get back. He's going to call in eight minutes."

"No hurry," the F.B.I. director said casually. "Dr. Exley will
take the call."

Paul put the bullhorn in Whitfield's hands. "You talk to
the press, then. I'm leaving."

Alone, he walked down the eerily empty street to the
Civic Center, Whitfield's amplified voice trailing after him
like a ghost on waves of hot desert air. Stopping at the reception desk, he asked Jeannie if she'd seen Ellen.

"Not for a while. Maybe she went home."

"Call her house. I'll be in the squad room." He looked at
his watch: 6:57. Who would the kidnapper ask for? He
turned again to Jeannie. "He's going to call in three minutes. Whoever he wants, you stay on the line and record it."

Jeannie nodded and took a call. "Las Cruces Police De
partment."

He listened long enough to ensure that it wasn't the kid
napper before going into the squad room. Harris was star
ing at his phone. "Think he'll ask for the squad room?"
Harris wondered aloud.

Paul shrugged. "Here or Dispatch." He glanced over a
the large wall clock: 6:58.

Two of the black-clad members of the rescue team cam
in for cups of coffee. They nodded to Paul and stood watch
ing the clock.

The phone rang.

Harris lunged for it and almost immediately his face fell
"Tell him he'll have to wait until tomorrow, Jeannie. I know
I know. We'll put it out over the radio, but he's going to hav
to wait to talk to anyone." He slammed the phone down
"Liquor store on Magnolia was robbed. The owner wants u
to drop everything and come out and hold his hand. That'
the sixth robbery since noon. The bad guys know we can'
respond."

Paul looked at his watch. Seven o'clock. He turned an
checked the wall clock. Exactly. Whitfield and Bishop, both
looking out of place in their hand-tailored suits, came int
the room. Changed their minds about the press, Pau
thought. Or, more likely, checking up on him. In a deter
mined tone, Whitfield said, "We've been through this, Chie
Whitehorse. I want this call transferred immediately to D
Exley. I insist."

Paul crossed his arms and rested against Ellen's desk.

One minute past seven. The kidnapper didn't seem th
sort to break his promise.

Whitfield, the president's pal, wasn't accustomed to bein
ignored. He puffed himself up—like a cat trying to loo
larger, Paul thought—and came up to Harris's desk. Ther
was a line of sweat prickling his neck, and his eyes narrowe
as he stared into Paul's face. "That wasn't a request, Chie
I'm telling you."

Bishop said, "I think we sort of agreed on protocol, Paul. The phone would be Dr. Exley's concern—"

Paul nodded. "He wrote a book."

"He's an expert," Bishop insisted gently.

The phone rang and Harris picked it up. "It's Dr. Exley. Wants to know if we took the call."

Whitfield grabbed the phone from Harris. "I think it would be better if you came down here, Doctor."

At five minutes past seven, Exley and LaSalle came into the squad room. "Who's looking for the survivalist?" Paul asked sarcastically.

Exley immediately sized up the situation and tried to act as a moderating influence. "We build profiles using the best available evidence. That's all we can do. Are you sure he has not called? Authoritarian personalities always stick to schedules. Perhaps it was forwarded elsewhere in the building."

As Exley was talking, Middleton came in and stood by himself, leaning back against the wall with his arms folded on his chest.

Exley darted a glance at the clock. "He must have been held up somewhere." His face was strained, and he began to pace around the room.

"He might be dead," one of the rescue team members said from the back of the room. "Then we'll never find the kids."

Paul turned and saw Ellen standing rigidly by the door; she was pale and looked as though she was going to vomit. He felt a mixture of relief and irritation. "How long have you been here? I thought you went home."

"He said he'd call," she said stiffly and everyone twisted around to look at her. "Why doesn't he call?"

Paul heard something in her voice. More than concern. Panic, almost. It wasn't like her. She took two unsteady steps into the room, seemed to waver, eyes not focusing.

He grabbed the swivel chair from behind the desk and spun it around as her legs began to give way. "You better sit. You don't look well."

Still pacing, Exley again looked up at the clock. "I don't

like this. Not at all. It's asymptomatic, not the way he should be behaving."

"Another victory for the behavioral sciences," Middleton said calmly into the gloom.

"Maybe it has something to do with his call to the press about the police not cooperating," Whitfield said. "He's angry about something." He stared at Paul, his face reddening. "He's upset, so he's changing his plans."

Paul felt his temperature flare. "When didn't we cooperate?"

"Why the hell did he mention it, then?" the F.B.I. director demanded in a rising voice. "There must be a reason."

Paul seemed to snap. His head jerked forward and his body twisted toward Whitfield as though to strike him when Harris, alarmed, said, "Paul," and he halted.

Concerned at the escalating anger, Bishop said, "I don't think we should start making accusations." And the room fell into an uncomfortable silence. Then Middleton stalked to the far end of the room as though to distance himself from the others.

At 7:20, Paul turned to Harris. "I'm going up to my office. Stick to your desk. If the phone rings, you get it." Turning to Ellen, he said, "Let's go."

She didn't move.

"Ellen!"

Her mind a fog, she turned and looked at him. What was he saying to her?

"In my office," he repeated hotly.

LaSalle put his hand on her shoulder. "Do you feel okay?"

Paul stepped toward them aggressively, a mixture of emotions in his mind but wanting most of all to yank LaSalle's hand from Ellen. At the same moment, she pushed to her feet. Why was everyone staring? What was happening? Paul stopped in front of her. "Well?"

She looked at him, then at LaSalle. She wanted to say something, do something. But she couldn't figure out what it was. She nodded finally and followed as Paul left the squad room and strode rapidly to the elevators in the rear of the building. Pressed in by the tense silence of the elevator, they rose to the third floor, then walked quickly past Maggie's desk and into Paul's office. As he slammed the door behind them, she sank onto the couch. Still standing, he looked at her, his face flushed. "You want to tell me what's bugging you?"

"Just sick," she said, weakly waving her hand. "Something I ate."

"Bullshit. You're upset about something. What the hell is it?"

Her anger flared. "Don't fight with me, Paul."

"Go home if you're sick, then. Jesus, you're not doing any good hanging around here looking like a goddamn corpse. I can't even find you half the time."

Her eyes snapped up at him. "I'm not going home."

"Do it, Ellen. Go home. Go to bed. What good is it having you around here if you're sick?"

"I'm staying—" she began but Paul's phone buzzed. He reached over and snatched it off the desk. "It's him," Maggie said excitedly. "He just called."

Harris punched a button on the reception desk tape recorder. "He didn't ask for anybody and didn't explain why he was late." The tape recorder switched on:

"Monica Ochoa has a four-inch scar on her neck. Listen to me, put the money and jewels in a single soft-sided suitcase. Have a car with a full tank of gas; you'll be going on a long, long drive. I want you ready to move at exactly two A.M. No delays. No bullshit. And I insist that it be delivered by Dr. Walter Exley. Do you remember Charles Singleton II, Dr. Exley? Do you understand that the government is destroying this country? Two A.M. And just the two of us." He hung up.

Paul, in a fury, ran to the squad room and confronted Exley. "Why you?"

The man seemed perplexed. "I wish I knew. But it obviously has something to do with Singleton. Another survivalist, you see—"

"It's not right," Ellen said, and everyone looked at he
standing small and alone and staring at the recorder.

Misunderstanding, Exley said, "He seems to know me
It'll be okay, though. I've done this sort of thing before."

But Ellen wasn't paying attention. This didn't make an
sense. He said he'd call *her*. He wanted something from he
in exchange for Denise. Why'd he ask for Exley? Somethin
had gone wrong, terribly, terribly wrong. That must be wh
he called a half-hour late.

Oh my God, she thought, maybe something's happene
to Denise and he doesn't need me anymore. She had to ac
She had to do something.

Standing next to Bishop, Whitfield said, "Singleton'
body was never recovered, was it, Doctor?"

Exley shoved his hands in his pockets and looked ur
comfortably at him. "No."

"Then maybe that's who we're dealing with," the F.B.I. d
rector said. "Maybe he's not dead. Maybe he got out afte
the explosion."

No, that's not who you're dealing with, Ellen wanted t
scream. He's right next door. His name is Lowell Alexar
der DeVries and he works here.

"Monica Ochoa has a four-inch scar . . ."

Someone had punched the button on the recorder agair
and everyone stiffened as they once more heard the voice
Ellen retreated to her desk and sank down on the chair.

*". . . understand that the government is destroying this country
Two A.M. And just the two of us."*

Whitfield turned to the other F.B.I. agents and nodde
anxiously toward the door. "Let's move!"

Paul whirled on them angrily, but there was nothing to say
The kidnapper had asked for Exley and was setting up a pay
off outside of town. The Las Cruces police were out of it.

Sensing his fury, Bishop said, "Chief, we'll keep your res
cue team at the ready. Just because the pay-off's miles from
here doesn't mean the kids aren't being kept in the city lim
its."

Whitfield, in a conciliatory mood now that he had the

upper hand, turned from the doorway. "Wherever the hostages are, unless it's a siege situation and we need the army rescue team, we'll let your people move in first. The Las Cruces police can bring the children home. You can even use our choppers if you have to. That okay?"

Paul felt an overwhelming surge of anger. Bones being thrown to keep a barking dog quiet, he thought and started to say something but changed his mind. Whitfield hadn't needed to offer even what he did. Everyone was staring at Paul, and he said what he knew was expected. "Yeah, thanks. We'll do that."

The F.B.I. agents hurried out, and Paul turned angrily toward Harris. "Goddamn them. Unless it's a fucking siege situation and they need professionals . . ."

Ellen's mind was racing. DeVries! DeVries! What had he wanted? What was he doing with Denise? Maybe he's still next door, she thought suddenly. My God, maybe he's in his office. She jumped from her chair. Next door!

Paul spun around as she hurried out of the office. "Now where . . . Jesus."

Harris said, "She don't look well."

Paul had already lost interest. "We're checking those bomb shelters. I'm not letting them box us out on this, and I'm not sitting in my goddamn office until two A.M."

Harris said, "The sheriff used their helicopter to check the shelter in the desert. The place had caved in and was unusable. I had Durand run over to Old Town to check out the one there. It's been empty for years."

"I'll take a look at the Hawkins place," Paul said. He glanced at his watch. Ten minutes to eight. "I'll be back before nine. If you need me, use the radio." He stared toward the door the F.B.I. agents had disappeared through. "Goddamn them!"

7:51 P.M.

Ellen hurled herself out of the squad room, past the reception desk and Jeannie, who said, "Hey, where you off to?

Bring me a pizza when you come back, okay? I'm starving.'

Without responding, not even hearing, Ellen raced into the marble-floored lobby. The large open area seemed unnaturally bright and glossy as the overhead lighting streaked across the windows and walls. Through the glass Civic Center doors she could see the back of a uniformed police officer and beyond, a dull green line of National Guard vehicles, just visible in the quickening darkness of the night.

Her steps echoing loudly and rapidly on the floor, she hurried to the city side of the building, pushed through the entrance door, and into the reception area. No one around. Where was the building inspector's office? To the left, she thought vaguely, then down the outside hallway. Half stumbling, she rushed along the corridor, past a woman operating a floor polisher, to the suite of offices occupied by the city administrative officer and several smaller departments. The door was locked. She shook it furiously, then pounded on it with her fist but no one appeared. Again, she pounded on the glass, then took the door handle in both hands and yanked back and forth as if she could force it open. A man with a mop stepped from the office across the hall and looked at her irritably. "Hey! Cut that out! No one in there. Who you looking for, anyway?"

"The building inspector," Ellen said feverishly.

He squinted at her. "You a cop, right? From next door?'

"Yes."

"You want to call him at home? The inspector?"

"No. Yes! Yes, I want to. Do you have his number?"

He motioned her inside the office he was cleaning. It was some sort of tax department, she recalled. The man, about sixty and white-haired, handed her a thin spiral-bound notebook. "Probably in there," he said. "It's got all city workers' home numbers, 'cepting police, of course."

She snatched the book out of his hands and started fumbling through it, quickly finding the right page, her fingers racing down the columns of type. DeVries, DeVries. . .

There it was, his home number. Without a word, she dropped the book on a desk and rushed out, the custodian staring after her with irritation. "Well, you're welcome."

Racing down the hallway, she realized she couldn't go next door to make the call; someone would overhear. The phone at the city reception desk next to the lobby, then. Hurrying behind the counter, she snatched the receiver and punched out the number. After three rings she heard, "This is Lowell Alexander DeVries. I am not able to come to the phone right now, but if you leave a message, I'll get back to you."

An electronic beep sounded in her ear as she screamed, *"Where are you? Why haven't you called me? What do you want?"*

8:11 P.M.

Pipeline was a two-lane road that ran like a straight edge along the eastern side of town adjacent to a string of aging, isolated ranches and date groves. The Hawkins place was a decaying single-story wooden structure with a separate garage off to one side and an ancient corral on the other, where two ragged burros stood motionless in the overheated twilight as flies circled their heads. The total isolation of the property made Paul uneasy as he jerked the Jeep Cherokee onto the gravel drive and rolled to a stop. The hairs on the back of his neck bristled. Something wasn't right. The front door of the house stood open, but there didn't appear to be anyone around. A forty-year-old Ford pickup, its paint long since burned off and its tailgate missing, sat in front of the garage, a fairly new white Toyota sedan behind it, up on blocks. As he watched, a man slithered lizard-like from underneath the car, grabbed a rag to clean his hands, and scrambled to his feet as he noticed the Jeep.

Paul quickly seized the short-barreled Remington 12-gauge from the rack between the front seats and stepped outside, holding it at waist level. "Las Cruces police. Just stand right there a minute."

The man squinted across the fifty feet to Paul. "What the—"

"Turn around and walk backward toward the sound of my voice. Hands in the air."

"The hell you talkin' about?" He threw the rag angrily on the ground and took a step forward.

"Goddamn it, turn around!" Paul jerked the shotgun to his shoulder.

More angry than frightened, the man did as he was told, Paul saying, "Back, back, back, further," until just two feet separated them. "Keep them up." Paul quickly patted him down with his left hand, then said, "Take out your driver's license."

The man put his arms down and turned around. He was about sixty-five, grizzled, dried-up looking, with thick rimless glasses, bad teeth, and a thin, mostly bald head. He was also mad as hell.

"Maynard Hawkins," Paul read aloud from the license. "How long have you lived here, Mr. Hawkins?"

The man snatched his license back and jammed it into his wallet. "Thirty-two years. I know who you are. Seen your picture in the paper. You wanna tell me what in damnation this is all about?"

"You alone here?"

"Wife's in town playing bridge. The hell you getting at?"

"What do you do for a living?"

"Retired. Used to own the Mobile station on Heap's Road." The man was clearly annoyed and said again, "Goddamn it, what the hell are you doing here? I got a right to know. This here is my property you're on."

"You got a bomb shelter, Mr. Hawkins?"

Hawkins stared at him in disbelief. "That ol' thing? You're out here because of a bomb shelter?"

Paul stared at him, waiting impatiently.

The man shifted his shoulders. "I don't get it. Do you want to see it? That's why you're holding a goddamn shotgun on me? 'Cause you wanna see my *bomb shelter*? What in hell for?"

Paul tried not to show his irritation, but he didn't want to spend any more time than he had to out here. "I'm looking for those missing school kids."

For the second time, the man looked at him in disbelief. "The kidnapped kids? You think I got 'em in the *bomb shelter?*"

"I don't think anything at all, Mr. Hawkins, but the sooner I see your shelter, the sooner I'll get out of here and you can go back to working on your car."

"Hell, I haven't been down in that dump in twenty years. Damn fool thing to begin with, thinking there'd be a world to come back to after an atom war. I used it for storing lumber for a few years but got tired of having to lug it up the ramp every time I wanted some. Locked it up back in the seventies and never looked inside again."

Paul waited a moment, but the old man didn't seem inclined to go on. "Mr. Hawkins." He motioned with the gun.

Hawkins spun around. "Jesus Christ! Come on! I'll show you."

The old man shoved his hands in his jeans pockets and started to shuffle off toward the garage. Keeping his finger on the trigger guard of the shotgun, Paul followed a half-step behind. One of the doors was off its hinges and the other was dragging badly. The building looked half a century old and stank of hay and animal waste. Even in the diminishing sunlight it must have been a hundred and ten degrees inside. The man kicked at some half-decayed straw on the floor, exposing a rusted padlock and a metal panel. "That's it," he said. "The doorway to hell."

"You got a key?"

"Hell, probably lost the key when Carter was president. You still wanna get inside, I reckon."

Paul said, "Yes."

"Well, let me get my sledgehammer and knock that sucker loose."

There was a long-handled hammer leaning against a wall. Hawkins grunted and grabbed it, coming back to the trapdoor. Dropping to one knee, he lifted the lock on its side so it presented a larger target. Then he straightened, hefted the hammer over his head with two hands, and took a mighty swipe at it. The lock flew free.

"Better get a light," Hawkins muttered and took a flashlight from a large, rusted toolbox. Paul reached down and pulled the trapdoor all the way open. A cool, faintly sick smell rose uneasily from below. The old man walked up and stood next to the opening, pointing his light inside. "You can see from here there ain't no one in there."

Paul said, "I'd like to take a look."

Hawkins shook his head. "Do what you want, but I ain't going down there after twenty years. Could be a hundred rattlers living there now."

Paul nudged him with the barrel of the shotgun. "You first. Now!"

Hawkins swore furiously. "Police brutality, is what it is. Goddamn abuse of power. You just wait till the mayor finds out." But he had walked to the top of the ramp and, keeping his flashlight beam moving quickly around the underground room, took three tentative steps down. Paul eased up behind him, and the man hesitated and aimed the light into each corner of the shelter.

There was no furniture. A single piece of decayed plywood rested against the wall. But no people, no sign that anyone had been there for years.

Paul sighed. "All right, Mr. Hawkins. We can go." It had been a long shot, anyway. But now he was out of options. He turned back up the ramp, Hawkins following him out to the Jeep. Paul opened the passenger door and secured the shotgun in its rack. Hawkins said, "What made you think about bomb shelters, anyway? Not too many folks left that even remember them."

Paul slammed the door. "Running out of places the kids can be. Thought we'd give it a shot."

"Only other one I know about is the old Larchmont place. I know they got an identical shelter because they used the same plans."

"Larchmont?" Paul pulled the list of shelters out of his pocket. "That the place in Old Town?"

"No, no. It's out on Ranch Road, got that God-awful barn with the corrugated metal roof you can see as you drive past. You know the place I'm talkin' about?"

Paul felt his pulse quickening. "What makes you think they got a bomb shelter? It's not on my list."

"Folks I bought this place from told me about it. Said they borrowed old man Larchmont's plans when they built their shelter. You shoulda talked to the city building department. They coulda told you. In fact, the inspector was out here a year or two ago asking me how many shelters I knew about."

"The building inspector?" Paul tried to contain his excitement. "You remember his name?"

"Nah. Big fella, though. Maybe six-two. Forties."

Paul tried to remember. "DeVries," he said at last. "Lowell DeVries."

"That's it," Hawkins replied and smiled with sarcasm. "Lowell *Alexander* DeVries. Kind of an uppity fella, fancy clothes and shiny shoes. Walked around here like he was afraid of getting donkey shit on them."

"And he knows about the Larchmont place?"

"That's what I'm telling you," Hawkins said as though he was talking to an idiot.

Swearing angrily, Paul snatched the car radio and got put through to Harris at the station. "Pull two cars and send them code-two to the Larchmont place on Ranch Road. Tell them to wait for me with their lights out on the highway about two hundred yards south." Trying not to sound as pumped up as he felt in case nothing came of it, he told Harris what he had learned. "Maybe it's something, maybe not. But I want an A.P.B. on DeVries, also. Find out what he's driving from the D.M.V. If he's spotted, I want him followed, not stopped. Use as many cars as it takes and notify me immediately. And tell the rescue team to go on standby. We may need them."

Harris's voice rose with excitement. "What about the F.B.I.?"

Paul hesitated just a second. "No point in us getting all fired up and bringing them in. So far, we're just checking an abandoned bomb shelter. I'm not going to cry wolf." But his heart was pounding. The kids had to be there. Where else could they be?

He put the radio back and hurried around to the driver's side of the vehicle. "Thank you, Mr. Hawkins. You've been a big help."

"No sweat—" Hawkins began, but Paul was already backing up.

"Goddamn it," Paul muttered as he aimed the Jeep toward the road. He knew now where he had seen DeVries's name before: on the inspection slips he had so carefully gone through. *L.A. DeVries.* Paul was furious with himself. An inspector, not a worker. And the terrible realization grew and grew until he could think of nothing else. If he had thought of it last night, Bobby Muledeer, Linda Sowell, and Kim Zeigler would still be alive.

8:23 P.M.

Pacing back and forth in the conference room, LaSalle looked for the hundredth time at the wall clock. "Five and a half hours until he calls." The room was warm, dry, and brittle with tension as everyone's eyes followed his to the clock. He stifled a yawn and wished he could grab an hour's sleep but knew it would never happen. On impulse, he grabbed the phone and punched out the number for the conference room on the other side of the building, where his computer people were on line with the two surveillance teams.

"Twenty-six names so far," a woman told him. "Twelve cars drove past one or both sites twice, eight cars three to four times, and six cars five or more times. Records checks are coming in now. Who's going to follow up?"

"Tell LaPorte to bring in some of his people from the door-to-door. This is more vital." He hung up and dialed the number for the aerial surveillance.

"It's an embarrassment of riches, Matt. We give 'em to the sheriff as soon as we turn up anything suspicious, but it'll take days to check out all of them. We just found something we're sure's a bus along an old mining road, but there's no way of telling if it's our bus. Sheriff's heading out there now."

"Let me know either way," he said and put the phone down. He turned to Exley. "How far along are you with your sex offenders?"

The psychologist waved an arm in the air. "We haven't even made a dent. I told you this could take weeks."

"And the judges?"

"They gave us six names. None of them look promising, I'm afraid." He looked sharply at LaSalle. "That doesn't mean it's not a survivalist we're dealing with. After all, he mentioned Singleton. That patrolman, Muñoz, is checking everyone out for us." With obvious annoyance in his voice, he added, "Where's Whitfield? He should be here with us."

"He and the A.G. decided to talk to the press again."

Middleton laughed derisively, but LaSalle, uncomfortable with criticisms of his boss, ignored him as he crossed over to the coffeemaker and poured a cup. The table was littered with a two-day accumulation of Styrofoam cups and empty pizza and donut boxes, the air fetid with the stink of day-old coffee and human confinement. The ransom suitcase, sitting on the table, had already been bugged and another transmitter placed inside a stack of hundred-dollar bills. From behind him, Middleton asked, "Whose car are we using?"

LaSalle smiled grimly but didn't turn around. "It's a rental. We didn't tell Avis what we had in mind."

"I'm not going in armed," Exley said as though expecting an argument. "If I'm to gain his trust, I have to give him mine."

LaSalle nodded as he came over to the table with his coffee but didn't sit down. "Your choice. Army rescue's on standby. They can be airborne in two minutes." The director had already instructed them to do whatever the kidnapper wanted. No heroics, no special measures. The world was watching: they weren't about to satisfy the Bureau's critics by screwing up. Just find out where the kids were and get them back.

"Are you really going to let Whitehorse's people make the rescue?"

"Whatever Whitfield wants."

"Always the good soldier, huh Matt?" Middleton said. He stood up, stretching his arms high over his head as though lifting weights. Then he reached over the table and hefted the soft-sided suitcase with one finger. "Twenty million dollars doesn't weigh much, does it? Ever wonder what you'd do with that much money? What do you think, Exley? Set up a nice little clinic somewhere, where you can test your theories of criminal behavior?" He let the bag drop to the tabletop with a thump.

LaSalle looked again at the clock. After a moment he said, "Nothing left for us to do until two o'clock." Unless the reconnaissance or computer people came through. Or the agents in El Centro questioning the construction workers turned up something; so far, they had managed to eliminate just two of the men they'd taken in. That left sixteen, as well as the nine they still couldn't find. The phone buzzed again, and LaSalle picked it up. "Zach Harris downstairs. Carpetown came up with a list of seven buildings in town with a carpet like ours. What do you want we should do? Chief said it's your decision."

"Any of my people down there?"

"You kidding? Every place I look there's a gray suit talking to another gray suit."

He ignored the sarcasm. "All right. Put one agent in charge of each building, have them get a list of employees, and call me back. We'll handle it from there." He hung up as Exley threw his pen down on the table and said loudly, "Damn, I hate waiting."

LaSalle began to wander about the room. Where was Ellen? Something was wrong with her, something had happened. But before he could give it any thought, Howard

Stines ducked his head in the open doorway behind them. "Chief Whitehorse around?"

"Isn't he downstairs?" LaSalle turned around to look at the man.

"Didn't check, just glanced in his office. I ought to let you folks know anyway: Sacramento called with the results of the lab test on the shoes the Torres girl was wearing. Vomit, urine, excrement, and dirt. About like you'd expect. And faint traces of jet fuel."

"Jet fuel?"

"Interesting, isn't it? I gotta find the chief."

Stines hurried away, and LaSalle turned at once toward Exley. "The abandoned airfield."

"But how could jet fuel get on her shoes?" Exley wondered.

"Hell, there'd be traces of fuel everywhere out there," Middleton said, coming over to them. "Especially if they were inside a hangar."

Exley was flustered. His voice shook as he turned on LaSalle. "You think Singleton was just a ploy, then? They're at the base and not the mines?"

The phone rang. "Someone from Washington for you, Mr. LaSalle," Jeannie said. He sat at the table while she transferred the call, then heard, "Monica Ochoa has a four-inch scar on her neck."

LaSalle stiffened and covered the mouthpiece. "It's him!" he whispered, and added at once, "Yes. What do you want?"

"I want you moving now! Do exactly as I say."

"But you said two o'clock."

"Don't fight me, LaSalle. You're professionals. You're ready. For whatever I do." There was a slight pause, and LaSalle thought he could almost hear the man smile. "Flexibility. That's the key to good law enforcement, isn't it, Matt? Always ready to react? Okay, show the world what you can do. Just the two of us, me against you."

"How do—?"

"Shut up. Just listen."

LaSalle's voice went soft. "Tell me what you want. We'll

do it." Exley was on his feet, watching, wondering what was happening.

"There's a white 1985 Oldsmobile with a dented fender in the parking lot. It's been there for two days. It's got three pounds of *plastique* explosives hidden inside the fenders and headliner and door panels. That's the transport car. Take the tracking devices out of the ransom, all of them, LaSalle. Then put the suitcase on the passenger seat with the door unlocked. No fireflies or infrared on the suitcase or money. No tailing or swarming. No radio or electronic contact at all. I mean complete, one hundred percent air silence until tomorrow. I want Ellen Camacho driving. She's to go out of the Civic Center at precisely forty-five miles an hour until she sees a white Toyota pickup truck with its hazard lights flashing. Then she stops and turns off the engine. If the Oldsmobile is not out of the parking lot in four minutes, I'll blow it up like I blew up the van. If you attempt to follow her or there are any tracking devices in the money, or if you attempt to find the children, I'll kill Camacho and the children just like I killed the others. I've got enough *plastique* around town to destroy half of Las Cruces. Do as I say and you'll have the kids back unharmed by midnight. The clock starts now. You've got four minutes." He hung up.

LaSalle hurriedly recounted the conversation while punching the button for Dispatch. Exley began to wander anxiously around the room, looking baffled. His voice tense, he said, "We have to do it. We have no choice."

"We'll see," LaSalle said, then barking into the phone, "This is Special Agent LaSalle. I need to see Chief White-horse and Ellen Camacho immediately."

"I'll transfer you to Officer Harris," Jeannie said, and a few seconds later he repeated his request.

"Chief's out. Ellen's at her desk, but she don't look too good." Harris nodded to Ellen, who picked up the phone.

"The kidnapper wants you," LaSalle told her. "Better get up here pronto."

He put the receiver down and suddenly felt very, very afraid.

8:24 P.M.

Paul met Louie Sharperson and Fred Durand two hundred yards south of the Larchmont ranch. They pulled off onto the unpaved shoulder of the road and stood by their cars in the quickening dusk as the chief told them what he knew. "If DeVries didn't give us the address of this place, there must be a reason."

"Maybe he just forgot," Sharperson said.

"Maybe. But we're going to check it out." They could see the outlines of the darkened house and barn from where they stood. The ranch looked as though it had been abandoned for years. "We'll go in without lights or radios. I'll drive up near the barn. That's where the bomb shelter's supposed to be. Lou, you park thirty yards to the left and Freddy thirty to the right. Bring your flashlights and shotguns and stay behind your vehicles. We'll decide what to do next when we get there."

They slipped back into their cars and, Paul leading, moved slowly and without lights down the highway to the driveway. Paul let his Cherokee drift to within twenty yards of the barn, the tires seeming to loudly crunch the gravel underneath, then watched as Durand and Sharperson took their positions to either side.

Without a sound, three car doors swung open as the men stepped out with their shotguns and flashlights, and hurried to the rear of their vehicles.

Paul stood still for a moment and listened. Crickets. Coyotes probably a half-mile distant. No cars nearby. No sign of habitation. No light except from a quarter moon. It was almost too quiet, he thought as a primitive warning system came alive and sent a chill racing down his spine. After a moment, he motioned Durand to his side. Crouching low, the patrolman ran to the Jeep. "I'm going to check out the house, Freddy. Go around back in case someone tries to leave."

Durand's eyes were wary as he stared at the building. "Someone's here, Chief. I feel it."

Paul nodded. "Got any extra shells?"

Durand patted his shirt pocket.

"Get moving, then. I'm going inside."

Durand nodded and took off silently for the back of the house. Paul motioned for Sharperson to watch the barn, then hurried to the front of the house and up the steps to the wooden porch. He stood still for a moment in the darkness and again listened. Nothing.

Flattening against the exterior wall of the building, he reached his left hand out and tried the front door. The handle turned. Giving it a push, he watched as the door swung open. He held his breath and waited. Then, with the shotgun in his right hand and flashlight held high in his left, he stepped suddenly into the opening.

The living room was vacant, he could see at once as his light ran rapidly over the walls and ceiling. Moving without noise, he crossed into the kitchen. Empty except for a small television on the counter and a lawn chair. He went back to the living room and crossed into a short hallway leading to a single bathroom and two bedrooms. The bathroom was empty. No furniture in the bedrooms. He checked the closets. Nothing.

Walking back through the kitchen, he motioned Durand inside through the rear door.

"Someone's been here. We're going to take a look at that bomb shelter. Tell Louie to go around back of the barn. You come in front with me. I'll go in through the door. If it's clear, I'll signal with my light and you can follow."

Paul waited in front of the barn while Durand positioned Sharperson, then hurried back. For a long moment, the two men stood completely still, listening, before Paul abruptly took hold of one of the large double doors and pulled it all the way back. The door sagged on its hinges and loudly scraped the ground. From where they stood they could see moonlight drifting into the front half of the building. Paul waited, breathing silently, then, adrenaline pumping and the shotgun raised to shoulder level, he stepped quickly into the open doorway and bumped face-first into a cat hanging by its broken neck from a rafter. His heart hammered violently, and he angrily muttered "Jesus!" before stepping to the side of it. "The bus is here," he whispered to Durand, still standing behind the door.

Flicking on his flashlight, he let the beam dance around the barn. A large American car, its front end badly banged in, was partly visible on the other side of the bus. It looked like someone had left in a hurry rather than attempting to dispose of obviously damaging evidence.

A slight breeze came up, rustling some of the dry straw on the barn floor and chilling the sweat on Paul's neck. Behind him a car passed down the highway. Twenty years of training reverberated in his mind: Don't rush. Take it easy. A step at a time. "I'm going in," he said softly and stepped tentatively into the barn, his light moving in front of him. *Slowly, there's no hurry. First the bus.* He went up on his toes and glanced in the rear window. Empty except for a few lunch boxes scattered on the floor. The car was empty, too. Dropping to his knees, he glanced quickly underneath both vehicles. Nothing. Pulling open the passenger door of the car, he rummaged through the glove compartment for the registration. Lowell Alexander DeVries. A strange feeling moved within him. Why would DeVries allow himself to be implicated like this? Unless he's making a run for it and doesn't care. Or had he decided he was cornered and gone off to commit suicide rather than spend the rest of his life in prison? In either case, what had he done with the kids? And then he remembered what Exley had said: the kidnapper will want to ensure that the world knows who's responsible for this by some grand megalomaniacal act.

Paul crossed quickly to the open front door of the bus, stepped inside for a hurried look, then stepped out again.

Where was the bomb shelter door?

He shined his light around the barn floor. Nothing. Under the Buick? He dropped to his knees again, pointed the flashlight, and swept away a scattering of straw until it came dully into view—a rusted metal plate identical to the one at the Hawkins place. His excitement mounting despite himself, he straightened and raised his voice. "Freddy, Lou," and waited impatiently for the two patrolmen to join him. "Help me push this car out of the way so we can get at the door. Lou, bring your unit around to the barn door and shine the headlights inside so we can see what the hell we're doing."

Durand looked at him doubtfully. "You think those kids are down there?"

"The bus is here. There's a lock on the trapdoor. Yeah, I reckon they are. If so, you call in, Louie, and get the army medics out here by helicopter right away." How would the F.B.I. react when they found out he'd discovered the kids? he wondered. Pissed! They'll be royally pissed! Hick-town Wyatt Earps besting the feds. Too bad Ellen wasn't here to help; he could have used her with the children. He didn't even know where she was, he realized. At the station house? Maybe she went home sick after all. Something was going on with her, though, something he didn't understand but also didn't have time to worry about.

Paul and Durand began to push the Buick forward, exposing the rusted trapdoor, as Sharperson hurried off to move his car. Nudging the padlock with his foot, Paul could see it was not latched. Why hadn't anyone answered when he'd called Ellen's house earlier? he suddenly wondered. Mrs. Garcia was spending the night; he had heard Ellen talking to her about it. So why didn't she answer?

"Guess the kidnapper felt he didn't have to lock up," Durand said, bringing Paul back to the present. He walked over to the passenger door of the Buick, flipped open the glove compartment, and hit the trunk release. "No one around to see it. That way he wouldn't have to worry about unlocking it each time he wanted inside."

Paul stared at the metal door as Durand headed back toward the trunk. "Why'd he put the car over it, then?" he asked and looked up suddenly as he heard Freddy mutter, "Holy Christ."

"What?" Paul asked, and stepped quickly over to where Durand was staring at Manny Rios's bloody body crammed into the Buick's trunk.

"My God." He felt as though he had been struck and put his hand out to steady himself against the car.

Durand gently touched the body. "It's been a while. Twenty-four hours maybe." He turned around as Sharperson's patrol car maneuvered up to the barn door, illuminating the two men in the twin beams of the headlights.

"Better get the medical examiner from El Centro out here before we move him," Paul said, feeling both sadness and inevitability. Then he remembered the children. "Let's hurry it up. I want to see what's down there." He crossed back to the trapdoor and dropped to one knee as Durand moved around to the other side of the car.

As Paul pulled upward on the hasp, his mind suddenly flashed on Bobby Muledeer opening the rear of the van in the parking lot earlier in the day. Instantly he knew what he had done and screamed *"Down!"* as he dropped the door. But it was too late and it exploded off the hinges as the words flew from his mouth.

8:25 P.M.

His heart racing, LaSalle slammed the phone down. "She'll be here in a minute. Tell army rescue to stand by. We're moving."

Hurrying to the window for better reception, Middleton barked into the walkie-talkie, then waited impatiently for a response.

Exley sounded agitated as he began to pace rapidly about the room, staring at the floor. "I don't like it. I don't like it at all. Why does he want the policewoman to do it? He'd been asking for us. Me! How do we know he won't kill her after he gets the ransom?"

"Of course he'll kill her," Middleton said sharply, then shouted again into the walkie-talkie as static filled the room.

LaSalle's thoughts wouldn't stay focused. Of all the possible scenarios he had played out for tonight, none involved Ellen. Why would the kidnapper even know about her? And what difference did it make who brought the ransom? He tried to work it out, but there was no answer, no logic to any of it. All he knew for certain was that events were suddenly spinning off in a direction that no one had planned for and that they couldn't send Ellen. "We have to use someone else," he said with determination. "We can't risk her going in by herself. It's not safe."

Exley whirled around, and his voice rose to a scream. "No, no! We must do exactly as he asks. Don't you understand? Exactly! No deviations. None! Don't upset him, don't provoke him. We want those children back alive. It is possible he won't harm her—"

"Army's in their chopper," Middleton said. "All they need is the word from us."

"Find Whitfield," LaSalle snapped. "He's down with the reporters somewhere. Get him back here in a hurry."

Middleton hesitated, looking at LaSalle's sweaty face. "Something's not right. I got a feeling we fucked up, Matt. Somewhere, I don't know how—"

"Goddamn it, get Whitfield."

Middleton's eyes were impassive as he stared from LaSalle to the psychologist, then he turned and left at a trot. Exley said, "We have to remove the transmitters. He told us!"

LaSalle was beset by doubts. For the first time in his professional career, he didn't know what to do, and the realization paralyzed him. He looked at the psychologist, trying desperately to weigh the risks but aware that there was no way to do so. "I don't want Ellen out there by herself," he said at last. "If we take out the transmitters, we won't have any idea where she is."

"We can't risk it," Exley said. He grabbed LaSalle's arm, imploring and demanding at the same time. "We must do what he wants. We must."

LaSalle stared at him, then at the suitcase before impulsively grabbing it and dumping the money and a small blue cloth bag with the diamonds on the table. "We'll take the transmitter out of the money and leave the one in the lining of the suitcase."

At that moment, Ellen, half frantic, rushed into the room. "What is it? What does he want?"

LaSalle looked at her briefly. "He wants you to deliver the ransom." Hurriedly searching through the piles of cash, he repeated the kidnapper's demands.

She stared at him, her anxiety spiraling out of control. "We've only got about two minutes then. Give me the money." She looked to where he had spread out the stacks of bills, and her voice leaped up again. "What are you doing?"

"We had a radio transmitter in one of the bundles." He found what he was looking for and withdrew a stack with a paper Federal Reserve band around it. Ripping off the band, he fanned the bills until he saw the transmitter and removed it, dropping it on the table.

She stared at the tiny device. "Do you have any others?"

He hesitated, looking at her.

"Do you?" She was screaming at him.

"No."

The room was silent for a moment, then Ellen swept the money and the bag of diamonds into the suitcase. "Where's the car? He said four minutes. It must be that long now."

LaSalle was suddenly galvanized into action. "Let's go."

The three of them hurried down the stairs, coming out into the darkened rear lobby. Pushing on the exit door, Ellen ran into the parking lot and the nighttime desert heat. She looked frantically for the Oldsmobile, vaguely noticing that part of the lot was still taped off as a result of the bombing.

Exley pointed toward the west fence. "There. Last row."

They hurried over to it. Ellen yanked on the front door. A key was in the ignition. Throwing the suitcase and her purse onto the passenger seat, she slipped behind the wheel. Suddenly she froze and stared at LaSalle through the open door. "There's another transmitter, isn't there?"

He shook his head. "We took it out."

Her eyes went wild as she saw the truth in his face. "No,

you didn't," she screamed, and sweat swam across her forehead. "You're lying to me! Goddamn it, where is it?"

Exley, standing behind LaSalle, said, "In the lining on the bottom of the suitcase. On the outside."

She stared furiously at LaSalle. "Goddamn you! Goddamn you!" Grabbing the suitcase, she ripped at the bottom with her fingernails, pulling away the fabric. The transmitter fell onto her lap. She threw it at his chest.

As she reached for the door, Exley said hurriedly, "Don't argue with him. Do whatever he says. Whatever—"

But Ellen wasn't paying attention. She slammed the door and jerked the car into reverse. The F.B.I. agents jumped back quickly as she threw the gear shift into Drive and raced toward the exit. As if to himself, LaSalle said, "Something's wrong. Something's happened. We shouldn't have let her go."

Middleton and Vince Garibaldi came running up with Whitfield and another agent. "What's going on?" Whitfield demanded. "Where's she going?"

LaSalle watched her disappear. "I don't know."

8:38 P.M.

Sirens . . .

Someone shaking him roughly by the shoulders, yelling. Head spinning, pain.

"Paul! Paul!"

He rolled on his side and moaned. His face was burning, and there was a tremendous ringing in his ears, making his eyes blink again and again as flashes of light exploded in his brain.

Durand muttered, "Jesus."

Paul's eyes fixed at last on the other man. "It blew up," he managed to say.

"It blew off!" Durand said. "Look."

The metal trapdoor was tilted against the barn wall, where it had landed, twenty feet away. Sharperson said, "How do you feel, Chief? I got an ambulance coming."

Paul pushed himself to a sitting position, took a breath, then rose unsteadily to his feet. "I moved aside as I dropped it."

"Otherwise, it would have gone through you," Durand said.

"You sure you're okay, Chief?" Sharperson persisted. He was staring into Paul's eyes as if he didn't believe him.

"Yeah. Fine, Louie. Must not have been a very big charge."

"Not big enough to cave in the bomb shelter," Durand said. "Didn't even do any damage except to the entrance here."

Paul walked over and stared into the dark hole. "Anyone in there?"

Sharperson shook his head. "Five dead children, including a girl with a bullet hole in the back of her head. No trauma I could see to the others, but I didn't look too close. Probably died from a lack of medication."

Paul swore to himself. "DeVries knew we were on to him and cleared out. I wonder how the hell he's transporting the kids without a bus?"

The ambulance drew into the yard and cut its siren. Sharperson went out to greet it. Durand said, "Looks like he didn't care if we found this place or found the bodies inside. He coulda used more explosive and put us all on the moon. Maybe he wanted them found."

"Like he wanted us to find Manny," Paul said. His ears continued to ring, and he had trouble focusing his eyes.

Two ambulance attendants hastened into the barn carrying a stretcher. "Down there," Paul told them, nodding at the ramp, and added, "You'll need light." He told Sharperson to bring a lantern from his patrol car.

One of the attendants looked at Paul and said, "You've got abrasions on your face," and began to go through his medical bag.

Paul waved him off. "There's some dead kids in there you'll have to take back to the medical center. We'll need autopsies on all of them."

Sharperson hurried back with a battery-operated lantern, and the five of them headed into the shelter, the circle of light jumping nervously ahead of them on the walls and ceiling. A small boy in shorts was sprawled on his back and side at the bottom of the ramp. One of his knees was drawn up to his chin, a pool of vomit under his head. A girl lay face down on the floor a few feet away, her hair caked with blood. Another girl in a wheelchair. Two other children, a boy of five or six and a girl about eleven, on the floor; the boy's fingers were bloody and broken, the girl nude, her French braid unraveled, as though someone had clawed at it. Disarray and confusion followed the light everywhere: empty wheelchairs, torn clothes, vomit, excrement, pools of urine. The stench of illness and death was overpowering. The lantern wavered as Sharperson held it aloft and tried not to breathe. A TV lay in a dozen pieces on the floor. Paul flipped a light switch, but nothing happened. "The bomb must have blown out the electricity."

One of the ambulance attendants whispered "My God" and knelt next to the nude girl.

"I'm going to puke," Durand said and disappeared, his hand to his mouth.

As the other medic brushed past him to check the bodies, Paul turned back toward the ramp. "I'm going to call it in. F.B.I.'ll have to know." He looked at his watch. "Almost five hours to the pay-off. If it's still on."

"At least now you know who you're looking for," Sharperson said.

"Who," Paul agreed softly. "Not where." Still shaken by the sight of the dead children, he went out to his Jeep and called in to an agitated Harris. "Christ, boss, everyone in the city's looking for you. You have your radio off?" As he hurriedly explained the kidnapper's change of plans, Paul felt his spine grow cold. "Ellen took the ransom?" Confusion and fear muddled his thinking. "Ellen's gone?" It didn't make any sense. Why would Ellen be involved?

"She left about five minutes ago. The F.B.I.'s sweatin' bullets waiting to see what happens. No one knows what the hell's going on. We also found Manny's car, Paul. I'm sorry. A transient discovered it inside a gas station repair bay. Blood on the steering wheel and door handle but no body. I've got two cars on the scene now."

Paul said, "Manny's dead, Zach. Get LaSalle on the line. And hurry it up."

Harris's voice wavered. "He's outside with all the F.B.I. guys—"

"Well, get him to a phone, damn it!"

Paul's agitation grew until he heard LaSalle's, "Yes?"

"The kidnapper's a man named Lowell Alexander De-Vries," Paul said without preamble. "He's got the kids with him." Quickly, he explained what he'd discovered and added, "He's running. I don't know how many people he's killed now. Eight. Ten. But he sure as hell won't stop at that if it helps him get away. He's got to have a truck or a van to be carrying the hostages. I'll have my people pull over every large vehicle they see. You get the army and sheriffs' people out in the county. Set up road blocks. Any multi-passenger vehicle has to be stopped and searched. You understand what I'm saying? Any truck or van or bus. You've got Ellen bugged, haven't you? You're going to have to go after her. There's no way he's going to let her go now."

There was a silence, then LaSalle said, "The bugs are out."

"What?"

"He told us no bugs. Ellen insisted—"

"Then you don't know where the hell she is?"

"No."

Paul lost control. "Jesus Christ, he's going to kill her, LaSalle! Don't you understand that? Her, the kids. He's got nothing to lose. He's insane! He's out of control. He doesn't care who dies as long as it keeps us away from him."

LaSalle's voice wavered, then began to race. "She's in a 1985 white Oldsmobile, Chief. Get a statewide bulletin out." He gave Paul the license number. "She's going to switch to a white Toyota pickup truck. At least that was the plan."

Paul was sweating. He gripped the microphone and tried to rein in his fear. "Listen, LaSalle. You get the army and sheriffs and your people looking for Ellen in the county. I want everybody out, your field agents, lab techs, everyone. My people will take the city. DeVries is a psychopath, and he's on some kind of rampage. If you find him, don't hang back. Go in after him because he'll kill Ellen and the kids and anyone else if he has a chance."

LaSalle drew a breath. "She can't be that far from here. We'll find her." He put Harris back on the line. Paul told him to pull everyone from whatever they were doing and get them on the street looking for Ellen. "Find out where DeVries lives and send Howard Stines out there with an F.B.I. evidence tech. Maybe they can find something that'll tell us where he's headed. I'm coming in."

As he put the microphone back, he stared out at the darkness of the desert all around him. DeVries was out there somewhere waiting for Ellen as she hurried toward him with twenty million dollars. He knew now how the man thought. The moment he had the money, Ellen and the children would die, just as Bobby Muledeer and Manny and at least half a dozen children had already died.

8:39 P.M.

Feeling as if her head would explode, Ellen sped up Civic Center to Old Town where it became First Street and continued on, leaning over the steering wheel, searching frantically for a Toyota pickup. Nothing, nothing, nothing . . .

Sweat broke out on her forehead and dried at once in the heat. I'll do anything he wants, she thought. Anything. As long as he doesn't harm Denise. She's all I have, and—dear God, this sounds horrible—but I don't care what happens to those other children as long as Denise isn't hurt. I know it's terrible, but it's how I feel. I just want her back.

Her body began to tremble, and when she heard an electronic beeping she jumped in her seat. What was that? It sounded again, panicking her until she realized it was a phone. The car was littered with trash—empty paper bags, french fry containers, beer cans, newspapers. She brushed at a filthy towel on the seat next to her and saw the portable cellular phone. She snatched the receiver. "Yes?"

"Are you alone, Ellen?" A whispered, denatured voice spoke to her, maddeningly calm, unlike the last time she had talked to him.

"Yes."

"Unarmed?"

"Yes."

"And the electronic transmitters?"

"Gone."

"But they lied to you, didn't they, Ellen? LaSalle and the others. They lied about the bugs. It's how they are."

"Yes. They lied to me." Fury at LaSalle's deception made her scream. "But they're out, gone. I threw them away."

"How sad it is we can trust no one nowadays. The only constant is inconstancy. Everywhere there is betrayal. But I will not lie to you, Ellen. I never do. Where are you at this moment?"

"On First, near the city limits."

"Forget the earlier instructions. I was merely playing into their highly predictable mindset. There will be no 'treasure hunt.' And no Toyota truck. Continue east until you get to a two-lane road called Agua Fria. That will be in approximately seven miles. You'll have to look for it; it's just a ranch road. Take it into the hills until you see a Ford Explorer parked off to the side. Stop and put the ransom in the Explorer, without the suitcase. Continue on in the Explorer with your lights off for eleven point eight miles, at which time you'll come to a fork in the road. Turn left and follow it for exactly four point four miles. Stop, turn off the engine, and wait for further instructions. Do you have that? The whole trip is twenty-six and one-half miles. I have driven it many times, and it never takes more than thirty-three minutes. If you are not there in thirty-three minutes or if you attempt to use the car phone, I will have my way with pretty little Denise. You do know what I mean."

"Please," she began to weep.

"I never lie, Ellen. Remember that. There are no excuses. None. If you are late by even a minute, Denise is the penalty. She is with me this very minute, as it happens, in her sexy little sun dress. Such a grown-up girl, her skin so soft and warm and tantalizing. I put just a hint of perfume behind her ears. You don't mind, do you? I've always loved perfume on little girls. So Lolita-like, isn't it? So alluring. Do you want to speak with her? Perhaps you have some motherly words of wisdom for a child about to grow up."

Ellen's heart leapt. "Please."

"Mommy—" Denise cried into the phone, but DeVries came back on. "That's enough. No need to get maudlin. From your standpoint, it's regrettable I've had to do this, but it was the only way I could arrange for a courier I could trust completely. And I do trust you completely, Ellen. Did you hear about the other children, by the way? There's been an explosion where they were being held."

"An explosion? What—"

But when Ellen heard the dial tone, she broke down in sobs.

8:42 P.M.

Hurrying back to the parking lot where Ellis Whitfield was waiting impatiently with a group of agents, LaSalle recounted what Paul had told him. "Get all our planes up," the director barked furiously at Vince Garibaldi. "Tell Army Rescue we'll need them, too. I want everyone looking for those kids. The policewoman we'll worry about later. We're focusing on the desert: a truck, a van, any sign of life at all out there. I want those kids found now!"

LaSalle shook his head. "I don't think that's a good idea. We haven't had any luck trying to locate the children. Anyway, we don't know how this man will react. We need to get to Ellen before he does, then worry about the hostages. At least we know what she's driving—"

"Didn't you hear me?" Whitfield shouted at Garibaldi,

who immediately raced inside. He turned again to LaSalle and seemed about to lose control. "This is your fault, Agent LaSalle. You allowed that woman to go out there alone, with no support and no surveillance. It's unbelievable. Unbelievable!"

"We had bugs—"

"And you took them out because she told you to?" The director's pale face was red with fury. "You sent an unarmed woman—"

"A police officer."

"A woman! A single, unarmed woman after a lunatic kidnapper and mass murderer."

Middleton grunted and shuffled away, his hands in his pockets, leaving LaSalle alone with Whitfield. It's the press, Matt thought. The director doesn't want to explain if things go wrong. Or worse, be dragged up to Capitol Hill for a public lynching with cameras excitedly taking it all in. A dead police officer he could explain away; two dozen dead children would cost him not only his job but his beltway lifestyle. With determined calmness and relying on a rationality that had long since vanished from the investigation, he said, "We didn't have time to consult. The manual states—"

"Don't tell me what's in the manual, LaSalle. I goddamn know what's in the manual."

"Decisions are to be made in the field, using the best possible information at the time. The judgment of the agent in charge has to be relied on."

"Judgment, it seems to me, is very much the issue here. Did you ask anyone for their opinion? Did you ask B.S.U.?"

He wasn't going to pass the blame to anyone. Even though it was Exley who had insisted that Ellen take the money and that the bugs be removed, he had been in charge. His responsibility, and he wasn't going to distance himself from it like the time-servers and ass-covering bureaucrats he'd so loathed the past twelve years. He looked into the director's eyes and kept his voice calm. "It was my decision."

Whitfield was livid. He pressed his sweaty, reddened face

close to LaSalle. "Twenty million dollars," he said in a hoarse whisper. "You sent this unarmed woman, this hick-town patrol officer, off with twenty million dollars. How do you even know she's not in on it? Christ, it would be the perfect crime. How do we know she isn't the goddamn clown? She comes back in two hours and says she delivered the money and the kidnapper told her the kids are at the XYZ mine. Jesus, it'd be beautiful!"

LaSalle looked at him as though the notion were not worth discussing.

Whitfield stepped back and swore loudly to himself, then said, "Maybe you let your judgment be compromised by your personal life."

LaSalle felt a rush of anger. "What does that mean?"

"That means you've been sniffing around that Camacho woman when you should be working. I even heard about it back in D.C. You think it's a secret?"

He stared past Whitfield. Middleton and the other agents had moved out of hearing, and Exley was heading back toward the building. He wanted to ask who had complained but wasn't going to lower himself to that level.

"Mixing business and personal lives is a particularly egregious form of unprofessionalism, wouldn't you say, Agent LaSalle? Especially during a case where people's lives are at stake? No wonder you want us looking for her rather than the kids—"

"There was no mixing. I've done nothing other than talk to her and mostly about the case."

"Talk? What about those flowers you sent her? You always send flowers to police officers you're working with? What about calling her at home after midnight to whisper sweet nothings in her ear? What about snuggling up to her in the Xerox room, for Christ's sake?"

He felt a tightening in his chest but didn't trust himself to respond. Near the rear entrance to the Civic Center, Middleton stopped and looked back at the two men, seeming to nod across the darkness, and LaSalle heard Paul's *Never leave wounded* echo in his mind.

Whitfield turned as if he was going to stalk away, then spun around again. "I read your file on the way out here from D.C. Eighteen commendations, glowing reports from superiors, an admin job at headquarters coming up in four months. And you throw it away because you can't keep your hands off some bitch with a sexy smile. She'd better be the best fuck in the world, LaSalle, because she's cost you plenty."

"And maybe," he said, barely controlling his temper, "she'll come back with the kids. That's our objective, isn't it—getting the kids back?"

Whitfield had already started toward the building. He turned and took a step back. His body was trembling. "Listen to me, LaSalle. You're the agent in charge. It's your ass on the line, your name in the reports. But from this moment on, I make the decisions. Do you understand what I'm saying? I'll make the decisions."

"I still think it's a bad idea to send planes into the desert," LaSalle said, giving it one more try. "They'll have to fly too low. Anything under ten thousand feet and DeVries will know you're trying to locate him. The minute he does, he'll kill Ellen and the kids."

Whitfield was fifteen feet away by now. He shook his head in disbelief. "You just don't get it, do you?" He stalked into the Civic Center, leaving LaSalle alone.

8:45 P.M.

Danny Varig heard the A.P.B. on the '85 Olds just as it shot past him three miles outside the city limits. He hit the lights and siren and checked his computer screen to make sure he'd gotten it right. The car was driven by a Las Cruces police detective named Ellen Camacho. She was to call in immediately. Urgent.

Well, hell, this'll be a first, Danny thought, pulling over a goddamn detective. A woman detective at that. Might be fun.

But the Olds didn't seem to see or hear him as it continued south at ninety miles an hour. *What the fuck's going on? She goddamn blind and deaf? Well, hell, I got a brand new super-charged Chevy. I'll be on her ass in half a minute.*

Which he was, siren blaring, lights flashing. Still, the Olds didn't slow.

Danny pounded on his horn. *For Christ's sake, lady, stop!*

God, no, no, no, Ellen thought. *What could he want?*

I'm not going to pull over. I'm not going to do it. Thirty-three minutes, DeVries said. If you are late by even a minute—

The sheriff's car was suddenly beside her, honking, the driver gesturing wildly at her.

I'm not going to stop. I'm not going to! I can't—

The deputy pounded on his horn and pointed to the shoulder.

Oh God, I can't let him follow me. DeVries will kill her if he sees a police car.

The Oldsmobile's brake lights suddenly splashed across the darkness. The car slowed, pulling noisily onto the gravel shoulder and swerving almost out of control as the driver stopped too quickly.

This wasn't an enforcement stop, Danny reasoned, so he cruised up in front of the car and got out. *Nice-looking woman in there. Always liked pulling over the lookers.* He walked up to the driver's-side door, maybe swaggering just a little, struttin' his stuff, but taking it easy, too, watching, still not sure what this was all about. The window was down, and the woman was staring at him, a wild glint in her eyes. *Kinda weird-looking,* he thought, now that he was up close. *Hair all frizzy, eyes red like she's been crying. Sure as hell don't seem like no detective.* He bent and peered through the window at her. "You Sergeant Camacho?"

"What do you want?" Her gaze jumped from his face to her watch, then back to his face. She was sweating like a heroin addict going through withdrawal. *Or she's scared shitless about something.* "There's an A.P.B. out on you. Your department wants you to call in. Some kind of emergency, I guess. You can use my radio if you want. Maybe they want you to teach a driver education course."

For a moment, she didn't respond, just stared at him like an idiot, fingers opening and closing on the steering wheel. "I can't take this," she mumbled, and he had to bend his head to hear. "I can't—"

"Ma'am?" He began to feel uneasy. *This is too fuckin' weird, man. This ain't no cop though; that's for sure. And look at that car; it's a pigsty.*

The woman turned suddenly and fumbled with her purse, finally pushing the door open with her left arm and stepping out, the whole operation not taking two seconds. Danny breathed a sigh of relief, then blanched as he saw her lift a 9 mm automatic in a two-handed grip and hold it just inches from his face. "Turn around."

"What?" Sweat broke out on his forehead and his throat tightened so much he could hardly speak.

"Turn around, goddamn it!" She jammed the gun against his cheek. *Jesus, a nut case, practically jumping out of her skin. No wonder they want her back. Why the hell didn't they say she was dangerous?* He did as he was told, turning his back to her and wondering if she was going to put a bullet in his skull.

"Put your hands on your head."

Don't argue, he warned himself. *Just do it, she ain't in no mood to listen.* As he lifted his arms and pressed his palms on the back of his head, he felt sweat drip in a thin cold line along his ribs to his waist. He'd always wondered if it was going to end like this. He heard her fumbling with her purse again, then felt one wrist yanked down and handcuffed, then the other.

"In your car," she ordered, pushing him roughly toward the black-and-white. Opening the rear door, she shoved him in the caged compartment, then slammed the door and ran back to her car.

11. *Finale*

DeVries couldn't keep a sense of euphoria from surging through him. At long last, it was all coming together, and his soul sang with the headiness of victory. In just minutes he would have twenty million dollars. Jesus, think of it! Think of it! Twenty million! To spend in a country where the per capita income averaged fourteen hundred dollars. And he would be there sooner than expected. Of course, he couldn't slip leisurely out of town now, but that mattered little. Before the night was out, he would be in Mexicali and, the day after, in Chihuahua, where Thomas Clarkson, a high school teacher from Indiana, had arranged to stay with a local family for a month to brush up on his Spanish. It was a precaution that had cost him nine hundred dollars but money well spent, even if never used.

Again, the benefit of careful preparation was manifest. It had been time-consuming, to be sure, but worth it. It had all been worth it—the months, years, of studying and planning, the countless dry runs, the risks he had taken learning how to steal cars, learning about explosives (how pleasing that had been, watching things disassemble, their atoms rearranging into nothingness), planting the bugs in Ellen Camacho's house (listening to her most secret moments, taking part almost).

Ellen. A smile spread across his face, and he began to tap the steering wheel with the tips of his fingers. Sounded a little panicky there, didn't you, my dear? Just a tad *worried* about lovely little Denise, I imagine. Wondering what I might be planning to do to her. Perhaps you should worry more about the other children; they are my epitaph and my glory.

He suddenly reached over and laid his huge hand on

Denise's bare thigh. "Having a nice time? You've probably never been in a truck like this, have you? People rent them to move their household goods, you see."

The girl squirmed out of his touch and toward the door. Her hands were tied behind her with duct tape. He took his eyes off the road and focused on her face as it appeared indistinctly in the darkness. "Feisty little thing, aren't you? So full of life."

"I want to go home," Denise said with more bravery than she felt.

"I'm sure you do. In just a few minutes, you will meet your mother. That should please you."

A familiar stirring between his legs brought about an unwelcome shifting of thoughts. Perhaps there would be time after transferring the money to make use of the marvelous Ellen, after all. The idea had recurred so many times the past few days that it might be best to act on it just to get it out of his mind. The tapes of her and Whitehorse kept playing and replaying in his mind, creating visions that teased and tantalized horribly since he had only sound to base them on. But he had listened so frequently, over and over (how she moaned!), removing his clothes as he lay on his bed, sharing their pleasure.

Don't do it, Lowell, he told himself. Don't. Plans are meant to be adhered to, not deviated from, especially for so transitory a pleasure as sex with someone you have to kill moments later. Still, it would provide an extra measure of thrill, a sexual frisson not available elsewhere, even at Miss Violet's, to put a bullet in her head at the exact moment of climax. Bang . . . and bang. Timing it just so. *God yes! Yes!* His heart began to beat loudly (surely Denise could hear), and his foot went down harder on the accelerator as he thought about it. Perhaps young Denise could watch. Pay attention, child. See how your mother thrusts her hips and cries in delight. We could invite the other children to take part also. Or Denise could even be first. Yes, of course! Much better! Make Ellen watch as he does her daughter. Then do Mommy.

Such a marvelous child, he thought and then had an idea so logical and so wonderful he couldn't understand how it hadn't occurred earlier. Why waste so singular a treasure as Denise when she could continue to bring pleasure for years in the future? He could take her with him, a sort of living souvenir, an offering from Eros to Chaos—Eros, who softens the sinews and overpowers the mind. Yes! Of course! Denise might object, but children are ridiculously easy to intimidate. Just scare the living daylights out of her and she'd do anything. Hell, after a while she'd learn to love it, just like the children at Miss Violet's. He'd read about kidnapped kids who came to so identify with their kidnapper, even when "abused," that they didn't want to go back to their real parents. The four-year-old mind is like a new computer that has yet to be programmed. All you need do is start typing.

He turned excitedly to the girl. "How would you like to live with me? A great big house, all the toys you could want, a swimming pool, other children to play with all day. Think about it. You wouldn't even have to go to school. It'd be perfect. Perfect."

He didn't wait for an answer. He could hear what she was thinking. Yes. Yes, she was saying in her mind. *Yes!* And he stared straight ahead as Chaos gently whispered through his lips, "Of course. After the others die . . . Denise and me. Together forever."

8:55 P.M.

Hurrying to make up for lost time, Ellen at first shot past the unlit road, then slammed on her brakes in anger, spun wildly around on the loose dirt, and headed back. Turning quickly onto the narrow lane, she checked her watch. It'd taken sixteen minutes to go seven miles. She'd never get there in time. That goddamn deputy! she swore to herself. A rock flew up and hit the oil pan. "Damn it!" she screamed aloud. What if she had a flat tire? DeVries would never believe her. He wouldn't wait. *There are no excuses. None . . .* A sliver of moon in front of her revealed the outlines of the

low, jagged hills thrusting up on either side of the road. This
was somewhere near the bombing range, she knew, though
the actual impact site was on the other side of the mountains, at least ten miles east. Coyotes were howling very near,
warning each other of an intruder. She flicked on the radio.
". . . no one was hurt in the explosion although Chief of
Police Paul Whitehorse suffered bruises and cuts on his
face."

Ellen felt as if she had been kicked in the stomach. That's
what DeVries had meant. But no one hurt? Could it be
true? It must be. Paul would never have given out false information. The report continued:

"Five children, two boys and three girls, were discovered
dead in the bomb shelter. The remaining children have not
been found as of this time."

Five dead. Oh my God! Then DeVries has the other children with him. But why? What is he going to do with them?

Briefly, the starlight picked out something far in front of
her. A red light, she thought, visible for an instant only, then
gone. Taillights? Rear reflectors, maybe. She couldn't tell.
Turning off the radio, she concentrated on the road ahead.
The Oldsmobile had dipped into a declension that ran for
a quarter of a mile before gently rising again. As she crested
the hill, a Ford Explorer came abruptly into view on the
shoulder of the road, its lights out. Ellen hurried up behind
it, killed the engine. Only thirteen minutes to go sixteen
miles on unpaved mountain roads. She'd never make it.

If you are late by even a minute . . .

Grabbing the suitcase and her purse, she hurried out of
the Oldsmobile, ran up to the four-wheel drive vehicle, and
peered inside. Empty. Keys in the ignition. There was not a
sound anywhere, not even the wind. Hands fumbling, she
tossed her purse inside; then zipped open the suitcase and
dumped the ransom on the passenger seat. Turning
around, she threw the suitcase into the desert as DeVries
had ordered. Just then, coming from the blackness of the
night, she heard the faint but unmistakable rhythmic
thumping of a helicopter.

The F.B.I., she thought with alarm. Oh my God, the bastards followed me. They followed me! Then they hadn't taken all the transmitters out after all. "You lying goddamn bastards!" she screamed into the night. Clenching her fists, she lifted her face to the sky in the direction of the sound and flailed at the air. "Goddamn you, Matthew! Goddamn—" Her eyes flew to the two vehicles sitting on the road. They'll see me for sure. There's nowhere to hide.

But just as abruptly as it came, the noise faded. Her heart pounded wildly; she could scarcely believe it. They were gone, looking somewhere else.

She ran to the Explorer and turned the key. Move, damn it! she told herself. Damn it, *move!*

9:01 P.M.

Barely able to control himself, Paul stood behind his desk, hands clamped on the back of his swivel chair to keep them from shaking. Across from him, LaSalle and Whitfield squirmed in their seats. Paul's rage filled the room as he looked from one to the other. "What the hell were you doing taking out the transmitters? How in God's name did you expect to get to her?"

Whitfield's face was glowing; without turning to LaSalle, he said, "Perhaps you could explain it to the chief, Agent LaSalle, since you were in charge."

"We thought it best," LaSalle replied with strained reserve, "to do what the kidnapper wanted. He asked for Ellen and she agreed. We didn't pressure her to do it."

"This isn't just a kidnapper," Paul cried. He couldn't believe what he was hearing. "DeVries is a sociopath, for Christ's sake. He's already killed at least ten people. He doesn't care who dies. Do you think he's going to let Ellen go?"

"The plan was to send Dr. Exley," LaSalle reminded him. "We felt he could have talked to—"

"Talk?" Paul exploded, striking the chair with his fist and sending it spinning toward the wall. "For God's sake, this man's out of control, he's a multiple killer, he's psycho. Can't you get that through your goddamn head?"

"We've got aircraft looking for her vehicle," Whitfield interjected. Since sitting down he had determinedly not looked at LaSalle. Sounding almost conciliatory, he added, "We'll find her."

"The aircraft," LaSalle said, holding Paul's eyes with his own frozen gaze, "are not looking for Ellen. They're searching for the kids."

Paul stared at him in disbelief, then turned on Whitfield. Before he could open his mouth, Whitfield said, "Agent LaSalle is fantasizing again, I'm afraid." The fingers of one hand angrily gripped the arm of the chair. "Our planes have orders to look for your detective or any vehicle large enough to transport the children."

LaSalle shook his head, still watching Paul. A feeling of inadequacy and impotence had gripped him, robbing his voice of animation. Only fear sounded through. "They were given no instructions about the car. She's alone, Paul, unarmed. There's no help—"

"A white Oldsmobile!" Whitfield snapped. His face had gone red, and he came half out of his chair. "They're goddamn looking for it!"

Paul couldn't believe what he was hearing. As though Whitfield weren't there, LaSalle added, "There was something wrong with Ellen. She was keyed up, about to snap. She also didn't seem surprised that she was taking the ransom."

"We'll find her," Whitfield repeated, though no one was listening to him now.

Paul's knees felt weak. The phone rang but he ignored it. "She won't be in the Olds anyway. Or the Toyota. DeVries will have her switch cars. Christ! You people act like he's an imbecile. He's been ahead of all of us for two days, playing with us, and you still think you can outsmart him." He snatched angrily at the phone. "Howard Stines on three," Maggie said. Paul jabbed the button and said, "What?"

"It'll take us days to do a complete search of his house,

Chief. DeVries wasn't planning on leaving, from the looks of it. All his clothes are here, a thousand books in the bookcases, food in the cupboards. And kids' clothing, too. Underwear mostly, panties, and so on. I think he's got some weird sex thing for children. Also electronic eavesdropping equipment. He was obviously surveilling someone. There were some photos, too, of the inside of Ellen's house. I recognized it at once." His voice raced on before Paul could interrupt. "And the F.B.I. guys came up with something else interesting."

"What?" Paul said, feeling rage and fear race through him at the same time, wanting to know and not to know.

"A map of that abandoned airfield north of town. DeVries had written today's date and ten P.M. on it, next to what looks like where one of the hangars would be."

Paul's heart skipped a beat. He looked at his watch. Less than an hour from now.

"And something else, Chief," Stines went on. "I flicked on his computer and took a little tour of his files. I found one called 'Children' and thought I better take a look-see. It's a list: 'DO IT,' 'LOCK UP,' 'WARNING,' 'PATIENCE,' and so on. Each one refers to a separate subfile. 'DO IT' is the snatch, all laid out in detail, just like it happened. 'LOCK UP' is the hideaway. You understand what I'm saying? He has a damn list and he's following it, one, two, three. Every damn thing he's done is on that list."

"Then we know where the pay-off is," Paul realized. His eyes darted to LaSalle.

"Right. The list even says 'PAY-OFF.' So I went to that subfile. I'm looking at it right now. It's the airfield, all right. He's going to meet the courier, grab the money, and run. You better hustle out there."

"With the choppers we can be there in fifteen minutes," Paul said, his mind working it out.

"Hey, don't hang up, boss. There's one more thing on the list. The last item: It says, 'KILL ALL.' He means the kids and the courier. I guess he's not taking a chance on witnesses."

Paul slammed the phone down and told Whitfield and LaSalle what they'd found. The director bolted out of his seat. "We can get there before she does. We'll get army rescue to change direction and go in with us. Get your team ready. They can come, too." LaSalle had also come to his feet, and the room pulsed with hope for the first time in hours. But something moved in Paul's mind, and he stood motionless. Whitfield looked at him with annoyance. "Well?"

A sinking feeling, like the queasiness after a high-speed pursuit, settled in his stomach. His voice unsure, he said, "DeVries knew we were on to him hours ago. Why would he leave that computer program where we could get at it?"

Whitfield stared at him impatiently, his anger again escalating. "What are you getting at?"

"How do we know it's not a diversion? Why would he leave something so incriminating around? It doesn't fit."

"He didn't plan on us being this close behind him. Criminals never do. For Christ's sake, if they thought the authorities were going to be on their tail, they wouldn't be criminals."

LaSalle said, "The Torres girl had jet fuel on her shoes, Paul. I think this pretty well seals it."

"But DeVries is a thinker, a planner," Paul said. He began to pace behind his desk. It was all beginning to make some sense now, the lineaments of DeVries's thought processes just visible through the layers of deliberate obfuscation. "The lunch box, the lost shoe, the fuel, the telephone calls, the computer. It's too pat. Think about it: Everything leads north—toward either the airfield or the mines. But DeVries has been planning this for years. Remember the knife with the governor's prints? Do you think someone that methodical is going to leave a trail for us to follow? This is a man who deals in misinformation. He creates confusion. He's used the press to keep us from looking for him. He killed people just to divert attention from the kidnapping. He changed the pay-off and—"

"Chief," Whitfield said with smoldering impatience. "He

did not plan on you finding that bomb shelter. He wouldn't have gone ahead with the kidnapping if he thought you'd figure out who was behind it and where the hostages were being kept. He did not plan on being on the run with the kids. According to your man, he left in a hurry, didn't have time to clean out his house. If he's done everything else on that list, why would he change now?"

Paul was subdued. But he was certain he was right. He knew suddenly how the man thought. "DeVries understands how the police operate. Just like Exley said. He knew we'd go through his house. He wanted us to find the list. It's all part of the plan."

"But he couldn't know we'd get into his computer," Whitfield said with exasperation.

"It's exactly what he would expect."

Calmly, LaSalle said, "Where do you think he is, then?"

"Anywhere but the airfield."

"That's not very helpful, is it?"

Whitfield's voice rose. "We're wasting time. We need to move. The one thing we're agreed on is he'll probably kill your officer. He's already facing the death penalty. He's got nothing to lose." He began moving toward the door. "How many did you say he's killed? Ten? Maybe more? Well, we're not going to let him kill again. I'm sending army rescue to the airfield. We're going in, too. Do you want to send your team or not? They can go with us."

Paul had only a second to make up his mind. With a sinking feeling he said, "Yes."

The two F.B.I. men disappeared out of the office.

Feeling as though a major mistake had just been made, but not knowing what to do about it, Paul walked over to his windows and stared out toward the darkness.

9:15 P.M.

How long have I been driving? Ellen looked at the dashboard clock. Dear God, I'm late already! The rutted dirt road was difficult to maneuver on in the darkness, and she had already run off onto the shoulder twice. Wait for me, DeVries! Please God, make him wait! The road seemed to lead due east, running along a dry creek bed for a while, then crossing it and meandering into the hills. A vague light appeared as a sudden flash in front of her from somewhere well behind the mountains. Not so much a light as a hint of light, briefly illuminating the topmost edge of the farthest ridge. Then it occurred again, and again, and again. After two minutes it stopped.

Gunnery practice or low-level bombing.

The road would have to stop soon. She'd be at the range property, and it was protected by a twelve-foot chain-link fence with barbed wire along the top. She and Pete had come four-wheeling out here before Denise was born. Pete had a twenty-year-old Jeep Wrangler and he'd drive out from Los Angeles, fired up with Coors and machismo, and beat the hell out of the desert, racing bare-chested and half drunk up and down hills and through the dry river beds. He didn't want so much to enjoy the desert as to possess it, dominate it, as he dominated everything.

Her throat tightened. Don't start crying, she warned herself. Need to think clearly. Concentrate on facts. Be as professional as you would be in any other case. What is DeVries planning when you get there with the money?

With an effort she tried to clear her mind. I need to know. I need to know what you're planning, DeVries.

But it always came back the same way: You're going to kill me. You'll have to. You're going to kill me and Denise and the other children if you haven't already. I know you, goddamn it! I've dealt with people like you before. Human life means nothing, literally nothing. You've seen ten thousand people killed on television or in films; you probably collect videos of people dying or being tortured. You run to auto accidents and fires and disasters. You worship pain and suffering and death.

And you're going to kill me. The minute you get your hands on the money I'll die. I'm not going to let you do it, you bastard. I'll kill you first. I'll make you suffer like you made Linda Sowell suffer.

Her eyes went to the floor in front of the passenger seat, where her purse lay with the 9 mm automatic inside, and aloud she said, "I'm going to kill you."

Something silver and metallic rose up abruptly fifty yards down the road. She slowed and rolled to a stop in front of a gate set in a chain-link fence that ran in either direction as far as she could see. Getting quickly out, she went up to it. A sign said:

DANGER DANGER DANGER
U.S. Government Property
Live Ammunition
NO ADMITTANCE
Trespassers Will Be Prosecuted

She gave a yank on the gate, and it opened. Hurrying back to the Explorer she continued on the dirt road. Suddenly she felt exhausted, as though she had been running and running, and a sob escaped her throat.

What if DeVries hadn't waited? What if he wasn't there? What then?

9:16 P.M.

Paul remained standing at his floor-to-ceiling window, watching the army rescue helicopter hover at the edge of town as three smaller helicopters lifted off with a half-dozen F.B.I. agents and the Las Cruces police team. DeVries is not at the airfield, he told himself. He's playing with our egos, relying on that rush of self-satisfaction we feel when outthinking the bad guys. Every law-enforcement officer in the country secretly sees himself as another Sherlock Holmes, able to piece together disparate bits of information that meant nothing until he devoted his considerable intuitive powers to the problem. *Elementary, my dear Watson. I've made a study of bicycle tyre tracks.* Once you get that burst of insight and the simultaneous pumping of ego, it's hard to back down. The lunch box, the boy's shoe, the jet fuel, the map—it's inescapable. But you're playing with us, aren't you, DeVries? You're too sharp to leave clues around. Clues are for Sherlock Holmes or Hercule Poirot. Or the goddamn F.B.I.

But if not the airfield, where? What did LaSalle say—eleven thousand square miles?

Where, goddamn it?

He turned suddenly and kicked his metal wastebasket, sending it flying across the room. Reaching over the desk, he flipped through his Rolodex until he found Ennis Cooper, then punched out the number on his phone. When it was answered, Paul hung up.

Ennis Cooper lived adjacent to the reservation on a ranch large enough to support his crop dusting and myriad other business ventures. Although only one-quarter Indian, he was a full member of the tribe and had been on the council for years. He was also, Paul reflected on the way out, probably the only person over fifty who supported gambling, seeing it as a last desperate chance to bail out the pisspoor gas station/trading post/motel he'd operated for more than thirty years. A grocery store adjacent to the dirt runway had been boarded up months ago, after Wal-Mart came to town, and even people from the reservation had quit coming by.

Before gambling became an issue, Paul and Ennis had been friends, even used to fly up to Idaho each year in Ennis's plane for a week of camping and deer hunting and whiskey drinking. Lately, they hardly spoke to one another.

Ennis was walking from the house to the garage when Paul pulled off the highway and onto the gravel drive. A grizzled, heavy-set man in his sixties, he was wearing faded Levi's, a white T-shirt, and a Dodgers baseball cap. The stub of an unlit cigar stuck aggressively out of the corner of his mouth. When he heard the Jeep's tires on the gravel, he turned and gave it a look, then put his hands on his hips and stood without expression as Paul parked and began to walk up to him. "Something you need, Chief?"

"Your plane, Ennis," Paul said, still a dozen feet away. He looked toward the runway. "You and your plane."

"She-it!" Cooper snatched the cigar from his mouth and spit on the ground. "Shoulda called before coming out. Woulda saved you a trip. I'm busy tonight. Gotta do my laundering. Today's sock day. Got me 'bout twenty pairs needs washing and fabric softening. Always do 'em in the 'gentle' cycle, you know, so they last longer. Then I gotta dry 'em. After that, I gotta match 'em up. You know how that is, usually one missing. Can take all night to find it."

Paul stared at the man with more composure than he felt. "Let me tell you how it's going to be, Ennis. That way it'll save us a lot of time playing games. Ellen's missing. You and I are going to go up in your Cessna and search for her. Those missing kids, too. We'll be looking for a white car or a large truck. We'll start on the highway south of town. If we don't see anything, we'll try somewhere else. But we're going to look until we find her. You understand what I'm saying?"

Cooper's sparse gray eyebrows jerked angrily together. "I ain't one of your peons, Chief. So get the hell off my property." He spun around and started to walk away.

"I know you aren't too happy with me," Paul said, raising his voice. "I know you think you've got a reason to dislike Ellen, too. But this gambling thing's a difference of opinion, Ennis, and that's all it is. It's not life and death. But Ellen being missing is. She went out to meet the guy who snatched those kids, and now no one knows where she is. He's already killed at least ten people. He's sure as hell not about to let her out alive. You want that to happen?"

The old man jammed the cigar back in his mouth and took a book of matches from his pocket. "Ain't my problem. I'm a crop duster, not a cop."

"What about those kids, Ennis? You don't care about them?"

Cooper's hand stopped in mid-air as he was about to

strike the match. "Kids? You want me to worry about some damn retard kids I never even seen?" He took a step toward Paul. "Look around here. Go on, do it. How many cars you see? Look, goddamn it." He waved an arm angrily in the direction of his dilapidated buildings. "You know how many people I got in the motel tonight? None. Not a goddamn one.

"You and your high and mighty friends in town—and I mean Ellen, too, and the city council—don't give a rat's ass about us folk out here. You turned all the old people on the reservation against us, talking about the fuckin' Mafia coming in here like it's goddamn Las Vegas or something. Now you want me to help?"

Just then the screen door to Cooper's house banged and a well-built young man wearing Levi's, a sleeveless black T-shirt, and a black cowboy hat came down the steps. Paul waited as the man walked up to them, then said, "Evening, Hek."

Hek Gomez, looking as if Paul was the last person in the world he expected to see, stared from Paul to Ennis, then back to Paul again. "What the hell you want?"

Paul was beginning to lose his patience. "I'm having a conversation with Ennis, Hek. Why don't you go on back inside?"

Cooper half-laughed. "Wants me to take him up in my Cessna, help look for them missing retards."

Gomez turned a disbelieving look on Paul. "You're shittin' me."

Paul was near the breaking point. Still trying to keep his temper in check he said, "Ennis, you get that plane of yours fired up or I'm placing you under arrest for obstruction of justice and interfering with a police officer."

"Don't do it," Gomez said, turning toward Cooper. "You don't work for the fuckin' Las Cruces white-folk police."

Paul took a step forward. "Get in the goddamn house, Hek, or I'll arrest you, too."

Gomez laughed and said, "Fuck you, old man. You ain't even going to be chief once—"

In one furious move, Paul seized the man's wrist and spun him around. Gomez resisted instinctively and tried to break free, but Paul yanked violently downward on his arm, forcing him to the ground. Dropping to one knee, he quickly snapped a handcuff to one wrist, then the other. Gomez howled in pain and kicked with his feet. "You broke my fucking arm! Jesus, get me to a hospital."

Without a word, Paul grabbed Gomez's wrist and hauled the man roughly to his feet. As both Gomez and Cooper hollered at him, Paul pulled his prisoner toward the Jeep. Opening the front passenger door, he took another pair of handcuffs from the glove compartment and quickly hooked one end to the front roll-bar bumper and the other to Gomez's handcuffs.

"I'm calling the F.B.I.," Cooper yelled. "Don't worry, Hek. I'll have the feds out here in no time." As he headed for the house, Paul said, "Ennis, you get the plane fired up or I'll have you in jail on more counts than a lawyer could handle in a week. If you could get a lawyer around here after refusing to help look for those kids."

The man stopped and turned toward him.

"I mean it, Ennis. Once people hear about that, how much business do you think you're going to get out here?"

Cooper mulled it over a moment, shifting from foot to foot, then waved an arm aggressively toward his friend. "You let Hek go first. Then I'll take you up."

Paul shook his head. "When we get back."

The old man stood motionless, staring uncertainly at the plane a hundred yards away. In a subdued voice, he said, "Where exactly you figure on going?"

"South along the highway toward Mexico. If we don't see what I'm looking for, we'll head east."

Cooper's eyes turned suspicious. "How far east?"

"Up in the hills," Paul said, walking up to him, close enough to see the webbing of creases on the man's face.

Cooper squinted at him, then became aggressive again. "Maybe you better be a little fuckin' more specific."

"We're looking for Ellen and those kids, Ennis. We'll do what we have to."

"F.B.I.'s been looking for more than a day. Big fuckin' operation going on north of town right now. Been listening to the radio traffic. Sounds like three or four choppers. What makes you want to go south?"

"Ennis," Paul said, trying not to lose control. "Get the goddamn plane up and I'll tell you."

The old man considered, then shook his head. "No deal. If you wanna go south, I'll take you. Or west. Or I'll take you north as far as that F.B.I. activity, as long as there's no shooting. But east is off-limits to aircraft, always has been. I try to go in there and they'll pick me up on radar as a drone, a target plane. We'll get blown out of the sky with a sidewinder missile. It's a firing range. That's what they do."

Paul grabbed the man by the arm. "Ennis, get in your goddamn plane. We're going up. You just follow the highway south. I'll keep you out of the target area."

And he thought: We're finding her. I'll fly the damn plane if I have to.

"A wrongdoer is often a man that has left something undone, not always he that has done something."

—*Marcus Aurelius, 2nd Century* A.D.

DeVries remembered this morning's aphorism as he looked at his watch. Yes indeed. Leave nothing undone. One last check, then. Not that it was necessary. All the pieces had fallen perfectly into place. Perfectly. Still, one can't be too careful.

He took the bulky cellular phone with its heavy battery pack from the floor of the truck in front of Denise. He knew from repeated trials that reception was poor out here and required a powerful set. Even so, making connection was a matter of trial and error. He switched on the receiver and checked the power indicator. About eighty percent. That should be enough. Putting his hand on Denise's knee, he squeezed painfully. "Don't say a word," he ordered, and dialed the number.

"Las Cruces Police."

"Hi, babe."

"Lowell! Hi! Where are you? On the cellular? You sound funny."

"I went out to Thrifty Drug to get a prescription for this fever. What's happening with the kidnapping? They get the kids back yet?"

Her voice was excited. "Not yet but I think pretty soon. A few minutes ago everyone ran out of here like the building's on fire. The F.B.I., the army, our rescue guys. It was like a war movie, all the helicopters taking off for that old air base—you know, the one we went snooping around last year. The kidnapper's got the children there. Zach told me Ellen left with the ransom about forty-five minutes ago, so I guess they'll all get to the base about the same time. I wish I could be with them."

He was feeling chipper. "And Chief Sitting Bull? He out there, too?"

"Lowell, don't talk like that. The chief's a nice guy. I don't know what he's up to. He radioed in a few minutes ago to say he's going to go in some guy's private plane to follow Highway 15 south. I'm not sure why. He sounded kinda antsy to me, all out of breath like."

He smiled to himself. "Sounds like everyone's busy."

"You can say that again. Hey, when am I going to see you?"

"After tomorrow I think you'll have your fill of me, babe."

Jeannie giggled. "I hope so, superman. It's been a long time. Oops, I gotta go, got another call."

"Hey babe," he said quickly. "What's the twenty-four-hour record for murders?"

"Huh?"

He clicked off the phone and turned to Denise. "Everyone's kinda busy elsewhere. We won't have to worry about being interrupted. Just you, me, and mamma alone in the desert. How's that sound?"

He laughed out loud. I've done it, he thought. Goddamn, 've fuckin' done it!

Maybe he'd celebrate a little, strut some . . .

9:30 P.M.

Paul was waiting impatiently for Ennis Cooper to get the eys to the plane when he heard the cellular phone in the eep ring.

He hurried over and grabbed the receiver as Hek Gomez wisted at his handcuffs and swore loudly. "Whitehorse—"

"Pretty informal for the chief of police."

Paul felt his flesh grow cold. He tried to speak but ouldn't.

"Lowell Alexander DeVries," the voice said, and added, I know your phone number, as you see. As well as much lse about you. Are you displeased? Don't be. It was all nec-ssary, as was keeping track of you and Ellen and your rather njudicious affair. Electronic transmitters can be such fun, lon't you think?"

"DeVries, goddamn it—"

"Calm yourself, Chief."

"What have you done with her? Where is she?"

"She? Who? Which she are we talking about? Ellen or the xquisite Denise? I have them both, you see. I have them. ou've lost. They're mine now. Mine."

Paul gripped the phone as Gomez kept yelling obsceni-ies and threats from five feet away. "I'll kill you, DeVries. ;oddamn it, I promise."

"In fact," DeVries went on as though Paul had not spo-en, "Denise has decided to come live with me. I'm so leased. At this very moment, we've been having a fasci-ating discussion of sexuality. You have no idea how grown p she is. I'm about to make her a young lady. Think of us, nd our life together, as we enter the future."

"DeVries—"

The line went dead.

9:31 P.M.

Traveling with the lights off, desperately trying to make up for lost time, Ellen almost didn't see the branching of to the left of the main road. She wrenched the wheel sharply, accidentally jamming her foot on the accelerator and ran the Explorer off the road. Swearing furiously, she put the vehicle in four-wheel-drive and shot back onto the dirt road, glancing at the odometer in the moonlight. Another 4.4 miles.

Although unpaved, the road she had turned onto was well maintained, as if used with some frequency. She was almost certain she had reversed direction and was heading west now. What the hell was DeVries doing? Leading her back to where she began? Wherever it was, she'd arrive in less than ten minutes. You'd better be there, DeVries, she thought. Goddamn it, be there!

She reached down and snatched her purse off the floor. She couldn't hide the gun on her person, so she'd have to take it. With her right hand, she opened the clasp, removed the pistol, and slipped off the safety. Then replacing the gun, she closed the purse without snapping it.

But even with a gun, how was she going to deal with De-Vries? He was insane, an out-of-control psychopath who had already killed and seemed determined to kill again. The only crazies she'd ever been involved with were the homeless and generally harmless derelicts roaming the streets of downtown Los Angeles, people who thought they were Napoleon or who held nonstop conversations with God. DeVries was very much another sort, someone who knew exactly what he was doing but with no feeling at all for human life, a man who saw other people only as game pieces to be manipulated for his own advantage. She tried to think back to her college courses. People like that crave notice and attention. They want to be told how smart they are, how much they tower over the rest of humanity, how the world will soon recognize their genius. Yet their egos are as fragile as glass.

Whatever you do, don't upset him, she told herself. Don't annoy him. Agree with anything he says, anything at all. Admire his skill and ingenuity. But don't overdo it, don't appear patronizing or manipulative. They're sensitive to that, it infuriates them.

She looked at the odometer. Another mile.

She had an idea and hit the brakes. Getting out, she hurried around to the other side of the Explorer, opened the passenger door and picked up the small bag of diamonds and as much money as she could carry. Then she turned and looked around. A dead joshua tree lay on the ground thirty yards distant. Already dangerously late, Ellen ran over the rocky terrain and dumped the ransom out of sight behind the tree. Two more trips and it was all there.

This definitely will enrage him, she thought. But it's the only leverage I have, using his craziness against him.

As she began to shut the passenger door, she noticed something amid the trash on the floor by the front seat. Her heart pounding, she quickly reached down and picked it up. A pair of little girl's panties. She began to shake all over. Oh my God, no! They were Denise's. They must be. Her fingers fumbled and her head felt light as she looked at the label.

He put them here on purpose. To scare me. He wants to scare me, he enjoys it. That's all. He hasn't hurt her. He hasn't.

She hurried back into the driver's seat. But she couldn't keep her body from trembling as she maneuvered the final mile, carefully watching the odometer, then killing the engine at the exact place DeVries indicated. Where was he? The road twisted out of sight around a huge outcropping of boulders a hundred yards in front of her. No one around.

Dear God, he's not here, he's not here. He didn't wait! But it wasn't fair; he hadn't given her enough time.

Through the open window a hot, dry breeze gently blew against the side of her face.

Coyotes stalking somewhere outside, yelping, watching her from a distance, wondering.

Denise is okay. She's okay. DeVries wouldn't harm her. He wouldn't. He needs her.

A jarring of the ground and a distant light in the rearview mirror. More bombing practice. He had directed her in a westward route, then, away from the range but still several miles east of the highway.

Silence.

She waited, glanced at her watch.

Where are you, DeVries? Please be here. Be here!

Turning suddenly, she stared out the rear window but could see nothing. Too dark, too dark. She heard a sound and spun back toward the open window at her side but no one was there. She shivered.

I'm coming, Denise, wait for me.

Her hand shook as she looked again at her watch. Nine fifty-two.

What was Paul doing? Or Matthew?

Where are you, DeVries? Damn it, where?

Jerking abruptly on the door handle, Ellen stepped outside. Too much tension. Have to walk it off. She strode rapidly down the road, in the direction she had come from, the muscles in her legs and back painfully cramped. Turned suddenly around. Came back, breathing deeply, clenching and unclenching her fists. Stood by the car, heart pounding, looking, looking. DeVries was gone; when she was late in arriving he spooked. He took Denise and ran. *If you are late by even a minute, Denise is the penalty.*

Her head snapped back, and she stared up at the limitless sky. "Where are you, goddamn it?" she screamed at the top of her voice, and the words disappeared into the void.

She climbed back in the car, hugged herself, rubbed her icy arms.

Ten o'clock.

What did he do with the children? Why booby-trap the bomb shelter?

He's crazy, he's insane, he has no right to live, no right . . .

Five after ten. Oh, God! Ellen shuddered and sank back against the door, staring out the passenger window. She was thinking, I'm going to kill you, as DeVries's moist lips gently touched her ear and his warm breath stirred the fragile surface of her flesh. "I have you, Ellen," he whispered, and let his tongue caress her skin. "Both of you."

9:37 P.M.

The army rescue team arrived at the airfield first with only the moon for light. Jet engines roaring horribly, rattling the vegetation and shaking the long-abandoned buildings, their helicopter made several swift low-level passes over the grounds to see if there was any obvious place where the hostages might be hidden. It negated any chance to take the kidnapper by surprise, but Whitfield insisted on speed rather than stealth. Seeing nothing, they set down near the south gate, and a dozen black-clad soldiers streamed out beneath the still whirling rotors, with automatic rifles at the ready. Running softly through the night, they set portable lights on the other three sides of the base, marking out landing zones for the F.B.I. helicopters.

After a hasty conference between the F.B.I. director and the major in charge of the army team, it was decided to erect a collapsing perimeter, with the army on the south, the Las Cruces police on the north, and the F.B.I. on the remaining two sides. Keeping in touch with one another by walkie-talkie, they would have to go through the base building by building. Even a cursory search, they felt, would take hours.

At 9:55, after checking their equipment, the four teams slowly began to advance. LaSalle, with the F.B.I. squad, looked at his watch and wondered why they hadn't seen Ellen on the road outside the base. It wasn't possible for her to have driven here already.

Whitfield, waiting alone in the passenger seat of a helicopter, realized too late: It's too easy. We screwed up someplace.

9:39 P.M.

Ennis Cooper nodded his craggy head toward the road below. "That's it. We can follow her all the way to Mexico if you want. Or pick up the road to San Diego. You call it."

"Just stay on the highway. If you spot a white Oldsmobile or a truck, try to get low enough to see inside."

"Look, Chief, I can do some pretty good tricks with this bird, but we ain't going to get low enough to see who's driving a car sixty-five miles an hour in the dark. It can't be done."

"Damn it, Ennis, if it has to be done it can be done. We'll set down on the highway if we have to."

"Not unless you pull your gun on me. I ain't losing my pilot's license after forty years because you got a hunch about something."

Paul wasn't listening. He bent over the side window, scrutinizing the sparse traffic moving along a few hundred feet below. Nothing matched what they were looking for. Ellen had probably switched cars. But if she saw a plane buzzing the highway, maybe she'd figure out who it was and stop. Or would she? She hadn't tried to communicate with the police station, even though she'd probably had an opportunity to stop at a pay phone for a hasty call. She must be convinced the kidnapper only wants the money and will let the kids go once he has it.

But, damn it, Ellen knew better than that! She knew enough about psychopaths to realize they never do the predictable or simple. DeVries had murdered not because he had to but because he wanted to. It was a demonstration and why he'd called Paul: Look at me. I can destroy, I can kill.

Then why hadn't Ellen checked in?

His head swam. None of it made sense, and he couldn't calm himself sufficiently to think clearly. What if Ellen wasn't on the highway? Where should they try next? He wondered if DeVries might have set the rendezvous at the border. Then he could be in Mexico in minutes. Of course. Mexico! He said, "Ennis, you keep heading south."

10:06 P.M.

Thirty miles north of Ennis Cooper's rapidly disappearing plane and fifty miles south of the abandoned airfield, Ellen's car door flew open and DeVries, holding a .38 revolver against her head, smiled excitedly and said, "Where's the money?" It was all he could do to keep from dancing along the desert floor as he imagined his first look at it: twenty million dollars!

Ellen took a breath. "I buried it back on the road. I'll take you there when I have Denise."

DeVries exploded and struck her furiously across the face with the barrel of the gun. "Goddamn it, get it! Now, now, now!" His heart began to race wildly, and he felt suddenly as though he was about to lose control. This was horrible; an intolerable delay. He hadn't anticipated her not having the ransom; that's what taking the daughter was supposed to ensure. There was no time to waste. He had to move quickly now, while everyone was looking for him in the wrong places.

Ellen felt a warm flow of blood along the side of her face, but she held firm. "Get Denise!"

There was no time to work this out; DeVries knew only that he had to move. Quickly making up his mind, he said, "She's over there. On the other side of the ridge."

Ellen leaned over the steering wheel, peering through the windshield, but could see nothing in the darkness.

"In a truck, damn it! You can't see it from here. They're all there. This is a military road. I came in from the other side. I've been waiting, watching you, making sure you were alone." He spoke rapidly, irritably, not wanting to prolong the delay.

"A truck? You put the children in the back of a—"

"They're okay, goddamn it! You think I'd risk their lives before I had the ransom?"

"I want to see them," Ellen demanded.

DeVries's eyes darted to the open purse on the passenger seat. With his left hand, he grabbed the hair on top of Ellen's head, painfully jerked her face in his direction, and shoved the barrel of the revolver in her mouth as far as it would go. "Don't turn your head. Pick your purse up by the handle and pass it to me."

For a second she hesitated, then tentatively reached her right arm over to the passenger seat and felt for her purse; carefully she lifted it to the open window. DeVries quickly glanced inside, immediately dropping it to the ground as he saw the gun, and howled with rage. Pulling the revolver back, he struck her furiously across the mouth with the barrel, breaking three teeth and ripping open her lip. Her head snapped against the seat-back and pain seared through her. "I want Denise!" she managed to say as blood gushed from her mouth. Her forehead fell sharply against the steering wheel. "I want to see her, I want to see . . ." Suddenly she spun in his direction, slashing out with her hand and spitting blood. "I want to see her!"

Swearing angrily, DeVries hurried around the back of the car to the passenger side and yanked open the door. "Get moving," he shouted, climbing inside. "You can see the truck around the bend. Move! Move! Damn it! Now!"

But she didn't respond, evidently didn't hear, her chest heaving with emotion and her head bobbing back and forth as she tried to keep air in her lungs. Suddenly she muttered something he couldn't catch, and her body jerked as though jolted with electricity. At the same time she pushed on the door handle, leaped from the car, and began running wildly down the dirt road toward the truck. He swore and took off on foot after her.

Panting for breath, she raced toward the huge outcropping of boulders to the right of the road that separated her from Denise. Her mind in a panic, she had no idea what she was going to do but knew with absolute certainty that Denise would live only so long as DeVries needed her. The moment he had the money, he would complete the killing. But if the children were here, she realized through her hysteria, everything changed. If the children were here, there was no reason for DeVries to live!

As she reached the base of the rocks, she felt dwarfed by their immensity. There were scores or hundreds of them, many as big as a house, thrown on top of one another by some prehistoric cataclysm and extending back in the hills as far as two or three football fields. It looked like the ruins of a monstrous Neolithic religious structure that had been half-covered with earth and overgrown with scraggly cactuses and pine.

She felt a tremor of hope. She was used to the desert, had climbed and explored all her life. DeVries in his soft, custom-fit suits and polished wing tips looked like a city boy, uncomfortable with the outdoors.

I'm going to kill you, you bastard.

The truck suddenly sprang into view not thirty feet away as she rounded the bend.

DeVries was fifty yards behind her, the gap increasing by the second. The bitch runs like a fucking coyote, he thought. His heart was going crazy and his breathing came in painful heaves he could feel all the way to his groin; he was in danger of hyperventilating but couldn't stop, couldn't allow her to open the truck. If she did, it would all be over. Everything! All those years of preparing.

He came to the boulders and scanned them briefly as he raced past but could see little in the darkness. It didn't matter. She was heading to the truck, to Denise. An ingrained motherly reaction: genetics over reason. Like a lioness and her cubs. Seconds later he rounded the bend and the truck was in front of him, outlined in the faint starlight. Where was she?

He stopped, breathing hard, and lurched over at the waist as he tried to catch his breath but instead felt a cramp knot his stomach as though he had been shot. He vomited violently onto the ground. Bile caught in his throat, and he angrily spit it out. "Can't be sick! Can't be!" he said aloud, then forced himself to straighten and stare around. Where had she gone? Fear and anger rose in his mind and adrenaline pumped wildly through his veins. He turned back the way he had come and stared up into the boulders. Goddamn it, he thought, what the fuck's she doing? "Where are you, bitch?" he whispered. Wasn't she after her kid? Or was she more concerned with saving her own life?

His eyes darted back to the moving van.

There!

Cautiously, the hairs on the back of his neck bristling with fear, he approached to within twenty feet of the truck. She could be hiding in the cab. She's a cop, she could have another gun and be scrunched down waiting for him to appear. Go around to the back side then, he warned himself. Never do the expected. Holding his pistol at the ready, he moved slowly past the cargo compartment, the sounds inside muffled but audible, to the passenger door. He stood, listening. Finally, he took a breath, eased up on his toes, and peered in the cab. Nothing. He angrily yanked open the door and light flooded the interior. Key still in the ignition. Snatching it out, he turned and threw it into the desert. Walking around to the back of the truck, he dropped to one knee and inspected the roll-up door. Untouched.

He straightened, looked around, wiped sweat from his forehead. "So what the fuck are you up to?"

Still laboring for breath, he tried to reason it out. Think! Think! She didn't try to set the kids loose. So she's trying to get away. Or is she after me? Of course! The bitch figures she knows where the hostages are, so kill me and she's home free. The hunter becomes the hunted. Faulty fucking reasoning, but if that's what you want, I'll play along. You and me together, babe. Then you, me, and Denise. Together. Bang . . . and bang.

So how did she expect to accomplish this reversal of roles without a weapon? Some sort of Indian magic?

As he rested against the truck, a pebble tumbled down in the darkness from the boulders and bounced to a stop fifty feet away. She's up there, he thought. Yes! And she wants me to know it, to follow. Then as I'm picking my way through the underbrush, she pops out. And what? Hits me on the head with a rock and splits my skull open? He smiled at the primitive simplicity of it all. Even if she succeeded, she wouldn't get her precious kid back. He'd seen to that already.

Okay, Indian bitch, he thought, we'll do it your way. You lead, white man follow. But white man has firestick that goes boom and all you have is rock. Let's see who wins.

Unfortunately, he needed her alive long enough to discover what she'd done with the twenty million dollars. So the firestick would have to wait. He jammed the pistol in his belt and felt in his trousers for his lucky pocketknife, the one he'd used with Annie, from the projects, and Maria, the seven-year-old he'd taken out to the desert years ago. Removing the knife from his pocket, he ran his thumb along the edge of the blade and, staring into the darkness, shouted, "Are you ready, Ellen? Are you?" He waited as the words floated into the night.

"Are you ready?"

Slowly, he began to walk toward the boulders, his voice the only sound for miles.

"Your boyfriend's looking for you in Mexico and the F.B.I.'s up at the airfield. It's just you and me, Ellen. And Denise. I need her. Do you understand? Not the others. Just Denise. I've been talking to her, getting her ready, telling her how much she's going to enjoy this. She can't wait. Neither of us can. How about you? Anxious to join us?"

Excitement joined fear in his mind as his pace picked up.

It doesn't matter, Ellen told herself. I don't need Paul. Or the F.B.I. I can do it myself. I've never needed anybody.

She was barefoot, moving quickly and noiselessly among the boulders. She couldn't see DeVries but knew he would begin to follow any second. As she ran, her eyes swept the ground for anything she could use for a weapon. Seeing a cantaloupe-sized piece of granite, she quickly picked it up, abandoning it a minute later as she noticed a triangular-shaped rock about seven inches across; more than two inches thick at the middle, one edge was as sharp as an iron-age axe. It fit her hand perfectly. If she could manage to come up behind him, she could slice through the side of his neck with a single blow. But she would have to let him go past her first.

Holding the rock aloft, she practiced bringing it down. It'd work, it'd be as easy as slaughtering a sheep, something she had done a dozen times. She needed a place to hide though, a place to surprise him as he went past. She stood completely still and listened. DeVries had turned quiet. He must have begun climbing. Below on the desert floor, coyotes were calling to each other, a mom and her pups. Then silence. Nothing else. Not even wind. It was almost calming in its nothingness. Stepping lightly, she began leaping from rock to rock, moving upward past emaciated pines that had managed to sink roots in the cracks between rocks, until she came to a crevice not more than a foot wide between two towering boulders. It was completely dark inside. She could slip in and wait for him here or try to get to the top, where it would be possible to overlook the entire area.

Still no noise. Why? Where was he? Had he left? It was impossible to see the truck from here. Putting her hand to her lip, she felt the ripped tissue, the blood and broken teeth.

Making up her mind, she stepped between the rocks. I'm ready, DeVries. Where are you? What the hell are you doing?

Approaching the outcropping of boulders, DeVries shuddered as the starlight was blotted out by shadows from above. He tipped his head back and stared up at the massive rocks. There was something menacing and primordial about it all, something oppressive. A volcano must have created it eons ago, though he couldn't imagine a volcano having that much energy. Probably a hundred places to hide up there.

He was reluctant to begin the climb and instead walked along the base of the rocks, feeling the darkness like a weight on his chest. What would the bitch do? he wondered. Hide and come up behind me? Smash, and I'm dead? Or go to the top, where she could watch me approach?

He had covered thirty yards, trying to think it out, when he saw her shoes.

She was barefoot. Why did that bother him so?

Ellen, standing frozen in the crevice, turned her head to listen. Movement somewhere below. Leather soles on loose gravel. The hairs bristled on her neck and made her shiver. This is no good, she told herself: it's too obvious, he'll expect you. Get higher, where you can watch him.

Swiftly, silently, she moved off again, leaping and climbing in the darkness.

Move, he told himself. Goddamn it, move, now, before you completely lose track of her.

There was a sort of a trail where he could see she must have begun climbing between the rocks. He set off, his heart still beating with the exertion of running, but trying desperately to make no noise. He traveled forty yards into the collection of boulders and was probably twenty feet above the desert floor when he halted. Should he try to follow her route? She'll be expecting that. She'll be waiting somewhere. He'll round a bend and she'll leap out screaming like a savage and slashing with her weapon. *Smash!* Or she'll be above him, and drop a rock on his head.

Don't follow her. Don't do the expected. Get to the top and work your way down. Make sure she's not above you. Then wait for her to make the first move.

He peered up into the darkness, barely able to make out

the topmost rocks. *There!* he thought as he saw the summit. Get up there, now, then decide what to do next.

His heart pounding with exertion and fear, he moved off, trying to be quiet but finding the climb difficult. Rocks slipped under his shoes, upsetting his footing and almost sending him sprawling. Don't stop, damn it, don't worry about it. Keep going. Keep going. Push!

Fifteen minutes later, covered with sweat and gasping for breath, he reached the top of the tallest and most massive of the boulders. He collapsed onto his hands and knees and heaved with exhaustion, then rolled onto his back and his eyes stared up at the sky. "Black sky" he knew astronomers called it, a phenomenon known only one or two other places in the world, multiplying by thousands the number of stars visible. *Black sky!* Coming alive and pressing down on his chest, smothering him, sucking his breath away. Don't look at it! He sat up. Get moving! Now! Find the bitch! Hurry! Where is she? Where? Think!

To the rear the foothills loomed, stretching back into the darkness, and in front the rocks he had just traversed. She wasn't behind him. So somewhere in that several acres of rubble and brush and pathetic trees below she was waiting. He sat, caught his breath, and stared. After five minutes, he knew where she was.

Crouched like an animal on her hands and knees in a low cave between two rocks, Ellen closed her mouth and breathed silently through her nose. She wiped blood from her face with her left hand and held the axe-like rock with her right. For several moments everything was silent.

Where are you, DeVries? Goddamn it, what are you doing?

Then she heard pebbles being dislodged as DeVries slowly, patiently, worked his way in her direction, and a wild fear suddenly took hold of her mind: He's coming from above! Oh Christ! Somehow he's gotten behind me. Her stomach tensed. It didn't matter, she told herself over and over. He'd be coming in the wrong direction, but she could still surprise him. Noiselessly she pushed to her feet, her head and knees bent under the low ceiling. Two more minutes, she guessed, and he'll cross by. Wait . . . wait . . . don't move, don't breathe. Keeping her eyes open, she visualized his neck, her arm crashing suddenly down, the rock slashing his carotid artery, warm blood hemorrhaging onto her hand. Like a sheep, like a slaughtered lamb . . .

More noise. Her heart was pounding out of control now. My God, he can probably hear it. Footsteps, moving slowly, cautiously thirty feet away . . . twenty. . . . She braced her feet and raised her arm as far as she could, ready to leap. It wouldn't take two seconds. Ten feet. She could hear him breathing heavily, grunting. All at once he wasn't trying to be quiet anymore, his pace picking up, almost a run. But instead of going past, he turned when he came into view and rushed straight at her. Surprised, she leapt forward from the cave, at the same time bringing her weapon down in a vicious slashing motion. But he was ready and struck her wrist with his hand, sending the rock flying into the darkness. He swore loudly as his other hand thrust suddenly upward and the knife blade pierced her palm, coming out the other side. She screamed, pulling her hand back, the knife still embedded in it, as he hit her as hard as he could in the face with his fist, hit her again and again, until she crumpled to the ground, sobbing with pain. Howling with rage, he lost control, kicking and kicking at her with both feet, screaming "Bitch! Bitch!" until spent. Then, remembering his purpose, he reached down and jerked her up by the collar. "Get up, damn it, move, move, move!"

She tried to stand, stumbled, steadied herself against a rock, and moaned as she saw the knife thrust through her palm. With her left hand, she drew it out and stared at it in shock. She was about to lunge at DeVries when he knocked it to the ground. Fiercely seizing her by the bicep, he yanked her face within inches of his own. "We're going back to the truck. When we get there, you've got one minute to tell me where the money is or I'll kill the kids. Pretty little Denise first."

Half falling and slipping on the steep rocks, they worked their way to the desert floor. DeVries grabbed her by the arm and was about to drag her to the truck when he remembered the Explorer a hundred yards back on the road. They had to go back: the Explorer was the only way out now.

Pushing the sobbing Ellen in front of him, he retreated up the unpaved road to the car. Coyotes, aroused by the commotion, seemed to be all around them, moving closer, howling and barking in the darkness, coming out on the road and challenging them, their eyes huge, luminous, and frightening in the starlight. He screamed at them and waved his gun but was unwilling to attract attention by shooting. Ellen pressed against her right hand, trying to stop the bleeding from the knife wound, when they reached the Explorer. He yanked open the door and shoved her into the driver's seat. "I won't even bother with you if you try to escape again," he said, climbing into the other side. "I'll go straight for Denise. How's that sound?"

She turned her head to look at him. He was filthy and bruised from when he'd fallen, and her blood was on his sleeves and shirtfront. She could feel consciousness start to slip away when he struck her in the face with his left hand. "Where's the money?"

Her head banged against the steering wheel.

"Where?" He had lost control again, screaming, grabbing her arm and shaking her body.

Her eyes closed as she fought for consciousness.

"Denise has thirty seconds to live."

She said nothing, began to sink into a blackness more calming than life.

"Goddamn it!" He grabbed her hair again and painfully yanked her head in his direction.

"Let me see her," she managed, speaking automatically, incapable of thought.

"Where's the money? Then you can fucking have her."

"I'll tell you where the money is. I don't care any longer." It was difficult to keep air in her lungs, and her mind both sought and fought the peace of unconsciousness. "I'll tell you, but I want to know she's alive. I have to know."

He threw his body back against the seat. "Goddamn it! I'll take you to her. Drive!"

Ellen didn't seem to know what to do.

"Drive, damn it!"

She shook her head, trying to clear her mind. Turned the key. Accelerated slowly down the dirt road, scattering a dozen coyotes, until the truck came into view.

"There," DeVries said with finality. "In the back. She's okay."

"I want to see her. I want to see she's all right." Her foot slipped from the brake and the car lurched suddenly forward.

"All right, goddamn it. But you can't talk to her until I have the money. When I do, I'll take the Explorer, you can have the fucking truck."

Ellen wasn't paying attention, her eyes riveted on the vehicle thirty yards in front of them. "Get her!" she screamed. "I want to see her."

He opened the door and hesitated. "It'll take a minute." He sounded unusually subdued, and she turned on him at once. "A minute? Why!"

He gave her an uncomfortable look. "I have to disconnect some wires."

"Wires? You booby-trapped the truck! It's set to blow up when someone tries to open it!" Her mind turned over and over as she tried to grasp what he had done. "You're going to kill the children and anyone who tries to save them." The enormity of it overwhelmed her.

DeVries took a breath and stood at the open passenger door, not looking at her. "It's only a precaution. In case I was stopped on the highway." He slammed the door. "I'll get Denise."

He walked rapidly along the dirt road to the rear of the truck and bent to manipulate wires obscured behind the rear bumper. Her body stiffened, and she hunched forward, watching the darkened figure through the windshield with rapidly mounting panic. He had planned from the beginning to blow up the children. All of them. For no reason. As soon as he had the money he was going to kill her and leave the truck out here until someone noticed it and opened the doors. Then the whole thing would explode.

The metal door rolled suddenly and noisily upward, and DeVries disappeared inside. "Here she is," he yelled from the darkness and Denise appeared in the opening. She was nude and crying and trying to break free of his grasp. "Mommy!"

Ellen screamed her daughter's name. Her foot pressed against the brake so hard she could feel the blood as it pounded through her leg.

Abruptly, Denise disappeared. DeVries grabbed the door and pulled it shut as he jumped to the ground. Then he began to reattach the wires.

No! Ellen thought as she realized what he was doing. "No!" No matter what she did, he was going to kill them, all of them. "My baby!" she screamed at the top of her voice, blood roaring in her ears, and her body ached and trembled with fear. Unthinkingly she jammed the car into gear, her foot crashing down at once on the accelerator and her mind filling with horror.

Oh God, please don't let him, please!

The Explorer spun out on the loose dirt and leapt forward like a cat. DeVries whipped around at the sound, his eyes surprised, then filling instantly with fear; he seemed to falter and shouted something, the words weak, drifting into the night. The car continued roaring directly at him, aiming at him, trying to crush him. It was coming too fast, there was no time to use his gun—the curtain ripping just a little and Chaos seeping through. (Is that laughter you hear, Lowell? Laughter?) Desperately he tried to leap out of the way but tripped, and the edge of the bumper struck him furiously on the arm and hip, ripping his flesh and flinging him like a doll to the ground as the car slammed into the truck's tailgate.

Pain sharp as an axe blow seared through his body, and

his left side was soaked in blood. He tried to move his arm but couldn't as it sprawled at an angle from his body as use-lessly as if it had been amputated. Lying on his back, he could see the huge deeply grooved tires of the four-wheel-drive Explorer just inches from his eyes. The grooves deep-ened magically as his perception suddenly intensified. He could see the perfect zig-zag pattern of tread, individual grains of sand trapped far inside, tiny hair-like wisps of rub-ber trembling as the wheels began to spin. No, no, no, he thought and frantically squirmed out of the way under the truck as the Explorer's wheels continued to whirl noisily, and dirt and sand splattered like buckshot against the side of the truck. Liquid gushed and steamed into the air from somewhere above his vision, dropping into shallow green pools on the ground. Coolant! She'd ruined the radiator, wouldn't be able to drive!

Go! he commanded himself. *Do it, Lowell! Move!* Forget-ting his pain, adrenaline pumping madly now ("The test of a man lies in action"—Pindar), he scrambled on his stom-ach toward the other end of the truck, pulling himself for-ward with his one good arm, finally emerging near the front wheels.

Gasping for breath, grunting, trembling violently with the uncontrolled passion of rage but triumphant again—free, free, free—he raced back toward the rear of the truck. Twenty million dollars! But the Explorer had already backed away from the impact. Steam hissed and shot from the ruined radiator, and he could smell the acrid metallic stench of an overheated engine all around him. The car's wheels spun wildly, and it lurched drunkenly backward, repositioning itself. Aware again of the pain in his useless left arm, he lifted the revolver, aimed carefully, and shot once from thirty feet at the figure behind the steering wheel. The windshield shattered, a mosaic of spidery cracks spreading instantly across its length. He squeezed the trig-ger again and again, but the vehicle had shifted gears and was rushing forward now, jerking rapidly and wildly from side to side but coming right at him, trying to crush him.

Lowering his arm, he aimed at the radiator, fired, hitting it, but nothing happened. The car wasn't more than ten feet away now, roaring loudly. He leapt aside, the right headlight striking his thigh, spinning him around. He screamed in a fury of impotence and frustration and screamed again in pain as he sank forward on his knees as though shot, his forehead striking the rocky ground.

The Explorer skidded at once to a stop. Terror held him powerless as he heard the gears grinding loudly into reverse, and he looked up to see the car leap backward again in the loose gravel, turning quickly in his direction. Its headlights snapped on unexpectedly, like two huge suns in the desert darkness, illuminating him, he knew, like a target, paralyzing him with their horrible, isolating intensity as the car again began to bear down on him.

Stumbling painfully to his feet, he jumped aside, but the lights continued to follow him. Desperate, wanting now only to get away, not to die, he began to run, the Explorer just thirty feet behind, then twenty. Dr. Stephen Weir's bearded face suddenly filled his mind, yelling furiously at him: *Get off the road, Lowell, get to the loose dirt. She won't be able to follow.* He raced into the desert as earlier he had run after Emily Scranton. The Explorer faltered for only a second as it hit a soft spot, but it was enough to enable him to lurch to the right and fire two more shots at the passenger side. One of the shots seemed to hit something, and the car stopped sharply, not two feet away, spraying up sheets of dirt and gravel that struck him in the face, momentarily blinding him. But then the engine revved again, the headlights swung around as though on a pivot and illuminated Lowell Alexander DeVries against the massive, black sky, holding his body rigid and still.

Panic seized him. His heart was racing uncontrollably, pain throbbed in his left side, and his bloodied arm hung uselessly. Too many mistakes. Too many mistakes. He gasped and gasped, unable to keep air in his lungs. Mustering all his will—his body mastered—he managed to force himself to stand once more and aim the gun at the form behind the steering wheel. He needed just one shot. He pulled the trigger and heard only a click. Howling with rage, the sound rising from deep inside rushed up all around him in the still, thin air, enveloping and wrapping around him like a desert whirlwind, buffeting his body again and again. The revolver tumbled from his hands as once more the headlights grew huge and bore down on him.

The cop's gun, he recalled suddenly and all at once hope rushed back. Yes, of course! The one in the bitch's purse! The memory energized and elated him; he spun around and began to run toward the dirt road where she had been parked. On the other side of the rocks, he thought. I can get there. He almost laughed: I can beat her. I can get there first. Yes! And again Dr. Stephen Weir was in his mind, an angry look on his face as he leaned forward in his chair: *Did you prepare sufficiently, Lowell? Did you think everything out? Were you rational? Talk to me, Lowell! Talk to me!*

Yes, goddamn it, yes! I planned it all. Everything. And I can beat her. I can do it.

Racing across the rocky terrain, breathing so hard his whole body trembles, DeVries's foot comes down in a hole and his ankle snaps and twists painfully; he hears it break but gives it no thought. *The gun!* All at once the Explorer rises behind him, roaring, roaring, its lights holding him in their grasp like two giant fists. He hears the engine pounding in his ears, pistons rising, falling, Chaos, Chaos, smells the radiator, senses the ground beneath his feet heave and roll.

It's gaining, Lowell, gaining. Do something! Hurry!

The gun, he thinks wildly as the curtain rips further—he hears it, too, hears the horrible *rippppp* of God's curtain in his ears, as loud as an explosion—and this time Chaos rushes through, laughing.

The gun . . . I can get there . . .

Can . . .

Can . . .

But the car's too close.

He stops suddenly, yes, spins around, throws his hands in the air and screams, "I'm not armed, not . . ." surrendering, seeking rationality, order.

The Explorer rises up and crushes him to the ground, brakes, shoots backward, and comes at his body again and again and again, driving it into the earth, into the primordial sand of the desert, beneath the curtain, into silence.

10:30 P.M.

Lights break the darkness, snapping on one at a time— click, click, click—from every direction, illuminating her like a solitary actor on a darkened stage.

Ellen, alone, lifts her bloody head from the steering wheel and tries to make sense of what is happening. Odd spectral shapes are stalking silently like wolves all around her. Footfalls sound in the sand, sound, she thinks, like babies slapping their cribs with tiny soft hands. Her fingers are frozen to the steering wheel so tightly she can't move them. Noises now, shouting, people running. She closes her eyes, lowers her head, dreams.

"Out!" a voice screamed and Ellen's door flew open, a man in Marine desert fatigues pointing a .45 automatic in her direction.

"Jesus, it's a woman."

Ellen looked at him, unable to speak.

Another man appeared, the passenger door abruptly banged open, and suddenly soldiers were surrounding her, rifles pointing. "Jesus Christ, look at the blood," someone says.

"Ma'am, step out, please," the first voice repeated angrily, but Ellen didn't move.

"Ma'am?"

She looked at the young man. After a moment, he holstered his gun.

"Ma'am—"

"I'm a police officer," she managed to say.

"Step out, please."

She looked at her bloody hands and lifted them from the steering wheel. "I can't close my fingers." She stared at them as though they belonged to someone else. Then she maneuvered out of the Explorer.

Someone was kneeling over DeVries, what remained of him. He came to his feet and shook his head.

The young man with the gun said, "What the hell's going on?"

She felt cold and shivered, stepped uncertainly onto the ground.

The soldier said, "Is there dope in that truck? You transporting?"

She turned in the direction of the truck. A soldier was about to open the rear door.

"No!" she screamed. "Don't touch it! It's booby-trapped." She began to race toward the truck. The soldier turned toward her. "Don't touch it," she shouted. "It'll blow up."

"We'll get the bomb team out here," the man with the gun said. "What's in there?"

Ellen told him and he said, "Jesus Christ."

DECEMBER 16

An icy wind that had its origin somewhere in western Alaska shot down through the San Jacinto Mountains, dropping a foot of snow on Idylwild before cutting noisily across the desert floor as it hurried on to Mexico. Ellen ducked her head against it as she slammed the car door and hurried toward the house.

"Jeez, shut the door," Julie Garcia said as Ellen bustled inside. "It's crazy out there."

Ellen took off her parka and gloves and draped them over the back of the couch. Julie and Denise were playing Chutes and Ladders on the floor in front of the fire. Denise was home because Ellen had decided not to enroll her in school a year early after all, wanting to prolong their time together as long as she could before losing her to the school system for several hours each day. Whenever work allowed, Ellen came home for lunch or stopped by to pick up Denise and Julie and take them to McDonald's. She looked toward the kitchen. "Anything cooking?"

"Quesadillas and vegetable soup," Julie said, getting to her feet. "Both hot and ready."

The three of them went into the kitchen and sat at the table while they waited for their soup to cool. Denise said, "I won Chutes and Ladders three times."

"Yeah, yeah," Julie replied. "So I owe you three dollars. Big deal."

Ellen said, "You didn't—"

"Joke," Julie told her. "So how's the chief? Troubles, they're saying on the radio."

"The tribal council has their election tomorrow. He's going to lose. Next year we'll have gambling on the reservation. It'll mean more work for us—burglary, car thefts, stick-ups. Nothing we can do about it now though."

"Maybe he'll retire after you get married. He don' need the money. Both of you could retire, take life easy, go to Hawaii or Tahiti in the winter, lay in the sun and sip those weird drinks with flowers in them."

"I don't think so, Julie. Paul likes working too much. Me, too." She slid a glance at Denise who was holding a quesadilla like Bugs Bunny held carrots, and nibbling furiously at the end of it. "But maybe I'll take off a year if I get pregnant—"

"What?" Denise turned suddenly in her direction.

Ellen smiled at her. "I'm talking about a couple of years from now, Denise. We're not even getting married until June."

Her daughter made a face. "I think you should get married now. And I want a sister. No dumb boys. They're too loud. And they fight all the time."

"Well, you're just going to have to wait. The wedding's set for summer. I'm not ready to share you with anyone until then."

Julie said, "Guess who I saw on TV this morning? That F.B.I. guy who was here, whatsizname? LaSalle. The good-looking one. Remember him?"

Ellen tried her soup, her face blank. "Yeah? On TV?" It was still too hot. She stirred it and glanced at Denise, who was directing a long, low gust of breath at her bowl.

"In Detroit. They arrested some bank robbers. How come he was in Detroit? I thought he worked out of L.A.?"

"The F.B.I. likes to move people around. They think it gives them experience, I guess. Pretty stupid, huh?"

She had not talked to LaSalle since returning to the police station the night of the kidnapping. He had been there, along with Whitfield and Bishop and all the others, but she could find nothing to say to him. Whatever had existed between them died the moment he lied to her about the transmitters. He had been prepared to risk her daughter's life for the sake of an arrest and willing to deceive in order to do it. She didn't care what his reasoning was. "Complete honesty in all things. All things," she'd told him furiously. Not just the easy and convenient. Honor isn't a question of "sometimes." She'd seen him again a couple of hours later at the hospital, where she and the children were being checked over by doctors. Except for those who had missed their medication, there was little wrong with any of them. DeVries had made the children take off their clothes before putting them in the back of the truck but hadn't harmed any, though Ellen shuddered to think what he had been planning, especially with Denise. LaSalle had taken her aside and tried to explain what he'd done, but she wouldn't listen. He seemed as blind to the truth as Pete had been. Couldn't they understand? Without trust there could be no love. How could anyone not see that? For weeks afterward she'd refused to respond to his phone calls, until finally he'd given up trying.

She'd never told anyone in detail what had happened out there that night. She'd given a short statement to the sheriff's department and the attorney general but hadn't elaborated on it. Paul had asked once, but after she'd shaken her head he'd never asked again. She tried every day with all her will not to think about it, just as she tried with all her will to force a veneer of normality on her life. But it still returned every night in her dreams. Every night. DeVries and Denise. It made her physically ill to think about it. A week after the kidnapping, she'd ended up in the hospital with an emergency ulcer operation. She still had trouble keeping solid food down and had lost fifteen pounds. Her color had come back, though, and she could sense herself slowly returning to normal. But it had been a long road.

How much better to be a child, to whom it all seemed to have little more reality than a TV show. Bugs Bunny chasing Daffy Duck, Wile E. Coyote after Road Runner. Within days Denise had been back in preschool three mornings a week and seldom even mentioned that night. Of course, she had been in the back of the truck most of the time and had seen nothing. Some of the other children, those who had spent so much time in the bomb shelter, found recovery more difficult, however.

Concerned about long-term effects, Ellen had taken Denise to a child psychologist in Palm Springs several days after the kidnapping. After talking to the girl alone for an hour, the psychologist said, "Read to her."

"What?"

"Read to her. It's what makes her happy. You don't need me. She'll be fine."

And so Ellen did every night. Read to her. *Hop on Pop, The Cat in the Hat, The Little Train That Could, Are You My Mother?*

The psychologist was right. It all seemed to leave little permanent effect on Denise. Ellen's constant battle had become not to overcompensate by watching the girl too closely. But she had almost lost her twice now.

"You can take off a little early tonight," Ellen said to Julie. "We're going to have dinner at Paul's. If it warms up any, maybe we'll go horseback riding."

Denise's ears perked up. "Really? Can I go on Denver again?"

"I think so, hon, if you wear your bike helmet. Let's see what the weather's like." She turned to Julie. "Did the real-estate agent come by today?"

The baby-sitter nodded while spreading butter on a warm tortilla and handing it to Denise. "This time eat it, don't nibble like a bunny." She turned back to Ellen. "They always want you to spend money fixing things up. She wants you to do something about your grandfather's old room. Paint it or something. It's too gloomy. Smells, too."

Ellen had shut up the room when her grandfather had died, a week after the kidnapping. "I'll wallpaper it, I guess. Maybe Denise can help."

Julie laughed and gave her a look. "You ever wallpaper with someone? My husband wouldn't talk to me for a week after doing the bathroom, and it was only about six feet square."

Denise said, "I want Winnie the Pooh paper like at preschool."

"We'll see," Ellen told her. "It's only for six months. Then we'll be living at the ranch."

Denise hopped off her chair and raced over to hug her mother around the waist. "And I get my own horse. No one else can have her. Only me!" She pranced back to her chair. "I like it, Sam-I-am. I do, I do, I do."

And Ellen looked at her daughter's face and thought, Yeah, me too, Denise. I like it.

I do, I do, I do.

THE ONLY ALTERNATIVE IS ANNIHILATION . . .
RICHARD P. HENRICK

SILENT WARRIORS   (8217-3026-6, $4.50/$5.50)
The Red Star, Russia's newest, most technologically advanced submarine, outclasses anything in the U.S. fleet. But when the captain opens his sealed orders 24 hours early, he's staggered to read that he's to spearhead a massive nuclear first strike against the Americans!

THE PHOENIX ODYSSEY   (0-8217-5016-X, $4.99/$5.99)
All communications to the *USS Phoenix* suddenly and mysteriously vanish. Even the urgent message from the president canceling the War Alert is not received, and in six short hours the *Phoenix* will unleash its nuclear arsenal against the Russian mainland. . . .

COUNTERFORCE   (0-8217-5116-6, $5.99/$6.99)
In the silent deep, the chase is on to save a world from destruction. A single Russian submarine moves on a silent and sinister course for the American shores. The men aboard the U.S.S. *Triton* must search for and destroy the Soviet killer submarine as an unsuspecting world race for the apocalypse.

CRY OF THE DEEP   (0-8217-5200-6, $5.99/$6.99)
With the Supreme leader of the Soviet Union dead the Kremlin is pointing a collective accusing finger towards the United States. The motherland wants revenge and unless the USS *Swordfish* can stop the Russian *Caspian*, the salvoes of World War Three are a mere heartbeat away!

BENEATH THE SILENT SEA   (0-8217-3167X, $4.50/$5.50)
The Red Dragon, Communist China's advanced ballistic missile-carrying submarine embarks on the most sinister mission in human history: to attack the U.S. and Soviet Union simultaneously. Soon, the Russian *Barkal*, with its planned attack on a single U.S. submarine, is about unwittingly to aid in the destruction of all mankind!

Available wherever paperbacks are sold, or order direct from the Publisher. Send cover price plus 50¢ per copy for mailing and handling to Penguin USA, P.O. Box 999, c/o Dept. 17109, Bergenfield, NJ 07621. Residents of New York and Tennessee must include sales tax. DO NOT SEND CASH.

HORROR FROM HAUTALA

SHADES OF NIGHT   (0-8217-5097-6, $4.99)
Stalked by a madman, Lara DeSalvo is unaware that she is most in danger in the one place she thinks she is safe—home.

TWILIGHT TIME   (0-8217-4713-4, $4.99)
Jeff Wagner comes home for his sister's funeral and uncovers long-buried memories of childhood sexual abuse and murder.

DARK SILENCE   (0-8217-3923-9, $5.99)
Dianne Fraser fights for her family—and her sanity—against the evil forces that haunt an abandoned mill.

COLD WHISPER   (0-8217-3464-4, $5.95)
Tully can make Sarah's wishes come true, but Sarah lives in terror because Tully doesn't understand that some wishes aren't meant to come true.

LITTLE BROTHERS   (0-8217-4020-2, $4.50)
Kip saw the "little brothers" kill his mother five years ago. Now they have returned, and this time there will be no escape.

MOONBOG   (0-8217-3356-7, $4.95)
Someone—or some*thing*—is killing the children in the little town of Holland, Maine.

Available wherever paperbacks are sold, or order direct from the Publisher. Send cover price plus 50¢ per copy for mailing and handling to Penguin USA, P.O. Box 999, c/o Dept. 17109, Bergenfield, NJ 07621. Residents of New York and Tennessee must include sales tax. DO NOT SEND CASH.

THE SEVENTH CARRIER SERIES
BY PETER ALBANO

THE SEVENTH CARRIER   (0-8217-3612-4, $4.50)
The original novel of this exciting, best-selling series. Impris-
oned in a cave of ice since 1941, the great carrier *Yonaga*
finally breaks free in 1983, her maddened crew of samurai
determined to carry out their orders to destroy Pearl Harbor.

RETURN OF THE SEVENTH CARRIER
                            (0-8217-2093-7, $3.95)
With the war technology of the former superpowers still crip-
pled by Red China's orbital defense system, a terrorist beast
runs rampant across the planet. Outarmed and outnumbered,
the target of crack saboteurs and fanatical assassins, only the
Yonaga and its brave samurai crew stand between a Libyan
madman and his fiendish goal of global domination.

ASSAULT OF THE SUPER CARRIER
                            (0-8217-5314-2, $4.99)
A Libyan madman, the world's single most dangerous and
fanatical despot, controls the fate of the free world. The brave
samurai crew of the *Yonaga* are ready for the ultimate kami-
kaze mission.

*Available wherever paperbacks are sold, or order direct from the
Publisher. Send cover price plus 50¢ per copy for mailing and
handling to Penguin USA, P.O. Box 999, c/o Dept. 17109,
Bergenfield, NJ 07621. Residents of New York and Tennessee
must include sales tax. DO NOT SEND CASH.*